LOGAN D. IRONS

OATHS OF BLOOD

aethonbooks.com

OATHS OF BLOOD

Aethon Books
www.aethonbooks.com

Print and eBook formatting by Steve Beaulieu. Artwork provided by Vivid Covers.

Published by Aethon Books LLC.

ALSO IN SERIES

Oaths of Blood

Sands of Bone

City of Wolves

Check out the entire series here! (Tap or scan)

CHAPTER 1

The darkness reeked of bitter piss. Armored footmen and knights were packed inside the wooden siege tower, shoulder to shoulder, a full quiver of arrows overlapping one another. The suffocating heat had stolen every last droplet of sweat from them, saturating their thick woolen tunics and breeches, pouring into damp irritating linen coifs that padded beneath their helms. Now only a dry crust embedded their garments, chafing their skin under the weight of their armor.

Muffled breaths filled the stinking air as the men tried to breathe, every inch of space smothered by the men around him as if they'd all been buried alive in the same rotting coffin; left to bake in the brick oven of the Eastern heat. A splash of vomit splattered down a footman's chain hauberk, adding fresh salt to the wound of every man's misery. A misery that promised to continue as the siege tower rolled painstakingly slow over the rocky ground toward Jerusalem's inner walls.

Light slipped from the trapdoor above them, blanketing them in shadow. The stomp of boots and the cries of battle came in muffled waves from the covered roof of the engine. There was an abrupt thud as a body hit the platform above. Blood dribbled through cracks in rough planking like a newly forming mountain spring, splatting on a helm drop after drop, the man beneath unable to move from its path.

Mercenary captain Robert Cutnose knew what it meant to be in the front line of a siege tower. He steeled his insides against it and clenched his hard jaw as he waited. His only comforts were his shield, his hand axe and the iron warriors around him. Men who understood, even if they succeeded, many would fall on the walls, holding bloody wounds and punctured bodies, dying in the land where Christ had died for their sins over a thousand years before them.

For many in the tower, it was the power of God that had brought them on crusade. The priests and bishops had lit the kingdoms of Europe afire with Christian zeal to take up arms and free the holy city of Jerusalem from the vile grasp of the infidel, drawing together a cultural patchwork of 30,000 men and women to partake on the militant pilgrimage. That had been three years prior, and now, within sight of Jerusalem's walls only 9,000 crusaders remained for their final test. With but a few of the least holy placed at the tip of the Christian spear.

Cutnose and his men were there to get rich. Richer than beyond even a mercenary's drunken dreams. The cities of the East were overflowing with enough coin for a man to pay another man to do the fighting while he lounged in a throne made of gold with a woman on each arm. Pretty women too, not the worn out, weather-beaten ones with rotten teeth he might run into at a dock-side tavern. Pleasant ones with pretty smiles, perky tits, and white teeth, who would feed him grapes, pour him the finest wines, maybe even cut his meat for him. All they had to do was survive the deadly hailstorm of spears and arrows hurled from the city's limestone walls. Then live through the onslaught of Saracen swords and axes as they fought to drive them into the city. And survive whatever resistance crept up in the streets.

Below them the crudely-built wheels creaked out a slow and

repetitive groan as each span forward threatened to turn the slipshod three-story engine into a pile of wood and bodies. The siege tower was actually taller when you included the makeshift archer enclosure on the very top. Men shouted as they whipped the oxen driving them onward, the siege engine's pace painstaking at best, an agonizingly uncomfortable wait before death at worst. The labored encroachment of living death to the city. There was no deception in their attack now. This would be their final attempt to take the walls. The crusade would triumph or collapse with the men inside the engine. If their courage failed them in the face of death, all was for naught, and they would have but the thrum of a bowstring to contemplate the sin of defeat.

The desperate Christians had scoured the land for timber to build siege engines before being forced to scuttle Genoese ships to collect enough wood for a ram and two towers—one for each of the army's main divisive factions, Godfrey of Bouillon's men to the north and Raymond of Toulouse's men to the south. The only benefit of the fractious army of the crusaders was that a third of their army assaulted the southern wall, splitting the defending garrison in half.

In a cunning maneuver, Godfrey had ordered the siege tower constructed in one place, then in the chill of the night had his engineers deconstruct it and rebuild it in front of a different section of the wall, denying the Fatimid defenders the use of most of their wall-mounted stone hurlers. Raymond had not employed such deception and now the southern Frankish tower was engulfed in an inferno. Every man crammed inside the bowels of this tower knew they were the army's last hope. A rolling tomb of crusaders willing to be the first warriors fed into the breach's brutal bosom.

Cutnose rested the point of his almond-shaped shield, rounded at the top and curving down to a point at the bottom, on the wooden floor. Holding it at rest would only waste precious energy before the battle. The knight behind Cutnose braced his shield against his back. He audibly prayed to Christ and all the saints as piss dribbled down his legs.

One of Cutnose's men leaned closer. "How much piss can a man have in this heat?" said Roger Maule, his voice as gravelly as the ground they rolled over. The brutish soldier had a broad face punctuated by a smashed nose, having been broken so many times it was almost flat. His cheeks were hairy, his head shaved, and he had small dim eyes. He wielded a long-flanged mace he'd stolen from a dead Turkish nobleman, and Cutnose never doubted him in a fight. He was a man to swing first and ask questions later. Deep chasms circled Roger's eyes beneath his helm, the nose piece reflected no sunlight, only ashen metal.

"Maybe he'll bleed less when the Saracens stick him," Cutnose said. A few of the veteran men softly chuckled around him. About half the men on the platform were his, the band of mercenaries hired by Lord Bohemond of Taranto to ensure that his nephew, Tancred, survived the coming siege of Jerusalem while Bohemond consolidated his lands around Antioch. Their task was to attach themselves to Tancred like a shadow, never leaving his side, which was proving a dangerous order. Along the campaign trail they had fallen under Tancred's command, the young lord offering to pay them in Bohemond's stead. Cutnose eagerly accepted the offer, hoping to garner payment from both lords.

Now the young lord, head swollen with songs of glory and poems laced with valor, threatened an easy payout by wanting to be the first son of a bitch onto the walls, dragging Cutnose's men with him. He'd known plenty of young men with the exact same disposition, now dead young men, windswept bones bleaching pale like a felled forest of birch left to rot in the domineering desert sun. Yet most of those young men didn't have Cutnose and his company at his back. Even then the outlook on survival for any of them was grim.

"How close are we?" Tancred asked him. He was almost a half-head taller than Cutnose and the mercenary captain was not short by any means, the mercenary more of a robust weed next to the flower of Taranto. Tancred was a young nobleman, well-bred and fed, fit for the bards to sing of, striking jaw line, cleft chin, hair the color of straw worn down to his shoulders despite the hinderance in combat, and piercing blue eyes. He was akin to many of his Norman ancestors, whose stock came from long lines of adventuring Norsemen. Like many of those Normans who had settled in the lands south of Rome, his ancestors had come to serve and tasting victory and gold, stayed to rule.

Cutnose tuned out everything except the tempo of the archers and crossbowmen on the very top of the tower. Shaded by an overhang of wood, wattle, and animal hide, they kept the Saracen archers on the wall from having an easier time peppering the siege tower with arrow and fire. "The archers are loosing faster. I'd say forty paces."

"Some men have a longer pace than others," Roger said. There was more laughter from Cutnose's men. It was impossible to tell in the intermittent dark, but he was sure a grin appeared somewhere on the young nobleman's face too.

"Soon the infidels will fall beneath our blades. It is God's will!" said Tancred.

Murmurs of "Deus vult" trickled from the men beside them. Despite cutting the battle's edge with deadman's humor, most of them were dry-mouthed, hearts beating like a mad blacksmith, despite scarcely being able to scratch a flea out of one's beard.

Deus vult, *God wills it,* was the rallying cry of the crusade. No matter what language the diverse crusaders spoke, every single one understood the phrase. The words were meant to fill them with God's fury, yet inside the siege tower, it was more of a plea for mercy. The few that had space, blessed themselves with the sign of the cross over their heart.

"God's will won't matter once the bridge goes down," Cutnose said to Tancred. He'd seen pious men slain, stuck with bolts, feathered with arrows, cleaved from neck to groin, speared through the midriff only to linger for weeks and die the same as the unrighteous and much of the time worse. "Keep your shield high, my lord. When we charge the breach, they will throw everything they have to hold us back." The last thing he wanted was to get pinned in the siege tower with the bridge down like stalks of wheat for the Saracen scythes of arrows, rocks, and spears. Bodies falling over the sides to smash onto the rocky ground below.

"Today is the day we liberate Jerusalem from the infidels' grasp. You shall see, Cutnose. God will grant us victory. The priests have foretold it."

"God's glory will be seen." Two weeks prior, the crusaders had made their first assault with a single ladder the outcome all but assured. Cutnose had held his men back and let the household troops of Godfrey scale the ladder into the waiting blades of the defending garrison. Brave Sir Raimbold Creton, with more brawn than brains, had been the first man to top the wall and lost the hand that crossed the summit to an axe. He lay back in the camp now, cheeks aflame, eyes wild with fever. The knight wasn't long for this earth.

The slaughter on the scaling ladder had made even a veteran's stomach turn over and spill bile-filled bread. The men grasped for a hold as they plummeted through the air, calling their death cry before they cracked apart like men made of sticks, splintering upon tan rocks turned reflective crimson.

Cutnose was sure bards and righteous clergymen would sing songs of their bravery and scrawl epic accounts of God's embrace of his mortal warrior martyrs one day, but there was no glory in a falling corpse crashing into the earth, and if God watched, he'd shown no mercy upon those battered men in life. After the second wave rushed in, the ladder was shoved from the wall and broke into pieces of kindling, a handful of men twisted beneath it, bones jutting out of arms and legs. Fellow crusaders had tried to drag their wounded comrades to safety, but a shower of arrow tips quickly silenced the cries for help and the Fatimids ensured there were no wounded left remaining on the field. The flimsy assault ended with only those who had run early.

One of his men, who simply went by the name Henry, called

from the back. Everything about the man was long, his nose, his face, his height, arms and legs. He was able to speak over the other men inside. "You been all over these lands. You ever have a Saracen woman, Cutnose?"

"Can't say I have."

"You think they're like regular sheaths?"

Cutnose reflexively shrugged beneath his hauberk. "A woman's a woman. Suppose they be the same."

"Don't think they got teeth or nothing like a succubus?"

"By Christ's fingernails, I doubt that."

"I had one near Antioch. Furry little black-haired all down there. Felt the same," Pagan said from the mass of men. He wielded a fine sword, and his body was covered in pale blue tattoos he claimed was an ancient custom from his homeland of Jut. His Christian faith was doubtful at best. He was the first man to scale the ladders in the night assault upon Antioch, and his bravery in the face of death was never in question, bordering on reckless.

"Quiet your men or my lord will have their vile tongues removed. To speak of such depravity when we march for Christendom is a sin," said the knight behind Cutnose.

"And what man would run to their lord and tell him of such blasphemy?"

"It is I, Sir Ludolf of Tournai, knight and friend of Lord Tancred." He leaned closer. "Do not cross me, mercenary."

"You want me brain him?" asked Roger.

"Stay your mace," Cutnose said. "I have heard of brave Sir Ludolf. He should remember he stands among my men."

"I stand unafraid in Christ's palm," Ludolf said, his voice cracking near the end.

The men laughed around him.

"What will you do, drown the enemy in piss?" asked Pagan.

Ludolf sucked in a breath. "I demand a duel with any man who names me coward."

"You want me to brain him?" asked Roger again.

"Cutnose, quiet your men," said Tancred. "They will wet their blades soon enough."

"Aye, my lord," Cutnose said. He had heard and seen enough of Ludolf to not wish to have the arrogant coward dressed as the part of a knight at his back. Fine helm, shining mail, a sword, his shield checkered blue and white. He, and his brother Engelbert of Tournai, were landless knights, their father having but a few tracts of land to hand down to his eldest, which neither of the brothers were.

Engelbert had found himself deathly ill back in the camp, leaving his brother to attack the city alone. Ludolf had a horse earlier in the campaign. Cutnose thought the knight had eaten it somewhere near Edessa. Not many of the knights had a horse left between them, most marching to Jerusalem on foot as well armored men-at-arms. Cutnose supposed having a horse mattered little when assaulting a city wall.

Yet somehow Ludolf had found himself in Tancred's trust, becoming his confidant and ally. Then when Tancred insisted that he be the first warrior of Christendom as the bridge dropped, he implored his friends and allies to join him. Ludolf regretted trying to advance his station on behalf of the young lord, but honor had held him to his word. So now, Cutnose had a flaccid, landless knight at his back ready to take cover behind his torso and shield rather than cutting down the enemy on the walls.

"You heard the lord, no more talk of a man's sword or woman's sheath," Cutnose said. He wrinkled the stiff scar tissue running down the center of his nose in irritation. It tapered to the right at the tip. He hadn't lost his nose, but it had made him what many considered ugly. Unironically how he'd come by his name.

An archer screamed as he fell from the platform above, drawing their eyes upward. The men became quietly sober as they listened to his final cry. The wheels ground. A man coughed.

"Do I hear a woman's sheath whining?" came a voice.

Men chuckled, a bold attack against the fear suffocating in the darkness. "Who dares utter those words?" Ludolf leaned over

Cutnose's shoulder. "Your man will be found and flogged or will feel the wrath of my sword."

"I'll see the man found and flogged, when this battle is done." The blamable comments would be heaped upon the shallow grave of any one of the breathing dead men standing inside the tower.

Thunder crashed through the side of the siege tower. Wood exploded inward and a projectile struck the skull of the nearest footman. His head snapped to the side. Blood and brain spattered the men around him. He crumpled into them, and they used their shields to shove him upright, his head flopping, chunks of gore running down his face. Spears of light thrust through the gaping hole, blinding them and then harshly glinting off their swords, helms, axes, and armor. The broken footman was shoved to the corner, his body held upright by the men around him, no more than a limp scarecrow.

The siege tower limped through the breach in the shorter exterior walls of the city. The breach was produced by a successful assault from the army's battering ram. Only an hour prior, the ram had been set alight by the garrison, and put out by the crusaders, who then to their horror discovered the ram was barricading the tower's path to the inner walls. Hastily the crusaders relit the siege ram and now the defenders scurried to dump water upon the flames. In the end, a steady stream of crossbow bolts and two mounted charges had driven the defenders back to the interior, and both sides watched the ram burn.

The main walls of Jerusalem were taller than the outer walls, spanning over three stories of white limestone, sprawling to the east and west before them. Turbaned archers scrambled to shoot arrows, searching for prey in the cracks and holes between the planks of wood.

"Stand fast we will soon be too close for their rock hurlers," Cutnose said. They only need pass the threshold of the wall and the rock hurlers would have no angle to launch upon the siege tower.

Tancred shouted down the ladder to the next floor. "Faster men, we are near!"

A footman pressed his eye against a hole in the wall, holding his helm with one hand. "They're lighting arrows!"

"God will see the camel hides complete the task," Tancred said with a tone of reverence.

"Let us hope," Cutnose added. Every man knew this time would eventually come yet feared it all the same. Fire was the most mortal of enemies to a siege tower. The men held their breath, and Cutnose clenched his jaw harder, hand squeezing the top of his shield.

Flaming arrows softly pattered on the sealed bridge. A whisper as the flames crept along the door. Smoke flooded between the planks. The crusaders had so little water in the camp they hadn't had enough to drink let alone dampen the hides. A flaming arrow blazed through the hole in the tower. It struck a man in the cheek nestling into his jawbone. His hands leapt for his face as he dropped his shield and sword. The fire illuminating the wide-eyed men around him. His screams came seconds later.

"Dump him!" Cutnose screamed at Henry. A fire inside the platform would annihilate them all and doom the entire siege.

Using his shield, Henry forced the man back into the hole, straining. The other men-at-arms and knights smashed at the man with their shields until his flaming skull and shoulders were outside the siege platform. He continued to scream, high-pitched and shrill, arms flailing as they hoisted his legs, and he disappeared to the ground.

"Cover that gap," Cutnose ordered. Henry shoved his leaf-shaped shield into the hole sealing the exposure. The shield vibrated as more arrows struck it. He gritted his teeth with a grimace at them. "Roger's girth is better suited to fill this void."

"You're harder to hit with your skinny bones."

"I'd rather not have them practice on me," Henry said. He jerked his head back as an arrow struck his shield.

Through the gap Cutnose could see they had almost reached

the walls. "Keep your shields up. Weapons ready. Whatever you do, keep moving forward." Men hoisted their shields, helms sticking out over the top. Sweaty hands gripped handles and arms were run through enarmes.

Cutnose touched the long dagger at his belt. Tested the weight of his shield. His heart raced, his whole arm feeling numb. Despite fighting a hundred battles and the heat, his hands were cold. No matter how many battles he'd fought in, it was always the same. His chest beat in time with the turn of rough shod wheels.

Liquid dripped from the ceiling above. Cutnose looked upward and a droplet fell to his face. He wiped it away, crimson staining the leather of his gauntlet. Their archers were taking casualties, and it came as no surprise, as the infidels were excellent with a bow and the tower was a scarcely moving target as it struggled foot by foot closer to the walls.

He spoke quietly to Tancred. "Don't charge ahead. Stay with me and my men." Not only was it his task to keep Bohemond's nephew alive, Cutnose would say he'd grown rather fond of the young nobleman, and he wasn't fond of many nobles. They were as treacherous as the next man and even more entitled. With Tancred, he may go as far as to say he felt a bond with the lord, the way one feels with a younger brother or other close kin. As long as the kin paid handsomely to be his kin.

"You are far too old to keep up with a man in his prime," the young lord said, the gleam of determination settling upon his face.

"There's no easier man to keep up with than a dead one."

Tancred lifted a noble chin mail rustling. "Have faith. God will grant us victory."

"He'll grant us something," Cutnose said under his breath. Arrows, spears, and swords aplenty awaited them with the eagerness of a well-paid whore. Years on campaign, killing and leading men into battle, had seasoned Tancred to the crusade, making him a dangerous holy warrior, but he did not understand the horrors the top of the city walls could bring.

"The Lord rewards those who slay the enemies of God, regardless if they do it for coin or His blessing."

"All wars come down to coin." War and coin went hand in hand. There could be no war without coin and too much coin usually wrought more war. It kept men fed and armored. And a fed man would fight. It also supported men in less savory activities. To say that Cutnose was motivated for anything other than gold would be a sin. He loved a good woman in a tavern and strong drink, but above all, he liked living. So far, he'd done a fine job at it too. He'd lived far enough in life to reach the old age of about thirty-eight. Give or take a few years. His mother had once told him he'd been born during a blood moon of 1061, but the memory was lost to time. The truth lay in a shallow grave outside the city walls of Taranto for over thirty years.

The siege tower's pace slackened, the tower swaying, then rocked forward to a halt. Screams permeated from outside. The archers above performed their dastardly work. Now they were roughly the height of two men higher than the wall itself. Crossbow bolts sung a short and deadly song as they burst into the enemy archers, now that the crusaders held the high ground.

"We must cut the ropes," Tancred hissed.

"Patience," Cutnose said. "Give our archers a minute to clear the walls."

Every footman who carried a spear or lance had left it in the camp, gripping their melee weapons for the close and dirty work. Cutnose held a long hand axe at his side. The shaft was longer than most to give him better reach, especially from horseback, but still short enough to be wielded in close quarters. The axe-head was rounded with a short beard. It was as perfectly proficient at hewing a man as it would a tree branch. The shaft was wrapped in leather all the way to the axe-head to ensure a grip anywhere afforded extra purchase. Off the end of the shaft there was a leather loop that he would wrap around his wrist in a fight as to not lose his weapon in the melee.

"Hold men," he growled.

The crusaders steeled themselves with the words of their God. "Deus vult."

A violent and nervous energy gripped them. They must muster forth with all their speed. The dead shoved to the side. To be stalled on the bridge would promise death. Everything predicated in establishing a foothold on the wall. Then Godfrey would feed more soldiers into the gap. For if they did not, the whole effort would lie to rest with their corpses. Lifting his eyes in silent aid, Cutnose prayed the archers and crossbowmen found their mark.

Leather creaked as men regripped their weapon hilts. Mail armor whispered. Boots shuffled beneath them, restless soldier's energy with nowhere to relieve oneself, trapped inside a crumbling tower a hundred hands high. The worst thing a lord could ask his men to do was remain unmoving while a battle raged around them.

Jars smashed into the bottom of the secured draw bridge. Smoke puffed through as the fire ate at the coated furs and wattle screens made of laced branches of wood.

"The Greek fire," Tancred said with awe in his voice.

Roger raised his deep voice over the din of desperate men. "If any gets through, we'll have Ludolf put it out."

Despite his grin, Cutnose stared upward at the wood ceiling. *Hurry you poor bastards or we'll all be burnt to dust and ash.* Yet the enemy did not have real Greek Fire, at least he'd prayed as much, a magical flame that water could not drown. He'd heard it burned so fast and hot, men would simply turn to mounds of bony lard. The Saracens had a sort of devilish cousin that the Christians had been told was not nearly as effective. One that would have burned all of them alive had it not been for a Christian defector who had found his way into the camp three nights prior. He'd told the lords of the

Saracen plans, and that when doused with vinegar, the flames would be snuffed out. Jars of vinegar had been stored on the roof of the tower waiting for the Saracens to execute their wickedness.

Men breathed harder around him, battle fear coiling around their insides and squeezing. The smoke seeped inside the tower, slipping through the cracks and under helmets. It tormented their lungs, stung at their eyes until they were parchment and cracked their lips like brittle kindling.

"Bloody Christ," Henry cursed as an arrowhead punched through the shield covering the hole.

The smoke took on a tainted vinegarish stench as the flames were doused. Cutnose exhaled forcefully. Men coughed around him, the odor overcoming them. It worked, they had willingly traded one hell for another, and he'd take a hell trading blows with an infidel over cooking in his armor until his flesh melted from his bones every time.

"Cut the ropes!" Tancred cried over his shoulder.

A knight in the back vigorously sawed a piece of rope holding the bridge in place. With a crack, the drawbridge crashed onto the stone ramparts.

Are we too soon? But it was a fleeting thought that had no place here on the walls.

Bright light struck them as arrows to the eyes, making the men flinch and turn away with blindness. Cutnose hunkered lower behind his shield. They did not wait long before a cluster of arrows and stones crashed into them. An arrow slid upward off his shield. A rock clanged like a bell as it hit a helmet. A man cried out in the back. The men were so tightly packed Cutnose could not turn to see if it was one of his. Only time for God's work. No way but forward.

Terror-eyed and bloodied Saracens formed a ragged line, spear points aimed toward them, round shields stopping arrows from the crusader siege tower. One lurched backward as an arrow lodged into his skull, spraying blood in its wake, sending him off the wall. For a brief moment the two groups of enemies stared at one another, but that moment quickly passed.

Tancred lifted his sword and cried, "Deus vult!"

The crusaders surrounding him returned the battle cry, and Tancred raced onto the bridge, sword pointed over his shield, breaking any semblance of a shield wall. His blue-and-red shield vibrant as the sun's rays. *Brave fool,* Cutnose thought.

"Kill them all!" He shouted, and his men were the fools that followed a step behind into the enemies' waiting blades.

CHAPTER 2

An arrow blurred past followed by another. Saracen bows twanged over the shoulders of the footmen in front of them furiously slinging their deadly darts into the mass of crusaders. Along the length of the wall, archers popped upright loosing quarrels then crouched down to avoid the arrows flying in their direction. More Saracen archers leaned dangerously over the side of the wall to shoot the crusaders along the flanks of the bridge.

Mail armor jangled as Tancred's men raced over the short bridge suspended dangerously in the air, the single link between attacker and defender. Keeping his head just over his shield as to not obstruct his vision, Cutnose charged after the young noble. His hand axe cocked ready to strike, but not extended too high to risk becoming an easy target.

A crusader screamed as an arrow lodged deeply into his thigh, barbed point punching out the side. He clutched at the shaft before he tumbled over the side of the bridge. Shouts of 'Deus vult' deafened Cutnose's ears, drowning out the crunch of the man on the rocks beneath the tower.

Tancred collided with the line of defenders with a clap. His sword flashed as a lightning bolt striking left and right among them. The weight of his body and the fierceness of his attack wavered their line. He parried a spear thrust with his shield, another spear grazing along his shoulder in a half-hearted jab. The nobleman's sword crashed into a turbaned skull, the defender crying out as he was laid out upon the stones. Tancred raised his shield to protect himself from the onslaught of spears before cleaving through a defender's arm. The spearman screamed as his hand still holding the spear parted from his body. Tancred swept his sword wide at the Saracen's partner driving them both backward in an avalanche of force.

The crusaders surged behind Tancred, rushing to follow him onto the walls. *Pfffhff!* An arrow flew over Cutnose's shoulder and thumped into a shield behind him. At least Ludolf had enough self-preserving sense to keep his shield high. Cutnose leapt off the bridge to the battlements, slipping on slick blood as he deflected a spear thrust.

He regained his balance as a dark-skinned Saracen in a loose blue surcoat over a mail shirt and a conical bronze helmet, shouted something heathenish in his direction. He swung a straight sword in an overhead arc toward Cutnose. Cutnose lifted his shield to deflect the blow, but more importantly he whipped his axe downward into the man's unprotected ankle. He ignored the crack of bone as the Saracen was cleaved off his feet. He gave the man a single swing to the neck, turning his screams to gurgles, and scoured the battlements for his charge. Shields crashed together, and his men hacked their way around him.

"Stay together," Cutnose shouted. Ahead of him, Tancred was a serpent through the grassy stalks of defenders, his sword his deadly bite, felling men with dashing speed. He charged for the tower. Arrows continued to rain death from above onto the crusaders.

"Form on the Captain!" called Cutnose's second in command. The men called him Ralph the Gray; he was the eldest soldier in their company. He had a sun-burnt and tan face with a short gray-and-black beard jutting out from his chin, shield and sword in hand. He shoved a man into line joining Cutnose. He had been stuck in the rear of the siege tower and a sense of ease took hold of Cutnose knowing his oldest friend and battle-brother had finally reached his side.

The crusaders closed shields around him, hammering at their foes. Hermann screamed as he took a spear in his groin, pinning him to the ramparts before Henry shoved a sword through the Saracen's breast.

"Drive them off," Cutnose said to the men. Each swing pushed the enemy backward with their whirlwind of force. He kept darting his eyes from enemies to Tancred worrying the noble would be cut down and Cutnose could do nothing to prevent it.

Tancred beat two men backward toward a tower, his battle fury luring him further away, but more defenders rushed from the steps below. He slowed as slashing swords and thrusting spears put him on the defensive. He fought wildly to stay upright against the renewed spirit of the reinforcements.

"To Tancred!" Cutnose sprinted for the young lord. Age and experience made him a step slower in his pursuit, despite his long strides to catch the young noble. Garrison reinforcements wedged themselves in the middle, blocking his path.

Baring his teeth, he battered through a small buckler to hack a defender's shoulder. With a scream, the defender fell to the stone. He dodged a trio of spear thrusts, before Roger's mace smashed the spearman's shield to pieces. Cutnose bashed a spearman off balance with his shield and Geoffrey of Bari pierced his belly. The wounded began impeding their progress toward the tower providing unstable fighting grounds.

Time passed slowly in battle, but it was only slow in the eye of man, most everything that happened was chaotic and wild. Still to Cutnose it felt like an eternity had galloped past him before Cutnose could hack his way to Tancred's side. Using his shield, he shouldered into a man on Tancred's flank, pushing him backward until he had brought Tancred back into the fold. He felt the violent energy of his men around him. They wanted to break free like their lord, to run down their foes and slay them.

"Hold them back!" Cutnose shouted. He stood on his nobleman's right, protecting his unshielded side. The garrison soldiers continued to force their way onto the walls. More Saracens screamed obscenities as they navigated the steps from below. The two groups stalemated, neither able to gain leverage over the other.

Yet time was on the crusaders' side. Every moment they held a foothold Lord Godfrey ushered more men into the breach. Then it would become a weight scale of men, and mass equaled might. Once the walls were taken, the battle would quickly become a rout.

"The heavenly Father will rejoice at our brave deeds done in his name," Tancred breathed. An arrow ripped into his shield and the lord flinched. With a laugh, his voice grew louder. "Deus vult!" He bulled over the spearman in front of him and raced for the steps, cleaving the defenders in two groups, Cutnose was his shadow only a step behind. Defenders pushed their way onto the battlements and the rival soldiers met with a crash.

Cutnose hacked through a man's neck as he crossed the threshold of the battlement from below. Blood sprayed and the man fell forward. The man behind him stumbled, and Cutnose threw his weight into his shield to push him back.

A spear darted over his shield twice, and Cutnose tugged at his axe, still in the first Saracen. A sword clanged off the side of his helm staggering him, and the Saracens forced him backward. Tancred was there, a golden shadow of death, his sword biting viciously into the Saracen's neck, blood bubbling from the wound. Cutnose barked a thanks at the young lord. "It was me who was supposed to watch for you."

"There is still time to repay your debt," Tancred yelled, throwing himself back into the fray. He hacked at Saracen shields with such fury they shied away, stepping awkwardly upon their fallen comrades to escape.

"Dickless," Roger shouted at the enemy. He shouldered past Cutnose and swung his mace with brute violence. It caved in a man's skull, sending bone and gore airborne. Ralph the Gray skewered a man through the chest and the enemy was driven down the steps. A Saracen fell from the stairs to the streets below.

Bodies rolled down the steps, hindering the defenders. Cutnose's men formed a wall of wood, metal, and man, severing access to the walls from the city. The Fatimids in the streets hesitated, unable to navigate the steps, and saw the wall for what it was, certain death. Fear seized control and they broke for their homes or the Citadel. It mattered not. Those still on the walls were finding no mercy from the attackers and were massacred by the zealous swords and axes of the crusaders.

Cutnose allowed himself to catch his breath for only a moment. He ducked behind his shield as an arrow almost took him in the head. *Never ends.* It pierced William behind him, biting deep into his arm. The mercenary dropped his axe hunching over to clutch his wound.

Arrows continued to fall upon them from the rampart tower. Another company of crusaders emerged from the siege tower floor beneath them and raced to join the fray, eyes enraged and ready for bloodletting. Two fell as arrows pierced exposed necks and faces. Another man lost his balance falling from the bridge.

"Cutnose! The door!" Tancred shouted.

Cutnose lifted his shield. "To the tower!" His men followed, shields covering their heads from the projectiles above. They hugged the wall of the tower like old friends.

Tancred breathed heavily, his eyes alight. "We must take this tower. I want my standard to hang from the ramparts for all to see. It will give the men courage and send terror through our enemies!"

His shoulder fatiguing, Cutnose kept his shield overhead. Better than catching an arrow through the eye. He flinched as an arrowhead plunged through the wood. "We're on it." He called down the line. "Roger!" He jogged forward, his mace slung and two-handed axe in hand. Cutnose and his men shifted tighter, covering the colossal man as he hewed the door.

"God wills it!" Tancred shouted. The third wave of soldiers emerged from the siege tower with a yell. They joined the others, shields shoved into backs, driving the defenders away from the siege tower by sheer weight while others made for the city. An arrow splintered on the ramparts and the young lord ducked with a grin.

"Keep your head down, lord. An arrow can kill a rich man as much as a poor one."

"Nonsense. We have better armor. Hurry man! We must be the first."

Roger puffed red cheeks as he worked. The wood was thick and sturdy, reinforced to prevent easy incursion inside. "As fast as I fucking can." The axe-head chewed into the wood door. With a thunderous crack, the door gave way. A spear point darted through the doorway and almost ran Roger through the neck. He rolled away onto the ramparts and Cutnose brushed the doorway as he forced himself inside, shoving a spear aside and sticking the man between the eyes. Henry pushed past the dying spearman, and the band of men rushed the defenders, hacking and slashing in the close quarters.

The men inside had little fight left. They were poor archers. No armor. No helms. Only bows and tunics. A few wore thicker robes. Nothing that would stop the Norman blades from cutting them down as a farmer versus wheat during harvest. Cutnose's men swept over them in a mercifully quick fury of death holding near the ladder leading to the tower roof.

The Normans shielded themselves as the remaining archers shot quarrels down the tower ladder. Shields held high, Henry crawled rung over rung followed by Roger and Pagan. The crusaders were an inevitable slow-moving death, their war song complemented by the thudding drum of arrows into their shields.

Cutnose's men pushed through the trap doorway to the tower roof. He followed behind, a witness to the slaughter. Fatimid archers breathed their last, butchered to mere limbs and pieces, gurgling whispers to their God. Pagan threw an archer over the tower walls, his screams cut short by the rocks below. Cutnose's men stared at one another in the exultation of battle. Giving Pagan a nod, Cutnose raced to the tower battlement.

Ladders were slammed against the city walls below. Men climbed, free from stinging arrows and crushing stones. Another surge of crusaders spilled from the siege tower, followed by the most famous crusading lord in the army, Godfrey of Bouillon and his champions, gleaming in their white surcoats and armor, unstained by the grime and gore of battle. He marched toward the tower entering below.

Cutnose caught his breath. Despite the familiarity with the weight of his kit, a fight always tired a man out. A few of his men searched the dead and dying. Henry drew a knife over a man's throat as the archer grasped at him. "Shh, Hell awaits."

"Ludolf? Where is Ludolf of Tournai?" Tancred asked. He seemed almost recovered from the exertion.

"Don't know, my lord," Cutnose said. Roger handed him a bladder of wine. Cutnose upended the bladder before handing it off to Ralph the Gray then wiped his mouth.

"That man," Tancred said with a quick shake of his head.

"Here my lord," came a shout from below.

"Always a bit behind, that one," Henry said with a raise of his eyebrows.

Ludolf emerged from the tower floor below. His armor and clothes mostly clean. If any one of them were clean at this point it was undoubtedly an act of God.

"My standard, sir," Tancred demanded.

Ludolf opened a leather bag, removing a man-length tri-tailed flag of blue with red tips and a white-and-red checkered stripe running diagonally. It matched the crest upon Tancred's shield as the noble house of Hauteville. A house of Norman adventures turned southern Italian nobles. He whipped the flag as he unfurled it.

"Hand it over," Tancred said. He ripped down the green Fatimid flag covered with Saracen writing and tossed it over the ramparts. It fluttered as it fell to the rocks below. He took his own and draped it over the tower edge. Crusaders outside the city gave a cheer and Tancred raised his sword high into the air.

Godfrey of Bouillon emerged from the trap door followed by four of his knights. Three wore surcoats of white, an armoring tactic that was being adopted by the crusaders to keep them cooler in the unforgiving sun. Their shields bore a green tree on a field of red. They all had the same hawk-like appearance, making it clear they were brothers. Henry, Godfrey, and William of Esch.

The oldest of the three brother knights was Henry, the current lord of Esch, holding the castle of Esch-sur-Sûre in the Ardennes. To use the term lord to describe them was a stretch. They led a band of brigands terrorizing the citizenry of a rival lord on behalf of the Count of Luxembourg and were rewarded with a keep for their crude efforts. They were ever eager men to bear the cross and see what riches lie in the East.

Godfrey's last knight had a red cross sewn upon his white surcoat. His mail coat was dirty, his clean-shaven cheeks dirty, his eyes beyond wary. A thin red scar encircled his neck.

Sir Clarembald of Vendeuil was a knight who traveled with the commoners in what was being called the People's Crusade. The pilgrims had been treacherously cut down in Anatolia, any survivors sold as slaves. Clarembald was one of the few trained knights traveling with the peasantry and had managed to survive, getting his throat slit by a Turk then laying amongst the dead for over a day in the heat, his armor baking him, before he stumbled to the nearest town where friendly Greeks took him in. He then rejoined the nobles and their armies as they passed through Anatolia after the first pilgrims. Unable to speak, he always stood as a silent sentinel near Godfrey and had become a sort of hero amongst the crusaders for his silent dedication to the cause. Cutnose took a knee followed by all his men lowering their heads in deference. Tancred bowed to the leader of the Crusade.

Godfrey of Bouillon was a tall man for his age, he held fierce, calculating eyes, set beneath a stern brow, and a gray beard with a black mustache sticking overtop the mail coif encompassing his face. He wore a conical helm with a nosepiece, a white surcoat bearing a red cross encompassing his entire chest. The mail visible from beneath the surcoat glittered in the sun, and he wore a cloak of red and white. He eyed the city for a moment before his eyes found Tancred.

"Tancred, my son, you've done well. First over the walls. First to plant God's standard. First among my knights. This day will be remembered throughout history." Brazenly he contemplated the holy city over the wall, a king surveying his new rich domain. "Let us send a message to the rest of the army of our success. Henry, you may return brave Tancred's standard to him." He paused. "Then raise my own."

Tancred bowed his head without hesitation. "The honor was mine, lord." Yet his eyes harshly found Henry as he tugged down Tancred's banner. The standard was shoved back into his hands while the youngest knight of Esch, William, rolled out Godfrey's red and white one.

Godfrey grinned at its sight. "The glory is yours, but the men know my standard and fight in my army."

"Yes, my lord."

Godfrey surveyed his army rushing to pour through the siege engine then turned, eyeing the city with a satisfied grin. Screams and shouts over the clang of metal swelled beneath the walls. "You may carry forth your assault, Lord Tancred. The end is near, but the enemy is not beaten yet."

Tancred dipped his head in deference. "No heathen resistance shall survive the wrath of the Lord."

"Indeed."

The rest of the crusader army swarmed across the open grounds toward Jerusalem. They bottlenecked in the rubble of the exterior wall, clambering over broken stone. Once through the exterior, they sprinted over the remaining land between the walls. Arrows were still launched at them, but the defenders were falling back further and further through narrow city streets.

A fire started in an open-air market near the western walls. Colorful stalls all blazed orange-and-yellow flames, and black smoke snaked its way into the sky. Terror embraced the city. A torrent of crusaders flooded inside the walls. Godfrey sucked in air with a fierce nod. "Christendom has won a great victory this day." He presided over the city that collapsed before his men. "There is much work to do." He nodded to Tancred and left the tower followed by his bodyguards.

Tancred turned on Cutnose. "Prepare your men, we strike deeper into the city. Tend your wounded quickly. Godfrey is right, we must push our success even further this day."

Cutnose turned to his second in command. "Who's accounted for? Ralph?"

Forty-two footmen had served in Cutnose's band. Most hailed from the lands around Apulia in the southern end of the Roman peninsula near the island Kingdom of Sicily, but adventurers from all over the western and northern kingdoms and duchies had found themselves in the company: a couple Danes, an Anglo-Saxon, a Fleming, and a few of the northern Normans.

About a dozen had fought on the island of Sicily and in the far east with Bohemond against the Turks and the Eastern Romans. Men with the eastern campaigning experience were highly desired by every noble on crusade, and the men who had served with Bohemond had the most.

The rest of Cutnose's men were new to the band, although no virgins to the ways of violence: warriors, adventurers, and a few cutthroats and men who wouldn't discuss their past. They stunk worse than shit, they wouldn't back down from the devil himself, and they were ready to unleash a religious-sanctioned fury upon the holy city becoming rich men in the process.

All their sins would be absolved so what did it matter how sinful they were in previous lives? Cutnose had his fair share of un-Christian like behavior, surely enough to send him straight to a fiery eternal death in Hell so a pardon of sorts suited him just right. As did gold, plenty of drink, and a woman or two, or three. He supposed all his men were like that in one way or another.

His band alone had lost ten men to a fever during the siege of Antioch. Those afflicted shook themselves violently until they died. Another seventeen fell to Saracen and Turkish blades and arrows. Simon, a sturdy former household guard for the Count of Rossano that had grown out of favor when he'd lain with too many of the household servants, had a grazing arrow wound to the arm that turned it green and then black becoming useless as a eunuch in a whorehouse. Cutnose knew he would die then, but the man kept living, a corpse marching along beside them until he fell, never rising again. His body lie under a pile of rocks only a mile from the walls of Jerusalem. Cutnose could make no sense of it. He'd seen men lose a hand or take a blade to the belly and live. Yet this hearty soldier fell to a mere scratch and the foul spirits.

Much like every Frank who remained for the final assault on Jerusalem, they were all harder, leaner versions of themselves. Men ready to see the campaign completed and finally get paid while reaping whatever riches they could from the city.

"Hermann took a bloody spear to the groin," Ralph said with a grimace. "Don't suspect long before he moves to Heaven. William took an arrow through the arm."

The normally jovial company surrounding them became more somber.

"Which one? Bow or axe William?" Cutnose asked.

"Axe."

"Get him water and see if he can keep up. Check on Hermann. We're going to miss his bow."

"Aye." Ralph climbed down the ladder and disappeared below.

Only thirteen men left including myself, and that's if William can still fight.

Tancred grasped his standard between his hands. His men handed around a bag of wine. Cutnose joined his young lord staring at Godfrey's banner. "Tancred. This is his army. Think nothing of it."

"My standard will fly this day."

"You fought well, lord. Although I wouldn't recommend charging *so* far ahead."

"I am just faster than you, old soldier."

"I've lived this long for a reason, my lord."

Tancred turned to smile at him. "The day isn't over yet."

Cutnose's men started to laugh now as Roger picked up the fallen corpse of an archer. He danced with the body in his arms, humming a tune, making a circle around the rooftop. "Dance with me?" he asked Henry. The tall soldier chuckled and shook his head no. Roger swept to the side. "A dance?" he asked William. The archer leaned on the wall trading his long knife for a bow and quiver. "Not today, my lady." Roger danced his way over to Cutnose. "Captain? One last dance?"

"Next time," Cutnose said.

Roger bowed, making sweeping steps to the wall and dumped the body over the edge.

"Your men have wicked souls," Tancred said.

"Wicked and sin free," Cutnose added with a grin.

Ralph reappeared. "I have made Hermann as comfortable as I can, but we must make haste or the other men will gain at our loss."

"Aye, they're going to get all the best plunder after we did all the dirty work," Roger added, wiping the archer's blood on his sleeve.

A bandaged axe William poked his head through the trap door to the roof, red seeping from the rags on his arm. "Captain, if I'm going to take a bloody arrow, we best get something for it."

"This is a big city," Cutnose responded. "Let them drive the enemy back. Drink water, it will help with the blood loss."

He turned back to Tancred, and the lord still clutched his standard. "They are right. We mustn't delay." He scanned the rooftops of the city. "There is much wealth and power here. We should secure our share."

Cutnose nodded in agreement. He wasn't there to say no to his lord. Guide him, yes. Protect him, yes, but not stand in his way.

"I sent Humbert and Bertrand to gather our mounts. They will arrive soon. There is more to be done," Tancred said. He climbed from the tower.

Roger slapped Cutnose's shoulder. "We're going to be rich with gold and have a dozen bastards in different bellies by the end of the night."

"More than we can say for Hermann."

Roger frowned at the thought, an ugly face turned uglier. "Every man knows the risk. I don't like to see a man wounded especially down there, but we all know the risk."

"You wouldn't be saying that if it were you," said Henry.

"You're right. I'd slit me own throat if me yard was gone."

"We can hope it ends this night and we can put our man's yard to use." Cutnose loved to fight, but he loved living and women so much more. One could always find a fight, but women and gold were harder to come by. "I will seek out a priest for him."

"Look out for our coin pouches and our souls. A rare trait from a free captain."

"You just look out for infidel archers, and we'll call it even."

Roger gave a hearty laugh rotating his mace in a circle. "Me mace never met a skull it couldn't crack."

Cutnose stared out at the holiest city in the world. Every major religion of the world claimed it for themselves yet only one could rule it. Most of the buildings were constructed with a softer pinkish-white stone, everything bordering upon the same bland colorlessness. However, it was not devoid of color.

Dark green foliage was inviting, especially around pools and fountains. There were enclosed gardens and lonely pine trees standing straight, but the trees were few in and around the city, long since taken to build siege engines and defenses. Spires of churches loomed triumphant. A gold-domed building sat on a hill surrounded by gardens. Green Fatimid flags flapped in the smoky haze of a city under assault.

Screams permeated the air, and Cutnose smiled. Lords played their games, but so did the common man. It meant three things: women, gold, and relics to be sold. Three years on campaign may as well have been a thousand, and it was time to get paid with the blood price. It was time to reap the divine rewards of a successful pilgrimage.

CHAPTER 3

If Jerusalem were a bride on her wedding night, she was breached, but the sacking had yet to consummate. Resistance sprang out from buildings and towers, each instance viciously suppressed by the crusaders sensing the end was near for the garrison. Crusaders flowed through the streets only deviating to loot and pillage.

Bloodied boots splashed over wet stones as Cutnose's men trailed behind Tancred's mounted knights. Darkened bodies lay splayed in the streets, draining tributaries feeding the rivers of red, washing over the stones. The men waded in and around the fallen with as much feeling as they would give butchered animal carcasses. Although he was accustomed to the sight of the dead, the smaller forms of children tugged at his gut. He ignored them, nothing could be done now. He was many unsavory things, but a child murderer he was not.

The view directly ahead of him was slightly more palatable than the dead, almost eye-level with a horse's ass. The stench of shit and blood dominated the air. Their mail coats susurrated as they jogged, chests heaving beneath the weight. A few of his men had picked up spears from the fallen, but the rest still carried their bloodied melee weapons.

William held his bow while Peter lifted a bow and quiver off a dead archer. He was proficient enough with the weapon to make him a threat and since Hermann had been grievously injured on the walls, they needed at least one other archer in their ranks, otherwise the Saracens could rain arrows upon them from afar with no fear of reprisal. Both archers slung their plain shields behind them and stayed in the interior of the formation where they could fire protected over the armored men.

The streets narrowed and widened at will as if the city were not made by men but by a sculptor who packed clay repeatedly in the same locations. A Frankish soldier with a long black mustache emerged from inside a home. He gave them a bloody smile beneath his helm and hefted a robed woman over his shoulder, disappearing back toward the walls.

The road gradually sloped upward, the blood running along the streets and the angle making the stone slick. He tried to focus on keeping pace with the mounted knights.

"God damn this man," Ralph breathed next to him. The elder warrior had seen many campaigns and served many lords. He knew that the most profitable time to be a soldier was sacking a city, not running exhausted through the city streets on a lord's whim.

"We should be pillaging," Henry sounded off quietly from behind. "That Frank had a fine-looking woman on his shoulder."

"We are owed our war-gift," Pagan said with a frown. "Or we will take it. No man may say we are not owed."

The air burned in Cutnose's chest, but he kept his outward features calm. "Better than walking around the city barefoot waiting for God to allow us entry." He referred to the multitude of religious processions put on by the crusaders around the walled city. Heavy breathing and a few smiles met him. His men had watched the pilgrims in morbid amusement, they were about as pious as a pack of wolves having caught the scent of a wounded stag. Even Ralph had declined to march, his years on campaign outweighing his piety. Most had returned without wounds, but the risk of an errant arrow finding its way inside them was enough to keep them back. "Tancred will take care of us. He swore it." Their boots thumped the stones, splashing through crimson puddles.

"Better. Everyone else is getting all the good loot," Roger said, his mace resting on his shoulder as he jogged. The young nobleman's entourage slowly outpaced them until they were opaque shadows in the black smoke. His men coughed around him, the smoke stinging eyes and noses equally, bringing on streams of snot and tears.

A woman cried out in a building next to them. Men laughed in the distance. An elder man in robes sat in a pool of blood next to a smashed door, his white beard stained red. He blinked at them as they passed. Many would not survive the night, of that Cutnose was sure.

They finally rejoined the mounted knights near a lower ten-foot stone wall. Tancred's collection of followers had grown over the campaign as the young lord had taken chances in growing his wealth and lands. Many lords and knights had shifted from beneath Bohemond's command to Tancred's with the desire to complete their pilgrimage as the uncle had stayed near Antioch to assert his claim. Most were second and third or bastard sons of lords seeking to claim lands and secure riches deprived of them by their birthright.

In Tancred's *conroi,* personal guard riding with him in battle, the highest-ranking lord was Lord Robert of Limosano, his leaf-shaped shield was painted red with three black circles stretching diagonally across. He was a man of middling height, with a hooked nose and a pock-covered face. Mounted near him was a small dark-skinned Greek, Sir Attropius, who used a round metal shield and carried a cluster of javelins on his horse's saddle. There was the bastard of Lord Richard of Salerno, Rainald, a permanent scowl on his face as if he couldn't decide what he hated more, being a bastard or the infidels. Then a trio of landless knights like Sir Guarin and Sir Hermann and the brave Ludolf of Tournai. Ludolf gave them a petty glance as Cutnose and his men caught their breath.

A short outer wall made from tan stone stood in their path. *Something of value resides within,* he thought. Merlons lined the top of the wall providing men cover during an assault. A thick wooden postern door with a rusted iron ring barred them. It was no citadel but could deter men easy access to the golden-domed building looming on the other side.

"What is this place?" Henry asked between breaths. "Looks rich."

"Aye," Roger grunted. "Dome made of gold."

Cutnose gasped for breath. A few put their hands on their knees. Intrigue alone kept them from splintering apart to find their own loot.

Tancred turned his steed pointing, "Cutnose. Get a ram and break down the door."

"You heard the lord," Cutnose said with a glare. The young lord intended to keep them tired. "Hurry." He pointed at a nearby home, a two-story building made of pale stone.

Roger lowered a shoulder into the house's door, bludgeoning it open. He disappeared inside to the screams of the occupants followed by William the archer.

Ralph spoke softly. "The men are right. Perhaps a few of us should peel off in case this cause is not fruitful. The men will not be happy to get whatever is left."

"No. Stay with me. We may need everyone for a fight inside." He eyed the dome with determination. A handful of archers atop this short wall would cause them serious problems, and Cutnose only had a dozen men left at his disposal. "If this place is made of gold, men will fight for it. Bohemond and Tancred will ensure we are paid."

Ralph clenched his jaw. "You place all your trust in these lords.

I've known noble low-born men and low noblemen, but seldom do I meet a noble lord. For both our sakes, I hope your faith is not ill-placed." An angry band of mercenaries could elect a new captain by any number of violent means.

Cutnose squeezed his oldest friend's mailed shoulder. "Stay the course. Soon we will be rich men."

Ralph gave a small grin. "Not rich enough."

"Enough to last until the next campaign."

Ralph's wary eyes searched the short wall for any movement that indicated an ambush. "I'm not sure I will travel back."

"No?"

"If a man is to meet the end of his life, what holier place could he die?"

"Always thought I'd need to replace you after you were cut down. Who would have thought it would be Jerusalem that took you from me?"

"My fighting days are not finished. They will need swords if they hope to hold this city." Ralph gestured with his head at the mounted knights. "These men didn't come here to give it all back when they were done. Tancred wants to make a name for himself, and he might be just brazen enough to do it."

"Perhaps he will." The young lord had enormous potential, he was Bohemond only younger, equally as brave and ambitious but with a greater sense of the politics of the East. If he stayed alive long enough, he not only was a potential employer, but an excellent ally to have. "And he will get there on the backs of men like us."

"That is a mercenary's life. The longest road and shortest route you'll ever travel."

Roger and William returned with a sturdy table hoisted between them. "Line 'em up." He gripped a table leg, and his men surrounded the makeshift ram and raced toward the gate.

"Hurry along men," Ludolf called at them.

"That man can kiss a whore on the arse," Cutnose said to Ralph. He placed himself along the rear of the table. "Make quick work," he said to his men with a glare for the knight. He'd love to flog a bit of bravery into him but held back.

They pounded the gate and on the tenth ram the door relinquished with a shower of splinters. Swords released from scabbards. Cutnose removed his axe from his belt, gripping it as he prepared for a fight.

With a nod from Tancred, they rushed inside the compound expecting arrows and spears. Instead, they were brought to a halt by the beautiful majesty of the courtyard. Lush gardens spanned to either side, with exotic fauna grasping for the sky, greenery that had been immaculately groomed and in the center of the garden plaza rested the gold-domed building. The entire place reeked of divine regality fit for lords and ladies, not a band of mercenaries. His men couldn't help but stand and stare at the colossal building, power and glory ebbing from the stones as a bell rung and left to rest. Then further south another giant building stretched its arms wide.

"Would you look at that?" Henry said, using his sword pommel to scratch dried blood from the side of his neck. "Just one shingle off the dome could make me richer than even Godfrey himself."

The knights walked their horses past them until Tancred halted them. He removed his helm and wiped his glistening blond beard and forehead. "Templum Domini." The men gasped. The Temple of God. He eyed the southern building. "It is as written in the bible," Tancred said. "Templum Solomunis." The Temple of Solomon. While the heathens had taken the use of such buildings for their own, these were in fact important places for Christians first. One of the most sacred places in all of Christendom, and here these men all stood before it.

"My eyes have shown me the glory of God," Ralph said, blessing himself. "To be in its presence is an eternal gift."

"Imagine what they might have inside," Roger muttered, tossing down the ram. He licked his lips. "We're gonna be richer than the pope."

"Saracens!" William shouted. He drew his bow, stretching the bowstring past taut. On the roof of the Temple of Solomon, shadowy forms peeked over the edge of the building.

"Stay your bow!" Tancred shouted, holding out a hand. He pointed. "You!"

The people shrank before his voice. He shouted in the Saracen's tongue, his words both slow and calculated. His understanding of the heathen language had been learned from many years warring against the Muslims in Sicily. A language Cutnose only understood a select few phrases of. *How much? Where's the gold? Sit. Stay. Die.*

"Remain here, men." Tancred walked his horse closer.

"My lord, there could be archers all over the rooftop," Cutnose said.

"The old man has assured me there are no soldiers here."

"An infidel's word means nothing," Ludolf hissed.

"God is with us this night," Tancred said. He turned his horse away approaching the structure, peering upward at the old man.

"One hand-size rock dropped over the edge, and we've failed our oath to Lord Bohemond," Ralph said.

"I would say one the size of one of Roger's plums would send him to Heaven." He watched intently, ready to spring into action as the elder called to Tancred and they conversed over the side of the building.

"Keep an arrow on him," Cutnose said to William.

"Aye, captain." His archer kept the bowstring pulled tight, experienced strength allowing the man to hold the position with an eye narrowed as he settled his aim.

Tancred turned his horse away from the temple. Cutnose let out a sigh as the lord walked out of bowshot. Then he shouted to his men. "Get the ram." They leapt to obey, running back to the gate.

"Stop," Tancred commanded.

The mercenaries slowed and turned, unsure of which man to obey.

"My lord?"

"We will not enter this Temple."

"Lord, this holy mount belongs to God," Ludolf said. "The presence of the infidels inside desecrates its sanctity."

Cutnose considered Ludolf briefly, debating whether or not to give credence to his words. "We are in agreement, lord, we should ensure the enemy does not plan a counter-attack from within its walls." *And ensure any riches are collected quickly.*

Tancred raised a hand. "Enough. The Temple and these Holy Grounds are under my protection. Woe to any man who threatens those who reside within."

"Has he gone mad?" Henry said quietly.

"Plenty of riches in there," Roger grumbled.

A killer's vibe pulsed from his men. A lord died as easy as any other man when riches beyond worldly measure were involved. Yet, twelve footmen versus twelve mounted knights were not favorable odds for a renege on their contract.

Cutnose weighed the situation. He had little to gain by turning on his lord now. They'd traveled to the ends of the world together. He even liked the young noble enough to not let him take an arrow through the neck, but a mountain of gold could take any man in its shiny avalanche. Money over loyalty or was it the other way around? It only worked well when both were high. Riches to warriors kept them loyal and marching on campaign.

"Sir, the town is being pillaged. If it is harm to those inside, then none shall be harmed, but let us have our reward. You may protect the innocent. I am sure your uncle would be proud of such a just display of mercy," Cutnose said. A couple of his men chuckled into their shields. They knew he flattered the lord. The knights and lords were just killers and thieves pretending to be something else, preaching God and chivalry while they did it.

Tancred pressed his horse near Cutnose, forcing the captain to step backward, then he loomed over him like the Archangel Michael over Satan's minions. He lifted his chin as he peered at his hired soldiers. "I know what kind of men you are. I know why you are here." He removed his helm and pulled back his coif. He shook out his sweaty blond hair, then regarded Cutnose again. "I do not trust the other lords and knights. They are in a blood rage. But I know I can trust you, as I would trust you with my own life. Have I given you any reason to not be loyal to me?"

Cutnose looked at his men then his eyes ventured back to the young noble. His features were calm and chiseled. "You have not."

"Have I not paid you more than my uncle would?"

"You have, my lord." The young lord was almost paying them enough for Cutnose and his men to never consider fighting for anyone else, even Bohemond. But in the manner of sacking a city, a man stood to gain drastically in his loot outside of his immediate employment. "This is where men feed their families. The looting, my lord."

Tancred squinted at him in harsh measurement. "How many riches do you think you can secure from plundering this city?"

"My lord?"

Tancred gestured over the breadth of the city. "How much can you squeeze from these people? How much before you are satisfied? Speak truthfully or so help you God."

Cutnose exchanged a glance with Ralph. Roger frowned, gripping his mace. The others shifted uncomfortably. There was a conflict brewing between their captain and an employer, the man whose life they were supposed to protect, a very wealthy man that stood in the way of acquiring a king's wealth. "The people of Jerusalem are known for their hoarding ways. I'm sure they've buried enough silver and gold to feed a man for a thousand lifetimes." Cutnose scratched his itchy beard with the edge of his axe. When on campaign, his men would let theirs grow, but during the down times in the cities, the men would shave their faces clean of hair. The hair on his head he kept in Norman style, shaved along the rear and longer on top that a linen coif would cover, as to not allow his hair to rip out while wearing a mail coif or a helm. *May as well ask for double.* "Two hundred tarì a man. Four hundred for my second. Six hundred for me. We'll take half as many dinars." Twenty-five tarì could buy them a fine horse. One hundred could secure land. It was a steep price and he doubted any of these men would do that. It would be less after they secured passage back to their homeland.

Tancred's eyes were cool chips of ice and unreadable, a prince in every form, unfeeling of the adjudication he was about to give. "I would see you knighted. There's plenty of land here. Your men could form my guard."

"A knighthood?"

"I would see you be an honest man yet."

Mutters came from his men. They were a free company, sold to the highest bidder. Soldiers of fortune, not claimed men, tied to the land.

Ralph leaned closer. "It is not every day a common man is offered a knighthood."

Ludolf balked behind Tancred. "He is far too common to be elevated."

"Quiet, Sir Ludolf. All men are common until a title is bestowed upon them."

Cutnose lowered his head for a moment. "You do me and my men great honor."

Tancred eyed him harshly.

"Yet, my men came here for riches, not employment."

Tancred nodded his head. "You have shown your virtues, captain. I will give each man two hundred more than what you ask."

A soft murmur rose from the smirking lips of Cutnose's men. Twice as much as they could hope to thieve from the townspeople. Perhaps less than whatever relics were housed inside the temples, there could be nothing, or the greedy infidels could have swallowed every valuable in the place, not knowing his men were willing to cut them open to find even a speck of gold. It was one thing to survive until they'd been paid, but it was another to be promised far more than the expectation. Ralph's gray eyes were hard, holding a wary hopefulness.

"You are going to give us two hundred more?"

"Four hundred for each man, six hundred for your second and eight hundred for you. But you must not stray from my orders."

"And what's that my lord?" Cutnose smirked to himself. With eight-hundred pieces, he'd need a chest best carried by two men or in a cart, a reinforced lock, and perhaps a dog to watch over it. A man didn't carry eight-hundred pieces on his person or his back, not a man bearing armor and weapons. He could buy a title when this was done.

"You mustn't allow a soul to harm the people inside the temple." His horse stomped a hoof in irritation. Its nostrils flared. The smell of the blood and bodies unsettling the animal. Putrid smoke formed over the city like an ebony tempest.

"Captain," Roger said, leaning closer. "They're only Saracens. What do we care?" Cutnose waved him away.

"You have but a moment to make your decision."

The calls of a dying city still echoed. Fires crackled. The cries of a despairing people. The sword song of men battling was faint in the distance.

Jerusalem was a large city compared to most Cutnose had seen, all save for Rome and Constantinople, but was filled with enough riches for every man to be his own king. Yet eight hundred pieces was one hell of a sum.

Perhaps he would buy land near Taranto. Money could change a man like him, or so he'd been told. Or he would just spend it on every curly dark-haired, perky-titted whore in Apulia until it ran out, then find his way into another war. Finding a fight was never a problem. Finding one you were guaranteed to win was the difficulty. Bohemond would have found another campaign by then. "I promised your uncle to watch over you."

Tancred's grin was as broad as an axe wound, splitting his face. He lifted a hand. "I assure you I will not fall this night, but if it is your honor at stake, I release you of any oath save for my own. You will protect these innocent people like they were me and you will be rewarded."

Cutnose nodded softly, mail jingling. "We will do what you ask. No harm will come to these people." He lowered his head. "You have my oath."

"No one. I repeat no one, noble or otherwise, may harm these people. Under my authority."

"Lords, my lord?"

"Brave Cutnose and his band shying away from killing nobles now?"

"Course not but we risk much to deny a lord."

"I will make sure there is no retribution."

Ralph spoke over Cutnose's shoulder. "That's a lot of gold if he speaks true."

"Not sure we can refuse," Cutnose said with a tired grin.

"Very well, Captain Robert Cutnose. We are sworn to one another in more ways than one." Tancred turned back, gesturing at Ludolf. "Give him my standard."

"But I bear your house's symbol, lord, with honor."

"We have other matters to attend, my friend. Hand him the standard."

Ludolf stepped his steed over the finely polished stone path. He handed the standard to Cutnose waiting for him to grab the pole before bending over his mount. "Be vigilant, Cutnose, or risk disrespecting Tancred's noble name and bring dishonor to your own. Although I'm not sure such a low-born cur as yourself could understand the meaning of it."

Ludolf's words rolled off Cutnose and he retorted without hesitation. "Be vigilant, Sir Ludolf, or risk letting harm befall our lord. For if he falls, I know who to present to Bohemond." Ludolf's mouth settled upon a sneer and Cutnose snatched the flag from him, handing it off to Ralph. His lieutenant marched it to the double door leading inside the temple. He hung the standard through a hook making it clear to all that a noble had staked his claim here.

"When the Christian storm blows over, you will be paid your sum. Come men." Tancred raised a hand, and his entourage of knights spurred their horses to a gallop through the gate.

The holiest city in the world was being ravaged by the brave knights of Christendom and Cutnose's company could do nothing but watch with stinging eyes and empty purses, putting all their faith in a single lord to uphold his promises.

CHAPTER 4

As the day breathed its last, so did the inhabitants of Jerusalem. The smoky tendrils of slaughter carried on into the waning light. The crusaders had bled both Jerusalem and the heavens of all its life blood leaving only a pallid pink sky in its wake.

The screams continued to erupt in the chaos that had swallowed the city, both poignant and jarring, as the waking of an ancient man. The people's cries were ones with which Cutnose was familiar, the distinct pitch of a pig squealing or the screeching of a wounded calf, all blending into a single hellish choir. The gut-wrenching tumult were accompanied by the shod-hooves and boots echoing over stone streets from outside the enclosure of the Temple Mount.

Opposite the dying city, the inner courtyard of the Temple Mount was almost peaceful, if one could ignore the raping and pillaging raging outside its walls. Cutnose had posted men atop the gate as lookouts, for every crusader had seen the golden dome and wondered how many riches he could pry from its walls.

William the archer pointed out a growing inferno in the Jewish part of the city and Cutnose joined him to watch. Fire leapt around the edges of the giant building zealously reaching for the roof. "Buildings like that burn hard on their own," Cutnose said.

"Aye."

Cutnose turned to peer at the golden dome. "We may be next. Keep your eyes sharp."

"I will, captain."

Cutnose left the archer to his watch.

He found Pagan and Roger laying on their bellies across the stones of a cistern, cupping their hands and slurping crisp water from the fountains. Cutnose knelt to wash off his face and scrub his hands then proceeded to clean the blade of his axe.

He dipped the axe blade beneath the surface and used a calloused finger to scrub. Left for too long, blood and gore corroded the metal, weakening its edge over time until it broke under pressure. Rubbing a finger along the blade, he noticed an uneven chip. He'd need to see a blacksmith when this was through and have him sharpen the gouge out. He secured the axe back on his belt.

He rolled his shoulders out, wishing to be free of his mail coat, but any veteran knew that residing in a captured city presented a whole other set of dangers than the assault itself. A sharp whistle came from across the courtyard. Every man turned toward William crouching on the wall. Cutnose wiped his hands on his soiled reddish cloak, stolen from an Eastern Roman soldier long ago. He stood to get a better view of the archer.

William knelt along with Peter, spying between the embrasures. William signaled to Cutnose opening and closing his fist spreading his fingers five times. Twenty-five against his twelve. He growled; *Tancred should have left more men.* He eyed the Temple of God with its gold roof and blue sides. It bequeathed utter and total commanding opulence. It was only a matter of time before more men wanted a piece of the heavenly riches for their own.

Cutnose gave no orders to Ralph, his second was already on the move. Both men understood what was at stake. It was the tightness of two warriors who had fought together for over a decade. There was a trust between them. A shared knowledge that one could be relied upon in life and death.

Ralph pointed at each man, his scale armor dully glinting in the dying light. The men hustled upright from where they rested, ignoring the exhaustion of campaign, donning helms, hefting weapons, and banding together into a cohesive unit.

Shields kissed as they interlocked close to one another. The men brandished their weapons ready to do the devil's work. Roger centered the line and Ralph took his place upon the other side. The best warriors would anchor either side, more likely to withstand a flanking attack. They kept the men situated and presented an organized mass of soldiers.

William and Peter ducked along the wall moving into an angled position to shoot down at the enemies' flanks, and to a degree that would avoid hitting one of their brothers if the shot went wide or high. They looked to Cutnose waiting for a signal, arrows nocked, bows half drawn.

If he could stop Christian blood from being spilt, he would, especially with poor numbers. In the same vein, he'd rather burn in Hell than let these men pass through without a fight. Any man who stood in the way of a payout was a dead man.

It was not long before a band of crusaders drenched in blood from helm to boot approached the walls as demons crawled from Hell itself. The rival crusaders skulked into the courtyard one by one through the gate. Without as much as a word, they quickly noted the men barring their path and formed a rival wall of man, metal, leather, and brawn. Spears dipped forward, their line bristling like a hedgehog.

Cutnose peered at Ralph. The old warrior's eyes hardened. Their opponents were experienced soldiers. Then there were the spears, almost every enemy soldier carried one, giving them an extended reach, which would cause his numerically inferior company an issue. If it came to a fight, things would turn ugly fast.

The two groups stared at one another. Neither approaching the other. A man forced his way from the back, shouldering through his men. His frame was broad and thick with muscle and a bushy black beard ran down the front of his lamellar scale armor. Each scale was metal including rounded pads that were tied over the shoulders to allow flexibility and protection. He held a long axe with a bearded blade. He sneered at them.

"There be riches and Jews in those temples. Now step aside and let us pass," the leader said, his voice throaty and deep. He gripped his axe as if he couldn't decide if he wanted to squeeze it to death or throw it end over end into Cutnose's skull. With wild eyes he glared at the mercenaries daring them to respond.

Cutnose tucked his helmet beneath his arm, taking unconcerned strides to meet him. He settled for a distance that would give him an extra moment to react if the talks ended poorly. "These temples have been claimed by Lord Tancred of Hauteville, nephew of Prince Bohemond of Antioch." He wasn't sure Bohemond was technically a prince yet, but he would be soon. He gestured to Tancred's standard draped over the temple door. "You must know his standard. He is a champion and leads a sizable faction in Godfrey's host."

The hulking war leader chuckled and pointed with his axe. "I, Frumold, say Lord Tancred should have left more men."

In that we are in agreement, brash Frumold. "He left all he needed and has faith that Christian men will not kill each other in such a holy place."

"Christians not kill Christians?" Frumold laughed, a guttural sound. "We killed Christians before we had Jews and Saracens to kill. We'll go back to killing Christians after we return to our lands."

"Aye. There's always a man to kill." Cutnose gestured toward the gate with his chin. "There's plenty city left to loot. Move along and there won't be violence." Cutnose's eyes shifted to William. If this battle was going to happen, he wanted an arrow through this man's back first.

"No one ever teach you how to count? We have more men."

Cutnose's men would fight to the death, there was far too much gold on the table which gave them an edge. They hadn't marched hundreds of leagues over hill and mountain through valley and forest, desert, grasslands, and crossed rivers both mighty and small; they hadn't survived the Turkish arrows and swords nor Saracen spears to come away with nothing. "We will bleed you. At least half your men won't walk away from this, but you have my oath that you will die."

"No one kills Frumold. I've been blooded dozens of times, yet no man has ever come close." He pointed his long axe at Cutnose. "Who dare speaks of Frumold's demise?"

"Robert Cutnose."

"Curthose? Godforsaken Norman dogs, this will be over quick."

"No, Cutnose." He ran a finger down the length of his nose and Frumold's eyes narrowed, and Cutnose donned his helm and raised his shield. The time of talking had reached its end.

Frumold snarled rotting teeth, and he charged, axe held high over his shoulder. He moved with alarming speed for a man his size. Cutnose tightened his grip upon his hand axe bracing himself for a fight.

A gory arrowhead emerged from the nape of Frumold's throat, and his steps slowed. Blood burst forth like a broken dam, his mouth opened and closed once, before he crashed into the stones, armor rattling. He'd made it less than ten strides.

Cutnose moved rearward and his armored men rushed to form around him. Shields clanked as they closed ranks. "Stay together," Cutnose called to his men. "Forward."

They stepped over Frumold's bloody corpse. The rival crusaders held rank but eyed the gate over their shoulders. They knew a deadly archer held them in his aim and that death could fly for them at the tip of an arrow at any moment.

"Hold!" Cutnose shouted to his men. He pointed at the other crusaders with his hand axe. "You don't have to die here. Plenty of loot elsewhere."

A few of them appeared ready to charge, a few of the wiser ones stayed their hands gripping weapons fearfully.

"Only death will find you here."

Each man waited for the other to make his decision. Dark eyes ran over them. A few of them juggled their lives inside their chests debating the odds of riches versus a blade in the belly.

"This is Tancred's claim. You will answer to him even if you overcome us."

One by one the rival crusaders lowered their weapons. They backed slowly toward the gate. Shadowed eyes scanned the walls. Like black spirits they disappeared into the night and Cutnose exhaled. He turned toward Ralph, shaking his head in little spurts. "Could have been a bloody way to end the campaign."

"Aye, could have been," Ralph said.

"Bloody for them," Roger called over. His men rushed to loot any valuables from Frumold's person.

Roger held Frumold's helmet in the air. Round eye guards hung down in Northern fashion centered by a nose protector. "A fine helm. Fit for a new lord like myself." He tossed his dented helm to the side, admiring his find.

"Won't fit your huge head," Henry said. "But these boots." He held fine leather boots. "Christ, they smell terrible, but they're better than these ones. Mine are more worn out than an old whore in Rome." He promptly sat on the ground, kicking off his hole-ridden boots.

Roger wriggled his head as he tugged the helm over his coif. "A little snug."

"Can you get it off?" Henry smirked. He wiggled his toes in his new boots.

Roger pried it off, wrinkling his nose. "Don't matter as long as it prevents some goat's arse from putting a dent in me head."

"It's my armor. I claimed it first," said Geoffrey of Bari. According to the mercenary himself, he was a bastard of the brother of the viscount of Bari, with his red shield, a sooty black cross crudely painted on it. Based on his darker complexion, Cutnose assumed he had Greek or Saracen blood in him or an escaped Slavic slave from the slave markets Bari was famous for.

The only certainty in his parentage, was that he was someone's bastard.

Geoffrey planted a finger into John of Lecce's chest. John wouldn't relent, keeping a hand on Frumold's lamellar scale armor.

Ralph separated the two. "I will judge. Pick your competition." The two men decided to conclude the matter by throwing dice with Ralph acting as the noble adjudicator, administering fair judgement. They laid the armor on the ground and took turns throwing the bone dice on it.

"Nice shooting, William," Cutnose shouted at the wall. "Extra tarì for a shot well made."

William beat a fist on his chest. "Maybe I'll stick a few more before we're done here."

"Just make 'em count," Cutnose said. He gestured at Henry, and he jogged the arrow back to the archer.

Cutnose left his men to rest. He walked through a small garden, finding a semblance of peace in the green sanctuary. Half palm trees sprouted from the sandy soil and taller palms' leaves spread like drooping green spear heads. Water bubbled in a small basin inviting him closer.

He propped his shield along on an evergreen pine tree, then lowered a heavy knee to the stone and removed his helm, setting it to the side. Pulling back his coif, the dying sun faded behind a black cloud of fiery smoke. He let himself relax for a moment and dipped his hands into the rejuvenating water. It washed over his blistered and battered hands, the wounds and dry cracks stinging as he cupped them together, drinking the crisp water. It poured a breath of life into his belly, soothing his parched throat and temporarily cooling him despite the reigning heat. He splashed some on his face and rubbed it through his beard flecked with gray, that ran along his jaw like windswept snow on a recently plowed field.

He stood like a growing oak, slow but with strength, and found a place to lay beneath an evergreen tree, its pine scent unable to withstand the domineering black smoke. He pushed the screams of the dying away and checked his surroundings for any insects or snakes before settling in for a well-earned sleep.

When he awoke, the sky above was charcoal, favoring the darkness of night. He lay still, listening intently for danger. He caught faint cries in the distance then a clash of arms, but the tempo was decreasing.

He smacked his lips finding them dry and swollen. "Need more water," he muttered. He stood, feeling his muscles and joints complain with every movement. The weight of his mail coat was heavier than normal, the battle on the walls catching him like a man fleeing a stampede of Arabian horses. He hoisted his shield onto a sore arm, never smart to leave it unattended for long and navigated the garden to join his men.

His men appeared bored. A few dozed under trees. Henry and Roger sat near a fire roasting something over orange flames. Cutnose joined them. Weapons were at their sides or propped on trees, but close enough to be snatched into waiting hands at a moment's notice. When the enemy employed lightning hit-and-run tactics, raining arrows upon them only to disappear moments later, a man could never truly feel at ease.

"You think that one up there," Roger said, gesturing with a handful of meat. He talked as he chewed. "The one Tancred spoke to." He swallowed. "You think she'd come down here?"

"Not for the likes of your ugly face," Henry said.

Roger frowned looking like an angry boulder. "I ain't ugly, me mother loved me." Cutnose was amused by the fellow, he took simple joy in every action.

"Didn't she abandon you?" Henry said with a grin.

Roger pointed his piece of meat at Henry. "Why don't you come over here and let me bash in that sweet mouth of yours. See how pretty you look when I'm done."

"I'd rather not," Henry said. Cutnose couldn't tell which man had the advantage in a fight. Henry was long-limbed, his reach giving him an advantage over almost all others and when he wielded his spear, he was almost untouchable in a fight. Roger was a brute, using his indomitable weight and strength to bash men to mush.

"Where did you find the meat?" Cutnose asked.

Both men regarded him for a moment and Roger raised his bushy eyebrows. "Captain, you know Germans taste the best."

Cutnose found his throat dry. "You jest."

Roger tore into his meat. "Just like swine, right?"

Cutnose's eyes found Frumold's naked body rolled unceremoniously near the wall twisted half on his back and half on his side. Flies buzzed about his corpse with interest in planting their eggs in his flesh to feast upon as they hatched days later. His legs and body were as pale as the fallen snow. His mouth open and tongue hanging out like a butchered pig. Yet he was untouched save for the hole from the arrow in his neck.

"We're cutthroats, but not that desperate," Henry said with a laugh. "We found a goat."

Cutnose breathed a sigh of relief. "Hand me some."

Henry cut him a hunk of meat. Roger continued to stare longingly at the roof. Every so often faces would peer over the side watching with fearful eyes as if every man bore horns and cloven hooves.

"Come down here my little lambskin." Roger waved at them. "Let me take a look at ya."

"Do you suppose it matters what she looks like?" Henry said. "For a man such as yourself certainly it doesn't matter."

Roger's eyes narrowed as he thought. "Aye, it does. I wouldn't just stick anything."

"A relief for all the goats," Henry quipped. "If she's a woman, wouldn't you try to steal her virginity no matter her appearance?"

Roger grinned, licking his lips. "You think there's virgin lambskins in there?"

"Very well could be why our noble lord has decided to 'protect' the temple." Henry smirked, his eyes alight with the prospect. "I hear it's the Temple where they keep *all* the virgins.

Maybe one of those ancient Greek all-virgin sects. You know the ones where all the most desirable women are kept virgins for the gods."

"You be lyin'." Roger picked at his teeth with a blackened fingernail.

Henry shook his long face. "I am as noble as our leader Tancred, I cannot tell a lie. Heard it from a poor knight in Gaston's army. He said the holy land is filled with ancient temples just like it where they hide them. Either that or perhaps the emir is keeping his harem in there. Hundreds of fine beauties all for a single man's pleasure."

Roger chewed the thought. "One man needs that many lambskins?"

"That's how they do it over here. Each man gets as many wives as he can afford."

"Cutnose?" Roger called over. He finished chewing his meat in a hurry. "How many wives do you think I can buy with two hundred tari?"

"One."

Roger grinned in confusion. "One? Surely more than that? I'd basically be a prince, and princes get what they want."

"You ever been married?" Ralph called at him, lifting his head from his prayers. He held a necklace with a small wooden cross in his hands.

"No. But I been with plenty."

Ralph shared a knowing glance with Cutnose. "Then you'd know that you can only afford one."

"Stick to your whores," Cutnose added. "Cheaper." He called to Ralph. "Has Tancred sent any word?"

The cross necklace slipped around Ralph's head hanging over his chest and he joined them, taking a seat. "Been quiet. Town burns. Riders have gone past. None stopped."

"Then we wait." While protected, the courtyard would prove difficult to defend. The gate lay smashed. They would need to fortify it, but the real issue was the breadth of the temple courtyard, and how long they would need to hold it. It was far too expansive to protect with twelve men even with the walls. He only had two archers. It would do them no good to spread men over an acre of the mount. No, he would keep his men close to the temple entrance and bar access that way. Anything else they would have to handle as it happened. "Why don't you take a rest? There's a fountain through those trees. Almost peaceful. We will wake you if needed."

A weight lifted from Ralph's features only for a moment before it returned. "Fresh water. Truly a gift from God."

"It is. Anything is better than the brackish wells we indulged on the way here."

"To think we tread the same paths as Christ did over a thousand years earlier. I can feel his presence. His power resonates in these stones. It clings to the very air like the smoke. We are closer to God in this moment more than any other." Ralph eyed the darkening sky swathed with black like the raven wings of night. The orange glow of flames lapped the eastern part of the city. He lowered his voice to keep the other men from hearing. "You think he'll pay?"

Cutnose cocked his head. He'd fought with Bohemond enough times to earn one another's trust. The family paid any warriors willing to fight with loot and lands aplenty, drawing any and all who dared to adventure in the East. Tancred would keep his word or neither uncle nor nephew would have an army to support their claims throughout the Holy Lands.

Lords who didn't pay their men became as welcome as a leper cook preparing ones' food. They were shunned for lords who fulfilled their contracts and provided additional opportunities for gain. "He'll pay. I do not know how, but if he is willing to pay that much to protect these people and this temple, then I'll do it."

Ralph nodded. "I know Bohemond is good for it, but young men often make promises they cannot keep."

Cutnose gripped Ralph's shoulder. "And old men worry themselves with things they cannot control."

"It's called experience," Ralph said, raising bushy eyebrows. "Something you should have more of by now."

"I only ever took well to a few things." He patted the axe on his belt. "This being one of them."

Both the men smiled at one another.

"Here we stand in the holiest city in the world. Talking of money and killing."

"We are but mortal men. Take your rest. Our dutiful vigil may stretch longer than one night."

"These old bones don't need the rest, but they will embrace it." Ralph took his leave, departing toward the pool.

Cutnose made his rounds and spoke with his men. He shared bread with his archers, William and Peter. Drank wine with John, axe William, and Pagan. The injured William was in high spirits despite his wound. Ralph had it cleaned and wrapped and bandaged, the wine dulling the pain. He flexed the fingers on his hand for Cutnose, showing him he still had adequate flexibility to fight.

Morale was high. They'd survived the long campaign road and a siege assault that could have slain the lot of them either by sword or pestilence. They had marched in a strange and foreign land and would live to tell the tale to their wives and children one day. Where many had fallen to sickness and blades, they could now enjoy the fruits of their pilgrimage. Rest, food, riches, and absolution of all their sins for their holy actions.

After he'd spoken to each man, ensuring they were well, he resumed his place near the fire with Henry and Roger. He welcomed the warmth even after the heat of the day. This land would bleed them of sweat during the day and freeze them at night. It was a place of contradictions. Holy and violent. Hot and cold. Muslim and Christian. When it switched from one extreme to the other, people died.

He entertained the idea of removing his armor. His thick woolen tunic that some men referred to as an arming shirt was stiff with sweat and blood. Without a heavier undergarment, the weight of the over thirty-litra coat of mail, equivalent to wearing a foal around his shoulders, would chafe a man raw. The undergarment also prevented damaged or bent rings of his mail from digging painfully into his skin during battle. It wouldn't stop a mace from breaking a bone, but every bit of armor blunted damage. His mail would need to be scrubbed with sand to remove the blood and sweat from rusting the interlocking rings, but it would have to wait. His men still wore their armor as well, warriors through and through, for it paid to be prepared for a sudden fight, despite the discomfort.

"Cutnose," Henry said. He gestured with his head toward the walls.

Cutnose's fingers found his hand axe, his eyes searching the wall. He'd carried it for over two years. No fancy designs, no decorations running along the shaft. Just a pure and simple tool for killing. Made for cleaving and bashing through armor and bone. The hook some men referred to as a beard, could be used to disarm a man or wrench free a shield, exposing his opponent.

His eyes found William crouched behind the wall's skirt. The archer held up a hand with one finger raised.

"One?" Cutnose mouthed. A messenger from Tancred. William the archer nodded, his features shadows of the night. Henry shoved his sword back into its sheath.

"Finally," Roger growled, standing and stretching his back. "We can get paid." He turned toward the temple. "You hear that, ladies? Roger Maule is about to be a rich man with a coin pouch hanging low enough for all of you." His voice echoed between the walls, and the people of the temple were silent.

"What you want to bet he's a messenger from Tancred saying to man our post?" Henry said.

"Bah, he's coming to tell us the sack is over." Roger pointed at Cutnose. "All the loot accounted for. Time for us to get paid."

"Tancred will keep his word," Cutnose said.

"Better or we'll break his lordly skinny arms."

"Brave words. Your ugly head will be an ornament outside his tent by the end of the day," Henry said.

Roger frowned, eyeing the men around him. "It's the principle of the matter. A man should be paid what he's owed. Contract was made. Oaths were sworn."

"Fact remains the lords will pay us what they want," Henry muttered. "It is the way of things."

"If they want to have an army, they'll pay us what was promised," Cutnose said.

Iron-shod hooves clopped slowly off the sand-colored stones. The rider emerged through the gate, ducking his head and lance as he walked through. His mount was a fine black destrier with rippling muscles that flexed as he walked. The horse was over eighteen hands high and the man atop the human equivalent of his battle steed. His skin was the color of a fresh snow with slight shades of rose on his cheeks. His nose was hooked like a thick beak of a bird of prey and his golden mustache hung off his face like a priestly mantle. His cheeks were rounded and his frame one that rivaled Roger in muscle and girth.

His helm was tied to his saddle and his shield bore a red boar's head on a field of green. A heavy war hammer hung from his belt. It was a weapon made to crush armor and helms, shattering bone and skulls with brutal strength. It was the weapon of a man who enjoyed ruthless brute force in battle.

Henry walked near the knight. "You come from Tancred? Let me take your reins, my lord."

The knight close-lipped smiled at him.

There was something unsettling about him that made Cutnose's hackles stand on end.

"What's he a German?" Roger grunted.

"I do not know."

"Can you talk, sir?" Roger shouted. "Or you lose your tongue?"

"Have you already entered the temples?" the knight asked, his voice clear and with the frost of a winter morning.

Even Henry appeared small next to the mounted knight despite his height. "No one is to go inside by order of Lord Tancred."

The knight nodded his head. "Who is your captain?"

"Cutnose," Henry said, looking over his horse at the fire.

The fire crackled. Someone cried out in the night from the city. "I am the captain of these men."

"Tancred has sent me to relieve you. You may go. Reap the spoils of your toil as you deserve."

Cutnose's eyes shifted to Roger and then to Geoffrey who stood shadowed by a palm tree. Hands casually found their ways to weapons cloaked by the darkness. "These temples are under our protection."

"And now they are under my protection." The knight's eyes flashed a shade of the sun in the darkness catching Cutnose off guard.

"Lord Tancred was clear. No one may enter the temple even such a noble man as yourself. You must wait."

The knight's horse shifted, a hoof clapping the stone. "You are mistaken. I *will* enter these temples this night."

Cutnose glanced at his men around the fire. Roger removed the mace from his belt. It thumped his hand impatiently. Geoffrey's finger stroked the pommel of his sword round and round. Henry slowly released the reins, his eyes not leaving the knight.

The knight's horse snorted, tugging at its reins. The knight easily controlled the beast, a silver stag and cross ring on his hand reflecting the night flames. "Woe to any man who bars my path. I do not wish death upon you but will do as I must."

Cutnose pointed toward the gate. "Turn around and leave this place. There are twelve of us and only one of you. The last knight who tried us is worm food. If his bones ever find a grave."

The knight gestured with his lance cocking his head to the side like an interested dog. "My patience thins. Step aside," his tone that of an emperor.

Cutnose laughed and it came across smaller than he felt, as if the man sucked away the power of his voice by his presence. An uneasiness implanted itself inside him. The knight must be maddened by war to even entertain fighting a dozen mercenaries that effectively surrounded him. He didn't even wear his helm. Cutnose's finger reached for the scar on his nose, tracing the length of it. It was an instinctual gesture that he did when preparing for a fight. The violent blemish was a reminder to move fast and aggressive on the enemy or risk gaining a wound that may never heal.

A lifelong soldier's confidence shone through the clouds of doubt. "We've already slain one knight." He gestured toward Frumold's fly-shrouded body. "Why not two?" He gave Roger the signal.

Roger grinned like a bear in mating season. "Me mace wants to make your acquaintance," he called to the knight before rushing him.

CHAPTER 5

Cutnose let his eyes drift from the knight to William on the wall. *Take the shot, kill this man quickly.* The knight lifted his shield. He covered his torso unaware of the archers. William's bow became taut then his arrow fluttered from his fingertips, propelling from the bowstring in a blur. In a sudden motion, the knight twisted his shield behind his head and the arrow pinned itself through the hide and into the wood.

Cutnose frowned at the knight's luck. He drew his hand axe. He expected the knight to spur his horse away from Henry and he did. Henry cautiously followed, sword appearing in hand.

Fighting from horseback gave the knight an advantage over dismounted foes, but a horse could be cut from beneath a man and a man cut from atop a horse, as the crusaders had found repeatedly throughout their campaign in the Holy Land.

An arrow flew over the knight's head as he guided his shield back to his side. Another arrow embedded itself in the wood. The great black destrier stormed toward Roger. Every man there expected the knight to lower his lance and attempt to impale the large mercenary.

Instead, he hefted his lance into an overhand grip, the shaft unwavering in his hand, and he threw the long spear like a common javelin turning to the side. He unleashed it with lethal force. Cutnose wasn't sure he could believe his own eyes, until the crimson spear head burst with a crunch out Geoffrey's back, taking him off his feet before sending him crashing into the stones. Cutnose had never seen such a feat attempted in a battle. There was only a brief moment to consider the strength required for such an effort.

"His horse! His horse!" Cutnose shouted as he charged. He prayed to Christ; William heard his calls. Arrows zipped through the air striking the beautiful animal in the hind quarters and then another in the chest. William and Peter stood upright on the wall drawing and loosing, yet slowing to ensure they didn't hit one of their own in the firelight.

The beast whinnied and stood on two legs, hooves flailing, each one as deadly as a boulder flung from a catapult. Jan, a quiet young man who'd joined from the Low Countries, rushed forward ramming a spear into the horse's breast. *Good boy.* The horse gutturally screamed, flecks of spit flying from its mouth, tongue flopping, and the haft snapped in the young man's hands.

The horse reared again, an iron-shod hoof snapped Jan's head back, his helmet smashed inward worse than if he'd been hit with a war hammer. Blood streamed down his face, and he fell to his back. His legs twitching as he died.

The knight could no longer stay in the saddle, and he toppled rearward, his hands grasping to brace his fall. They would have him now. On his feet, he was only a single man. And a surrounded man didn't have long to live. An arrow. An axe. A sword swing. A mace caving his helm. Any number of ways this knight would fall before them. Sensing victory, Cutnose's men closed.

The knight was back on his feet before Cutnose had closed with him. With an overhand swing, he crushed Jordan's helmet in. Blood spurt from underneath and he screeched as he went down, the force of the blow shortening his neck. An arrow thumped into the knight's shoulder, puncturing his mail coat. He didn't flinch, but smiled, reaching back to rip the arrow from his flesh.

"Face me!" Roger screamed at him, hefting his mace with two hands.

The knight took a massive blow from Roger on his shield, smashing it into unusable kindling. If a man could be a bear, Roger was that man. Fiercer and stronger than most men Cutnose had seen fight. The knight tossed the wrecked shield aside and in one motion caught Roger's mace in his open hand. *His bones must be shattered to dust.*

Cutnose slowed, momentarily stunned by the man's action. Roger gaped but swung his shield at the knight's bare head. The knight deflected the blow with his hammer, and like a giant serpent slithered his arms around Roger's body. The men struggled in each other's arms, but it was clear that the knight was stronger. Another idea unfathomable to Cutnose.

A man's certainty was his folly, and it was an error for the knight to believe himself untouchable. This man would pay dearly for his arrogance.

Cutnose closed on his right flank and slammed his hand axe into the knight's unprotected upper calf. *We will cut him down piece by piece.* The axe-face embedded itself through boot and flesh until it grated to a stop upon bone. A moment later, with a yell and force, Henry rammed his sword into the knight's side, penetrating his mail. "Gawww!" Henry shouted with a vicious twist of his mouth. He ripped the blade free. Nothing was better than striking the killing blow on an enemy who'd killed one of your brothers-in-arms.

The knight howled in pain, but he didn't release his death hold. Cutnose and Henry gawked. Roger's face turned red as the pressure built, his eyes bulging in pain. He pried at the knight's arms and pounded his fists in the crook of the knight's elbows. "Get me free," he spat, veins swelling in his neck.

Cutnose ripped his axe free and swung it into the knight's back. Roger's mouth dropped as metal crunched, sounding like two armies clashing on a battlefield as his bones popped inside him. Henry and Cutnose retreated backward.

The knight spun, growling as he tore Roger in half. Tossing his torso to one side and his legs to the other. Cutnose's hand went to the long dagger on his belt. "Deliver us o'Lord from this evil." His belief in God was tenuous, but if this creature was not of the devil, then nothing was.

He gaped as the knight grew in stature, tossing down his mail coat. His blond hair appeared to encircle his face. His form elongated, becoming more feral beast than man. His hands stretched into claylike daggers. He bared teeth that could only belong to Satan's own.

The knight's wicked spell ensnared them in fear. His men frozen before evil in its truest form. *How can we overcome this monster?*

"Garwalf?" Henry sputtered.

Cutnose shook his head silent.

Pagan rushed to their side. Axe in one hand, sword in the other. "He is varulfur. One with the wolf. It can be killed."

The spell breaking, Cutnose steeled himself. He wouldn't shame a man who ran from such a hideous creature, but he would not bear that shame. "If it bleeds, it can be killed!"

Another arrow bristled from its back and the animal didn't bother to respond. The archers loosed arrow after arrow with frightened eyes, feathered shafts bristling from the beast. Nothing slowing it down.

Cutnose drew his long dagger and gripped his shield in a white-knuckled hand, pushing down his fear. He charged. It was the only thing he could think to do. John of Lecce jabbed at the beast, but his spear did nothing. The beast chewed his throat out and blood sprayed into the air like warm scarlet rain falling from the sky. Blood streamed down John's new scale armor. Cutnose closed and a paw the size of a small boulder backhanded him off his feet. He crashed into the ground sliding painfully over the stones.

"Odin will be pleased by your hide," Pagan shouted. He leapt forward. He ducked a swipe and hammered his axe into the beast's shoulder, and ripping it free, he slipped his sword between its ribs. The blade stuck, and he spun away, his axe landing in the meat of the beast's thigh. Like him, his strikes were fierce and precise.

Cutnose pushed himself upright, collecting his dagger. Pagan dashed forward again swinging, and the beast caught him by the throat. He lifted the muscular mercenary off his feet. Pagan never let go of his axe, only gurgled as the animal closed massive jaws wrapping around his skull. With a crunch, Pagan was nothing but a limp carcass dropping to the ground.

Henry rammed his sword into the beast's back, the blade sinking in deep. The beast raised its muzzle skyward a low howl bellowing toward the heavens. Henry maintained a hold on his sword. Its howls grew quieter, and it turned on Henry raking a claw along his belly. The sound was linen ripping in two before Henry's bowels hit the plaza with a splash.

"Devil!" Cutnose shouted. The beast grinned, and blood dribbled from its lips. Arrows feathered it, but nothing made a difference. It felt like Cutnose swam toward it. His limbs were leaden rods, and those rods were mired in a thick honey.

The beast caught him in a coarse claw, nails digging through his armor as he pulled him closer to his jaws. With as much strength and fury as he could muster, Cutnose rammed his blade into the beast's chest, where its heart should be, the point biting through his taut mail.

The wolf-like beast held him close to his face. Its eyes shone gold. Its mouth gaped with fangs longer than daggers. Its snout drenched in his men's blood. Henry groaned as he tried to keep in his insides, but they slipped like naked snakes between his hands.

Cutnose bared his teeth and pushed harder on the hilt of his dagger. The beast's eyes glowed and it spit blood back into Cutnose's face in anger. Then with a snap of its jaws and a twist of its sinewy neck it tore out Cutnose's throat.

The beast tossed him, as easily as a soiled tunic to the side. Pain spiked through his body, but the pain wasn't what made him panic. No matter how hard he tried, he couldn't breathe. The taste of iron pooled in his mouth. His hand stuffed flaps of flesh into the wound trying to hold his blood inside. It found its way outside anyway, pumping in a rapid drum beat with his heart.

Fuck. Fuck. Panic fled before a stinking reality that tasted like shit. Cutnose was going to die. He never thought he would expire this way, trying to hold a flap of skin where his throat used to be in place. He tried in vain to catch one more breath, despite knowing it was his last.

With gaping eyes, he watched the beast leap onto the walls to kill his archers. William managed to jump to the courtyard out of its grasp. His leg twisted beneath him. The beast slaughtered Peter, tossing a hand and leg into the courtyard. Cutnose couldn't see where the rest of him disappeared to.

The ground shook as the beast landed on the plaza stones. Fire danced off its fur. William crawled away. Cutnose's vision began to blur around the edges.

Ralph's burnt and tan face hovered over his. While the other men kept their hair short over the campaign, Ralph had let his grow to his shoulders. *He could be a gray-haired Jesus, but with an unmerciful stare.* His eyes took in Cutnose's injuries with a pang of pity and then a glimmer of determination. *Banish it from life. Avenge us of this damnation.* Gurgles leaked from his bloody lips. He choked on his words. *Slay it.*

Ralph placed his sword near his lips and closed his eyes for a moment, praying to the blade. "You will be avenged, Deus vult," he whispered. William's screams broke his prayers. The beast savaged him with grunts and feral growls that came from no human. Meat and bone were savagely tossed into the air.

Ralph rose from his crouch, then charged. He ushered forth no battle cry, for if surprise carried the day against their opponent, then no more noble victory could be attained. Only bitter determination to end the threat driving him. His boots were the only sound aside from the beast's growls.

Cutnose's men were no saints. Honor be gone, this was life

and death. The moment Ralph took a step closer, the beast's eyes found him, glowing like flames over a hoard of gold coins. Bits of William fell from its jaws.

In face of fear, Ralph cried to the heavens for succor, "God wills it!"

The beast lunged at him from all fours and Ralph rolled to the side out of its way, barely escaping. He sliced and rolled away from knife-like claws, and he was as quick as Cutnose had ever seen him. He was an immortal, Achilles reincarnated, dodging swipes from the hairy devil and terrible bites from its devastating jaws. God was with him, perhaps his piety was the difference between victory and defeat. Cutnose had far too little time left to consider it.

Ralph slashed the beast's shoulder, swept his blade over its leg, then danced to the side and spun, the blade shone in the firelight licking the beast's flesh. Blood appeared all over the creature with a dozen arrows bristling from its back and chest, Cutnose's axe and dagger still sticking from it.

His sword bit deep. He tugged, unable to regain his weapon and unwilling to relinquish the blade. Massive jaws clamped upon his shoulder. With vigorous shakes of its head, Ralph screamed as his sword arm was removed from his body. Metal and flesh crashed to the stones.

Cutnose's vision turned to a red fog. His hand slammed the ground, grasping for purchase. The stones were slick. A man had only so much blood inside him before he bled himself dry. As far as Cutnose had seen dozens of times before, roughly four jars of blood resided in the body, and when that last drop hit the ground, most men were dead soon after. His moments dwindled and now his last hope for revenge died with his friend.

Ralph took a step back, staring from his shoulder to his missing limb. His mind was slow to connect with the reality that he was no longer in possession of his arm. The beast lunged for him, and Ralph reacted as the ever-good soldier, raising his shield to prevent its attack. Shield and man crashed to the ground and his screams were muffled by the beast's body.

The ground was warm and the air cold. Cutnose dug his fingernails along the wet stone trying to push himself seated, but he couldn't find any purchase. His cold fingers scraped the stone again gaining nothing. His ears caught the sound of a butcher at work, shredding with force. Something thumped near Cutnose, rolling over the plaza stones before coming to a rest in front of him.

Ralph's head. Mouth open in a wordless scream. Eyes unblinking. Gray hair dampened with blood, sticking to his face and neck. *Old friend, I am sorry it was like this. You fought as any good soldier would.* But no words were exchanged. Both men were speechless in death.

Faint banging resonated in his ears. Without seeing, he knew the door was being broken down. Cutnose spit blood in anger, trying to get air through his ruined throat. It pattered on the stones and down his chin into his beard.

Dying wasn't as memorable as living had been. It had come quick after a brief gurgling struggle. Bloody, painful, and a rush that flowed through the body like a surging tempest. Then it was gone. The long night embraced him, pure and utter darkness, endless, and ignoble. There were no lights shining from the heavens as he was told would happen by the priests. Angels did not descend from above with trumpeting fanfare to escort him to a place in paradise. He wished he could say he'd been surprised considering the life he had lived, but a small part of him had hoped that he had been forgiven his many sins for the part he played in freeing Jerusalem.

Death was a general enclosure of the darkness until it strangled the life from the light. His vision constricted tighter and tighter in a serpent's deathly embrace. It was cold. There was no joy or relief, only the pain of his body trying to live.

It grew quieter like men calling to one another as they drifted apart at sea. He was thankful for that, the shrill screams from inside the temple were not pleasant even to a man who had committed his fair share of violence. Even as they were drowned out by the faint pump of blood in his eardrums, he had a panic of regret for not fulfilling his last task.

This regret surprised him. He didn't know them. Nor did he really care if they lived or died, but there was something there that made him cringe as they screamed. Not the screams of the dying, but of people truly afraid.

His light faded around the oval edges of Ralph's decapitated head. He had fought all over the world for his thirty-eight years only to fall unceremoniously in the holiest city known to man. His hands dropped to his side unable to find the strength to hold in any more blood.

He gasped, the sound of a man snorting water. He couldn't feel his legs or his arms and Ralph's gray eyes pierced him with condemnation. *If you would have let us sack, pillage, and rape the city, none of this would have happened. We would all yet live. Sorry old friend, our road ended before our time.*

He desperately sought his fondest memory, some part of life he could cling to in death. And the best he could conjure was a memory of a whore in Rome.

Her coppery skin glistening with sweat, fine round tits bouncing off his cheek, her nipples aroused to spear points the shade of freshly tilled earth. The kind an olive tree would thrive in. Him trying to catch one in his mouth. Those hips rocking with the experience of a life in the saddle. A victorious moan escaping between her teeth as she sensed she had him in the palm of her hand. The swirl of her ringleted raven-black hair as she arched her back, her hips swaying at the gallop. It would have been nice to have her again or even gaze into her soft brown eyes as he crossed to the next life.

What was her name? Bonavera? Galita? No, those were others. His mind swam through the numbing quicksand of death. *Contessa. Her name was Contessa.*

Securing hold of her name in the tendrils of a fleeting mind, gave him the tiniest bit of relief. Perhaps his seed had grown in her and a legacy of his own survived. At least it would ease the crossing, but he was foolish to entertain such thoughts. A spear in the gut. A sword through the heart. A dagger in the back in a dilapidated port tavern. Those were always going to be the way he exited this world. Throat removed from a beast on the Temple Mount? Not an end he'd envisioned.

Ralph continued to stare at him bodiless. A red-soaked hand grasped Ralph's gray hair. A silver ring centered by the symbol of a stag and cross tightened around the strands and Ralph disappeared. *Christ came to take him. He deserved Heaven, of all of us he did.*

Cutnose tried to find Contessa once more and every inch of her lust but struggled to find the memory and that too was taken from him. Then black stole upon him like a horde of galloping Turkish horsemen, and his world faded from the feral darkness to the ebony of an eternal night.

CHAPTER 6

When Cutnose blinked back awake, he was sure he'd been banished to Hell. His vision was a hazy morning mist, but not crisp as the dawning of day, more smoke leaking from the fiery depths. Shadowy orange flames danced from beyond the walls. Ralph's condemning eyes and head were gone.

This cannot be Heaven. If it were, the priests lied.

His eyes began to see more clearly. The half-consumed bodies of his men lay around him in bloody piss-stained encirclements. More unmoving shapes had joined them in death, scattered in pieces of cloth and flesh strewn over the courtyard in splashes of blood, painting the stones in dark crimson.

Wood smoke and coppery blood stuck inside his nostrils dripping on his tongue and making his stomach roil. Still on his side, he took a half breath and vomited, adding his own putrid stink to the rancid stench swaddling him. He blinked his eyes and he tried to lift his hand to wipe his mouth. Only his finger twitched. His nose wrinkled stiffly as he tried to focus his efforts. His arm shifted slowly to his mouth, and he ran his mail sleeve over his foul lips. The coolness of the linked metal rings caught and ripped at his beard bringing pain, and he knew he had been condemned to Hell.

Pain shot from his belly through his chest and centered around his neck. It stole what little breath he could squeeze from his lungs. Did he even need to breathe if he was dead? His body felt as if he'd been stampeded by a herd of horses and left in the sun to rot.

Air whistled through clogged, blood-caked nostrils. *Air? I can feel it in my lungs. I live.* Two things moved near the temple. The beast. *Dear God, what have I done to deserve this mauling twice in my life?* He grasped for the ground ahead of him. His arm worked but was weak as a man who'd slept for years on his side. He sought an answer in the smoky night sky. *Don't answer that one, Lord. I thought freeing your city would wipe all those sins away. Sometimes there are a few too many to wipe a soul clean.*

There was movement on the edge of his periphery. Faint voices whispered in the distance. People. He wanted to shout but his throat was an open wound. He lifted his hand and gingerly ran it back to his throat. A strip of cloth encircled his neck, and his flesh screamed underneath as if his insides were exposed.

The voices grew nearer, and he let his hand fall to the plaza stones. Dirt clung to the sticky wetness wedged under his fingernails as he scratched the bloody stones. His fingers found nothing as the shadows closed.

Two faces appeared above him. A woman with a narrow face and slightly slanted eyes beneath thick eyebrows glared at him like he was just another corpse, a barely living inconvenience. Her hair was blacker than the death he'd escaped, and it was pulled back and tied behind her head. Her cheekbones were high and prominent, so much so, Cutnose knew she must be a lady of some standing. But her attire was that of a wealthy noble's squire or servant on military campaign.

The more he stared, the more baffling she became with her black kaftan with gold trim and a small round buckler with a metal emboss on her arm. Her sword had no guard and a slight curve in it, and an ornate scabbard was lined with silver sunbursts denoting it as a blade of immense wealth.

He'd been told of women warriors in the east but had yet to see a woman in combat. He'd seen women defend their young with their bodies as brave as any man standing shield to shield, but never dressed for war.

The man with her shared none of her looks. His hair was like the golden sands of a Thessalian beach. He was handsome with a dimpled chin and blue eyes, but his features were marred by four long scars running along his cheek. He held a longbow made from yew in his hand and wore an out of style seax, a long straight-edged knife, on his belt.

Cutnose tried to gulp and wanted to scream for the effort.

The woman's shadowed eyes rested upon the temple. "Ulf, he returns." Her eyes weighed him with indifference.

"You think he will live?" the golden man said.

"If he does, he will be the only one," came another voice, holding wisdom and experience. It was the voice of a king, and he joined them.

His years must have more than doubled the other two. Crow's feet indented the corners of piercing blue eyes encircled with gold beneath a domineering brow. A trimmed but long gray-and-brown beard pointed from his chin in a braid. A gold wolf-head ornament dangled from the braid's tip. The style was out of place in the Holy Land or anywhere Cutnose had fought, making the man appear far from home.

Bronze scale armor hung down to his thighs, a mail coat worn beneath draped to his elbows. He removed a plain eye-piece helm, and a leather circuit held long gray-and-walnut hair from his eyes. He reached a bandaged hand for Cutnose, the other holding a long Dane axe with a bearded axe-head that came to a devastating point.

Ulf's fingertips massaged around Cutnose's throat, and he choked back anger for he was unable to stop the man from handling him like he was a horse awaiting the decision to be mercifully put down.

The elder released him. "He will live."

"When will he be able to speak?" the young man asked.

Ulf's piercing blue eyes surged into him. "Maybe never, but we can hope soon. Can you write?"

Barely able to shake his head, the movement sent pain lancing through his body.

"Then we must hope his speech returns."

The woman spat to the side. "We shouldn't have helped this man. He is a mercenary and not worth our time."

"It was my choice to make."

Her eyes flashed at him. "One I disagree with."

"The situation warrants great risk if we are to succeed in our quest."

"I understand what is at stake, and this brigand will be far more of a problem than he's worth. I say we go back to the crusader encampment and sniff around there. One of them will show themselves before long."

"Not all men who sell their sword do so with ill intent."

Cutnose was silent. Killing was a skill he'd honed like the edge of a blade. He wouldn't say killing was his sole purpose to exist but being handsomely rewarded for it paid for other less savory pastimes. He supposed that in some instances the battles he fought benefited lords who were noble and had just intentions. He couldn't name one outright, but he was sure there must have been more than a few.

The archer bent down. "Can you stand?"

With every passing moment, Cutnose felt a little less like the dead. It was as if his body was remembering what it was like to be alive. *I was sure I was gone.* "Who…are you?" he managed grating, ugly words.

"I am Arnulf." He nodded toward the woman. "She is Marya." The archer hauled Cutnose to his feet with surprising ease as he was not light in his mail coat. He faltered, his feet numb like a newborn calf, and Arnulf gripped him tighter keeping him upright. "Be calm. You will be stronger soon."

Calm? Cutnose wanted to scream. *I was dead. Gone. Worm food.*

"We need your help," Ulf said. The man was taller than the rest and had a slight stoop in his back as if he'd worn armor for much too long.

"My help?" Cutnose gingerly rubbed his neck, his skin felt as thin as a monk's parchment. His men were nothing more than scattered remains, no different than the people in the streets. Tancred's banner lay in tattered ribbons on the ground. He felt the cloth around his neck. "The standard?"

"It was all we had," Arnulf said.

"Who killed your men? How many were there?" Ulf asked, his voice a command that would not be denied an answer.

The fog of war shrouded Cutnose, and the heavy odor of death surrounded him. His thoughts were simple and leapt for his companions. "I breathed my last. I should not have lived. Did anyone else survive?" He knew the answer but asked anyway.

"They're all dead," Ulf said. "Only the gods know why, but you had enough life still in you." His eyes regarded him with a flash of gold. "Those with a hardy spirit always linger the longest."

"We couldn't stop it." Cutnose's eyes narrowed, straining through the mists of his mind. He was not an unsure man. One did not survive many battles with confidence lacking. Everything that had transpired was beyond his understanding, shaking his clutch on reality. His men were dead, that was clear, yet somehow, he survived.

"Speak, soldier of coin," Ulf commanded.

The nightmare of fangs and fur flashed before him, ripping and tearing like a beast from Hell. "It was a beast. A devil in wolf form cut us down like we were men made of straw." He eyed the three warriors. They showed no indication of surprise or sympathy. His voice came out like a rasp of metal over whetstone. "My men were seasoned warriors. We had archers on the wall. No man could have done this."

"Your men were brave to stand before such a foe."

"You know this creature?" he spat, rubbing his neck.

"I may. What did he call himself?" Ulf asked.

"He gave no name, but on his shield was painted a wild boar. He was tall and broad. Long blond mustache and hair. Wielded hammer and lance." He shook his head, the images stubbornly branded in his memory. "Wore a stag and cross ring."

Arnulf exhaled forcefully shaking his head, and Marya eyed Ulf, her dark eyes burning. "Sir Bors," she said softly.

Ulf nodded, it was a grim movement, the corner of his lip twitching. "Was there anyone with him?"

"He was alone. We stabbed him no less than a dozen times. Arrows, spears, swords, axes. He would not yield before any blade. He tore my biggest man in half with his bare hands."

The trio ignored him. Arnulf regarded the gate as if he expected someone to enter. His voice came hurried when no one appeared. "If he's alone, we can slay him."

"He's not alone," Ulf said, he lowered his head as he thought. "He would not travel alone."

"What does it matter?" Cutnose interjected. "He slew twelve men in less than minute. It wasn't natural. We need an army. Poison and fire. A pit with stakes. A ballista may do it."

Arnulf spied over his shoulder. "It is time for us to depart this place."

"We do not wish to be connected to this massacre," Ulf said, his eyes taking in the slaughter easily. The two men walked into the shadows for the southern gate.

"Aye, but what harm can a mortal man do to the devil?" Cutnose called after them. The woman lingered, his eyes finding her. "I guess this is a night filled with all sorts of oddities."

"We've given you a second chance on life. I suggest you use it for something more than whoring and killing. Bors can be slain, but we must find him."

"My men deserve a Christian burial." It would take him time to collect their parts, and that was only possible if he could still identify them. Perhaps it would be better if he piled them high and set them alight.

"Others will see to it that their earthly vessels are cared for. I would suggest you hide yourself or they will name you murderer," Marya said.

"These are my men. I must see them through to the grave. My lord must know what evil lurks among us."

"Little thieves are hanged, but great ones escape."

"Do oaths mean nothing to you?" he spat at her.

"Oaths of blood are all that matter."

He shook his head at her. Pain ebbed through his neck, and he grimaced. He walked amongst the scattered remains. It was rare to not lose a man to something on campaign. Death always lurked around an army, disease, an arrow, a wild animal, anything could and would kill a man especially in a land foreign to him. It was never hard to find a warrior to take his place; you pay a man enough, he'll fight, but he'd never lost his entire company.

He was a mercenary captain with no men. There was little chance he'd be paid in full now anyway. One man could be held down and have his throat slit if he caused too much trouble. Without an armed band at his back, he was but a landless warrior with no way to demand payment. He would have to depend upon his reputation with Bohemond and Tancred to uphold their contract. He told himself that in these newly conquered lands, they would still need him even if he was but one axe.

He found his hand axe and discovered his long dagger near Ralph's headless body. He knelt and sheathed the blade then reached out to lay a hand on the man's lifeless chest. "You will not have died in vain." He searched the sky for God above. "I know you're in Heaven you pious bastard, guide me to your justice." He found Geoffrey's shield still intact with the crudely painted cross on it. Fitting to bear Christ's cross for a man reborn in his city. *I am Lazarus.* He turned and the three warriors were gone. His eyes strained in the darkness searching for them. *Unnatural folk, better to be free of them.*

The sound of shod hooves over stone preceded the mounted knights as they trotted through the broken gate into the courtyard.

He took cover in the shadowed garden trees waiting to see if they were friend or foe. In the dark, the riders cursed and shouted in dismay at the corpses layering the walkway. Torches were lit and the men gasped at the slaughter surrounding them.

Cutnose recognized the shield of Lord Robert of Limosano. *An ally.* He stepped out to greet him.

Marya's hand gripped his wrist like an iron shackle, turning him toward her. "You are you, but not the man you once were. You must come with me."

"The fuck do you know? That's my lord, and he owes me a sack of coin." Cutnose glared at her. He was not manhandled by anyone let alone this freakishly strong slender woman. Her hand did not relent, squeezing even harder. "Perhaps I must speak more simply. You resemble the dead," she hissed. Irritation filled her face that of a master scolding a bad dog. "They will not embrace you, mercenary. They will fear you and seek to destroy you."

"Unhand me, *woman*." He tried to shake her hand, and she begrudgingly released him. *Must still be weak from my wound.* "I'm walking and talking, aren't I?" He coughed and grimaced, his voice croaking. "You even said yourself, I didn't die."

"I regret letting Ulf save you."

"You and me both." *Still weak from the battle. No woman's grip had so much strength.*

"This will be a hard lesson for you. One you may not survive."

Torches cast a yellow glow over the fallen, the horsemen covering their faces in horrid disgust. Even in the darkness, he recognized Tancred's crest upon his almond-shaped shield. The young lord removed his helm. "I will have heads for this," came Tancred's voice. "Where is Cutnose? Find me his body. I won't believe it until I see his corpse. Search everywhere."

The sergeants and knights scrambled over the yard. "Can't tell whose body is whose, my lord," called a man. "They're only pieces."

"He was among the dead, my lord," Ludolf said. "I saw him

with my own two eyes." He walked his horse closer to where Cutnose had laid dying. "He laid here. His throat ripped out. I swear an oath to the Lord it be true." The knight turned fearful to his lord. "I know not what this means, but it reeks of the devil.

Tancred eyed the bodies before they rested on the temple. "I thought that enough coin would keep the man honest. I had sworn to these people they would be free from harm and now they lay massacred before me."

"I recognize this man; he was in his band. The overgrown one who did not know his place," Ludolf said, he pointed at Roger's top half. "God's justice has been administered upon the sinner."

Tancred regarded the temple in awe, the city and everything within left him in a surreal state, the death of his men even more. "Cutnose's men were killed. You tell me he was slain yet he is not here." He turned to his sergeants. "Someone must have survived to tell this evil tale."

Sir Rainald of Salerno and a handful of footmen hurried out from inside. A spearman leaned on the wall and vomited on the stones covering his mouth. "Desecration. Unholy."

"The slaughter is complete," Sir Rainald said, his face paling. "None live."

"No one?" Tancred shouted.

"Not one, my lord," Sir Rainald said. He hurried to his horse, clambering into the saddle. The mount tossed its head skittish from all the carnage. "Lord, the devil owns this place. I can only think of one reason Cutnose's body would no longer reside here and to utter it would be blasphemous in the eyes of the Lord. We must leave this place." Ripples of agreement traveled through the ranks of knights and sergeants. Killing was a part of their business, but this was butchery for the sake of butchery.

Ludolf urged his mount closer to Tancred. "He always spoke far above his station. He has been in the devil's hands since we met." Every word these men uttered drove a deeper wedge into his lord's mind, and it made his stomach turn over.

Tancred shook his head. "Men who value coin over the honor

of a lord often lack the virtues that we hold dear, however I enjoyed his brutish company. His betrayal wounds me deeply, but I will have no more talk of the devil. I would have him answer for this."

"He was dead, lord, I swear it," Ludolf said.

They were all wrong. Cutnose campaigned with Tanrcred's uncle many times. Served at Tancred's side with the same loyalty as a sworn man. He took money, yes, but he served well. He fought their battles. Killed the men they wanted dead. He would beat the blasphemous words straight from Ludolf's mouth. Cutnose stumbled from the garden, his legs reluctantly obeying as his boots squished through the pooled blood of his men. "Tancred!" He lifted a blood-stained hand.

Tancred squinted in his direction. Lord Richard drew his sword and Sir Rainald halted his mount, hands tightening on his reins. their Swords glinted in the torchlight, casting an eerie glow over the enclosure. Two spearmen took a step backward, spear-points wavering.

"Christ save us, he is risen as undead," Ludolf said, pointing his sword.

"Let us cut down this foul abomination," Lord Richard growled.

Sir Hermann and Sir Guarin leveled lances preparing to charge and Cutnose stopped. Attropius clutched a javelin in each hand, one ready to launch, the other prepared to be thrown second.

"I am not dead," Cutnose croaked which brought on a hacking cough that doubled him over until he spat. He ran a hand over his blood-stained mail then raised a hand for mercy, his voice grating. "It's me, Cutnose."

"The dead speaks with his tongue," Ludolf hissed. "It is the work of the devil!"

"The devil had his chance, and he cursed me to deal with you," Cutnose said.

Tancred stepped his horse closer, but still was over fifty paces from Cutnose. "I know not what evil possesses the body of

Cutnose, but it is our sworn duty to the Lord our God to destroy it," Tancred said. Raising his chin, his eyes wider than the Red Sea, determination settled upon his rigid face. "Bring me it's head!"

The Greek knight was the first to attack. His arm flowing in a fluid motion as his javelin sailed off and to the right, missing Cutnose and rattling as it skipped over the stones. It was followed by another, the point crashing between Cutnose's legs as he stumbled backward.

Knights spurred their horses, hooves crashing over the stone. Even had he been healthy he would never dare to stand before so many mounted foes. So he ran. His legs were weak, a foal during its first week of life, but they moved with the urgency of a desperate man. An arrow lodged into the Attropius's horse causing it to stumble shrieking before it crashed into the stones. Throwing the Greek knight, hands outstretched before him onto the ground. In the dark, Sir Guarin's mount slipped on the slick stone before falling on its side as Guarin twisted in the saddle clutching his reins. Hermann's mount drew itself onto its back legs rather than leap over the fallen, the knight clinging to its back. Confusion gripped the rest of the knights, and they were forced to slow and circumvent both rider and mount, giving Cutnose precious moments to dive into the garden and crawl on all fours. He stumbled back upright, reaching where Marya stood in the shadows of the courtyard walls. "You did not listen. Your death will serve no purpose here. Come. We have our own man to hunt." She disappeared through a postern gate, and he trailed her close behind. The gate fed them onto a narrow lane littered with dead bodies as if God was a puppeteer who had grown tired of making them dance to his music. Shouts of the knights sounded from the courtyard hastened his steps, but he could not see the woman or her companions.

The ghostly female's voice whispered in his ear. "Follow us, soldier of coin." Her eyes held an eerily seductive glow, but with the fierceness of a bird of prey toying with a mouse.

"How did you get behind me?" His instincts told him that something wasn't right with her, and his gut told him to run.

A shadowy smirk filled her lips. "Your kind no longer wants you. If you desire revenge for your men, follow me.

He blinked, feeling the bandages around his throat. His thoughts jumping to his comrade Ralph and the rest of his men crying for help as they were butchered. "Yes." *I cannot stay here.* Finding his feet willing, he trudged after her to the shouts of Tancred's men.

CHAPTER 7

Currents of blood ran freely over the stone streets. Roving bands of crusaders marched along alleys and lanes, between narrowly built homes stacked atop one another, many made of stone far older than Christ himself. They kicked in doors and looted the homes as they went. If anyone resisted, they were put to the sword, and if they were unlucky enough to be women, they were defiled before being put to the sword.

Cutnose and the three warriors avoided contact with the conquerors, dodging into shadows and alleyways to stay out of sight. He tried to quiet himself, sidestepping a body strewn over the stones. Despite a soldier's endurance, he stumbled along behind them barely able to keep pace with the warriors. Doors had been kicked in or hacked to pieces by axes. Furniture tossed to the side as the crusaders searched every crevice for hidden wealth. A woman cried out as they jogged by. Mouth twisted in agony, she reached gory-soaked hands to her face. Her clothes were ripped and torn; her face stained with tear-streaked soot.

Cutnose was numb to the destruction. The priests had been clear in their sermons. God would lay judgement upon the non-believers inhabiting the city. Show no mercy, have no pity, and take the city at any cost.

The sensation returned in his legs as they jogged, every step growing stronger, his head clearing away the fog of dying. His thoughts were muddled, a boat navigating a bog, and too many questions lingered.

"Where do we go?" he hissed at Marya from behind.

"Christian quarter is the only place they will not immediately search," she said over her shoulder. "Now be quiet. A deaf man could hear your mouth breathing from the other end of the city."

They passed the threshold of a church, and the violence dampened around them. There were still bodies in the streets, but there was far less looting and destruction. Most of the homes were empty or securely barricaded, people hiding behind doors, fearing the retributive slaughter. The warriors slowed near an alley and Cutnose finally caught his breath. Ulf tilted his head upward as if he tasted the smoky air swirling above them, then he disappeared into the alley's darkness.

The alley had barely enough space for them to walk single file. The homes were pressed and stacked atop one another, all made from the same pale stone. Lines stretched between the alley walls where the people would hang laundry to dry.

They moved silently before Ulf halted them. Cutnose checked the street behind with caution. Boots thumped and mail clanged as a patrol of spearmen walked past.

Ulf lightly rapped his fist on the door. He spoke quietly into the door frame, and the door opened a crack, revealing an older man with the reddish-tanned skin of a Frank who'd been exposed to the sun for many years. The four were ushered inside the humble home. No candles were lit, and its occupants sat in the darkness. A woman clutched two children in the corner.

"Rest easy, Hugh, it is only us."

Hugh bowed his white-haired head to Ulf. He was of middling height with shrewd eyes, and he wore a tan loose-fitting robe. "I thank the gods for that. Any word of it?"

"It's gone," Marya said.

"Water and bread and I will share our tale," Ulf said.

"Come Agatha, take William and Mary and bring them upstairs. These conversations are best left for my ears alone." He collected the woman and children and guided them out of the room.

"We squander time here," Cutnose said. "The beast's trail grows colder the longer we delay." He was no fool, he knew enough to be afraid of it, but revenge was a tall flame fed by righteousness of wrongdoing and he would feel the heat of its inferno before he breathed his last. At least that was what a vengeful man told himself. "And the daylight will do us no favors." Once word got out that he was a wanted man, it would be difficult to do much without fear of capture.

The trio ignored him as if he hadn't said a word. He stood irked, waiting in silence. Arnulf and Ulf sat in chairs while Marya sat on the floor, resting her back on the wall. She took a bowl of water and splashed some onto her face, washing away the dust and grime.

"That man is a Frank. We were told no loyal Christian man stood behind its walls." The ones he'd met on the road had been expelled from the city. Anger settled in Cutnose's gut like a peach pit swallowed whole. Any remaining Christians in the city could have opened the gates, alleviating many dead crusaders broken upon the rocks and walls. It mattered little now with all his men dead.

"Hugh is an old friend," Ulf said. His words definitive and final. A man who did not explain himself twice.

The elder returned with a tray and a jug of wine and water. He set a round loaf of flat bread on his modest wooden table.

Yet Cutnose's angst at having lost his men would not be overcome by Hugh's friendship with Ulf. "A single man opening the gates would have saved hundreds of lives."

Hugh regarded him like an annoying child who demanded attention. "Who says I wished the gates open?"

"You're a Frank. Why would you not help your own kind?"

"Once you could have called me that, but I gave that life up long ago." His eyes found Ulf. "My time had come to embrace a different life. Why don't you sit and rest, pilgrim?"

Cutnose shook his head. "All my men are dead. My lord wants my head. If there be no coin to be had, I'll take heads of my own, including that of this Bors."

"Did he say Bors?" Hugh asked.

"Aye," Ulf said with disgust.

"In the city," Hugh breathed. "They must know."

Ulf gazed at Hugh in silence, his eyes speaking tales untold.

"Slowing him down was the best you were going to do facing a man like that," Hugh said.

"I shoved my dagger into his heart, and he shook it off."

"You are not listening, mercenary. You did the best any man could do," Ulf said. He crossed his muscled arms over his chest, his blue eyes flashing gold.

Cutnose's belly jumped like a man realizing he was alone in a cave with a bear. Bors's eyes had flashed the same gold before he had begun his massacre. Like the sun cresting the horizon at dawn. "What is this witchcraft? Your eyes are the same as his." He took a step backward.

"Sit down and I will tell you what you want to know," Ulf said, gesturing at a chair.

"The only thing he needs to know is that he's lucky to be alive." Marya paused then added, "For the time being."

"You're worse than a long-winded priest speaking in riddles and lies. You promised you'd help me kill this knight," he said to Ulf with a momentary glance over at Marya. She smirked at him like a wolf seeing its pup try to bare its teeth, an unnatural sight, almost taking his words from him. "I only need to know where the ugly bastard is so I can kill him."

Arnulf half-smiled. "Foolish but brave. I think we should keep him."

Ulf was less amused. "You are not ready. If you do find him, he will easily kill you."

"It didn't work before, did it?" He slapped his chest. "I'm breathing."

With a brief glare, Ulf tore the loaf of bread and passed it to Hugh who waved him off and then to Arnulf. Between mouthfuls he said, "You were as close to death as one can come and return, but you did not die." He swallowed his food. "You surprised even me."

"I feel fine." Cutnose flexed the muscles on his arms and rolled his shoulders and adjusted his neck. It was still raw, but he felt strong, like he'd had a good plow followed by sleep in a feather bed.

Ulf eyed him. "Bors is no man."

"Of that we are in agreement. He is one with the devil."

"He is not the devil either. At least not the way you understand it."

"You would not speak so lightly of that creature had you seen it."

Silence choked the conversation. Everyone in the room exchanged glances with one another. The only sound was the chewing of bread and drinking of wine.

Marya brushed past him and grabbed a hunk of bread. "Better be careful who you're calling devil. Sometimes devils are the only company you keep."

"Or the only company that will keep you," Arnulf added.

Ulf eyed him with a stern gaze then leaned backward in his chair. "Some men have called us devils in the past. Some have worshipped us as gods. We are none of those things and all of those things. We are men but different."

"Stop with the riddles." Cutnose pointed toward the door. "If I'm going to kill this thing, then I need to know what you know. What is it? How do we kill it?"

"I will tell you in time." His answer made Cutnose clench his jaw. He was a soldier. He wanted simple answers for which he provided simple solutions, usually ending with a swing of his axe. "Many have tolerated our existence as long as we kept out of sight. Some have sought to destroy us. Bors falls into that category."

"He wants to destroy you?"

"He thinks our kind are a plague upon the bloodlines of man. A curse from God to be burnt away with fire or a pox to be cut away with a sharp blade. He is a member of an ancient order of knights that seek the eradication of our kind."

"Who are your kind?" Cutnose felt his back reach the wall. *Who and what are these people?*

"We've been called many names. I've always known us as Ulfhednar."

Cutnose gulped, the word was unfamiliar to him yet sounded like a harsh wind from the wintery north. "I do not know this word." He eyed them and then gave Marya a backward glance. "What are you?"

Her full lips curved in a short smile, her hazel-green eyes holding an unknown mirth, contrasting sharply with her snow-drift skin, her lips uttering, "Vlkolak."

Arnulf leaned back into his chair and fingered his wine cup. "Wiccan, werewolf, wolfskins, Sons of Cain." Then downed his cup, reaching to pour himself another. "Amongst other less flattering terms."

Cutnose's heart sped into a gallop while his gut plummeted. Witches, goblins, ghouls and werewolves were all meant to scare little boys and girls to keep them from the real dangers of the outside world. Nothing more than tales that old women told to gain compliance from children. "Old wives' tales."

"We are neither monsters nor men but something different."

Cutnose tugged his knife from his belt in what felt like a meaningless but comforting way to die. He pointed the blade at Ulf then Arnulf. "Stay away from me or I'll kill you." Arnulf lifted his hands with a mocking smile.

Hugh's eyes judged him calmly, a child with a toy sword, and he took a small sip of wine. "You are not in danger."

"The hell I'm not. Stay seated, or I'll kill you."

He slowly moved laterally toward the door, his eyes never leaving Ulf and Arnulf, the knife pointing from man to man. "Stay away."

Marya's voice came from behind him. "Sheath your blade, Cut. Nose." He felt the razor-sharp tickle of her sword edging his neck. He lifted his chin.

"He's already paid through the nose once," Arnulf said with a smirk.

"He keeps this up, he'll end up with more cut than just his nose," Marya said.

Cutnose gulped, sweat dripping down his neck. His eyes darted to the side trying to see her. "Let me leave. I will tell no one of what I've seen."

Ulf slammed his long axe onto the floor and his voice boomed with the power of a king. "You will not leave." He gestured with his braided beard. "Now, sit. If we wanted you dead, I'd have let you finish feeding the stones with your blood." His lip curled. "But we gave you a chance at life, and I intend to put you to use."

"Sheath your blade," Marya said. He spun away from her sword, and she snapped the flat of her blade on his wrist. The pain was sharp, vibrating through his arm, and his fingers relinquished the blade.

Christ's second coming. I've been disarmed by a woman.

"You want revenge for your men?"

It took every ounce of restraint to not dive for the weapon. His eyes betrayed him. "Yes."

"Then take a seat like Ulf said." She gave him a slight shove toward a chair. "You've been given more chances than a man of your knightly virtue deserves."

"I'm no knight." He eyed her in irritation.

"I can see this."

"You keep talking like a man, I'll treat you like one."

She laughed at that, and it was genuine and musical, pointing at a chair with her sword. Her strength was uncanny, ten times a woman her size. He gulped, feeling the rawness of his throat. His world spun around him like he'd drunk an extra jar in the tavern, everything an uncertain whirlwind. The chair creaked as he sat in it.

A glimmer of a smile danced around Ulf's lips unable to take shape. "The Norns were not kind to you and your men. It was unfortunate we hadn't caught his scent sooner."

Cutnose resisted rubbing his wrist where the she-devil had grabbed him. "Aye. It was. We were no better than a herd of goats taken to market."

"And to him you were. You stumbled into a war that has gone on for hundreds of years. A war between people like us and that of the Order. Bors's quest seeks to tip the scales in their favor and that is why he must not succeed."

"More than they already are," Arnulf added into his cup of wine.

"What does this have to do with the temple?"

Ulf continued. "Long before my time, my people told tales of a powerful relic that resides in the lands of Judea. A relic of renowned power made from rock not of this earth. It is said to have fallen from the heavens long ago when our race was born. The Order seeks this chalice, and if they do, it is our cause to deny them of it."

Cutnose searched for an answer. "What is the chalice?"

"There are many names. Christians know it as the Cup of Christ, the Holy Grail. We know it as the Black Chalice. I believe them one in the same. The Order will use whatever power the cup holds against our kind, and I have no doubt to subjugate the realms of men."

"The Holy Grail was in the temple?" Cutnose wondered if Tancred had somehow known this and that was why he assigned Cutnose's men to protect the people there. Surely, he would have posted every single one of his men if he knew this to be the case. He made the sign of the cross over his chest.

"Our quest is clear now. They must be stopped." Ulf shook his head. "Bors may be brash, but he is not unwise. Embracing his wolf form and slaughtering so many, was a risky decision. We can only assume he would be willing to place himself in such danger if it was within his grasp."

"He will not be alone," Marya added. "They never travel without brothers and sergeants, perhaps even hounds. I wonder if his loutish progeny rides with him. It would give me great pleasure to take both their heads."

"Whether or not he has the chalice does not matter. We must deny him. Bringing him down will be worth the risk to ourselves."

Cutnose eyed Ulf and then Marya. "This Bors is like you?"

"One would say we are distant kin, but most of the Order are mere men."

"Over pious zealots," spat Marya.

"Bors is one of the Twelve. They are the most powerful warriors within their ranks. They hold council at a round table as peers."

"Cockless dogs call themselves the All-Fathers," Arnulf said.

"You too will be like him," Marya said, with a wrinkle of her nose. "But weaker."

Ulf's eyes flashed at her. "He is not ready for that discussion."

Marya frowned, reluctantly obeying.

Realization of her words crept upon him. "That animal? That monstrosity?" He eyed his hands, expecting claws to burst forth from his fingernails and coarse fur to enshroud his entire body. "I've been cursed. A resurrected corpse doomed to become a vile beast. I would say kill me now, but I've never felt better." He squeezed his fingers together making a fist. He felt like he could punch through the house's stone walls then run in full armor for a day despite the gnawing pain in his neck.

"Many blessings come with curses. Your strength will grow," Ulf said. "These changes are rare, and with practice, extremely powerful. With time, you will become an even greater warrior than you ever imagined."

"If you don't control it, you will be dangerous," Marya said.

"If you lose control, you will be labeled for Culling, and then we cannot save you," Arnulf said. He held Cutnose's gaze, unafraid of the scarred soldier.

"I can't be one of those things." It was like new blood pumped in his veins, stronger blood, the blood of an old forest god rising from dark soil, decaying leaves dripping from him, ancient and reborn. After laying in a puddle of his own blood, he knew that whatever he was, he wanted to always be that way. Stronger, faster, and virile, like an animal whose needs required fulfillment at any cost.

"You will aid us in stopping Bors. Even now, you must feel his presence in your mind, for you are connected by blood," Ulf said. "Your powers will rise like the tides of the sea. Unchecked and uncontrolled, it will grow stronger until it consumes you during the moon's final hours."

There was worry hidden in Ulf's voice, Cutnose could sense it. Like he held back a step from the truth. Everything he said added the wood of change unto the funeral pyre of the old Cutnose's understanding of the world. And Ulf held the torch waiting to set him aflame. "I will know where Bors is?" He searched his thoughts and found nothing. "And what happens at the full moon?"

"You will be able to sense him if he is near. With a stronger connection, you may be able to tell the direction. I do not know. Most men who follow this path do not live long enough to tell the tale."

"You're a comforting man. I feel nothing." He grimaced and rubbed the back of his neck.

"It will strengthen over the coming days."

"Why the full moon?"

"At the full moon, the animal inside you will claw its way free. It will feed on the man until only the beast remains. Should you let this happen, only the wolf will remain. The man can never return, he will be lost to the Wilds. Men will fear you. They will tell tales of your terror, bar their doors in the night. The Order will hunt you and crucify you. They will bleed you drier than the desert plain, and packs of wolf-brothers will hunt you down and tear your heart from your chest."

"Wolf-brothers?"

"Our kind have not faded into the mists of day. Packs of Ulfhednar will slaughter you to protect their own. But that is if we cannot find Bors."

"Can't say I am feeling very wanted by this *pack*."

"We are not a pack," Marya said.

The weight of her words yoked them in silence. After several moments, Ulf spoke. "Bors must die before the next moon, and you must strike the killing blow and remove his heart."

"That's if you're quicker than me," Marya said. "Then I can be the one to take your head."

Cutnose narrowed his eyes at her. "I'm surprised no one has taken your tongue."

She smiled her blood red lips. "Who's to say they didn't try?"

"Best be wary, soldier. She's killed more men than you've seen in your lifetime."

"I'm not sure I like her."

"Feeling's mutual."

He tried to ignore her, but it was difficult. Her eyes were as piercing as arrows, and her confidence was that of a victor of a hundred battles. He'd seen men like that get cut down as easily as the next, but the way in which she said it made him believe her. And that unsettled him even more. Best to focus on the easy part. "I have to kill that whore's stillbirth by the full moon?"

"Many brave warriors have fallen before his hammer." Ulf's hands tightened around his engraved long axe. "But you will not walk this dangerous path alone. We will guide you, but for you to survive, you must take his head."

He sighed, and he eyed them. Arnulf stuffed a piece of bread into his mouth. Marya sipped some wine. Ulf stared unwavering, his eyes holding millennia of experience. All he had to do was kill the monster who slew all his men, as easy as a camp follower finding a man's bed to share. "A desperate man will do as he must." There was a desperate beast inside every man. He'd seen them kill for a bite of bread, stab each other over a drop of water, feather one another over a piece of silver. "I kill him, and I will be free of this curse?"

"You can never be cured of this," Ulf said, his voice rising in anger. "It requires no curing but a man of patience and self-control. It is a dangerous gift you've been given. But it is a gift."

"He's not ready," Marya said with a disgusted look.

"Many who are not ready rise to their calling. Only the man decides," Ulf said. His eyes judged him as if he were St. Peter descended from the heavens to provide him divine guidance. "If this is beyond you, I can end this swiftly." Ulf did not need to heft his long axe for Cutnose to know the assurance of his words.

The room became quiet aside from Arnulf's chewing. The walls closed around Cutnose suddenly and the air thickened like a stew, making it harder to breathe. Death loomed in every direction, but there was a glimmer of hope to live even if he could not fully comprehend all the tales these people told him.

"If killing keeps me from going mad, I am as good a man as any for the job. I would live long enough to see my men avenged."

Ulf's eyes flashed gold and a slight grin held on his face. "Then we will embark on this journey together."

CHAPTER 8

Bors's mount struggled with its head down even at a steady walk. It sighed heavily beneath him, unaccustomed to carrying such weight. Its shod hooves almost hesitating as it clopped along. The knight he'd acquired him from hadn't been feeding it properly, rib bones protruded from beneath its stretched skin. It would take months of heavy feeding to get the animal to full strength, one that could campaign or sustain multiple charges, especially under Bors's hefty frame. He wouldn't need it for that long, but he would take measured care of the poor beast as was his custom.

"You will be fed soon," he said softly, patting the horse's flank. The loss of his superior mount irritated his thoughts like a cluster of bent rings in mail, rubbing the flesh it was meant to protect. "You will not suffer the same fate as Segomo." *A sickening waste of trained horse flesh, but his death served a greater purpose.* His thoughts were accompanied by the soft thumping of the bag on his saddle and the strike of his mount's hooves. While the new mount was trained enough to adeptly ignore the bodies splayed on the street, it was still skittish with the trophies dangling from Bors's saddle. He steered the horse down a narrow alley barely wide enough to fit them.

He kept his back straight, but the numerous wounds still plagued his body. He'd been subject to much worse over his centuries of existence and he would eventually fully heal, but fresh wounds nagged at him nonetheless, as a murder of crows on a corpse. It would take a few days to feel like a new man again. Age dulled his ability to heal as it does all men, lingering pain becoming a lifelong accomplice, but he would not die from his wounds.

Barred doors and dark windows loomed out in the shadows. The Christian citizens of Jerusalem were terrified the crusaders would turn their wrath upon them, despite belonging to the same vagabond cult. The violence perpetrated by the religion sworn to peace, temperance, chastity and poverty was comparable if not far greater than the worshippers of pagan gods.

He halted near a wooden postern gate and dismounted, favoring his leg. He pounded his fist into the door and waited. There was a scrape of wood, and soon the doors were swinging open to a small courtyard. A tall man filled the opening, holding himself erect as a king wrapped in a cloak of red.

His gaunt, lined face was shadowed in the light of a single torch. Dirty, snow-colored hair hung to his shoulders. A plain sword was strapped to his belt. His mail coat rustling as he nodded his head to his companion. "Brother Bors."

"Brother Percival."

Bors led his horse through the gate. A sergeant offered to take his mount and Bors waved him off without a word and secured his animal in line with over forty others. *Must find my first brother and get a new shield.* Sergeants and brothers peered curiously at him as they oiled weapons and mended clothes and armor. Many averted their eyes from his harsh gaze.

"Is that still necessary?" Percival said, eyeing the saddle of Bors's horse.

"What is that?" Bors said. He busied himself checking the saddle, but he already knew the answer.

"The grisly trophies you insist on taking," Percival said, his voice was higher than one would expect from such a tall man, hints of an ancient aristocrat clung to his words.

Bors grinned, although one could hardly call the flat-lipped curve of his lip such, but for him it was an outward display of joy. He admired the three heads dangling from his saddle. The gray-bearded one gave him a warm feeling inside. He had fought well. Smooth for a man his age, like flowing water. He felt stronger carrying the souls of his enemies with him, especially those of worthy adversaries. The other two heads were almost rotted through, a Turkish warlord and a giant Syrian, one had been insulting, the other brave with the strength of a dozen men, but neither had fought as well as the gray-haired one.

"You would deny a dead man such an honor?" Bors asked.

"I care little for their honor. They are already dead. You should let their souls rest in peace."

"You always frowned on the old ways. Quick to adapt the prudish cultures. It is a wonder you ever procreated at all."

"A man who wishes the stability of companionship over pleasure, is a man who lives in peace." Percival bowed his head. "You would do well to adopt the same god as Uthur encourages. The Christians further our cause and weaken our enemies'. We are natural allies."

"Do not lecture me." He spat on the ground. "Christians." The word was a mealy apple crumbling on his tongue. "Their beliefs brought down the empire from within."

Percival showed no emotion to his harsh views. "Times change and empires fall while others rise anew. It was not that long ago that Islam was but a desert cult. Now it embraces all these lands."

"They both steal from the religions before." Bors snorted. "Will you be joining them next?"

"I follow Uthur's wishes."

"I keep what has been paid for in blood." The two men stared at one another, neither relenting. "Uthur cares not. He cares for success in our quest, and he shall receive what he seeks." He untied the rope securing the bag to the side of his saddle, being careful to ensure the knot keeping the bag closed was not touched.

Percival turned his head curiously. Bors knew he could hear the whispers now. "It cannot be."

"It is."

Percival dropped to his knees in reverence as if a forceful gust drove him to the stones. "Our prayers are answered. O'Lord, we are forever in your debt." He clasped his hands together, praying with hardly audible sounds. "Pray with me, brother."

What god preaches equality while asking you to kneel? Bors grunted and walked back to the gate and closed the doors. "Much blood was spilled. Crusader and infidel. I was forced to embrace the darkness."

Percival eyed him angrily beneath overgrown white eyebrows. "You put our position here in jeopardy."

"The city is brimming with blooded swords. The various factions will blame each other or the infidels."

"It could tarnish our reputation with the leading lords." Percival hastily stood, knees creaking like a rusted hinge. "I can speak with Raymond of Toulouse if needed, he would be grateful for our support, but I'd rather use discretion with so many crusaders within the city." The ancient knight stared at Bors with steel eyes. "How it sings? I would lay my eyes upon it."

Bors's nostrils flared, testing the scent of the air. It had called to him the entire time it was in his possession, but he ignored it. "Inside the chapel. You must have smelled them."

"The Hunted."

"They are near. I've been smelling their stink all night."

"How many?" Percival asked. His eyes examined the perimeter of the chapel and courtyard walls searching for means of egress. He feared they already stalked them in the shadows.

"No more than five."

"Five is too many for the two of us even with all our brothers

and sergeants. This is an ill omen. That we are so close, and they reveal themselves I fear is no coincidence."

"Any word from Galahad? My patience thins with his absence." His patience had been thin since they'd left England.

"I expect him anytime. He should have left Antioch three weeks ago."

"That young calf drags his feet. He knows the importance of our quest. Curse Uthur for making us bring him."

Percival held his tongue. "Only God knows what drove Uthur to send him with us. Our comrade is young but not without skills. Our party is strong and our quest noble in the eyes of the Lord. No devil may stand before us and live to see the morning's light." He lifted a weathered hand toward the small chapel. "Let us see it."

Bors followed Percival inside the chapel, bag in hand, his leg and side complaining, a chill settling around his hand as he walked.

The chapel was dank, the stone blocking the daytime heat, becoming even cooler in the night. It was empty save for a wooden altar. The floors were made of the same ashen stone most of the city had been constructed with and needed sweeping. Candles rested in nooks on the walls and from the altar.

Percival stood to the side. Colban, his young squire lowered his head, standing in the corner and avoiding eye contact with Bors. He was little more than a child, and he never looked Bors in the eyes, meaning he was afraid. It was a healthy fear, but he needed harsher training to encourage him to overcome it.

Colban was the sixth son of a minor lord in the midlands hoping to gain favor with Uthur. Bors was sure the man viewed the boy as a sacrifice to keep Uthur's wrath from purging his lands. Probably never expected to see the boy again. There were not many prospects for the sixth son of a backwater lord, but if he was lucky, this young man might have an eternity in the palm of his hand. While his father and brothers would be ground to the dust of time, he had the possibility to live for lifetimes and perhaps rise far above his station. Or he would be cut down by blade or arrow, most likely ripped asunder by one of the Hunted. Risk was the burdensome twin of reward.

Bors gently set the bag upon the wooden altar, uncertainty hanging in his gut. It thumped down with the weight of an anvil. He took a step back, reluctant and eager at the same time. His hand shook almost willing to betray him to grasp the bag again. He beat down his uneasiness, he couldn't recall a time in recent history where he'd held any doubt. He flexed his fingers and squeezed his fist, forcing blood back into his hand.

What is wrong with you? Bors is afraid of nothing. Man nor beast. He let his hand safely rest on the handle of his hammer, finding comfort in the shaft.

Percival stepped to the altar, his feet hesitant. His hands quivered as he hovered near the bag. "I can feel it. The holy spirit of God," he whispered. His throat rolled down and up, and he glanced at Bors, his features shrouded in dark wonderment. "It was sent from the heavens. A most powerful gift."

Bors nodded, it took every ounce of himself to avoid falling into the abyss of the bag. "It called to me with the voice of the gods. It sang no words, only notes that quake the bowels of the earth."

Percival exhaled, his lips quivering. Stress formed around his eyes. With two fingers, he parted the opening of the sack. Gradually with almost tenderness he shifted his hand inside. He let out a small gasp of painful ecstasy as his fingers grazed its surface. He removed the object with care and brushed the sack to the side, holding it in both his hands.

Men called it the Holy Grail, the Cup of Christ, but the brothers of the Order knew it as the Black Chalice. The interior was hollowed, giving it the appearance of a shallow and crudely carved bowl. It was made from a coarse sable rock, the surface cragged as if man had struggled to shape it. Specks of white embedded the sides. It was like no stone Bors had ever laid eyes upon.

Percival's eyes gleamed in the candlelight. "It is breathtaking."

Bors grunted an unintelligible answer. Percival abruptly set the object on the altar and exhaled forcefully as if the bowl had stolen his breath. He took a step backward, closing his eyes. "Come, brother. Let us repent of our sins," Percival said, his breathing unsteady.

Bors struggled to pry his eyes from its orbit. "We don't have time. We must secure passage back to England."

"There is always time to pray. He will show us the way," Percival's eyes found a wooden cross hanging on the wall.

"How many gods have you prayed to over the course of your life?"

"Many, but I have repented of those sins. I have found my way in Christ, and you must do the same."

"I've slaughtered men as they prayed to this Christ. He gave them no strength. He did not heed their calls for mercy."

"And they dine in his heavenly embrace for their martyrdom. Bors, kneel with me. What is one more god to your pantheon?" Percival lowered his eyes and began muttering the *Pater Noster*.

Bors suppressed a growl and joined his comrade at the altar. He knelt onto the hard surface ignoring the itching pains of healing wounds. His blood audibly dripped on the stones, but he ignored it as a mere annoyance. He clasped his hands together but struggled to lower his eyes.

The flickering candlelight cast no glow off the bowl's celestial surface, the light dying in its presence. It was as if the bowl stole the air from his mouth leaving him unable to breathe. His mind became obsessed by it, solely focused on it. Everything else faded away to the background. Its song was incomprehensible, yet his soul yearned to know every word.

His voice wavered under its pressure. "Its power is beyond me."

"The Chalice echoes eternity," Percival said, lowering his head. "The Lord has told me as much."

Bors forced himself to lower his eyes, an action demanding his full effort. He clasped sweaty palms in front of his body. He recited a series of prayers to the gods, both ancient and new, for an old man knew many prayers, and it seemed imprudent to leave them out. He finished with one he had learned long ago.

God of War, Son of One, Golden-helmed shield-bearer, spear thrower and axe wielder, blood giver and Master of the Hunt, give us strength to overcome your trials. We shall pay your tribute in blood and water the earthly domain. We give thanks for granting us valor and courage in the face of our foes. Father of soldiers, most blessed of warriors, lend us the fury to conquer man and beast alike. May the piles of our enemies be high, may their blood satisfy your hunger, and in the face of death may we find victory.

Satisfied with his adherence of the gods, Bors glanced at Percival. The old man's cracked lips bespoke silent prayers, but his old ally did not hold his gaze for long. The chalice could not be ignored.

The black bowl hummed of destiny. It brought a soft ring to his ears, a downpour of heavy rain on stone roof tiles in the night. He stared at it, more intently eyeing the bowl to see if it indeed vibrated. His eyes could not catch a tremor. He reached a hand for the bowl. *Perhaps I can feel it? What magic possesses this cup?*

"Stay your hand, brother," Percival said softly.

"It calls to me. It is a link to the gods," Bors said, letting his hand fall to his chest.

"Indeed, but we mustn't fall to temptation. Uthur was right to send us. The others might not be so stalwart in the face of God."

Bors pushed himself upright. "I care not to be in its presence." Its faint song mocked him like a clever woman, tantalizing and fooling him.

"That is why he sent his warrior. He cares not for objects unless their purpose is war."

Bors's lip twisted. "Do not mock me. I care for many things." Many of them were a warrior's possessions. He cocked his head to the side. The jangle of bridles, mail coats, and swords caught his ears like the faint trickle of a bubbling stream, barely audible in the presence of the chalice. "I hear them coming."

Percival blinked, overcoming the bowl's intoxication. "Yes, I hear them now as well."

"You are getting too old for adventuring," Bors said, staring down at the elder soldier.

Percival pushed himself to a knee, and Bors grasped his forearm helping him to his feet. "I believe you are correct, Bors. These many years have worn me down like a sword sharpened too many times over the grindstone."

"Yet here we stand. Alive."

Percival's dark eyes regarded him for a moment. "I can barely remember what happened two hundred years ago, but the Nox Umbrarum is still fresh." He shook his head. "I will never forget it."

"Nor I." The men held that night like a black stain on their memories. Never to be washed away, impossible to forget, a branding in their flesh or a battle scar that never healed.

"I will meet them," Bors said. "You may continue your prayers."

Percival gave him a wrinkled smile. "You've grown softer in your old age."

Bors gave him a short grin. "I have a soft place for my war-kin and so few of us remain." He left the chapel and stepped into the courtyard. He easily lifted a heavy bar on the gate and opened the doors. Riders appeared and he waved them forward.

The lead brother carried a shield with a black eagle on a field of crimson red. "Brother Bors," the rider said, a soft smile beneath a sharp nose and a closely trimmed black beard. His ear-length hair had a slight wave in it, like a painting of a black sea. A wolf pelt lined the top of his cloak, and he handed his lance to the mounted sergeant behind him and dismounted. His guard of twenty mounted brothers and sergeants crowded into the courtyard.

Each of the Twelve led his own guard of between ten and

thirty-two mounted brothers and sergeants, and together the three guards formed a banner, falling under the most senior member of their command, Brother Percival.

Bors did not return his grin. "Young Galahad. You've finally arrived."

The two men gripped forearms as the rest of the banner tended to their mounts. "My duties in Antioch took longer than I anticipated," Galahad said, releasing Bors's iron grip.

"Your task was simple and your delay harmful to our cause."

Galahad took a slight bow. "The Franks are as divided as they are stubborn. I came as fast as it could be arranged."

"And you missed all the fighting."

Galahad's eyes twitched and he scrutinized Bors's emaciated horse. "I trust your trophies weren't too difficult for you?"

Bors's skin prickled. *Damn child and his cutting tongue.* He imagined what it would be like to punch the smirk from his face, but as peers, he would not touch the boy for fear of drawing Uthur's wrath, even halfway across the known world. "All men fall before Bors, but few are worthy of adorning my saddle."

"Your mount looks destitute. What happened to Segomo?" His quick tongue drove a man like Bors mad, but he was forced to follow Galahad's direction or appear weak.

"The bastards slew him with arrows and spears. I would have gladly let them live to preserve such a magnificent animal. He deserved a better death."

Galahad nodded knowingly. "Alas, such a fine and well-kept creature did. Bors and his horses. Treats them better than he does his women."

"It's much harder to find a fine horse than a woman." Seeking to take the upper hand, he spoke briskly, surveying Galahad's men. He immediately recognized several brothers of the Order, men of high breeding and knightly training. Most brothers came and went over time, no more than names and corpses in the ground.

The best within their ranks became first brothers, noblemen

and veteran knights whom had tracked and fought the Hunted and lived to tell the tale. They served as a second-in-command in a guard or banner only outranked by a Second Son, a descendent of one of the founding All-Fathers, or an oath brother, and there were few men who reached such rank in the Order, but when they did, they were esteemed among all.

"Where is your first brother?"

"Probably two days behind with Brother Alymere. I had him replace First Brother Malcolm to command the banner of spear."

"What happened to Brother Malcolm?"

"A fever took him near Antioch." Galahad shook his head in disgust. "Full of vitality one moment, gasping for breath the next. God's will can be ugly to watch."

"And you left them?"

Galahad disregarded Bors's concern with a wave of his hand. "The infantry was slowing us down. He marches with fifty spearmen and two dozen crossbowmen."

"Leaving him with no horse was a mistake."

Galahad spread his arms. "I was torn between rushing to battle and the safety of our men. Apparently neither decision pleases my comrades."

"You protect your men. Always protect your men. Do not split your forces unless it is for a flanking maneuver. I would rather not see you for weeks than leave part of your command exposed." He pointed at him. "You need another century of war under your belt."

"If only we all had your longevity, brother."

Bors would have been much more comfortable if it was First Brother Mador standing before him instead of Galahad. "Mador is a reliable commander, he will ensure Brother Alymere reaches us."

Brother Alymere was one of the Second Sons, a rank and status unto itself with the brotherhood, one that caused friction within the Order, as their worth was wrought by blood rather than action. He was a slender knight of a diluted bloodline and descendant of one of the original founding brothers. He was braver than most, with a noble look to him and a grace that embodied his every movement. On most expeditions, he would be leading a guard under his own command, but with one of the Twelve in the field, he fell second to Galahad. Bors was tepid toward the man. The true loss to them now was First Brother Mador.

First Brother Mador was one of the best the Order had to offer, loyal, reliable, eager to get the job done, and an astute fighter. He believed in the Order's vocation and would carry out commands without hesitation. It had been the primary reason he had been paired with young Galahad. He was a true soldier, something that was hard to find anywhere these days, including within the ranks of the Order.

Bors blamed it on lack of discipline. Most of the men that came to them for service were hot-headed blowhards, told tall tales of their exploits, sang epic songs of their deeds, then shit themselves at the first sight of the Hunted. Few had put in the time in the field, let alone faced demons in the darkness clutching their blades like lovers. Then again there weren't many professional soldiers left in the world. Only rich aristocrats playing war with all the best equipment available. Nothing like when he was young. Oh, how milk-soft the world had become.

Instead of reliable Mador, Galahad stood before him, one of the Twelve, holding a venerated place at the table with Uthur, one of his champions and advisors, a peer to the others, but this man was not their peer. He reeked of youthful indiscretion. A glimmer of a smile attempted a raid upon his lips and was beaten back by the whiskers of his mustache.

The first Galahad had been quite the little *verpa* as well. Clever yet brash. A dozen generations and it appeared that the congenital trait had lived on, even if it was within the weak bloodline of a Second Son. Galahad was the ninth of his name, although it was surprising that one with such minimal abilities had gained such status within the brotherhood. In fact, he was the only one in the entire existence of the Order to become one of the Twelve while lacking the ability to embrace the darkness. It had caused quite a stir amongst the other eleven brothers. Yet Uthur had insisted. Now Bors was stuck with a man who should be taking orders not giving them.

"I need you to send one of your sergeant-brothers to the crusader camp. Find a Genoese ship captain named Arduino. Tell him to gather his crew and secure a ship. We will pay him whatever he asks."

"In such a hurry to leave this land of milk and honey? It seems as if we've only just arrived."

"Yes, and I don't mean to walk all the way back to England. Especially not through that wolves' den they call Constantinople."

Galahad read his features, his dark eyes contemplating his meaning. "Then we've found it?"

"Aye." His single word seemed to strike the young man. "Now, get your man to Arduino and join me when you are finished."

Galahad blinked back his shock but lost little time before acting. "Edwin." He waved a grizzled man forward. The senior sergeant-brother wore finely trimmed coat of mail. He bore the brand of the Antler on his neck almost masked by his beard, marking him as a sergeant who had survived enough encounters with the Hunted over the years to be inducted into their ranks. Not many men who entered the Order as laymen survived long enough to join this elite faction. He was just another stout warrior hand-picked to accompany Galahad to ensure he stayed out of trouble.

Bors sought Percival in the chapel. He pushed through the door and stopped. The sight before him struck him as utterly nonsensical. Bors had known Percival for an eternity. They had ridden together on countless campaigns and raids. Fought in battles ranging from riding down brigands to full-scale war between tens of thousands of men. They'd killed all kinds of men of every shade from white as snow to black as night. Men who worshipped snakes and rocks to men who followed the improvised teachings of the Christians. They were war-kin from the very beginning, and while they saw the world in a different light, they knew one another better than anyone else. He always knew what to expect with Percival, and the man was tried and true, set in his ways.

The scene before him was antithetical to Percival's nature. He loomed, a red-cloaked shadow over the altar. His squire lay before him, the same as a corpse ready for burial. The boy's foot twitched. It was clear the boy was dying or already dead. A simple slit in the boy's wrist dribbled blood into the ebony bowl. Percival held the bowl underneath, watching the blood fill it with the intensity of a desert sun.

"Percival?"

The old brother didn't look up from his task. "Do not interfere with God's work, Bors. His will be done."

Uthur had been clear. Do not touch the bowl and bring it back to England with all due haste. *It must have broken his mind. I was right to leave when I did.* His hand felt for the handle of his hammer. His voice boomed. "Percival, you know not what this may bring. Remember what Uthur said."

"I remember. I have read every prophecy a hundred times. Even those by the heretics."

Percival turned toward Bors, holding the bowl as it were a newborn babe between his gentle hands. His eyes gleamed with hope nearing upon rapture.

"We must get it back to England." Bors stayed his hand, fearing the man would attempt to destroy the relic.

"Do not fear, Bors. You will complete your quest."

Bors took a step closer. "What do you mean to do?"

Percival's eyes were tired, a man barely able to stand. "You ever wonder how many miles these feet have tread? How many mountains they've climbed? How many hills they've run?" He studied his hands. "How many lives these have taken? The oceans of blood spilled upon them?"

"Too many to count."

Percival lowered the bowl eye level. "Do you ever regret the killing that we've done?"

"No."

"That is the truth and there is no denying it. There is no end in sight. Only more killing. More marching. More fighting. And to what end? This world is worse than the one we came into. It lacks any semblance of civilization. There is no order. Chaos rules. We are a rock in the ocean being washed away with every wave."

"Eradication of the Hunted is the blood oath we swore. None of us have broken that oath."

Percival blinked, his lashes rapidly beating together. "It was." He nodded. "You aren't tired of this eternal war?"

Bors thought for a moment. War was the oldest of friends. Battle. Arms. Soldiering. He had always been a warrior. It brought him joy, even now. When love, companionship, kingdoms, and honor had all faded with time, war had always been there. Each war was different. New enemies. Old enemies. All manner of causes and all manner of men wishing to die. War had given him life. A reason to live. For what greater art was there than besting another general on the field of battle. Facing a champion and cutting him down. The thought of slaying those mercenaries in the melee was almost ecstasy. "It is as close as I will ever get to the gods."

"A warrior's blood has always run through your veins even from the beginning."

Long ago, men said those words to him. A warrior's blood did not run through every man's veins. Yet Percival had stood with them from the beginning, a shared bloody past together. Weariness shrouded his comrade's eyes. He'd seen men carry that stare with them like a weighted pack on campaign until it broke their backs.

"I alas, grow tired of this *existence*."

"What will you do?"

A strange look crossed Percival, the bowl shaking in his hands.

"There is only one thing that all men must do, and despite all this time here, I am still a man." He said the words as if he tried to convince himself that he spoke the truth. He gulped, his words sounding weaker. "I am a man."

Are we?

"All men must die."

"We made an oath of blood to wage this war."

"An oath is but a word. Death is the eternal oath." He brought the bowl to his lips. He tipped it upward as he drank, wholly but not greedily as if the vessel held the blood of Christ himself. None dribbled down his cheeks or chin, he held himself to a higher standard. As in life, the man was ruled by moderation. He quietly set the bowl back on the table and Bors watched him, expecting something marvelous to take shape.

Percival blinked half-lidded eyes. His words slurred. "Invictus maneo?" He held out his hand watching it shiver.

Bors shook his head. He had felt its magic. He had felt its alluring siren's song. It must hold some power here. Yet there Percival stood, invincible to its touch.

"It has done nothing," Bors said.

Percival fell sideways into the altar, trying to hold himself upright. Bors rushed for him and caught the falling man, aiding him to the floor. His comrade's breath came hard and slow.

"Go in peace, brother," Bors said.

Percival reached out a weathered finger and touched Bors's face. His words came softly with the voice of an ancient. "Ego denique cessat." A final gasp of relief forced itself from his chest and his eyes stared blank. The man withered in Bors's arms, his skin a drying parchment left in the sun for ages. His form shriveled, losing mass with each passing heartbeat, until his brother turned to dust in his hands. It had all happened so fast. He blinked and rubbed his fingers together, still holding the dust-caked red cloak. His sword belt and mail armor laid limp and shapeless.

Bors stood in quiet disbelief, his friend's belongings draped in his hands. The soft drip of the squire's blood pooling and the faint crackle of a candle were the only sounds. He eyed the black bowl with wariness reserved for a man staring down a lion in the tall grass. It held immense power.

"It is true," Galahad said from the doorway. He stepped quickly inside, closing the door. "The Black Chalice exists."

"It sings praise for the blood."

Galahad stepped closer, cocking his head. "I can hear something, as faint as a stream from afar."

Bors handed off Percival's gear, shoving it into Galahad's hands. The young man grasped the mail, cloak, and sword. Bors approached the bowl as a man would a viper. His hand neared its curved wall, his fingers shaking. Its power vibrated outward. Its song the deadliest notes he'd ever heard. His mouth formed a tight line as he opened the sack. He must cover it. He must silence it.

"What happened to Percival's squire?" Galahad asked.

"He died serving his order." The bowl screamed at him to be wielded, held, filled to the brim. Bors's hand neared the chalice.

"Where is Brother Percival?"

The chalice was a raging storm of energy forcing Bors to grimace to stand before it. He held out a hand. "He's dead. Quiet. I cannot think."

Galahad's brow furrowed. "How did he die?"

Bors took a step away, facing Galahad. "The chalice turned him to ash. This must reach Uthur. Only he will know what to do with such power."

"The cup destroyed him? So, the prophecies are true?" Galahad's dark eyes wandered over the chapel.

"Bugger the prophecies. Every slack-jawed wiseman has one. Now quiet." He took the squire's lifeless hand and used his fingers to help maneuver the bowl into the bag, nudging it along. Bors ground his teeth as the chalice's power continued to ebb outward over the room. It scraped the table like an anvil as Bors forced it into the bag. Ripping the drawstrings, he tied the top of the sack tight. He exhaled in relief as the song faded.

"What is it truly?"

Bors stood over the bag leaning on the altar. "I do not know, but it mustn't fall into the wrong hands."

"The Hunted are in the city?"

"Aye," Bors said. He caught his breath before he noticed it. His eyes were drawn to movement. The squire's pale hand jerked, three fingers flexing. Bors frowned beneath his long mustache. "What in the name of Hades?"

Galahad joined him at the altar. The boy's thumb wiggled. His fingers stretching for anything, but the rest of his body laid still, dead to the world.

"He is possessed," Galahad said.

"I used that hand to put the chalice in the bag."

"And now it moves like the living."

"We know not what magic is at play here. Best not to find out." He grabbed a candlestick and placed it close to the boy's clothes. Flames engulfed the boy.

"This was not meant to be seen," Bors said. He glared at Galahad. The young brother watched with fierce intensity. "This knowledge is to be kept a secret."

A meaty stench filled the chapel. Smoke overtook the simple wooden cross hanging on the wall. The fire spread to the altar, eating the wood. The two brothers were forced backward by the heat.

"My lips are sealed."

"Our ally Percival has done us a great disservice. We will need his sword before we are done here. Come."

"He should have waited until we reached England."

"In that we are in agreement."

The two men moved outside as the fire took over the chapel. They watched the flames, thoughts lost to the meaning of it all. Percival's first brother rushed forward, pushing past them. He was a spitting image of Percival, so much so the men speculated he was of distant or immediate relation. He was as tall as a warhorse, his face gaunt, with prudish eyes that judged every man for his many sins. "My lords, there is a fire," said Godric. He went to push his way inside the chapel.

"Hold, first brother. We must let it burn," Bors said.

"Where is Colban?" Godric's eyes were frantic as he searched the courtyard. "Colban!"

"Lower your voice, brother. They have departed. We will not see them until England."

Godric's eyes narrowed. "Brother Percival said nothing of this." He glanced toward the horses. "His mount and that of Colban are still here."

"They are on foot on an urgent errand."

Godric's face twisted in mistrust.

"The expedition is now under my command. Percival's Guard will attach to my own. You will lead them in Percival's stead."

Godric bowed his head, made a fist, and touched his breast in salute.

Sergeants came running, alarm in their eyes.

"Get water, but let it burn," Bors commanded. "Hurry to your task, sergeant." The sergeants saluted and rushed to find buckets of water, Godric following the men. The advantage to Bors was that half the city burned and one more fire would not draw any attention. "I will set up a meeting with Godfrey tomorrow," Bors said to Galahad.

"I have news from Bohemond to deliver."

Bors eyed him sternly. The young brother was astute at weaseling his way into the nobles' politics of the crusade. Diplomacy was not Bors's strongest skill, as Uthur had sent Percival to fulfill the diplomatic role of their mission. However, Bors would smile and do as needed to ensure their success.

"I will speak to Godfrey. I am the most senior member of this expedition."

Galahad grinned mischievously. "Right you are by far, but please let me do the talking, Brother Bors. It—" He raised his eyebrows. "While you have your hammer and swords, I have my tongue."

"You will be silent and wait outside. It is critical we hold this army together until passage can be found. Not whatever schemes you are implementing."

"Schemes? I only further our cause."

"Bah, this is our cause." He held the bag away from himself. "We must be gone and soon."

CHAPTER 9

A cold red sun shone between the stout olive trees atop the mountain ridge to the east of the city. Known as the Mount of Olives, it was a place revered by both Christians and Jews. In the city itself, the drum of boots marching, the metallic song of swords crashing, and the rumble of hooves pounding continued until the bells began to toll. It had taken until mid-morning before the crusaders were done sating their bloodlust and squeezing coin from the lifeless fingers of the dead.

While the Christian quarter hadn't been ransacked like the rest of the city, the crusaders had sought a different toll from their fellows in Christ. They had taken refuge in the empty homes of the expelled Latin Christians. Knights hung shields outside the homes, marking them as occupied by a new crusading resident. The crusaders drank their fill and slept in beds not their own, as they found comfort in any semblance of home in this alien land so far from their own. A small minority of the Greek Christians had been allowed to remain for their loyalty to the city's former rulers, the Fatimids, for leniency in worship. If they resisted occupation, they were shoved homeless into the streets, but there was plenty of vacancy now in the Muslim and Jewish quarters.

When a drunken man had pounded on the door in the early morning, he fell back and pissed himself when Ulf answered, crawling over the refuse in the alley before fleeing. The night had been quiet in their narrow alley, and the sleep of the dead took Cutnose into its own darkness. He awoke as soft voices pricked his ears. He kept his eyes closed as he listened to his new comrades speak.

"They could be anywhere," Marya said.

"Aye," Ulf said, running a hand along his braided beard. "If he indeed has it, he will be heading to the nearest port to hire a ship and depart as quickly as he can."

"That would be Jaffa," Hugh said with a nod. "About forty miles on the coast."

Silence filled the room and Cutnose spied them with half-closed eyes.

"Do you have anything to add, Cutnose? Can you feel his presence?" Ulf asked. Three heads turned in his direction, and he slowly opened his eyes, pretending to awaken with a yawn and a stretch. He pushed himself upright and rubbed his neck. The skin was raw, but healing, his voice croaked like a man dying of thirst. He thought long and hard if he could feel the knight, but he could notice nothing aside from his general well-being. "I cannot feel him, but I do know Jaffa's port is blockaded by the Fatimid fleet."

"It is?" Ulf said. His mouth formed a grim line.

"Aye, Godfrey built our siege towers from the last Genoese ships that made it to the harbor only two days before the Fatimids arrived. The priests called it divine guidance."

"Do you think they are still there?"

"If you want to drive the invaders out, cut their supply lines. We need food and men from Europe if we are to sustain our presence here." He'd been on enough campaigns to understand the hard fact that keeping men armed and supplied was almost as important as getting them to fight. He'd been in campaigns where lack of supply weakened morale to the point of desertion. A hungry man could only be asked of so much.

Ulf nodded. "Spoken like a true soldier."

"The boy knows a bit about war," Hugh said with a glance at Ulf.

Cutnose eyed him quizzically. He couldn't recall the last time anyone called him boy or even ever being a boy for that matter. He'd been at war as long as he could remember, whether it was struggling to find bread to eat on the streets of Bari or marching with Bohemond in Sicily and Greece, fighting had always been a craft he'd sharpened repeatedly out of necessity of survival. He held his tongue, these men were many years his senior, and men didn't grow old by chance in this part of the world, especially in a warrior's profession. But it still chafed him beneath the mail coat to be talked down to as one would a child holding a sword for the first time.

"Gods be good, the blockaded port is in our favor," Ulf said. "Bors won't try to leave over land. It's too risky with all the warring factions."

"He wouldn't dare cross through Roman lands," Marya said.

"No, he will find no aid in Miklagard. Nor south toward Egypt." Ulf's jaw clenched as if he tried to crush a stone between his teeth, and the three sat in silence as if they waited on Cutnose to reveal something.

"Miklagard?" Cutnose asked.

"The Great City. An old name for the place they call Constantinople. Do you know more?"

"I don't expect any massive Venetian navy to come and relieve us. Our enemy may be waiting for some time." Cutnose shook his head. "Especially since we've already taken Jerusalem. We ate our horses when they fell, after that, we marched with empty bellies. We pillaged what we could, but the Fatimids poisoned the wells and burned the crops." He shrugged. "Perhaps the Pope will send the Venetians or more Genoese. All that matters is that we have taken the city. We can defend walls far more easily than we can campaign."

"We hope that your Pope does not send aid. The blockade is our lifeline. It will give us time to track down Bors." Ulf nodded as if it were settled. "We begin now. I will take Arnulf. Marya, you take Cutnose."

Her eyes flashed green at Ulf. "Sticking me with the young pup?"

There was no humor in Ulf's words. "I am afraid at the trouble that Arnulf and him may find. I trust you can handle such a charge?"

Arnulf smirked at him.

"I'll go slow." Marya went to the door. "Come, soldier of coin."

He followed behind her, hefting Geoffrey's red shield from the corner, slipping his hand axe through his belt loop. He shaded his eyes to the sun. It was the color of flush crimson as if it bled across the sky. The heat didn't bother to creep upon them but charged blindly, increasing by the moment. It took many a pilgrim by surprise. It cared not for noble or common, it flogged them all with the same intensity, and too much exposure shoved many into an unmarked grave.

They weaved through the back alleys until they stood, shadowed before the carnage of the main roadway. Tan stones were stained brown with the blood of the city's citizens, puddles slowly drying in the sun as if the crusaders had drunkenly painted the city walls and streets red. Corpses lay where they were cut down, as if a wanton butcher slaughtered his herd haphazardly before he reached the market. Dying within hands reach of the holiest sites of three prolific religions had given them no extra virtue in death, and Cutnose covered his nose at the stench.

"These bodies will bring disease," Cutnose said. The stench of the dead lingered over them in a malignant cloud of piss, blood, and shit. To Cutnose there was nothing worse than the stench of the dead having been left to rot in the sun for too long. It churned his belly, and the bad air brought disease.

A woman lay spread across their path, her hands reaching for something unknown. Marya stepped over the corpse, sending a horde of flies airborne. Cutnose closed his mouth and brushed the buzzing flies away with his hand as he crossed the same threshold, ducking his head. "Pestilence will spread."

"We can hope that your leader Godfrey will be prompt in his undertaking or many more of his army will fall."

"And he won't have much of an army left when the Fatimids arrive to take their city back."

She regarded him over her shoulder. "Heaven forbid."

"It sounds as if you want that to happen. Where do your loyalties lie?"

"Not with the crusaders."

"You would rather see the infidels hold Jerusalem?"

"I care little who holds this patch of desert. Christian or Muslim it means little to me. Many times in my life I have seen the aftermath of Christians' piety, and it looks like this. A few less of them does not bother me."

Cutnose snorted his disgust at her words. He was honest with himself though, his presence in this army was based on the coin to be had, but it was difficult to not feel the piety of the men around him. The holiness of their quest to free the City of Christ. And the talk of being absolved of sin appealed to all. For a man who had done more than his fair share of sinning, it offered eternal rewards. Absolution was only second to gold.

A procession of men in soiled white robes marched toward them. Marya and Cutnose stood near the walls, allowing them space to pass. Mud and blood caked their attire, a sprinkling of holy violence. They were led by a priest holding a staff with a cross on it along with a thurible spilling white smoke. The rest of the men were unarmed save for daggers, but Cutnose saw them for what they were, knights and soldiers. Perhaps they were the purest among the army to have sheathed their swords and embraced the world of a pilgrim once more. The hard glint in their eyes made it clear that they were no camp followers, or part of the herds of pilgrims that followed in the bloody wake of the army. They were the fighting men of that, he was sure. Men that would be quick to draw their swords again.

Between the dozen or so men they carried half as many wounded on makeshift stretchers, the last man pushed in a hand cart. The priest chanted in Latin as he passed, voice rising in reverent song, singing of God's eternal glory. His voice echoed along the stone walls of the abandoned homes. The procession ignored the corpses lining the streets like they were trash. Dead eyes watched. Open mouths shouted silent curses. All condemning the righteous violence dispensed by Christ's army upon his very own city.

Cutnose made an obligatory signing of the cross as they passed. If only out of reaction to the priest and the dying men, he noticed Marya did not bless herself. The pilgrims ignored them, and Marya and Cutnose trailed behind. Most of the homes were single or two-stories and made of stone, but they passed some with three or four, some holding a family on each floor, others clearly owned by a wealthy merchant. The homes were all attached to one another, separated only by narrow alleys. They passed a wide limestone arch leading to an open-air market street, each of the shop bays were wooden covered with colorful awnings to shield the sellers from the sun. The bays were broken and splinted, wares stolen or smashed in the sacking. Above and behind the bays, stone domiciles where the merchants lived lined the street. Near the end of the merchant bays was a grain vault that had been left open. Rats scurried around the spilled grain on the streets.

"You do not make the sign of Christ," Cutnose said to her as they walked.

"I do not follow the Christian God or any man who perpetrates such fallacy."

"Careful or they'll take you for a witch." He glared at her wearing her armor and sword. "By your appearance, it will not take much to convince them."

She turned on him with a smirk and a lift of her eyebrows. "I am far worse than a witch."

He let an extra step linger between them.

She let out a laugh. "You know so little of the world."

"I know enough to know that any woman who does not believe in God and speaks of the devil is a witch or mad." *Best to be avoided on either account.* "You some kind of pagan? Heretic?"

"I tolerate your Christian cult. If only they did the same for others."

"It talks like a witch."

She stopped abruptly, turning on him causing him to have to catch himself from running into her. Her greenish eyes brightened in anger. "I am no infidel. I am no Christian. I follow old gods of the mountains and the sky, of light and darkness, love and hate."

"Pagans," he spat. Holy men often spoke of the followers of false gods with disdain. "They are thieving, devil worshippers." His words rang more hollow than he would have liked. He was willing to overlook a man's beliefs, really almost anything if a man could fight and follow orders. But outside of Pagan, he held much less tolerance for their kind.

"I am not interested in any of the gods who reside here. Just as you do not seek your God here. We are joined in our search for Bors that is all." She turned away, and they followed the procession in silence. If he could avenge his men and still get paid, then that was the best outcome for a man in his situation. "I will get paid what is owed."

"Forget what you know. Coins mean nothing in this war. All that matters is acquiring the relic," she said, pausing, "And if possible, the demise of Bors."

"War is business, woman, and I am owed coin. You gonna pay my wages? Man's gotta eat. Man's gotta drink." He hesitated for a moment wondering if he should be so crass with this woman, but only a moment before he plowed on ahead. "Man's gotta—"

She stopped him again, her hand iron on his chest. "Me allowing you to exist is payment, Cut-Nose. I could easily snuff your life out as one does the tiny flame of a candle. I grow tired of your petty qualms over coin." She released him, walking at a brisk pace. "If it is coin that motivates you, Bors and his comrades have more than enough to sate your basic needs after we put them in the ground."

"Perfect, I'll kill Bors and take my payment." Cutnose hefted his shield a bit higher. If she reached for him again, he would stop her, even with her unnatural strength.

The procession marched to an old church. A small dome covered the roof and a cross stood as a lookout at the highest point. The ground sloped to the limestone archway leading to the interior. The crusaders disappeared within its walls.

Incense poured from within, the sweet woody and earthy scent of frankincense and myrrh, but it struggled to overcome the stench of blood accompanied by wasting death, all singeing at his nostrils. He shook his head, the odor almost overpowering his senses, his stomach turning in disgust.

Marya went to follow, ignoring his hesitation.

"You think it wise?" he called to her. He tried to rub the stench from his nostrils.

She shrugged her shoulders. "I doubt Bors ended up in here, but who knows."

"That smell does not bother you? It is overwhelming." He shook his head trying to clear his nose.

She gave him a grim smile. "All the smells of the Holy City. You will grow used to it."

"I smelled death before, woman, but this is fiercer than anything I've experienced. It's like they are dying inside my nose."

"I suggest you grow a stronger stomach then." She stepped inside. He followed her, trying not to breathe. Men hacked and coughed, foul air enveloping them as much as the pungent incense eddying in the air. They lay in hospital beds in a long line, as a soldiers' barracks. The injured held their limbs as priests and servants tended them in the dry coolness of the hospital, stones dampening the rising temperatures outside the building. Candles illuminated the walls shedding dim light upon the patrons seeking divine intervention on their behalf.

A monk came forward in a brown habit, his hands shoved inside his drooping sleeves. A circular patch had been shaved around the crown of his skull, leaving dark brown hair hanging near his ears.

"How can I help you, brave warriors of Christ?" He stopped himself, realizing that Marya was a woman, his eyes widening as he took her in. His cheeks reddened in embarrassment at such an overt act, and he quickly turned them downcast. "Forgive me, my lady." He eyed the sword on her hip. "Usually only men carry arms."

She wrinkled her nose as if the heavy smell of incense and the dying offended her more than she let on. "Where I hail from, women often take up arms to defend their homes."

"Many people have odd customs, but as long as they have faith in the Lord they shall be rewarded," the young monk said.

"Not all things are within your purview of understanding."

"Many mysteries are better left in the hands of God." The monk bowed his head. "How can I be of service? Do you seek a patron here? Perhaps you wish to donate to the hospital?"

"I seek a knight if he yet lives," Marya said.

"Who may I seek on your behalf?"

"A knight by the name of Bors. His symbol is a red boar on a field of green, but he can also be known by a ring he wears bearing the stag and cross."

The monk took in her words and nodded. "I do not recall his name, but we have many recent newcomers. Let me confer with my abbot."

"Time is critical," Marya said. "I must speak with him, but if he resides here do not let him know I have arrived. Come straight to me first." She reached out a hand and the monk stared at her and accepted a coin. "A donation."

"Of course, my lady."

The monk hurried into the hospital, his robes whisking as he walked.

"If he heals as we do, why are we checking here?" Cutnose

asked quietly. A man erupted in a coughing frenzy echoing over the room. Two monks stood over him, wafting incense all around him in a hazy prayer. The man only coughed harder until he lay still, wheezing in exhaustion giving in to the smoke.

"It is possible he sought refuge to heal. He will not succumb, but he will be weakened if your men fought as well as you say they did."

"They fought better." He gently ran his fingers over his throat. "I healed unnaturally fast."

Marya's eyes flashed. "You may view this as a curse, but you've been given a gift." She continued to regard him with interest. "However crude you may be, it is clear you had some love in your heart for your men."

"I was their captain. Many I considered brothers."

"Yet you've made it very clear that gold is your singular motivator."

He frowned. "Not sure you would understand. War is my business. Lords need men, experienced soldiers, but they seek us because we have built a reputation to get the people that need killed in the ground. A reputation is all a man truly has in this world. Once a captain loses his reputation, his days are numbered. Men won't join. Lords won't pay."

"Your reputation seems to have diminished of late."

"I'm not done yet. I will find more men to join my company once this is sorted out. Then it is back to the best things in life. Fine things to eat, drink, and women to pass the time with until the next war."

She laughed quietly at him. "You wouldn't know a woman if she fell on your lap."

"Been with more than I can remember." The number of women only went up if he included all the ones he didn't remember. He had no wife. What woman would want to be married to a man who never stayed in one place for more than a few months before he was back on campaign. His home was foreign cities between wars, and like most men he required softer comfort where he could find it.

"That's because you are drunk more often than not." She side-eyed him. "Or am I mistaken?"

"I haven't found a wine I didn't like, but I've been with few women I'd rather have avoided."

"But no ladies."

The odor of the dying continued to breach his nostrils. He exhaled sharply, rubbing his nose. "Never been with a noble-woman. Don't suspect a low-born man as myself ever would. You may be noble, and everyone must bow and scrape, but I work for my coin. The low-born work and the nobles play."

"Then you do not understand what it means to be noble."

"I seen fleas on a dog's arse with more nobility than a man with royal blood."

The monk returned with an older abbot. The younger man reddening at Cutnose's last words which he had clearly overheard. The elder holy man must not have heard him or had chosen to ignore the vulgarity of the crusader. He had deep puffy circles under drooping eyelids. He glared at the Marya and her sword as if she were the oddest sight he'd ever seen, as unnatural as a pig in a dress come to discuss a cloud in the shape of the Virgin Mary in the sky. His frown drooped at the corners of his mouth as if he'd never tasted a grain of happiness in his entire life. Cutnose thought the abbot might bless himself in the presence of Marya just in case he stood before something evil. "Brother Beniface says you are looking for a knight?"

"Yes, abbot. Sir Bors."

"Sir Bors of?"

Marya smiled. "I don't know where he hails from these days, he has been a knight in the service of many lords."

The abbot tilted his head at her words. "Red boar on a field of green? I cannot say that I've come across him." His brow furrowed. "Stag and cross ring?"

"That's correct."

"I do not know that symbol. Is it from an order militant?"

"One could say that. I am afraid we must continue our search elsewhere, for he is a dear companion."

The two monks lowered their heads before the abbot said, "If he has been injured in the taking of Christ's city, perhaps if you check near the Holy Sepulchre. Our brothers have set up a hospital there near a holy spring that Mary bathed in. It has been known to cure most ailments accompanied by prayer."

"You have my thanks," Marya said.

"May you go with Christ," the abbot said, his voice a command. Both holy men bowed, revealing their shaved scalps.

Cutnose made the sign of the cross and nodded to the monks and they departed the hospital, both monks watching them go with curiosity.

They walked along the crowded streets as the morning eased to midday overhead. Drunken crusaders drifted from homes, happier to have survived the long campaign than anything else. There was the occasional shout and scream, but now the city was in a post-battle calm.

It was not hard to find the Church of the Holy Sepulchre. It resided near the heart of the city and stood taller than most buildings outside the Temple Mount and the Citadel of David. It was dominated by a rotunda with an open conical roof, apses on the north, west and south, and a new chapel in the east easily identified by the whiter gray stones.

A congregation of knights, archers, and spearmen had surrounded the entrance to the crumbling remains of the basilica. Most had shed their armor and only carried their weapons. A few of the men sat on stones piled along walls.

A finely-garbed man stood upon a stone block near the entrance to the church. He wore a tunic split in quarters of red and white, a red cross sown over his right breast denoting him as a servant to Godfrey. His hair was reddish-blond and matched the color of his goatee.

"That's Lambert," Cutnose said, recognizing the lord's servant. "Secretary to Godfrey."

Marya stopped near the edge of the crowd, folding her arms over her chest.

Lambert lifted a hand in the air, calling for silence over the din rising from crusaders and pilgrims. "Hear ye, hear ye." He held a piece of parchment far away from his face. "To the liberators of Jerusalem and its inhabitants. The council of nobles, through Godfrey of Bouillon, Raymond of Toulouse, and the papal legate have issued a decree against Robert Cutnose, a former soldier for hire under Lord Tancred's command. He is tall of height and broad of shoulder and known by the distinctive mark of a scar running down his nose, hooked to the right."

Cutnose instinctively brought a hand to his face. A clamor erupted from the men. He didn't expect many to know of him, but they knew him now.

"It does not appear that your employers wish to pay," Marya said softly.

He grunted his acknowledgement, waiting for Lambert to continue.

"He has committed crimes as a traitor and a murderer of his own kind. He has been excommunicated and is considered an enemy of Christ deserving neither mercy nor aid. If found, he should be apprehended or killed for his crimes against God and his people. Lord Tancred has offered eight hundred silver coins for the man who captures the criminal. Four hundred for his head." Cutnose's jaw dropped, and his world suddenly got a whole lot smaller. His men were dead. He was an enemy of the nobles and his fellow crusaders alike, who wanted him hunted down like a dog, his head mounted on a spear or atop the nearest wall spike. Tancred offered his hard-earned pay to any commoner who was brave enough to capture him.

Anger mushroomed inside him. To be condemned by your brothers in arms was a harsh reality while it lasted. One moment you were shoulder to shoulder with the men facing down the enemy, the next they were separating his head from his neck to send him to Hell. In one foul night, his reputation had been taken to the highest mountain and tossed from the top to splatter upon the jagged rocks below.

Lambert rolled his parchment, dipped his chin in acknowledgement of having been heard, and retreated from the doorway of the holiest church in Christendom. The pilgrims and soldiers funneled into the church to pay their respects.

"I'm thinking we should be going now," Marya said. She faced him with a half-smile. "The enemy of Christ." She nodded as if she were impressed. "It's been many years since I've heard that one. Your reputation grows."

"Enemy of Christ?" he spat. "No better than a pagan."

"I believe to be banished from the church is worse than not having been saved yet." The excommunication part worried him less, it may affect his standing for many of the more pious lords, but those lords were far less likely to need his services.

He gritted his teeth at the infuriating woman. "May as well sell my sword to the Saracens."

"I assure you, young Cutnose, seller of his sword, you'll be named far worse before we're done." She retreated toward the outskirts of the crowd. He followed like a whipped dog, his mind trying to make sense of what he'd just heard.

Enemy of Christ? Christ's shin bone, they are naming me no better than the devil himself. Is there a worse title? He kept this head low and hurried to catch the fleeting form of Marya, keeping his face lowered behind his shield. His mind dizzied. It wasn't the first time he had stumbled along and was tripped by powerful enemies, but the betrayal of his entire army, one he'd fought among for years, was enough to drown a man in disgust.

His next course of action should be to slip through David's Gate, disappear into the wilderness, and make for the sea. Alone, the lands surrounding Jerusalem would be dangerous to travel. Roving brigands or Saracens would prey upon him, not to mention the war bands of crusaders venturing to visit holy sites all over the area. Even a formidable warrior as himself would struggle fighting a group of men on his own.

Without a mount, he made even easier prey. There weren't enough horses to go around for the knights, let alone a wanted footman. A man had to sleep, and it was only safe to do that in lands such as these with someone to watch your back, and even then, it was dangerous. Tugging his bandages made from Tancred's banner over his nose, Robert Cutnose, excommunicate and Enemy of Christ, followed the mysterious heathen warrior further into the depths of the holy city.

CHAPTER 10

His eyes shot open, and he was surrounded by darkness. The room was entirely devoid of light, only the faint touch of the moon and stars crept through the window's curtain. Something unnatural inside him stirred. He raised a hand to his breast, a sense of dread taking hold of him. His heart raced.

A foul dream, that is all. But his body refused to believe him. An evil had risen inside, working its way from his belly to his heart. It dragged claws along his ribcage trying to escape. His heart responded by increasing tempo like a horse charging across a battlefield.

Scanning the room for enemies, there was nothing to have prompted such an intense disturbance in his sleep. Even in the darkness, his vision was clear. His hearing was crisp, every sound audible down to the soft whistle escaping Ulf's lips as he slept. The briefest escape of Marya's breath and the snore of Hugh from the upper floor's room.

They had scoured the city until night encroached, and neither pair had found any trace of Bors. Yet something unusual shrouded his being, a hooked fish dragging a line through water, its depths unknown. *Is this the connection with Bors they spoke of?*

He pushed himself seated, elbows on knees. He rubbed a hand

along his beard before finding his neck. The wound was healing almost as if it had never happened. He wasn't even sure if there would be a scar. He tugged on a fresh linen tunic borrowed from Hugh. He secured his hand axe and slipped through the door of the house.

Nothing stirred in the alley, not even a rat. Above, the glowing moon inched across the sky. It cast shadows from building to building, the darkness overlapping upon itself. The sight of the moon stirred the contents of his belly like a witch with her cauldron, and a primal consciousness took shape inside him. He choked down the growing impulse to howl, despite what it would do to his raw throat. He grimaced determined to resist its beckoning call. A call of the wild. His teeth clattered at the ecstasy of the thought, his breath deepening inside his lungs.

He pried his eyes from the moon and padded along the alley until he reached a main avenue. He searched for something, but he did not know what. His eyes caught the silhouette of every pebble, his vision unhindered by the night. The flutter of a curtain in the window. The ruffle of a dead man's robe. The ripple of the wind across a puddle of blood.

The stench of the slain made him want to vomit. Even now it loitered like a beggar near a church, always there, always waiting. His stomach growled fiercely as if it anticipated a meal of slow-roasted pig on a spit. And revulsion and hunger battled inside him. Then his nostrils flared as he caught the scent of something new carried in the winds. The sour stink of the living.

Desire followed behind. He lifted his head into the air, drinking it in repeatedly, emitting soft snorts. Soon he found himself bounding from shadow to shadow, avoiding the moonlight or anything that would allow someone to see him. Then he heard them. Two men talking in what they thought were hushed tones but may as well have been spoken only for him.

A nasally voice rasped from a small shadow. "You think they all were hiding gold in their bellies?" The larger man next to him stumbled on a stone in the dark, using a wall for balance.

"Aye, I do," he gruffed. He stopped, leaning against a home. "I bet when they burn the bodies, that dirty Patriarch has his servants rake the ashes searching for it."

Cutnose didn't need to squint to make them out in the dark even though they were concealed by dingy clothes. Daggers hung on their belts. Both were clearly Franks.

"I don't like the dead," complained the first man.

"Nobody likes the dead, but the dead can't do nothing about it."

"It's not right to harm them when they're gone. The spirits may still roam."

The larger man halted his comrade by force then gave him a shake. "Don't be scared of no stories about spirits or goblins. My pa always told me you got to be willing to do the dirty work if you're going to make it for yourself. He'd say, Adam, you want gold and silver, then you must be willing to go outside the law to get it done. 'Cause the lords make laws that benefit the lords. They make you grind grain in their mills. They make you bake bread in their ovens. You die your family has to pay a fine. Your son leaves the land for the city, he pays a fine. They tax you to farm a land the lord could never plant without us."

"I don't have no sons."

"That's not the point, my friend. We pay taxes and for what?"

"It is payment to live and work his land. He protects us."

"From who?"

"Brigands?"

"Aye. Brigands? Lords? Both one and the same. One operates outside the law, the other within it. Every law the lord makes benefits his station. You will never be truly free if we play by all their rules and laws." He regarded his partner fondly. "I don't want to bore you with all that. Fact remains, you want to be rich?"

The first man nodded vigorously.

"You want a woman on your flesh sword?

Cutnose closed on them, his steps silent as a mute and his breath shallow.

The man nodded again. "Course I do, Adam. Course I do. It's been so long. Where was it? The port of Genoa?"

"That tavern near the docks. Aye, Simon, that was a joyous time. Baldwin and Philip got in a fight over that whore?"

Both men stopped before Simon spoke quieter. "They're dead now."

The larger one clapped the smaller man on the back. "Their souls are in Heaven now; may they rest in peace. Focus, Simon. We do the dirty work for Baldwin and Philip. Don't you think they'd want to see us rich and living a lord's life?"

"They would. Well, at least Baldwin."

"Aye, Philip was hindered by the shakes. Twisted his mind." Adam spit after he said the word, shakes. "Once we get done splittin' their bellies and fishing out the gold and jewels, we'll have enough riches to buy as many whores as you want and then some. But you can't get the gold if you don't split the bellies. And women don't fuck men without no gold." He patted his friend's shoulder. "Bugger the spirits. They've no more power here than a Saracen's fart." When his friend still looked less than convinced, he continued. "I tell you now, Simon. I heard a priest say the Saracens don't even have souls." He spread his arms wide. "See, no souls, no spirits, easy as that. Besides, what do it matter if we're richer than Godfrey and that sniveling Raymond combined." The big man smiled broadly in the overwhelming darkness.

"You're right. Bugger the ghosts and the Saracens." The man flashed brown teeth at his comrade.

"Now, let's move along to the Jewish quarter and see if any are left on the street. I hear near the Temple is where all the rich ones lived."

The fire in Cutnose's belly surged like a volcano preparing to unleash ash and molten fire. His steps rapidly increased as the flames roared inside him. His vision narrowed as he closed on them, taking a reddish hue, wind rushing past. The beast raced through his veins, taking over his every move until the man Cutnose was only a brief memory.

The two Franks started to walk again. "They didn't seem so bad when we was killing 'em," Simon said.

Adam grabbed his friend. "It's that kind of thinking that will get you killed. If they ain't like us, then they're infidels. Infidels are the same as the devil, to be killed with impunity. They was thick as fleas when we came in the city. I wouldn't even trust those dirty Armenians. They look just like the—"

He never finished his last words, as Cutnose buried his teeth into the side of his neck. Blood instantly poured into his mouth, and he shook his head like a dog wrestling a bone. Soft flesh, watery blood, and leathery muscle came with Cutnose's bite. He tore away, and the thief fell into the wall of a house clutching at his neck as blood flooded between his fingers. The large thief groaned as he slid down to the street seated. Simon froze in fear, his mouth an open castle gate.

"I-I-I," Simon blubbered.

Cutnose spit the flesh from his mouth and lunged for him, knocking him to the ground and landing on top of his chest. The smaller man squealed beneath him, arms flailing wildly while he cried. Cutnose's hands ripping his tunic away in fistfuls.

A boot connected with the side of Cutnose's ribcage. The force of the blow sent him airborne. He rolled over the stones before gaining control of himself. Every movement was a reflex, a natural flow.

He crouched on all fours, snarling, before he lunged toward the newest threat. The man held a bow and stretched the string tight, muscles hardening in his arms and shoulder. Cutnose's ears perked at the sound of the string straining under the pressure. Simon scurried out of the way.

"Control yourself," said the man with the bow. Empty words to Cutnose.

He was more animal than human. He bared his teeth and threw himself at the bowman. He slowly recognized the man as Arnulf. The archer sidestepped as Cutnose missed, crashing into the wall. A speckling of orb-like lights flashed all around him. He shook his head in a daze. The anger, rage, and lust crawled back inside him like a snake coiling around his spine. There was something else there too. For the first time, he felt the lure of something in the city. It was splitting, as a piece of wood hewn in two by an axe. His mind was in a tug of war in opposing directions. He shook his head, attempting to clear the fogginess from it.

"Stay calm, Cutnose. Breathe. You must learn to control it, or you are no better than the animal you become," said Arnulf.

Metallic wetness lingered in his mouth. He wiped it away in disgust, smearing the sticky remains on his sleeve. The taste of blood started to rebel inside him, making his stomach churn. He regained his feet.

Adam had finished dying. He lay slumped on his side, bugged out white eyes staring away in fear. Simon ran down the street. He glanced back at his hunters, stumbling over an uneven stone before falling to his hands.

Arnulf was wholly unconcerned. "Can you hold the line? As a man of war, you understand this?"

"I understand this." Cutnose grimaced. "It tastes terrible." He spat again. He doubted his ability to control anything, let alone the animal inside him, but he held himself as steady as he could.

Arnulf gave him a grim smile. "Marya is wrong about you. You are smarter than you look."

In one smooth motion, Arnulf drew his longbow back, stretching the string across his body. His back flexed under the pressure. He tilted his arrow upward a fraction of an inch to compensate for the distance.

Simon had regained his feet, panting like a bitch in heat. Each gasping breath echoing in Cutnose's ears, even from this distance.

Thung! It was almost silent, but the string reverberated loudly for Cutnose. A second later, the arrowhead buried itself into Simon's back with a loud *thump*. Simon gave a soft cry as the arrow penetrated from back to front. The white feathers of the arrow quivered as he lay still. He didn't move once his body came to a halt on the stones.

"Nice shooting."

Arnulf lowered his bow. "It took many years to master this skill. My father was a master hunter, yet he never wielded his bow when we needed him most. A mistake I will not repeat when the time comes to avenge him."

Cutnose considered him for a moment. "At least you knew yours." He'd never met his father. His mother had only ever said that he was a soldier. And given Cutnose's propensity for violence, it all seemed like a natural profession for an orphan in a region filled with Norman adventurers teeming to secure more lands. There was always some speculation that he could be the bastard of some Norman lord even a distant relation of Bohemond or Tancred, but what did any of that matter with no proof? He was a fatherless bastard and the only woman who knew the truth lay in a shallow grave with many others who had died from the fever that plagued the city that year.

Arnulf stared ahead, lost in his thoughts.

"I'd take you in my company in a second." Cutnose's words were a stark reminder that he was a mercenary captain with no band, and a single mercenary was only a dangerous man with no allies.

Arnulf ignored him, removing his seax from its sheath. He bent near Adam and hacked the blade into his neck repeatedly.

"I think his death has been decided," Cutnose said with a half-smile.

Adam's body moved as Arnulf chopped his neck to pieces. After wiping his blade on the man's shoulder, he stood. "As much as I'd love to hack my way through the Order's men, the last thing we want is to give away our presence here. We must keep ourselves hidden, especially the wolf within. You should understand that now." He turned toward Cutnose, blue eyes judging him. "Men that look like they were mauled by a wild animal cause other men to be suspicious, puts them on guard. With the Order already in the city, it is best not to give them clues as to our location."

Cutnose nodded his head and scratched behind his ear. "I had no control. No choice. The beast just took over."

"You always have a choice. The mind controls the beast. The beast resides in the man. The man decides his fate."

"I am not one for riddles. How do you stop it?"

"It's no riddle. It is the only way." The archer turned and walked down the street. He put a boot into the dead man's back, pulling on the arrow. Simon's body lifted off the ground until Arnulf extracted his projectile. He held the arrow near his nose smelling deeply, nostrils flaring over his smile. "Hit him in the heart. A man will usually drop immediately if struck through the heart. Dies within a minute if not instantly."

Cutnose nodded his agreement. He'd seen plenty of men die in his brutal time.

"Long ago, I sought to inflict pain and torture upon my enemies, but I have learned to strike a man in the heart is a mercy."

"Is there such a thing in war?"

"There can be. If a man must be killed, do so swiftly."

"Easier said than done."

"Practical efficiency in combat. If I only have to use a single arrow on a man, as opposed to several, I can inflict more casualties upon the enemy."

"Like I said, easier said than done."

Cutnose had learned early, in battle, incapacitating an opponent was the primary goal. Striking a killing blow fulfilled this purpose. Any number of less timely woundings would remove a man from battle as well. Hamstringing, maiming of the hands or feet, any injury to the face tended to take a man out of the fight. The length of time it took for him to die was secondary as long as he was unable to continue fighting. Finishing him off was a mercy. But he supposed shooting a man through the heart was a type of mercy, not one he was used to giving nor wanted to receive.

He followed the archer back to Hugh's home where Cutnose stripped down his soiled garments, and Arnulf pointed him to a bucket of water where he washed the sticky blood from his hands and face. He crept back to his blanket on the floor, cautiously eyeing the other sleeping forms. They did not stir from their slumber. Cutnose lay flushed and sweating on the floor, his mind racing with every thought and unable to find answers. *What is happening to me? Control this beast inside me?* Even as he laid there, he could feel the beast growing stronger. He turned fitfully as he tried to find a comfortable position. Eventually, he managed to doze before the sun's vanguard drove back the horde of night.

CHAPTER 11

There was a certain envious peace to the dead in the streets. Save for the numerous mortal wounds blanketing their poor bodies that had released them from life. Those that had survived the sacking had it far worse in Cutnose's opinion.

The survivors were a hunch-shouldered, beaten people, moving in fearful exhaustion. Those left alive were submitted to their very own hell, slavery, and their first task was to bury their neighbors, some stiff as boards, others bloating with putrid gas, all surrounded by a horrible stench.

He had a great vantage point of the streets on the rooftop of an abandoned home. No one had been killed inside, but someone had ransacked the place, smashing the tables and chairs to pieces of kindling. All except a short three-legged stool that Cutnose sat upon, one foot on the waist-high stone wall as he watched the suffering of those below with disinterest.

The slaves fed giant pyres throughout the city, the dead tossed into heaping piles reminding him of a porcupine of bodies and limbs. Angry black smoke settled over the city like a thunder-cloud threatening rain that reeked of burning flesh. The stench clung to everything with its hellish odor. But it was Godfrey's mansion and headquarters for the nobles of his contingent that had drawn their eye.

Cutnose used a knife to pick meat stuck between his teeth. He scratched the blade along the crease of his teeth trying to remove the irritant while Marya leaned on the wall, one arm holding her chin.

"Tell me, seller of his sword, why are these men here and the others in the Citadel?"

"I'm not a man who cares much for politics unless it's which side to take. And I can smell a weak cause from a mile away. Raymond hides in the Citadel because his position is weak, and he seeks to stymie Godfrey's ambition by holding the fortress."

"Help me understand why you think it best to watch Godfrey over Raymond. Raymond is the richest, no?"

He'd do his best to explain the mind of a noble. "There are two main contingents in our army. Godfrey of Bouillon's and Raymond of Toulouse's. I don't know their rivalry, but I know that Godfrey's star has been rising and Raymond's falling." He paused, eyeing her to make sure she was following. "Men talk. Men follow riches and glory. You see Raymond is the richest, most powerful man in this army, and when we started, men flocked to fight beneath his banners. But after three years of fighting for a man, you begin to see his true ability, and Godfrey has proven the better commander. He holds the confidence of the other nobles and captains. He's a harsh man but understands how to win. A man that can get you paid. It's not too complicated, but you may not understand the politics of men."

She peered over her shoulder, ignoring his insult, and smirked. "I understand more than you know."

"Good. Godfrey built his siege tower in the north and Raymond took his to the south. The Saracens concentrated most of their forces on the walls to thwart Godfrey, but in the night before the attack, he had it taken apart and rebuilt in a different section on the wall. By the time the Saracens had awakened the next morning, their catapults and rock hurlers were out of position to strike until we were too close. Ha. The bastards didn't see it coming." He waited for her to join in the laughter, but she stayed silent waiting for him to continue. "Raymond didn't. His tower burned by the end of the day, and he only breached the walls after the men defending them fled into the interior to fight Godfrey."

"Why did Godfrey allow Raymond to take the Citadel then?"

Cutnose grinned. "Raymond is an opportunistic fool. He beat Godfrey there, and the Saracen commander would only surrender to him. They're clever. Even in their defeat they divide us." He peered south toward the fortress.

It had been built long ago in what was now the nearly empty Christian section of the city. The only fortress within the city walls. Two nights before, it had been in Fatimid hands under the Egyptian commander Iftikhar ad-Daulah and his remaining defenders who had rallied there. He'd proven a shrewd negotiator and capitulated the fortress for safe passage to the nearest Fatimid city, Ascalon, a formidable port city southeast of Jerusalem. Now Raymond's flags flew boldly from each of its towers. Each flag indisputably Raymond's with its distinctive yellow cross, each tip of the cross decorated with three ball-like *pomettes* on a red background. It wasn't a taunt but a dare to confront him.

"He would be a nightmare to remove by force. Many would die. It will come to a vote, and it is not clear who will emerge the victor. I'd bet on Godfrey." He freed the irritating meat from his tooth rolling it on his tongue. *Man or animal?* He spit it off the roof.

"I would not wager against a mercenary to pick the winning side."

"Aye, I got a nose for it."

"Half a nose."

He grinned at her. "My sense of smell has never been better."

"Human blood has an unusual taste, doesn't it?"

He leaned away from her on his stool. Arnulf must have told her of his nighttime rampage. "I like it no more than any man."

Her eyes told a different story, but he turned away to stand and face the city's fortress.

"And why would you not bet on Raymond? He appears to hold the high ground."

"All he's done is guarantee he has a say in the future of the city. Most have left his camp that aren't sworn to him. Godfrey holds the love of the men. If a line is drawn, I'd want to be on the side with more men and a proven commander."

"You are shrewd in your understanding of the army."

He took a slight bow. "It pays to land in the right camp." While his words were true, they were barbs aimed at his heart, for his company had all perished. The rapacious man in him knew being the lone survivor would have engendered a better pay out, if Tancred didn't want his head. Did the rich really have to negotiate with a mercenary without a company? Easier to have him killed and all the debts disappear.

"We shall see if your mercenary's intuition has any merit."

"Hasn't proven me wrong yet."

He joined her on the wall. A smoky breeze swept over the buildings, burning their eyes and stinging their noses. "Never get used to that smell," he said.

She continued to stare at the broken city. "No. It never really fades."

Men pushed wagons stacked high with the dead, their tunics and robes soiled from the bloody remains of their fellow citizens. A Frankish guard followed several paces behind to ensure the slaves did their job, a scarf wrapped around his face. It took four men to push the wagon, as all the horses had been confiscated by the invaders. They strained beneath the overburdened weight and one of the men slipped and fell. He laid as still as the dead he pushed, his robes soaking with blood and grime. The spearman stood over him, resting on the shaft of his weapon. "Get up, Jew."

The fallen breathed heavily, eyes closing in defeat.

"Get up," the spearman repeated.

A younger slave tugged at his arms. The fallen man resisted

them, but his fellows pulled him upright. "Hurry," the spearman said. With a brandish of his spear, he ushered them forward. The four men lay into the wagon, avoiding the bodies of the dead. The wagon wheels creaked under the strain. Each roll of the wagon threatened to be its last.

The quartet only made it another dozen paces before the man collapsed again. Exhausted, his comrades fumbled to his aid, but the spearman barked at them, and they held their place, hands clasped in front of them. The guard crouched down and cursed the fallen. After a moment, the guard stood, raised a spear over his head, it hovered in the air as he waited for the man to move, when he didn't, he rammed it into the slave's belly.

The others cried out, throwing their hands wildly in the air. Jerking the spear out of his belly, the spearman calmly pointed the bloody weapon at the others. "Get him in the cart with the rest." He gestured the spear back and forth. "Him in cart."

The slaves hoisted their fallen comrade, his hands holding his belly, and laid him across the dead. They then stood in silence. The injured man let out a horrible cry.

"Move or I'll see if you've got shit for brains," yelled the spearman. The three men lowered their shoulders once again driving painstakingly onward.

The fresh metallic scent of spilled blood tantalized Cutnose. He rubbed his nose violently, trying to free himself of it. The whole city had his mind on the verge of collapse with sensory overload. One moment it was the nauseating, putrid yet meaty smell of roasting flesh, the next he could hear two men talking about their wives from down the street.

"You can smell the blood?" Marya asked.

"Like I am choking to death on it again." He wrinkled his brow.

"It will get worse. Try and suppress it. We have no time to entertain the Wilds when we are scouting. Can you sense Bors?"

He gritted his teeth, letting the smells wash over him, attempting to control his breathing. There was something there, but it was far away, a grain of sand in a windstorm raging over the desert. "No, everything is intense." Her scent lingered in the air too. Fiercely feminine and seductive, a red thorny rose pushing out from a field of corpses. Her hazel-green eyes regarded him as he struggled to control himself. There were hints of violence and concern swirling in them, undecided as to what she thought.

"We still have time," she said.

He let the smoky air exhale in and out of his lungs. Then, as quickly as the onslaught of scents had come, they departed.

"It's less now."

"It will come and go until it is married in your blood."

"Married?"

"You will be unstable until the first moon. Your body wants to be man, but it will never be fully man again." She stopped herself as if she had more to say but thought better of it. He waited for her to continue, but he was left in her silence.

"Were you once like me?"

"It was different. I was born like this. The first time I answered the call was when I was but ten and three."

"You were born like this?"

"The ones that are born with it are strong like Ulf, Arnulf, and myself. Others that are born of impure lines are weaker. Ones that have been turned can be strong, depending on your wolf-sire."

"Wolf-sire?"

"The wolfskin you've slain to accept your own powers."

"Bors."

She was silent for a moment. "Once you've been blooded, there are only two paths to travel. You must kill him and embrace your new life or turn into a feral beast of which there is no return save death."

Cutnose rubbed his neck. The skin felt thin, but he healed exponentially. The bandages of Tancred's standard still covered the former wounds. "Bors has strong blood?"

"He is one of the strongest in the Order and almost as old as Ulf."

"They do not look the same age. Ulf can be no more than five and fifty."

A laugh burst from Marya's throat. Her greenish-hazel eyes still scanning the city. "He is much older than that. He has seen many moons and traveled to the ends of the earth."

Cutnose frowned. "Sixty?"

Marya's full lips pursed in amusement. "How old do you think I am?"

"Well into your breeding years." He thought for a moment then considered her wrinkles around her eyes then the shape of her lean body beneath her kaftan. She pursed her lips raising an eyebrow. "But not old. Twenty-four?"

She flashed a genuine grin, her teeth white. "I'm about as far as you can get from twenty-four, but you flatter me with your knightly words so you may continue to believe as much."

"I'm about as far as you can get from a knighthood," he said with a laugh. He supposed she could have called him much worse.

"That wasn't lost on me." She tilted her head, listening to the street below. A moment later, almost fifty knights trotted into view. Conical helms, mail coats, and lances in hands, many shields bearing simple crosses but not all, some bore their house symbols of animals, crossed swords or spears, keeps, eagles, lions, trees, and dragons.

"Can't be near my age." He took in her apparent curves hidden beneath her kaftan and leather-scale armor.

"How old is that?" she said with slight amusement.

"I think I'm thirty-eight. Perhaps thirty-nine."

"To be that young and naive again."

His brow furrowed. "You can't be any older. Look at you." An urge pinged inside his gut, he couldn't push it away, but he resisted it. He wanted to grab her, set her on his lap, whisper something sweet in her ear while massaging her leg.

She gave him a side-eye. "I'm a bit older."

"By Christ's nose hair, you are not." He eyed the curves of her attractive face and high cheekbones. Her black hair hung down to the center of her back. He noted he didn't even have to squint to get a good view of it. "Can't be. Not a touch of gray."

"Looks can be deceiving," she continued to smile as she eyed the streets.

"Well out with it then. How old you be?"

She turned toward him. "I never said I would tell."

"You, my lady, are a temptress in disguise."

She leaned on the roof-top wall. "And would you believe me if I told you the truth?"

Despite her unnatural behavior, she was at the least intriguing enough to talk to. "A woman's age would be the farthest thing from the unusual that I've experienced the last few days."

"You won't believe me."

He snorted his rebuttal. "Try me."

"One hundred and fifty-seven."

"You play me for a fool. You mean fifty-seven, but even that is a lie." He cocked his head to the side.

"I mean exactly what I said. One hundred and fifty-seven. I was born around 942."

"Nonsense." He turned and rested on the roof wall, draping both his arms over it. "I am no fool. It is impossible for one to live that long."

"People did so in the Bible. Didn't that Moses character live to be one hundred and twenty?"

"I thought you weren't a Christian?"

"I'm not, but I've read the Bible."

"You are the most unnatural woman I've ever met. An ancient woman who looks young and can read, running around with a sword. Any man would be lucky to make it out of his forties these days. I will not be mocked by your lies."

"Believe what you will, sword seller, but it is the truth."

"Prove it."

She removed her sheathed sword from her hip, handing it to him. "This comes from a Cuman warlord. He was the last man who put a hand on me when I wasn't willing." Her eyes read him as if she heard the echo of his earlier thoughts. "I took his hand first."

Cutnose smirked at this. "I know not of these people."

"A fierce tribe from the steppe."

He handled the sword with the care of an experienced practitioner. The scabbard was exquisite. Silver sunbursts were spaced intermittently along the black leather. He removed the blade from its scabbard. It had a slight curve near the tip. He'd crossed swords with some infidels who wielded such weapons, mostly Turks. He assumed they were only mimicking the symbol of their god, the shape of the crescent, much like the Christians and their straight swords forming a cross. When he thought about it more, he remembered the Roman cavalry used a similar-styled sword.

Yet it was clear that a master had made this blade. The pommel was hooked so it could grip the bottom of one's palm, thus preventing slipping with blood or sweat. "There's no cross guard." He handled the sword, testing its weight. It felt like a feather in his hands, a sword that could be wielded like the air itself.

"It was made to be wielded on horseback so you can slash better, and the blade won't stick."

He narrowed an eye at her in irritation that a woman would wield such a fine weapon. "Seems like a woman's weapon."

She snorted. "Tell that to that hide-covered monster I removed it from."

He ran his thumb along the edge. "Cunt," he whispered as it bit through his skin. He slammed the guard-less sword back into its sheath and handed it back to her. He sucked his thumb tasting the bitter iron of his own blood.

"They work the best when they are sharp."

"That doesn't prove nothing. Anyone can find a sword. Rob a grave. Rob a man while he sleeps. Find it buried."

"I am not lying to you." She turned to him, revealing a brooch from inside her kaftan with an emerald larger than his thumb. "This came from the Grand Princess Anna of Kiev."

He was no fool; it was clear the brooch had immense value. Enough value to buy an estate and the servants to run it for generations. "And how did you come across that?"

"Too long a story to tell." She tucked the brooch away beneath her clothes. "Believe what you will, but it is the truth."

He decided to play along with her game. "Will I live as long as you?"

"Depends if you can keep your head on your neck and your heart in your chest. And while Ulf is showing you a kindness, he does not tell you the whole truth."

"And what's that?"

"This is a dangerous time for you. Between the Order and your Turning, it is unlikely you survive the week."

He viewed the pilgrims on the streets below. One who wanted to live took threats of violence seriously. "Thanks," he said grimly.

"I only speak the truth, mercenary, prepare yourself for the afterlife and you will have no regret when the time comes."

He stared at her for a moment. There was no jest or hidden mirth within her eyes. "I'm not sending for a priest that's a bad omen." He shook his head. "Any man who meets with a priest before a battle was sure to be cut down. Seen it happen too many times."

Her gaze softened. "Ulf seems to think you have a chance, and he is wise."

"I think I prefer his outlook."

"The truth carries more value than pleasing lies."

"Sometimes a lie is the only thing that gets a man through the night." They stood in silence watching the knights dismount from steeds, handing reins back to squires to care for their horses while they made their way into the mansion. While she was pleasant upon the eyes, her truth was nothing he wanted to hear. He longed to be in the presence of men, simple and direct, desires the same as his own.

"If I need to kill a man to live, I won't bat an eye to do it. Point him out."

"Shhh," she hushed.

"I'm not talking loud."

She held up a finger, and he stopped speaking as she pointed. "Horsemen."

A dozen riders in a column of twos walked their horses through the streets, splashing through puddles of blood. Their mounts marched up an incline, heads bobbing with the effort. The mounted sergeants held their lances skyward with the discipline of trained warriors. While the men in front did not wear helms, the sergeants did, all identical, conical shining metal with nose pieces. Their shields almost all bore the same design: a stag centered over a cross, the antlers almost connecting near the top.

It was the knight leading them that drew Cutnose's attention. The towering knight had a long blond mustache that drooped off his chin. His red boar shield was clean without any scars of violence. His hair hung below his broad shoulders. His horse was brown and not nearly strong enough to carry a man of his stature, but it was hard to forget the man who ripped your throat out.

"That's him," Cutnose whispered. A pressure began to build in the back of his skull. "I feel him too."

"I see him," Marya said softly.

At his side, another knight carried a shield with a black eagle on a red background. His hair was closely cropped but had a wave to it like an unsettled ripple in a pond. His nose was pointed, and his beard was closely trimmed. He wore a wolf pelt cloak draped around his shoulders despite the heat.

"That one of your kin?" Cutnose asked with a laugh.

Marya didn't say anything, only stared, like if she lost sight of him, she would never lay eyes upon him again.

"No, it is not. Silence."

A fiery oil began to bubble in Cutnose's belly. It turned into the flame of anger fueled by the bloody fumes of revenge. It boiled through his chest, and even while knowing he would be cut down by a dozen men, he gripped the stone wall of the roof to throw himself down to the street.

"I'm going to go kill Bors."

"You're too weak," Marya hissed. "They will cut you down like a starving dog."

Red shrouded his mind, and the only cure was violence. Her words were an annoying mewing in the far distance. He recognized they were words and there was meaning attached to them, but they were foreign and soft, easily overcome by the urge for vengeance. "Weak," he laughed. He threw himself over the edge. Wind rushed him as did the stones below.

The man inside him cursed as the stones quickened for him. *You stupid slit.* But his legs absorbed the two-story fall as easily as if he tread a single step, and he landed in a crouch, his hand bracing him. He didn't bother to draw a weapon; he was beyond that.

The knights had finished speaking with the guards and entered the mansion courtyard, making for the stables. Cutnose wanted to run on all fours like a wolf, but his legs were strong, even carrying the extra weight of his mail. He felt like he could run back to Apulia by the end of the next moon. His hands curled and his fingers began to stretch into blades, fur sprouting along his hands.

The jangle of mail turned the eyes of the rear horsemen, and he felt himself ripped from his course of action. A force drove him into an alley. Broken doors chopped to kindling flashed past as he was driven further away from the enemy. He snarled as he was shoved inside a house and thrown on the floor.

He struggled beneath the iron grip of another. He growled and lashed out, only to have a palm shoved over his mouth. They reached a back wall. He exhaled forcefully, staring at the very angry yet beautiful Marya. Her eyes were alight. "You will control yourself, or I will cut you down here."

The rage inside him simmered to a boil, and he blinked it all away as his heart calmed. He nodded tersely and she reluctantly removed her hand. Shouts sounded down the alley. "We are not ready to engage them. Do not speak. Do not make a noise. Do not do anything. I'll handle this mess."

Cutnose removed his hand axe and crouched into the shadows. Dismounted sergeants ran past the door. More followed behind. One stepped near the cracked door. His gloved hand wrapped around the wooden door, and he gradually pushed it open. It grated. The sergeant's boots thumped the floor. Cutnose prepared to pounce.

The sergeant pointed his sword where Marya once stood. "Come out. We won't harm you." He took a step toward the shadow of Marya. He squinted and adjusted his grip on the sword, gloves moaning over the leather-wrapped hilt. A boot thumped down. *What is she waiting for?*

"Come—" the sergeant said. Marya was a blur over the room. A wraith swirling around the man, and then she was crouched near Cutnose, sheathing her sword in undulation.

"We must depart before the others find us."

The sergeant took a step toward them, his eyes bulging.

Cutnose raised his hand axe to strike the man, but the sergeant dropped his sword, and his hands leapt to his throat.

"We must go," she said.

The sergeant's eyes widened as blood trickled from a slit along his throat. Marya joined Cutnose at his side ignoring the man as he fell to his knees.

"Shouldn't we finish him?"

She cocked her head, watching the blood turn from a leak to flow. "I have no mercy for their kind." The sergeant gurgled as he choked to death. "Men are always looking for a reason to do evil. We must make haste," she said almost sadly, rushing for the stairs to the next floor. They climbed a ladder to the roof. "Try to keep up," she said with a smirk, and she leapt to another rooftop.

"Didn't seem to hurt last time," he called to her. Shouts sounded below. He exhaled and backed up to the other side of the roof. He sprinted and leapt into the air behind her.

CHAPTER 12

The bottom floor of Hugh's home was clouded with the stench of exotic spices and gut-wrenching worry. Everyone was standing, Ulf at the center, firing questions at them. "Tell me again. You think it was Galahad?"

"He appeared like the man you talked about slaying," Marya said.

Ulf's face was chiseled from stone in deadly seriousness. "Describe him and leave out no detail."

"Black hair swept to the side. Handsome face. Trimmed beard."

"Hooked nose?" he asked, eyes faint as he relived a memory.

"No, pointed like an arrow."

"Did he bear a symbol?"

"A black eagle on a field of red."

Ulf massaged his beard. "Must be one of his treacherous ilk. A Second Son."

"What's a Second Son?" Cutnose asked.

"It is a descendent of an original Order member. May or may not be direct. All I know is that it cannot be the original Galahad."

"How do you know?" Cutnose asked, rubbing the throbbing pain near the base of his skull.

Ulf's lip curled. "Because I ate his heart in a mountain pass, three hundred years ago."

"You sure you weren't followed?" Arnulf asked, he leaned on the wall, peering through the door slightly ajar.

"I saw to that," Marya said. "However, I was unreluctantly forced to spill the blood of one of their sergeants."

Arnulf grinned as he spied down the alley. "I don't believe you."

Marya's eyes turned upon Cutnose, looking him up and down. "Had little choice. Our mercenary lost control."

Ulf emitted a guttural growl. "You must restrain yourself. Your weakness has cost us surprise." He pointed to his head. "You must grow stronger."

"I will." It was all he could say. He was a dangerous man, and dangerous men needed to be in control or things turned ugly. A lifetime of war had not prepared him for the animal that grew inside him.

Church bells sang outside. More bells joined the first as they took up a metallic song."

"Attack?" Arnulf said.

"No," Ulf said, cocking his head. "These aren't urgent. They are joyous."

"I will check," Hugh said, he slipped out the door and into the alley.

Shouts in the streets were accompanied by trumpets. "Men cheer."

"A celebration?" Marya asked.

"Our time shortens," Ulf said. "The enemy is reinforced and has the relic. We must draw Bors into a battle we can win." Using his long axe as a walking stick, Ulf paced the confines of the room. Tension settled upon all of them, and Cutnose ran a finger over his hand axe. The elder warrior brooded in silence.

After a few minutes, Hugh slipped back inside, face alight with worry. "They crown the next ruler of Jerusalem this day."

"Where?" Ulf asked, stopping.

"Holy Sepulchre."

"Who have they chosen?" Cutnose asked.

The corner of Ulf's mouth twitched. "It matters not who. Yet sometimes, the gods grant us aid. If Bors has gained favor with crusader leadership, he will be in attendance. Therefore, so shall we." He thrust a finger at Cutnose. "You are not ready to face him. To him you are a legless goat. Not that you would be able to get very close without him knowing. You bumble around like a newborn calf."

Cutnose nodded. He could follow orders.

Ulf's eyes ate at him with the fierce contemplation of a pack of wolves. "Our quest is far too important to be cast away for an uncontrollable fool. Fail us again and I will take your head."

"You've made yourself clear."

"Then I will not tell you again." With a linger gaze, promising Cutnose he would kill him, if he failed, he continued speaking. "Spread out among them and watch for any servant of the Order. You are to track any of them you can. I want to know where they are based. They would never bring the chalice out in public without an army to protect it so we must find their camp." He tossed Cutnose the hooded brown cowl of a simple monk. "Wear the hood. Someone will recognize your scar."

"I'd have to say this is a first." He threw it on over his mail coat.

"Do not bring your shield or axe."

"I'd rather walk naked. I'm a soldier. I don't go anywhere without my kit."

Ulf's face hardened. "You are a man who would benefit from a disguise."

"A man who needs to be able to defend himself."

"A man who would do well keeping his mouth shut and his face concealed. If separated, we all meet back here when it is over."

Cutnose tossed his hand-axe down next to his shield with a

glare for Ulf. He slipped his hands into the sleeves of his robes and touched the hilt of his dagger still on his waist.

The four warriors made their way through the alley and onto the street. Where once it had been overrun with blood, now it was crowded with the Christian pilgrims. A happy fervor engulfed them like a saintly golden aura from God. Many were barefoot, others in no more than sun-faded tattered rags, every coin spent on the journey to reach this place. The crusaders were almost indistinguishable from the pilgrims save for a spear in a hand or a sword worn on the hip. Few donned any armor, helms, or shields. Instead, they displayed shoddily sewn red crosses on their tunics. Yet the only true way to tell pilgrim from crusader was the violent glint in his eyes acquired from years on campaign in a foreign land fighting foreign men.

Cutnose's group spread out, rubbing shoulders with the throng, but he kept his hood pulled over his head, and his hands clasped in contemplative prayer like a wandering priest, of which there was no shortage of in Jerusalem.

A song of praise pricked the lips of the righteous around him. The Latin words meant little to Cutnose. He gruffly hummed along with them, keeping his face shadowed. He trudged with the crowd until a hand grabbed his shoulder, and he tensed, his own hand slipping around the hilt of his dagger. *Don't care who Ulf is, if he thinks I am going anywhere without a weapon he is insane.*

"Priest?" the man said with a harsh accent.

"Yes?" Cutnose grunted in surprise.

The man's face was sickly and pale with dark circles beneath his eyes, and his arm was in a sling. It was his fingers that immediately made Cutnose hesitate. The man's hand had taken on a dangerously darker hue than his natural skin tone. An evil spirit had taken his arm, a true curse from God, decaying it from the inside out.

"I took an arrow scaling the wall. The surgeon removed it, but my wound has festered."

"You are a brave Christian." In all the battlefields Cutnose had fought on, he saw no worse violence than the creeping death that accompanied a wounding as such. The stench was wretched, making him want to cover his nose. This man did not have long. Even if they sawed his arm off and shoved the stump into the flames to stop the bleeding, he had been afflicted for far too long to live.

"Pray for me. For my arm to heal."

Cutnose gave him a slight nod. "I will, my son." Cutnose mumbled some words about salvation and God. "You have seen that Christ's City has been liberated. He will reward you in the next life."

"Thank you," the man said, tears forming in the corners of his eyes.

The procession continued its joyful march through the streets until it reached the heart of the city. Shouts rang as they neared the crumbling basilica taking shape before them. Thousands of Christians flooded toward the gates of the Church of the Holy Sepulchre, the church encompassing the places where Jesus was buried and rose from the dead. He could catch no glimpse of his comrades amongst the men around him.

Pressure magnified in the back of his neck. He twisted his head, trying to soothe it. *Bors must be nearby.* Keeping his head down, he shouldered his way through the crowd, blessing men as he passed with the sign of the cross, mumbling the best Latin he could remember.

The Church of the Holy Sepulchre grew in size as they neared. At the crumbling entrance the pilgrims pushed into were the remains of a once beautiful basilica. Gray stones were strewn about along the walls.

The mass of people crossed the threshold where two giant doors once stood, leading inside the open-air structure. Inside the rectangle basilica was a colonnaded atrium supported by a series of stone pillars arched to support the roof which was no longer there. At least half a dozen of the pillars had been deconstructed; the stones hauled away for use in other buildings.

Small individual chapels had been built near the walls in the ruins. Each one dedicated to one of the sufferings of Christ. On the other end of the ruined basilica was a covered plaza with steps leading downward, supported by white-stone pillars. The people all pushed closer to reach the dome they had seen from afar; the rotunda, the place where Jesus had resurrected from the dead.

Cutnose shouldered his way through the tight knot of pilgrims getting as close as he dared to the rotunda without causing too much chagrin to the men around him. The common crusaders tried to stand on their toes to get a better view of the ring of nobles and knights standing in front of a tomb carved from plain stone. Candles flickered around them on tall candelabras. He was taller than most, and despite his distance, he could make out the victorious faces of the lords.

The man nearest the front was a holy man named Arnulf. He was dressed in bishop's attire, white robes and gold and red shawls. Far too fine of clothes for a poor upstart priest owing his station to the death of the crusade's initial religious leader and papal legate Adhemar Le Puy. He clutched an object in his hands wrapped in silk.

Despite his fine attire, the bishop's hair was unkempt in stingy strands, and his beard was patchwork at best, skin waxy and pale, the only color a redness from exposure to the sun. He was just smart enough to be conniving and manipulative, and he was untrusted by most of the men, including Cutnose because of his rapid ascent in station.

When the Holy Lance was found near Antioch by rival holy man Peter Bartholomew, Arnulf had doubted its authenticity angering many of the men. Peter so believed in his discovery that he endured an ordeal by fire to prove he had indeed found the lance that pierced Christ's side. As the curious crusaders looked on, Peter entered the flames and became a screaming inferno of burning flesh. Even then, he survived almost twelve days in the worst pain possible before he perished, claiming it was the crowd that rushed forward to dampen the flames that caused his harm and that Christ had indeed protected him from the fires. There were even rumors that Arnulf somehow had something to do with Adhemar's death.

Godfrey of Bouillon stood near the bishop, making the holy man's common stature seem even more inferior. His cloak bore his house colors of red and white. He was a head taller than the bishop and held himself as a man of regal authority filled with the confident pride of a victor. Intelligent yet stern eyes absorbed the power of the soldiers, nobles, and pilgrims alike. He nodded tersely to someone in the crowd and gave a grim smile to another. On his other side stood Godfrey's younger brother, Baldwin of Boulogne, now the Count of Edessa, dressed in red, white, and gold embroidered finery. Much younger than Godfrey, he held the same intelligent eyes, yet less stern as if he had a joke he was waiting to tell.

Furthest away from Baldwin was Tancred, young, tall and proud, a long tunic of split blue and red, a sword hanging leisurely from his hip. The ambitions of both men had brought their contingents into bloody conflict earlier in the campaign, and Baldwin had been the victor with Godfrey the "neutral" mediator. Tancred's chiseled jaw held a mighty grin, and he waved a massive hand as he reveled in the cheers of the Christians.

Behind him stood Ludolf with an irritating sneer on his lips as if every man had come to see him. To Tancred's right was Lord Robert of Flanders, a portly fellow despite having been on campaign for years. Then stood Lord Eustace Grenier with a slender face, broad shoulders and knowing eyes, cheeks covered in a beard the color of dried hay.

On the opposing side of Godfrey's entourage stood a group of dour nobles as if they piloted a ship sinking beneath the waves. At their center was Raymond of Toulouse. His demeanor was that of a man condemned to face the gallows. Cutnose would go so far as to say he was downright miserable. His mouth frowned beneath a reddish-brown beard. His brow creased in worry. Dark circles hung beneath his eyes. His shoulders were slumped despite an effort to embody more space.

Cutnose leaned to the man next to him. "Godfrey is the one?"

The man looked up at him with a smirk. "Aye, you didn't hear?"

"Hear what?"

"Raymond turned down the crown. Stupid bastard said there could be no king in Jerusalem save Christ."

Cutnose bowed his head in reverence to the Lord. "That is the truth, my son." He quickly made the sign of the cross.

"It is father, but Godfrey jumped in and said that while Raymond is correct, he would stand as Defender of the Holy Sepulchre and Protector of Jerusalem, so the nobles granted him the crown. Ha!" The spearman shook his head in disbelief. "You ever hear of such a thing?"

"No, but God acts in mysterious ways."

"Course he does." The spearman tugged a cross necklace from beneath his tunic and kissed the wooden pendant.

The crowd continued to push closer to the tomb where Jesus's body had been kept before it was resurrected and ascended directly to Heaven from atop the Mount of Olives. Clergymen and guards formed a small circular perimeter around the tomb, keeping the growing multitude back.

Bishop Arnulf raised his hands toward the heavens in an attempt to quiet them. When the tumult did not lessen, he began shouting for the people to be quiet. He pounded a staff on the floor over and over. The sounds of chatter dissolved into a soft echoing whisper.

The bishop's voice grew louder. "We started this pilgrimage almost three years ago. The devil sent his minions to thwart us at every turn. From the back-stabbing Greeks, to the vile hordes of infidels, and the greedy Jews they all have failed to deny us our holy purpose." He paused lifting his chin. "We have vanquished each enemy of God who wished to deny us access to Christ's temple. This very tomb. The tomb of Christ himself." He placed a reverent hand on the tomb, embracing God's strength. Godfrey kept his head bowed.

"The devil reigns where Christian men do not wield their swords on his behalf. And I will tell you, the devil fears this place now. He hides because we have champions akin to the angels fighting on our side. He gestured toward the lords. "Champions such as Lord Tancred and Ludolf of Tournai. The first knights to breach the walls. They fought as an army of angels slaying any wicked Saracen who stood before them."

Tancred raised his chin and nodded at Arnulf's words. Ludolf beamed behind him. The crowd roared with cheers for the bravery of those men. Not the rotting corpses of Cutnose's men who'd done most of the fighting. No, for they were not heroes, not brave knights the bards would immortalize in song and poem. They were nameless footmen. The professional soldiers. The expendable common man. Their captain a condemned criminal of the highest degree. Their existence not even worth mentioning in passing.

"Leaders such as Bohemond of Taranto and Robert of Flanders, and the engineer of our siege engines, Gaston of Bearn." A bear-like man with keen eyes bowed his black, curly-haired head in honor. "We owe all these men a great debt for their leadership, for we would risk being cut down like poor Peter and his brave pilgrims without them." The cheers reverberated wall to wall. The crusaders had avenged the first pilgrims, mostly common men with no experience in war, that had been slaughtered in the hills of Anatolia. Fists jabbed the air. Spears and swords thrust toward the sky.

The newly made bishop turned, reveling in the crusaders' zeal. He surveyed the knights hovering beside their liege lords, then the soldiers, and finally his eyes lingered on the common pilgrims in the rear. "There is one man who deserves our ultimate praise." He held up a single finger. "A man of impeccable piety and devotion to Christ that deserves our prayers. A man that led us here when others balked at freeing Jerusalem. He took up Christ's banner and marched us here through trial and tribulation. The angel Michael came to him in a vision, lending him the foresight to assault a weaker section of the walls. Through God's will, he fooled the impetuous heathens. He truly has been blessed by God with ingenuity fit for a true king."

With a hand, the bishop ushered Godfrey to step forward. The lord did so with pious respect, reluctant yet brave enough to stand for such an arduous task. Bishop Arnulf gazed upward at the lord in adoration. The crusaders stood silently, eagerly awaiting each syllable of his next words. "But he turned down kingship for there is but one king of Jerusalem and that is Christ." His hand wavered over the lord blessing him. "He embraced the holy responsibility to protect this land in the name of Christ's chosen representative on earth, the Pope. He has sworn his sword to keep this land free of the infidel's evil influence, and to ensure that God's pilgrims have safe access to his stations. Only one man is befitted to bear the title *Advocatus Sancti Sepulchri,* and his name is Godfrey of Bouillon," his own voice growing louder with excitement.

The crowd exploded in revelry. Men beat their chests with clenched fists. The bishop bowed his head to Godfrey. The entire church vibrated with fervent rejoice. The ground trembled beneath them as the men stomped their feet. Even Cutnose, who knew the truth of Arnulf's words, felt the power of his false narrative.

Godfrey lifted a hand in the air, and all became as quiet as if they stood before God himself. "I humbly accept the title and station as Protector of the Holy Sepulchre and Duke of Jerusalem for there can be no King where God reigns supreme."

The bishop moved alongside the lord. "You may kneel." Godfrey knelt onto the stones before the tomb. Baldwin stepped forward and assisted Godfrey in disrobing from his red-and-white cloak, then stepped backward.

Bishop Arnulf took a pristine snow-white cloak with a red

cross and held it out. He stretched it wide for all to see. "Then I place across your shoulders the mantle of service to God's city. May you defend God's people with a mighty fury known only to the angels." With a flourishing sweep of the cloak, he draped it over Godfrey's shoulders. "You may stand as first among the defenders of Christendom."

Godfrey stood and the men's voices rang joyous. The Lord of Jerusalem basked in his title and the cheers, embracing their warmth and fervor. Guards wielded their spears widely, shoving back the crowds with spear shafts. Lords began the process of paying homage.

Tancred and his lackey Ludolf took a knee. Godfrey laid his hands on their shoulders, his lips moving. They responded in kind and stood again. Cutnose pushed closer through the crowd. He wanted to shout out to his young friend to let him know he was no traitor, but his thoughts were futile, for an outburst would lead to a brisk execution. The lords were followed by knights who honored Godfrey while others swore fealty to serve in his new lands.

A man stepped in front of Godfrey, catching Cutnose's eye. He was as broad as he was tall, and he was as tall as even Tancred. His tunic was a deep shade of green and his blond mustache hung long off his face. *Bors.* He could never forget the harsh stare of the knight. He knelt in front of Godfrey, bowing his head in deference. Godfrey bid him rise. The man leaned in and spoke earnestly into his ear. Godfrey cocked his head to the side but nodded slowly with a half-smile on his face. He waved an attendant forward, and he bowed to the knight. The two shuffled their way through the lords. Another knight took his place, and the ceremony began anew.

Godfrey and Bors are united. They must be. With the aid of the new Lord of Jerusalem, Bors would have free reign and the upper hand in escaping his pursuers. Cutnose couldn't locate a single one of his companions in the sea of heads.

With a growl, he pushed his way through the men toward the

exit. His only chance was to enlist the aid of another lord. One Cutnose trusted. He shouldered through more men. None cared, for all their eyes were focused on the coronation. He escaped the cramped quarters, the fresh air only slightly better than the stench of men packed together. He will listen. He must or all will be lost.

CHAPTER 13

Night fell upon the Holy City like an executioner's axe. The stink of death faded as the air cooled. The funeral fires dying down as most of the dead had been burned during the day. Cutnose used his hood to shadow his face in the darkness of a broken doorway. The city church bells were fatigued from the vigorous ringing and now lay dormant. The streets were devoid of crowds, only graced by the sauntering gait of the occasional drunken reveler.

Raymond's contingent of knights and retainers had left the citadel in a flurry of whipping cloaks, marching for Bethlehem to pay tribute there and see Christ's birthplace. He'd been outmaneuvered by Godfrey politically and militarily for years and the coronation was the final defeat for the lord of Toulouse. There was little to keep him in the Holy Land now that Jerusalem had been liberated. A full third of the crusaders traveled with him, a reversal of the Crusader army's composition from the beginning of the campaign. The only good that could be said of it was that it had not come to arms between the rival factions.

Cutnose had followed the lord's entourage to a mansion formerly belonging to a wealthy merchant. He stood in a splintered doorframe, and watched, waiting for the right moment to move. After a time, the darkness lulled the guards to complacency, and he shifted from his concealment, moving along the outskirts of the mansion.

Two guards stood out front, lazily leaning on spears. Anyone capable of threatening a lord laid in piles of ash around the city where the bodies had been burned. Others were held in confinement or had been sold into slavery. The lucky were being used as interpreters and household servants of the Frankish lords. The nearest enemy was over fifty miles away in Ascalon, and those men were not about to leave the protection of their fortified city.

Cutnose ran his hand along the mansion's courtyard wall. From his surveillance, he knew the courtyard contained a small stone stable, and a quick climb of the wall would gain him access to the rear of the building.

Checking his surroundings for anyone, he felt the wall for divots and finger holds. He found a groove; he scampered over the top. He landed in the courtyard with a soft *uff*. He pushed back his hood. A torch flickered near the stable, casting light over the rumps of horses. He hugged the inner wall and made his way to an unguarded door, gently pushing it open.

The interior of the mansion had a pleasant coolness to it. The corridor was dark, no servants had lit candles to illuminate it. He stalked into the home's interior then froze as a soldier crossed the intersection of the hallway. The guard didn't bother to look his direction, wiping his mouth as if he'd already drank a barrel of wine. Exhaling, he listened for voices as he walked.

For a man as old as he was, thirty-eight or so, give or take a few years, his hearing was the best it had ever been. He heard a man yawn from behind a doorway down the hall. He followed a servant carrying a tray of wine, waiting for the servant to pass him by before he hurried to the door. Gently, the door creaked open.

The chamber held a bed sizable enough for four people with a blanket spun with gold-and-green pillows. Finely woven floral tapestries of purple, red, green, blue, and orange decorated the walls. He slipped inside and closed the door behind him. A man in a plain red-and-blue tunic with shoulder-length blond hair and a lean broad back stood hunched over a table, pouring himself a glass of wine. *Tancred.*

He spied upon the young lord in silence. He had a certain fondness of him. The lord had the potential to be even greater than his uncle. He was just, had a sound military mind, and was brave beyond imagine. He would see the truth if Cutnose could have more than a few moments to explain.

If Godfrey was truly allied with Bors, then Tancred may be their only chance to survive this. Cutnose's words should still mean something. He had been as loyal as a mercenary could be, serving with the lord at the front of the siege tower, his men laying down their lives at the temple. Bohemond had trusted his nephew's life to Cutnose, making him swear an oath to protect him. The oath brought a fine payout, but it was an oath nonetheless and even mercenaries kept their oaths. *He must see the truth. I am not the monster they claim me to be.*

"Tancred," Cutnose said softly.

The young lord spun on him. Wide-eyed recognition transformed into rage. His hand inched for a knife on his belt.

Cutnose lifted a hand. "I am not a threat to you, lord."

Tancred's handsome face sneered. "Why would I believe a word from your mouth? You speak with Satan's own tongue. You are an oath breaker, and your soul is black."

"I did not kill those people, and you should know me enough to know that I would not kill my men."

"You reek of lies. Look at you. Wearing the clothes of a common holy man. Your treachery grows like a weed."

"I am no devil. There was another who killed my men and slaughtered those people. He almost killed me."

"Says the monster who rose from the dead. What proof do you have of such things?"

"The man responsible knelt before Godfrey today. He is a knight that goes by the name Bors."

"I know nothing of this man. You only come to sow dissension among us."

"Hear my words for there is much at stake."

"Speak the truth or you will answer to the Lord's justice."

"Bors has acquired an ancient holy relic, the Cup of Christ. He intends to carry it back to England for his own purposes. That is why he killed my men and murdered the people under our protection. This is the truth."

Tancred blinked at his words. "The Cup of Christ?" He blessed himself making the sign of the cross.

"Aye, the cup. It has magic too."

"Magic?" Tancred blessed himself again. "Is that how you inhabit this body? Through Christ's will?"

"I'm not sure Christ has anything to do with it, but you must know the truth. Godfrey is being deceived by this man. He mustn't be allowed to escape these lands."

"You would have me detain him?"

"Even if you do not believe me. Seek him. Search his belongings. Acquire the relic. Or even better, help me secure it."

"You want me to give you the Cup of Christ?" The young noble almost laughed with a shake of his head.

"He must be stopped."

"You are a bold man seeking me out in my own home. How did you get in?" Tancred's eyes flicked over Cutnose's shoulder. Hair stood on the back of his neck, but the soft rasp of the door gave the man away. Cutnose turned into a sword stab aimed for the center of his back. The sword missed; the weight the attack carried the soldier forward. Cutnose brought his hand crashing into the man's arm, and the soldier cried out as his sword clattered on the floor. He gripped the guard's arm and whipped him over his hip. The strength of the throw was far greater than Cutnose had imagined he was capable of; the guard crashed into the wall with a metallic thump of mail, helm, and man.

Another guard charged through the door, a roar on his lips as he back-swung his sword to avoid his comrade. Cutnose centered a kick to his chest, sending him back into the hall. The first guard attempted to regain his feet and Cutnose's fist connected with his cheek. The man collapsed.

Cutnose heard it coming from behind, like a soft breeze fluttering a ship's sail, but it was too late. He spun into a knife thrust from Tancred, the lord's arm extended, muscles flexing in a brutally efficient strike. The metal tip bit through his monk's cowl and mail into his chest.

He peered down and growled under the knife's force, the blade like ice penetrating the center of his chest. With a burst of violence, he threw an arm into Tancred, sending him to the floor. Eyes agape, Tancred crawled backward. For a lord in the prime of manhood to be thrown off his feet had stunned him.

"Christ's big toe that hurts," Cutnose said with a grimace. His fingertips examined the knife sticking from him.

"It is true," Tancred hissed. "You are a puppet of the devil."

"I assure you, this hurts," Cutnose said. He grunted as he removed the knife, inch by inch. The guard in the hallway backed into the wall before bolting like a scared calf.

Two spearmen burst into the room, and Cutnose was upon them in a flash, their spears much too long for effective use in close quarters. He slid through their guard, using Tancred's knife with deadly effect. He sliced a soldier across the arm, shifting behind him, then bent low cutting his hamstring. The other spearman tried to hold him against the wall with his spear shaft and Cutnose slammed the pommel of the knife into his jaw and the life faded from his eyes before dropping to his knees. When the guard tried to regain his feet, Cutnose cracked him again with the pommel, laying him out like a drunkard kicked by a horse. Guards lay in groaning heaps, grasping their wounds in shock.

Cutnose took a deep breath, turning on the young lord. "I did not come here to cause harm. I came to warn you about Bors. You offered me a knighthood once. You offered my men riches. We paid dearly in your service."

"I never should have trusted a man who would sell his soul for gold."

His words would have stung less had he not been innocent of the crime. "I would see justice yet done."

"You are but a demon wearing a dead man's skin. A corruption of life." Tancred spit, his eyes running to his sword hanging from a peg on the wall. "The only justice you will find is by the edge of my blade."

Cutnose approached Tancred knife in hand, the young lord crawling backward. "You think I would betray my men? Then you know little of me." His chest ached fiercely, and blood dribbled from the front of his robes. He put a hand over his heart, adding pressure.

A man silently stepped inside the room. Even with soft footsteps he drew Cutnose's gaze. *Bors's companion.* The knight's fierce eyes grew wider, his nose twitching.

Cutnose flipped the knife blade down and threw it. It spun end over end until the knight drew his sword, flashing like a lightning strike. The knife clanged into the wall.

"You will fall beneath my sword," the knight said. His blade arched through the air and Cutnose dodged to the side, reaching for the dagger on his belt. He jabbed and the knight sliced horizontally, smashing the dagger from his hand. The knight swung left and right, and Cutnose ducked and rolled toward the window. Tancred jumped to his feet, reaching for his sword.

Cutnose dove for the window, leaping through a gap in orange curtains. The air breezed past before he hit the hard stones below, rolling over himself. In a daze, he ran.

The black-haired knight stared at him from the window, a small smile curved on his lips. "Run along, you foul beast. Your end nears," he shouted.

Tripping over himself, Cutnose followed a street then veered toward an alley to the shouts of the guards.

Galahad wiped the blade of his sword on the surcoat of one of the dead guards.

Tancred raced to the window. "He escapes."

"You are lucky my lord that I was passing by when I did." Galahad sheathed his sword.

The young Norman lord turned around. "Who are you, sir?"

"An ally."

Tancred dusted off his tunic, making for the wounded guards. "How fare you men?" One of his guards assisted a wounded man bending down next to him. Two others lay still. Ludolf burst into the room, blond hair flowing behind him.

"My lord, I came when I heard," he breathed. "You've been attacked?"

Tancred raised a hand with a glance for Galahad. "I was saved by the appearance of this knight."

Ludolf's face twisted in envy. "A noble if convenient appearance."

Galahad smiled at him.

"Gather some guards and search the grounds for Cutnose, but I fear he has escaped into the night. Such is his nature."

"Captain Cutnose?" Ludolf asked with a gulp.

"In the flesh."

Galahad went to the window and peered out into the night. "No need to send your men, my Lord Tancred. My men will pursue it. They are well-suited in dealing with this sort of enemy." He twitched his nose. "Putrid smelling commoner, wasn't he?"

"My lord?" Ludolf asked.

"Make sure the grounds are secured and no one else is harmed."

"Yes, my lord," Ludolf said in relief. He gave a wary glance at Galahad and disappeared into the hall.

Tancred secured his sheathed sword to his belt. "I never

should have taken this off." Servants entered the room and carried the guardsmen's bodies away.

Tancred watched them with a look of disgust. "You could smell the man?"

Galahad gave him a faint smile. "Of course, my lord. The devil's ilk reek of him."

Color faded from Tancred's cheeks. He walked over to a table holding a pitcher and cups. He poured himself a cup of burgundy-colored wine and downed it. "How were you inside my residence, sir?"

"I came to speak with you and when I heard you in danger, I rushed inside."

Tancred nodded, his eyes narrowing a bit as he considered his words. "You got past my guards without challenge?" Galahad sensed his hesitation, hearing his heart beating in his chest.

"I believe your guards were already responding to the intruder. I pray I have not overstepped myself?"

"If saving a man's life is overstepping oneself, I am thankful for it." Tancred lifted a cup in the air. "Wine?"

"I would imbibe with you," Galahad said, he gave a faint smile. Tancred handed him a cup. Galahad swirled it around with a squint.

"I owe you a debt, good knight. By what name may I call you?"

"Most call me Galahad, my lord." With a wrinkle of his nose, he tried the wine. It was watered down more than it deserved, he guessed pitch, perhaps salt water had been added to preserve it on the voyage from by the taste probably Venice or Genoa. It was bloody difficult to find acceptable wine in the Holy Land. The Christians imported most of what they drank. Infidels with exception didn't drink it, and since they had ruled the region for some time, production was almost completely wiped out.

"Who's contingent? You aren't one of my retainers."

"I traveled here with Godfrey's men, but I am not famous, nor do I have grand estates." A smile stretched over his lips. "I am a most humble of servants."

Tancred poured himself another glass, the vileness of the wine having no effect on him. "The proud Prince of Galilee saved by a passerby." He snorted into his cup. "The bards will sing of it." He gestured with his drink. "I used to know that devil. I offered him a knighthood. I've saved his life and he mine. He was an excellent soldier, and I called him brother. Now, it parades around in his flesh, speaking with his voice. His existence is a curse that plagues me." His lips curled. "Evil is at work. That thing needs to be burned at the stake." He slurped down more wine, his eyes widening as he thought. "I put a knife through his heart. No man could walk away from that. Have you ever witnessed such a thing?"

"I know their kind well. They are unnatural beings, my lord."

Tancred made the sign of the cross. "Then maybe you can help me with this problem. What can be done to put his torment to rest?"

"I do not wish to alarm you, but he is one of many."

"Many? I will gather all the nobles. The beasts mustn't be allowed to live."

Galahad smiled; how easy it was to rally the support of the nobles against the Hunted. "There is no need. They will not return here this night."

"How do you know?"

Galahad started to pace. "My men and I have fought his kind for some time. One might say it is my knightly vocation."

"Witch hunters?" Tancred hissed.

"I would say they are more akin to demons and skin-changers. They are the living embodiment of the devil on this earth."

"Demons," he spat. "They bore not wings nor hooves or claws." Tancred poured himself more wine.

"The beasts live inside them. When it emerges, only death and destruction follow."

"I've lived to see the holiest of sites and the most wicked of creatures in a single day. We liberate God's kingdom, only to be plagued by the fallen angels. It makes me wonder if the infidels cursed this place when they knew they couldn't keep it."

"This war stretches far beyond the Holy City."

Tancred clenched his jaw. "How can we defend this land against the Saracens and this evil? Most of our army prepares to depart back to the continent. Soon only a few of us will remain."

"That is why I've come, prince."

"Speak."

Galahad rested a hand on the hilt of his sword. "We are not many, a humble order, but we would like to establish outposts throughout the Holy Land to weed out and eradicate such evils as they arise."

"Then you speak with the wrong lord, I am but a lieutenant on this crusade. As soon as the threat from the Fatimids in the south dissipates, I will travel back north with my contingent to Antioch and rejoin my uncle."

"The Saracens are close, lord. Closer than you should feel comfortable with."

Tancred gulped down some more wine, eyes watching him. "I've only heard rumors."

"It is true."

"Fatimid army? How do you know this?"

"I have sent scouts south; every merchant says the same. The Fatimids will not give away their prize without a fight." In his search to secure passage back to England, he'd come across several less scrupulous persons, men with connections to the Fatimids and enough coin in their palms revealed more useful information than a burning poker ever did. A Fatimid relief army was marching for Jerusalem and was far closer than the crusaders knew.

"I must see with my own eyes." Tancred slammed down his cup, standing taller. "It's ironic, for years this has been our only wish. To stand where Christ stood, lived and died for our sins, and resurrected."

Galahad nodded understandingly. This young man was a fool if he thought that his uncle wasn't positioning himself for a lordship north of Jerusalem and that Tancred acted as his representative here. While the other lords had bled themselves on Jerusalem's walls, Bohemond's men were ensuring his position was solidified, but alas, every man was another pawn in the games lords play. Even Galahad was here on Uthur's behest to find him the Chalice. He had pled vigorously to secure his position on the quest, for he knew that with adventure many opportunities would arise.

"Now that I'm here, I itch to be away," Tancred said. His eyes darted toward Galahad. "I have paid my proper respects to Christ. My pilgrimage is complete in the eyes of God."

"As have I, my lord. A young man as yourself is in need of adventure, no doubt."

A small grin took Tancred's face. "I've had years of adventure."

"None of us here want to know an army comes our way but come our way it does. Surely, we cannot surrender what we've fought so hard to take?"

Tancred's brow furrowed. "No, that wouldn't be right. Many good Christian men fell to free these lands." He gestured with his cup. "Perhaps cleaving a few Saracen skulls can take my mind off this mess with Cutnose. Those were good men he betrayed out there. Men in my employ."

"Less coin spent on mercenaries the better. You were rid of them at the right time."

"Less coin, but if what you say is true, we'll need every sword and spear in the coming days."

"Their loss has brought us together and with our chance meeting we have an opportunity."

"Join with me. Let us see this Saracen horde for ourselves."

"It would be an honor, my lord, to ride with you. My men have led me to believe that patrolling the coast near Jaffa is where the enemy marches. If permissible, my men and I would like to travel with you north when the threat has passed. Perhaps you can speak to your uncle on our behalf, he knows of my order. I carried a message for him from Antioch."

Tancred's eyes were fiery blue and his stature looming like a bird of prey with spread wings, talons ready to tear into the hunted. "It would be my honor, Sir Galahad, to speak in your favor to my uncle. Your cause is as noble as it is just, and you have more than shown your worth this day. We must silence any threat to God's land, together."

Galahad dipped his chin in deference. "No wiser words have been spoken." He rested his hand on his sword. "Then I bid you good night, Prince of Galilee. I will send word when my men discover the den of the unbelievers."

A pleased look crossed Tancred's face, the title clearly stroking his ego. "Let your men rest. Tomorrow we will ride in search of this Saracen storm. As much as it pains me, they pose the greater threat."

How little you know of the Hunted, Galahad thought. "As you wish, lord." He stepped outside the room. Guards jogged down the hall. "Your prince is well. Go man your posts." The two men slowed and continued down the hall at a brisk walk. This land was filled with opportunity. Ripe for the implantation of his Order upon its grounds. Opportunity for men to elevate their station as rapid as an arrow arching into the sky.

He should have traveled here sooner rather than later, but he needed this army of crusaders to carve out a path so he could nestle in unopposed. And Bors was so eager to depart with the bloody chalice. Fool. They could be the most powerful men in the world with that chalice, yet he wished to ride it back to Uthur, sitting in the cold damp mists of England.

He left the building and stepped onto the street. Guards near the door were surprised by him, the torches shining bright in their eyes. "The intruders will not return this night."

He stared at the moon in the clear skies. It cast a yellow glow, washing over all beneath it. Yet the moon had not completed its transition in fullness. A few more nights and this dog would show himself along with the rest of the pack, and without a den to hide in, they would be forced into the open. And when they did move against the Order, they would lose their heads, and Galahad would have a new pelt for his cloak. He would gain esteem in Order's eyes, but his ambitions were far greater. He would build an empire.

CHAPTER 14

Cutnose's footsteps echoed along the squat stone homes. His feet were numbing beneath him, unwilling conspirators in his escape. Blood soaked his hands, and he stripped his monk's cowl, tossing it upon the street in haste. *Tancred put a dagger through my heart.* The betrayal cut deeper than the flesh, piercing his soldier's loyalty to a good lord, no matter his age. *He thinks you're a monster. A demon. A thing to be burned at the stake. There is no absolution but a fiery inferno.* And one of the Order. *They may track me even now.*

He regained his composure, slowing and allowing the shadows to provide him concealment. Blood dripped from the bottom of his tunic, splatting on the street. He cut down an alley and checked over his shoulder. Nothing moved in the distance, but these men were trained hunters. He hugged the walls a bit closer, his mail coat scratching along the stone, trying to hide his movements. *I must tell them. Will they want my head? Who doesn't at this point? Bugger them all.*

He hurried down an alley then weaved across another street, avoiding a chapel. His neck began to throb, and he grimaced as he rubbed the base of his skull. The scent of smoke thickened. Not the putrid meat smell of the bodies but the rich scent of burning timber. This struck him as odd. Almost nothing was made of wood in the city. If a structure did burn, it was intentionally done by men.

Smoke hung in between the homes of the alley running adjacent to Hugh's. The alley was devoid of all people. Shields hung outside a few of the homes, marking them as occupied by a new crusading resident. His heart pounded with his boots, and his mind called in the background, knowing the truth before he rounded a corner.

Yellowish-orange flames leapt for the sky. The fire danced, pouring out of windows and the doorway of the home. Armored men watched from a distance, torches in hand, swords and spears in the other. A rank of crossbowmen eyed their surroundings, waiting to feather anyone willing to intervene. Two knights sat a horse, one with heads dangling from his saddle, his hammer resting on his shoulder. His face absent of emotion. *Bors.*

The pressure in his neck intensified. In the flight from Tancred, Cutnose had ignored it. Now with the man in front of him, it drummed his skull with pain. *Can he feel me as well?* Cutnose knelt in the shadows. *This is the beast I am to bring to heel.* He felt for his axe and found nothing on his hip, not even a knife.

Weaponless, staring at two dozen armed men, he'd finally located the man to enact his revenge upon. The man whom he and all his comrades needed to die. "Shit situation," he muttered. He scanned the rooftops expecting to see them preparing to strike back, but found only forgotten clothes whipping on lines, and black smoke. To charge in would be to die a foolish death and put all this madness to rest. He spied a shield painted blue-and-red stripe cutting the shield diagonally. He took it down from the door next to which it hung and shoved his arm through the straps, grasping the handle.

Then he waited for an opportunity. The soldiers were on high alert near replicas of the emotionless knight. Not one made offhand remarks. They only watched with benevolent eyes as they performed God's righteous work.

A slender knight, more spear shaft than man, spoke to Bors. "You think he will come out? Or submit to a coward's death?"

"He will come out. It is not in their nature to just die, Brother Alymere."

"Yes, of course, Brother Bors. My men are ready for when the time comes."

"You did well to get here so quickly. This Hunted has been a thorn in our side, especially after the untimely departure of Percival."

"It is dire news indeed. The Order will miss his wisdom beyond his years."

"More than you know."

Hooves galloped, and Galahad led an additional twenty mounted brothers and sergeants into view. He clenched a fist as he neared, drawing them to a halt. Cutnose would make it no more than a few paces before he was impaled upon a dozen spears, then hacked to bits by the footman.

"Where've you been?" Bors said with vitriol.

"Negotiating a deal."

"Always dealing," Bors said. "Never doing your job."

Galahad dipped his head. "It is necessary for our mission."

"You missed the hunt. Young Alymere tracked the beasts to this humble home."

"You have my thanks, Brother Alymere," Galahad said.

"He should. His value grows by the day. Uthur will hear of his fine work."

Galahad's eyes pierced Bors. There was tension and a rivalry there. "We are all thankful to have him in our ranks." He waited a moment as they watched the fires. "There is another Hunted."

"Another?"

"He attempted to assassinate Tancred."

Bors lifted his nose in the air. "I thought I smelled more. Smertrios guide our swords."

"As far as I can tell, he is not fully blooded."

"A pup? Easily brought down."

"I believe you may know of him. He was a mercenary in Tancred's employ."

The large knight's brow creased. "One guarding the temple?"

"Goes by the name Cutnose."

"That bleeding slit whose throat I ripped out? No man could live through that."

"It walks, and it talks."

"He should be a fly-covered corpse."

"Yet he's not." Galahad inspected his hand. "Threw a knife at me."

"It could not have been me. Must have been one of the others."

"Must have," Galahad said, his eyes betraying his disbelief. The tension grew between the two knights. "You're sure?"

Bors snarled at him. "Of course, I am."

Cutnose shook his head in confusion, not understanding to what they referenced. Silently, an arm wrapped around his neck, the point of blade pricking the side of his throat.

"What have you done?" Marya hissed. "Have you betrayed us? Speak true or I'll take your head."

Cutnose gulped, his impending death was a flick of the wrist away. "I haven't."

"Did you turn us over to the Order? Did you lead those bastards here?"

"I did not, I swear it." The blade remained in place, pressing slightly deeper. He gulped painfully. She released him with a shove and took his place peering around the corner. "A whole company of them all at once. This is no coincidence." She regarded him over her shoulder. "Did you see you Hugh or Agatha?"

"They wait for them to come out."

She eyed the doorway of Hugh's home. "He wouldn't just die. Not him. Ulf or Arnulf?"

"I haven't seen them."

"Our path forward is a jagged one. I cannot take Bors by

myself, especially not with so many brothers at his back. Even with your *limited* help."

"Where have you been?"

"Looking for you. You disappeared. Where did you go?"

"To speak with Tancred."

She pointed her sword at him. "To what end?"

Cutnose lifted a hand from his chest, showing her the ebbing flow of blood through his mail coat. "Ran me through."

"Men are slow to learn and quick to anger." Her dark eyes flashed green. "You must heed my advice if you wish to survive." Shaking her head like a disappointed owner of a dog, she studied the congregation of armed soldiers.

Cutnose knelt next to her. "Anger only gets a man so far in a fight, and I didn't survive this long by not learning from my battles. Tell me."

"Just do as I say. Starting with being quiet so I can think."

He did as she bade until the sound of a large mounted entourage carried down the street, hooves striking stones. Cutnose recognized the man in the lead, gray hair flowing, stern intelligent eyes, white surcoat with a red cross over his coat of mail. He wore no helm and held no shield. His face clear. Godfrey of Bouillon with two dozen knights of his personal guard.

"Sir Bors, I trust your expedition has ended well," Godfrey said.

"We have slain some and now use fire to smoke the last one out."

Godfrey eyed the humble abode. "Why not let it burn? Accomplishes your quest does it not?"

Bors gave him a stiff nod. "It does, Lord Godfrey."

"I would have my city wiped clean of all traitors before the Fatimids decide to show themselves again. You have done well to bring this nest of insurgents to my attention."

"As you wish, lord." Bors nodded to two sergeants, and they rushed forward to light more of the building on fire.

Godfrey grinned a flat smile and turned his horse to view the burning interior of the home. There was no hope now. The leading lord of Jerusalem and the entire crusade wanted them dead. Tancred wanted him dead. The Order's forces multiplied each day. As a veteran of countless battles both great and small, he knew there was little hope for defeating them in the open, or at all, for Marya and himself were only two warriors versus at least a hundred, of which one was the deadliest warrior he'd ever seen.

A noise behind drew Cutnose and Marya's attention. Three men on horses approached, an additional mount trailing behind. Marya leaned behind her buckler and pointed her curved sword. Cutnose raised his shield.

Ulf's scale armor glittered in the flames, his eyes a burning ocean, his voice a gathering swell. "There is no time. We must leave." He handed off the reins to Marya, and she bounded atop the mount. Arnulf nodded, his longbow in hand. A blackened soot-covered man kept his head down in the back. His clothes had been scorched into blackened rags. Hugh.

"Do not stand flat-footed, Cutnose. Mount with Marya," Ulf ordered.

Cutnose eyed the elder warrior. There would be no returning to his past life but was there ever really a chance to go back?

"Where is Agatha?" Marya asked.

"They're gone," Hugh said, his voice croaking. "They slaughtered them while they slept like the cowards they are."

"You will have your vengeance, old friend," Ulf said. "But not this day. It will only lead to your demise."

"That is all a man like me has left."

Ulf faced his friend. "I make this oath of blood to you now. Your kin will not go unavenged. Blood for blood until my last breath."

"Blood for blood." Hugh gulped, wet lines streaked his soiled face.

Cutnose turned back toward their enemies, all gathered in a single place for them to kill. He instinctually rubbed the tip of his nose. *Death awaits you if you choose to accept.* It would only be a matter of how many he could take with him before they finished him off. There was no delusion of surviving a fight this night. If he fought, he would ultimately fail in his quest for vengeance.

"Cutnose!" Ulf growled. His voice held less care than he had for Hugh. It was a command, soldier to soldier. "Death will come for us another day. Tonight, we ride."

"All the men we need to kill are here. I can feel him in the back of my skull throbbing. Oft times you do not get a second chance to kill a man." Ulf nodded to him and removed Cutnose's hand axe, offering it to him handle first.

"I took your weapon for fear of you returning for it before it was time."

Cutnose took it. The handle fit his hand like a glove. He spun it around in a circle warming his wrist. It was a good weapon, strong, held an edge, and reliable.

"You are no fool. You have two eyes that can see. I see over a hundred trained warriors and two of the Twelve worth fifty men each. You want that fight? The five of us versus that?"

"I weigh the odds more than most men. I can see it's a shit fight. But there's always a way to win. Even with those odds." Cutnose had weighed each scenario over and over, seeking a way to find vengeance and survive. Each time the scenario ended in a quick death. "If I don't end this now, I could end up a monster." He gave Ulf a morbid smirk. "That's if you don't take my head first."

"This war is far from over. Fate will see to it that we cross blades with them again."

"And if it doesn't?"

"We will bend the strands of fate to our will."

"And if we don't?"

"We will kill as many as we can."

Cutnose eyed Godfrey sitting in his saddle with his household knights, Bors flatly staring at the flames. Dozens of crossbowmen and footmen stood in rank. He felt robust enough to best ten men without even trying. He shoved his axe through his belt. "You just make sure we get our chance."

"You will get your chance, and if you should fall, your quest will become my own."

Cutnose grinned through the smoke. It was the way in which a man made his oath that told Cutnose he was worth following, and this elder warrior, whoever he truly was did not make oaths that he did not intend to keep. And if he lied, it mattered little, he would just be another man to kill or Cutnose would be dead. "I accept." He eyed Hugh, his eyes glistening with the tempest of rage. He nodded to Arnulf and grabbed the saddle, pulling himself behind Marya. Her hair smelled like dusky wildflowers.

"Stay quiet," she said.

He didn't speak. His choice had been made. The warriors tugged their reins away from the fire and quietly left the Christian quarter, walking their horses. They reached David's Gate, one of the two major access points to the city on the western wall, the one nearest the Mediterranean Sea.

While connected to the walls, the gate stood taller and was made with thicker stone, a squat tower in itself. The stones near the base were widely cut, and as the gatehouse traveled skyward, the stones became smaller as if the base had stood the test of time while the upper floors had been rebuilt. It was one of the last fortifications surrendered to the crusaders and would have cost many lives had it come to a fight.

Drunken guards diced by torchlight. They didn't look up from their game until a captain yelled at them from the gatehouse window. The threat to the city was from the outside, not within. Ulf spoke quietly and a bag of coin clinked into the guard's hands. Two guards disappeared inside the gatehouse and the gates that were normally closed at night were opened, granting them access to Jerusalem's countryside. The guard gave them a gap-toothed smile as they passed squeezing his newfound fortune in his palms. His men laughed loudly when he returned to the wall nearest the torch, and a new wager was put forth. The five warriors heeled the flanks of their mounts and disappeared into the countryside.

CHAPTER 15

"My horse will not last long, even at this rate," Marya complained at Ulf, but he didn't respond. The elder warrior stared forward silent.

The moon was two candlewicks from embracing its truest form. Its mellow glow blanketed them as they traveled along the road, known by the locals as the "Road to the City," westward toward the sea. After fleeing the shadow of Jerusalem's walls at a gallop, they walked their mounts to preserve the overburdened animals.

"Where do we go?" Cutnose asked, but it was a distracted question. He narrowed his eyes above. The moon called to him like a pack of wolves in the night. It beckoned him to become one once more with his inner wolf, a request he struggled to ignore like a tingle in his spine.

"Ramla," Arnulf said.

"It was a ghost town when we first went through," Cutnose said. "Stocked with food as if the people up and vanished. It was the last meal we had for days before we reached Jerusalem on empty bellies. Any forage burnt to ash and every well poisoned."

"There will be men there now," Hugh said.

"Mere field mice," Cutnose responded in disgust. "Scamper to their holes when danger comes, sneak back out when it has passed."

"They are men who do not wish to be slaves," Hugh retorted. "Or slaughtered while they sleep." His voice dripped with venom.

"I fight for the lord, not his cause," Cutnose said.

"Does that make you a better man?" Hugh spat.

"You campaign against the Saracens for three years, and you won't care much if they live or die either."

"My people were Christian, and they are all dead because of your army."

"And my men would be alive if it weren't for your kind."

Hugh growled at him. "Do not pretend that Bors and I are the same."

"And you should do the same."

Both men remained quiet, each regarding the other's words carefully until Ulf broke the silence. "Bors must pass through Ramla if he is to reach the port of Jaffa. He will expect us at Jaffa, not Ramla. It is there that we will ambush them."

"What about north to Acre? Or Constantinople? There are plenty of trading ships traveling back to Venice or Genoa or even beyond," Cutnose said.

Ulf and the others all shared a look with one another. "It would be a risky journey over this land, and Miklagard is no friend to the Order."

"The city isn't a friend to many. Bunch of lying, whoring Greeks. We were happy to be away from that place as quick as we could."

"Do not rush to pass judgment. Not all in Miklagard are driven by intrigue," Ulf said.

"I'm telling you how it happened. We were only mercenaries for their cause. We marched, fought, and died while they stayed in their own lands resting their heads on mountains of gold coin. They wanted us to swear an oath to *return* any lands or riches back to them. No better than a bunch of whores dressed in gold and silk."

"It matters not. They will not travel that way," Ulf said. "Bors is a direct man. I've never seen him shy away from a fight. He will make for the fastest route to return which is through the nearest port. He will cross Ramla to reach there."

"Any more of you hiding in the desert somewhere? 'Cause I'm out of men, and we need more." He rubbed the back of his neck again. "Can't kick this pain in my neck."

Ulf stared straight ahead. "What we have will be sufficient."

"It's not much different than in the city."

"We will fight on our terms."

"We have an archer, two elders, a woman," he hesitated as Marya stiffened in the saddle. "I mean no offense. And three mounts who won't make it another couple days."

"Do you wish this journey to come to an end?" Ulf said turning in the saddle, his eyes almost gold in the darkness.

"Our cause is the same. I only wish to live to see it through."

The glow in Ulf's eyes faded. "You must be patient until the enemy shows us his weakness. They are not perfect. Bors and Galahad will make a mistake and when they do, we shall be waiting."

Roughly twelve miles from Jerusalem, they came to a stop. "The Pool of the Palms," Hugh said, dismounting. "It is said Christ rested here as a child before he was presented at the Temple and those that drink from its waters are cured of their ailments."

"You think it will cure this?" Cutnose asked of them. But the others stayed silent.

Palms grew around the source, encircling it along with shorter, wider olive trees and rigid green pine. Grass sprouted from the ground growing around beige rocks and engulfing them in vibrant green growth. There were few such places in the Holy

Land and any water source was known by all who resided nearby.

"We shall make camp here. Twelve miles is enough for this night," said Ulf.

"I'll scout around," Cutnose said.

Cutnose dismounted, walking around the oasis with his hand on his axe, listening and scanning for people or animals. This would make the perfect place for an ambush. Everyone sought water while traveling. He hadn't worried much about bandits when marching in a massive army. Now, with thousands of men hunting him he was far more wary.

He walked through the trees. They had been thinned by men, leaving short stumps. The closer he walked toward the water, the denser the foliage became. The pool itself was more of a murky puddle with barely enough water to keep their party from thirst.

He dipped a finger in the water and tasted it. It was not poisoned from what he could tell but had enough sediment for him to consider trying to strain it through his clothes first. He carried on, quietly moving through the vegetation. He stumbled upon a cairn, elongated in the form of a person.

"Guess these blessed waters couldn't help you," he said quietly.

A wooden cross stuck out of the ground near the head of the mound. It was simple and crude, the sticks tied together with now brown cracking palm leaves that had fallen from the trees around them. It was but one of many who had fallen on their pilgrimage. They'd traveled so far only to succumb within miles of the city. Just out of sight of redemption for their soul. Valiant yet ignoble, and here he stood, a man who'd campaigned for riches, presiding over their bones, alive, although he should have been tossed into a shallow grave alongside the many slain in battle. His redemption assured by the priests for his violent actions capturing the city yet cursed by whatever form tormented his companions. Did God's forgiveness transcend his current disposition? Or was he now one of the damned? God's plan was an inexorable thing, choosing those that lived and died with as much thought as a flip of a coin. He was beginning to doubt good or evil had anything to do with it.

Satisfied with his inspection of the grounds surrounding the camp, he joined the others near the shallow source. Arnulf was building a very small fire, having gathered as much fallen wood from the limited saplings and runty trees. Marya gathered water in skin bladders. Hugh and Ulf spoke in hushed tones. They spoke words of solace that Cutnose could almost make out.

"The grounds are clear," Cutnose said.

Ulf gestured him with a terse wave. "Sit."

He took a seat on a blanket next to the older men. Hugh eyed him with mistrust, Ulf with contemplative thought. "You are like a baby."

"I have to disagree. Would you like me to show you?" he said, grabbing at his crotch.

"Quiet and listen boy," Hugh said.

Ulf continued. "You are unable to control your bodily functions."

"My movements are regular." He gestured at the water. "Maybe not after drinking this muddy silt."

Ulf's face retained its intensity, not breaking before Cutnose's jest. "I have tasked Marya with keeping you under control, but she has failed. Twice you have let the Wilds take you. Twice you have alerted our enemy to our movements. There will not be a third time."

"Do not flog the mentor for the ineptness of the student," Marya called from the water.

"If the student fails, it is the fault of the mentor." Ulf turned away from her. "Long ago, when I was young, I too had a *vǫrðr*. A guardian and mentor. One who guides us on our wolf journey. We all do. It was different for us. We were born with this, we grew into it, as a boy grows into a man. For you it is like a flood, for us it was like rain into a well, filling over time." Ulf's eyes stared far into the distance. "Nevertheless, you are not wrong. We are few.

We will need your axe in the coming battles. You must learn control. You must harness the wolf spirit inside you. The wolf is strong and bold, the man intelligent and disciplined, yet weak in body. If the man allows it, the wolf will consume him and only the wolf will remain."

"I've heard this all before."

Ulf took a stick from the flames. "Inside you there are two *hugr*." He frowned. "The Christian call them souls."

"Two? Thought we had only one."

"One should listen when an old dog barks." Ulf's lip curled. "Those that are like us have dual spirits. The man and the wolf."

"You don't understand. I have no power over it. It's like I become an animal. Nothing will stand before me and live."

"I understand." He touched his chest. "It is within me as well, but I do not rampage through the city streets. Everything depends on which soul you feed. The man or the wolf. Sometimes you must let the wolf off his chain, but you must cage him when his need has passed. Do you understand?"

Cutnose was intimately familiar with unleashing violence, but this thing inside him was unstable, unruly, with an impossible hunger to sate. "I do, but how?"

"You are a soldier, no?" Hugh said. The old Frank had washed the grime from his face, white hair pulled back and tied. He held a stick in his hands.

"As long as I can remember."

"How do you train a new recruit?"

"You teach them discipline. How to form rank. How to wield a sword. Defend himself with a shield. When to hold and when to charge. Then we teach him where an enemy's weak points are."

"Exactly. You must do the same with what's inside you. For the struggle will get stronger." Hugh glanced at the stars. "Your moon soon comes."

"Point me toward sentry duty."

The two old men shared a knowing look. Hugh shook his head. "He doesn't want to be taught. His cause may be a lost one,

Ulf. Perhaps it best if we snuff out his flame." Hugh's eyes hardened at the mention of violence. "It will be quick."

"He must be taught," Ulf said with a growl. "He *will* be taught."

"Are you sure he's worth it?" Marya chimed in. She took a seat near the fire, setting a bowl of water near them. Arnulf smirked over the top of the flames. Cutnose couldn't tell if she made a jest or if she meant her words.

"Only the wolf can overcome the man. The man can only keep the wolf in check. Yet he can only contain him. There is no other way," Ulf said.

"Many have tried to let the wolf roam free. To let them both exist simultaneously, but it cannot be. It is not possible. If you allow the wolf to roam at its will, it will come out for longer and longer, eating at the man's *hugr* until there is nothing left of the man and only the wolf remains," Hugh said.

"Every now and again it must be fed, but like all animals, the man must decide when the beast emerges. It must be harnessed or leashed or saddled. Pick your term. They are all the same." He eyed Cutnose. "Do you follow?"

"I do."

"For you, the wolf emerges whenever it feels the urge. There is no rope that binds it. It asserts itself at the man's expense," Ulf said.

"This is not the way. You must control it," Hugh said.

"But how?"

"Look here." Ulf waved the stick. "See this flame."

"Yes."

"See how it burns bright." The leaves of fire wavered, embers sparking off and fading before they touched the sand. "If I allow the flame to continue to grow, it will consume as much as it can. Unchecked, it will use the wood until it is but ash and dust. However..." He took the bowl of water in one hand and holding the stick level, he poured drops of water over the flame slowly. Steam fizzled as he worked his way to the tip of the stick, extinguishing the flame gradually. Near the end, a candle-like flame flickered. He took his fingers and squeezed the flame out of existence, looking at Cutnose with gold-flecked sapphire eyes.

"But the flame is out."

"It smolders. It waits to be called." The orange ember glowed at the tip. He blew on it until a flame appeared, small and manageable. "The flame is always there when I need it, but it is manageable because I control how much it grows. Then." He blew the flame back out. "When the time comes for the wolf flame to go away, it is easier to smother." He grinned as his words began to make sense to Cutnose.

"Eventually, the stick will be consumed?" Cutnose asked.

Ulf nodded. "If one is not careful, yes, but if one uses his wolf flame with reserve it will make him harder and stronger like the charred end of a wooden spear."

"But how can this be done? The wolf is stronger than me."

Ulf pulled a small drum from his bag. He handed it to Hugh, and the elder smiled, both grim and sad. He tested the drum by tapping his fingers along the hide surface. Then with a nod from Ulf, he began to drum softly.

He drummed a rotating tap between his fingers and palm. A song escaped Ulf's lips, his voice deep like a mountain cavern. His words were beyond Cutnose in a language he did not understand, but they felt familiar and raw like a wound exposed to the vicious heat of the desert sun.

"Let the wolf out," Hugh said softly.

Cutnose eyed Arnulf and then Marya. Both had their heads bowed, listening to Ulf's song. His eyes lingered on Marya and his loins filled with an unyielding lust. Her eyes would not leave his, as seductive as they were hardened, like jagged emeralds. His insides began to turn, and his breathing grew more intense as he fell into the rhythmic drumming. His skin prickled as he became aware of the wolf stalking him from the inside out.

Her eyes told him she sensed all of his thoughts. A smile curved on her lips, but she slowly shook her head, rejecting him.

He exhaled forcefully through his nose. The animal would be fed. He gritted his teeth, glaring around the fire. His hands flexed and his entire body quivered as it was consumed by the wolf flame. Jaw clenching violently, he could resist no longer. His throat vibrated as he howled at the moon. It was now the only object of his heart, a hoard of gleaming gold stretching endlessly.

The howl died on his lips. He had no recollection of time or space. He felt Marya near him, her voice caressing his neck. The drum tapped in the recess of his mind. "Feel the drum."

His eyes widened and he reached for her.

"No, Cutnose," Ulf said. "Harness your wolf." He resumed his chant.

Cutnose growled and the wolf grew stronger inside him a gust of wind swirling into a storm. The flame coursed through his veins like boiling water. He tried to stymie the fire, but it burned bright, needing more fuel. Only flesh and blood could satisfy it. In the recesses of his mind, he knew these beings would not do, man-flesh needed rendering.

He screamed as his fingers stretched into claws.

"Control the beast," Ulf commanded in a king's voice.

"I—cannot." Cutnose's screams turned into a shaking snarl. Spittle flew from his widening lips. Fangs as long as spearpoints revealed themselves to the moonlight.

Ulf's voice was harder than stone. "You must control it. See the flames. Douse the flames. Push the wolf back."

As Cutnose's vision eclipsed, he began to lose his internal battle. The man's fingers were pried off the leash of the wolf, one by one, the beast dragging him away into its den to be fed upon in leisure within the recess of his mind. Redness surrounded his vision, threatening to consume him whole.

"Cage it!" Hugh's voice echoed through the edges of his mind. Cutnose vaguely understood the words of two-legs. It was almost a foreign tongue, meaningless to the wolf's world of scents and primal desire.

Cutnose's eyes settled on Marya. The wolf grasped at the man

Cutnose, the animal tore at his soul in mouthfuls. Green eyes glittered in the flames. The flames were to be feared. The two-legs used them to hunt and drive out the wolf, to keep them away in the night. Cutnose howled at her in rage, but she tilted her head and joined Ulf's chanting. He lashed at the flames, claws gliding over fire. He snapped his jaws and tore out his fur to the beat of the drum. It thudded in his skull, a woodpecker pounding through the bone to escape, gradually growing louder and dampening the animal inside him, calming Cutnose's breath. The beast wanted to lunge, but the man grasped the reins and with every beat he gained control, straining for leverage.

"Hear me, Cutnose. Breathe with us," Marya said, her eyes glittering like the sea at sunset.

He blinked her in and felt the beast subside as it relinquished itself piece by piece.

"Breathe," Hugh repeated.

"Water the flame," Ulf commanded.

With every beat of his heart, he forced the wolf to yield, drawing it in tighter to his chest. The wolf snapped, but his mind collared around it, controlling every place it could go, the snare closing. The wolf raged furiously, and he felt himself slipping back into the scents of palm and musk and goat. The man faltered; the rope slipped in his mind. The drum and fire became prominent, and the wolf backed into the shadows, releasing a long and lonely howl that echoed over the hills.

The red fever around Cutnose's vision faded into the tiny campfire light. He grunted and stared at his hands, now a soldier's fingers, pink and round, nails short with black beneath the tips. The chanting died in his ears as Hugh drummed to a close.

"You have overcome him," Ulf said with an accepting nod. "It will get easier. When you control your breathing, it will help you control your wolf flame. You decide what it does and how it flows. It is waiting inside you always, but you must be able to bring him back when the need has passed."

"Thought I was going to have to rein you back in," Marya said with a smirk.

"Not sure that would have helped the situation," Cutnose said with an exhausted grin, running a hand through his blond hair, long on top, shaved along the back while still running along his ears.

"Not sure you understand what I meant."

He lifted an eyebrow toward her.

"Your training is far from done," Ulf said. "You must practice control over and over like a soldier does with a sword until it is second nature, an innate ability. You must build discipline."

"Is that what Bors did among my men? He embraced his wolf?"

"Yes, your men never stood a chance against him. Not without certain weapons or armor and training."

"Weapons?" Cutnose said, holding up his axe.

"Against men yes, but not when he is in the Wilds. Regular metal weapons are limited. It can still be killed, but it is an enduring process," Ulf said. He held up his long axe. "This has been crafted with a special metal called Lightsbane."

"I do not know this metal."

"Nor would I expect you to. The source is lost, but there are those among us including the Order that wield such weapons of power. It is deadly to us. We will die of wounds by it that regular men would survive."

"Like a poisoned whoring blade."

"It is, Crowfeeder must be handled with care."

"Why would you need such a weapon?"

"Not all my enemies are human."

Cutnose nodded after a moment. "What else can be used against Bors?"

"Pure silver has an effect, but it must reach blood which means it must be blended with other metals to penetrate his hide, weakening the effect. It will diminish your ability to heal, and if enough is in your blood, it can kill you."

"Inside," Hugh said, tapping his chest. "Or nothing."

"When the time comes, I will face him."

"I thought I must kill him?"

"You will, but his abilities are far greater than yours. Crowfeeder will drink his blood first." He gave Cutnose a grim smile. "The Order's herd needs thinning. You will keep them occupied while I incapacitate him."

"I will follow your lead." The elder warrior was undeterred and assured of the coming battle enough that Cutnose would not argue. But deep inside, he wanted that kill. He wanted to taste of Bors's blood, take his head, and hold it high in the air for all his men to see from Heaven above. Afterall, they'd been absolved of all sin several times by decree of the papal legates, bishops, and priests. The thought of his men peering down from clouds, white angel wings spread wide, golden halos, white dresses, singing in a choir, made him laugh at the absurdity of it all. Ulf's voice sobered him.

"You will or you're already dead. Now let us rest."

CHAPTER 16

In the grayness of dawn, they broke camp. Marya insisted on riding lead and Cutnose begrudgingly accepted her demand. There was little point in forcing the issue. These were his people now, and he was the newest member of the pack. He would be a good soldier and follow along until they let him off his leash.

The party walked their overburdened horses, Cutnose dismounting and walking alongside for long stretches. They made frequent stops and painstaking progress toward the sea. An entire day dragged by, and the sun was high in the sky before they reached Ramla, known as Rama to the Frankish crusaders.

Constructed almost four hundred years ago by an Umayyad caliph Sulayman ibn Abd al-Malik, to serve as a primary way station and military capital of Jund Filastin, Ramla had been the principal city for trade in the region, but now, was a misty morning shadow of itself. It rested at the crossroads of multiple empires, connecting Cairo with Damascus as well as Jaffa with Jerusalem, centered upon two thriving trade routes. And all that mattered to Cutnose the first time he had traveled through its narrow streets was that it held food and water for he and his men.

Crumbling buildings hunched like congregations of praying ancients. A portion of the city wall had collapsed toward the interior, stones strewn over the ground. Weeds had begun to squeeze through the cracks between the rocks. There were no guards at the gate; the heavy wooden doors were left open.

A pack of dogs trotted past as they entered the interior of the city, ignoring the riders. Men in robes disappeared into homes at the sight of armed warriors. The street was linear with only minor curves and led them directly to an extensive bazaar.

Blue, red, purple and orange overhangs covered merchant stalls and carts, only about half holding merchants hawking their wares. Goods were sparse and the empty stalls had been broken and smashed. Despite the destruction, a gray-bearded trader manned his post. He smiled at the newcomers and offered a tray of dates, asking his price in a tongue that Cutnose did not understand. Hugh spoke rapidly, and the man nodded and bowed.

Ulf gave the seller a coin, and Hugh handed the dates out to the party. The man bowed repeatedly to them with a smile on his face. Cutnose frowned at the fruit. The date had been dried so they would last longer, and he appreciated them better than one picked from the palm. A soldier would be a fool to turn down food because he never knew when his next meal would come. Or if he would ever eat again.

Hugh grinned at them. "The seller says the Prophet always broke his fast with dates."

"You'd think a prophet could find something that wouldn't make him run for a privy," Cutnose said.

Arnulf stifled a laugh. "Or maybe he needed it to facilitate the deed?"

"Men may kill you for uttering such words about the Prophet," Hugh warned.

"Ah bugger 'em. Add 'em to the list." He inspected his date. "But I won't turn down food." He took his axe, slit a hole in the side, and removed the pit before popping it in his mouth. They were satisfyingly sweet on his tongue, an acquired taste, yet one he'd become accustomed to in his years fighting in the Holy Land.

The companions traveled through the vendors, making for a

five-story white-marble tower spiring for the cloudless sky near the western edge of the market. The traders called to them. Others only managed to stare with mistrusting eyes.

"The White Mosque," Hugh said. He took in the breadth of the structure. "Marvelous. It is even greater than it was before the earthquake brought it down."

"There," Ulf pointed at the top. "We will be able to see in every direction for many leagues."

"Ah, yes, the minaret," Hugh said.

"The Saracens will surely bar our entrance," replied Cutnose.

"Do not worry yourself with such things," Hugh said. "I will handle it."

"More Saracen now than Frank," Cutnose said.

Hugh regarded him with bitter disdain. "They tend to be far more peaceful than *our* kind."

"Tell that to half my men."

"They defend their land from invaders. We were once safe. Now, that is all gone," Hugh said with a sweep of his hand. He shook his head as he calmed himself.

"What land has ever been safe from war? If it wasn't us, it would be someone else. The Turks owned Jerusalem until recently."

"Their exchange of territory was less vindictive."

"You can call me crusader, pilgrim, mercenary, whoreson, but I am a soldier first. I did not send the messenger to rally all the Frankish lords and their armies to Christendom's cause. You place blame on the toe for the man that kicks. I served a lord. Fight the men he wishes me to fight. And that's every man there is: Turks, Franks, Normans, Greeks, Romans, Saracens, hell even fought an Englishman or two. I am not responsible for this war."

"A typical soldier's response. I was only following my lord's commands. You're a killer for coin, no better than a common brigand."

"Sometimes I don't even kill for the coin." Cutnose followed his statement by spitting, wishing he had a bladder of wine to wet his tongue. This elder's mind had been cooked in the desert sun for far too long.

Hugh's face reddened. "And they call us monsters. We've just seen enough to truly value peace."

"Peace is bad for business."

Hugh turned away from him, muttering curses in a foreign tongue.

The band walked onward in bitter silence.

Only part of the mosque had been built on the adjacent side of the minaret tower. Near that, a temporary wooden structure served in its stead. The only completed part of the religious compound was the stone wall surrounding it. They approached a gate broad enough to admit three people shoulder-to-shoulder into the courtyard. It was made from cypress and cedar wood and carved ornately top to bottom with flowers. These were offset by fresh pieces of plain wood lining the door to cover a hole. The rest of the gate was covered in gouges from an axe, as if a carpenter had tried to maul his own work in frustration.

Hugh dismounted and pounded a fist on the door. He kept his head down as he waited. Then knocked again.

A voice came from the other side of the gate door. "God is great. Why do you wish entrance?"

"We seek to meet with you, father. It is an old friend, Hugh from Jerusalem."

A heavy door beam slowly scraped along the other side. Then stopped. Then restarted as if the man grew tired. The door cracked open and an ancient man with white eyes revealed himself. He turned his head to the side then gave a sniff, his mouth settling in a frown. "I can smell you well enough. You are not alone, friend. You reek of the Franks." His mouth twisted. "I know not why you bring them here, but you are permitted no further." With force, he closed the door, his body thumping to bar them entrance.

"Mohammed, please. It is me," he said, resting a hand on the door.

"They are not welcome here after what they've done. Now depart."

"I am sorry for that. There was nothing I could do." Hugh rested his head on the door as he spoke. "Please, Mohammed. I need your help. Agatha, the children, they're gone. The Franks murdered them."

Silence came from the other side. "You speak the truth?"

Hugh groomed his white hair. "I wish upon all that it wasn't."

Mohammed opened the door, granting them entrance. "Come in, we must be careful. The town is not welcoming to Franks of late." As Cutnose passed, the ancient man frowned. "You travel in such poor company?"

Hugh turned and viewed his comrades. "Most of them are good people. Old friends. The one that stinks, I cannot vouch for."

Mohammed stared blankly. "I will watch him closely."

"I will as well, old friend," Hugh said. "There is no need to worry. He will behave himself." Cutnose gave him an evil grin.

"Wonder if there's gold in here."

Hugh shook his head, but the old Saracen didn't hear him, shuffling on toward the minaret. The courtyard was lined with well-manicured gardens, the stones beneath their feet made with local limestone. A massive cistern rested in the center, stone walls curving like a bowl.

"You may tie your horses over there," Mohammed pointed, not bothering to look. "There is fresh water."

Cutnose made his way to the basin of bubbling water. He took a water skin and knelt, dipping it into the pool. He drank from the skin, letting the water sooth his raw throat, parched from the ride.

Marya joined him, filling her water skin. She was silent as the water bubbled. "Hugh is right. There is value in peace. But he forgets that there is a time for war."

"When you need to get paid," he said with a chuckle.

"There is more to life than riches and spoils."

"Coming from a woman wearing clothes and armor fit for a queen. If there is more to life, why does one value it so highly?"

He narrowed his eyes at her. "You can't avoid war. If you aren't marching on some poor whoreson, he'll be marching for you."

Her mouth formed a grim flat line. "We enter the world as one thing and often leave as something else, but we all leave the same way."

"An evasive answer, even for one of you and your comrades." He nodded his head and wiped water droplets from his mouth. "All men must die, but it's easier to die rich than to die poor."

She tied her water bladder. "Yet there are more important things."

"You mean God?" Cutnose glanced at the sky. He closed an eye, trying to make out the bearded fellow on his cloud. "You see enough of what men do in God's name you might rethink that."

She stood. "I've seen far too much what men do in his name. I do not speak of God or the gods. I speak of good versus evil."

"Good? It all depends on whose side you're on."

"It does, but in the end, there is good and evil. Light and darkness. Freedom and prison. I ask you this, which side do you fall on?"

"I get paid to not ask questions." It was impossible for a man not to consider what he was asked to do, but it was the coin that allowed him to look the other way. A man couldn't help but wonder if the men in front of him deserved to be slaughtered or not. It was always a fleeting thought, one that disappeared as quickly as it crossed his mind, because when they drew near to do the dirty work, the other side of a man's mind took over.

The one that would ram a spear through another man's belly and step on his face as he ran down his fellows, ignoring his cries. For then it was too late to consider anything except survival. "Maybe we're just different. Maybe I just think wrong. A soldier does what he's told. And that usually involves killing and dying for a rich man to get richer, but we do it all the same, to get the scraps from his table because that's the lot we've drawn. The commoner's lot. You tell me to fight for the good in life. What on God's earth is that supposed to be?"

She was silent, a queen considering her subject.

Seeing a gap in her shieldwall of morals, he sought to exploit it. "Is it supposed to be about what God wants? The Pope's the one who sent us here. We been killing in his name." He gestured over his shoulder. "Is it supposed to be what Godfrey wants? We been killing in his name too." He pointed at her now. "Is it supposed to be what you want?" His gaze hardened. "I'd only be killing in your name."

"Men can be killed to make the world a better place."

"Better for whom? You kill for three things, God, gold, or women. That's why we kill. There's no such thing as right or wrong. Just who kills and who dies, so you better be damn good at the killing part."

"Basic are the laws that govern men. I am telling you to search for deeper meaning." Her eyes viewed him with intense scrutiny. "The fight we choose to take is the most important decision we make. For we may fall or take life in its struggle." She walked closer. "You may fight for vengeance now and that is just. Fight for your slain men. But where will you fight when we are through? What purpose will drive you onward?" She turned away after a moment. "These are not easy answers. It takes men many years before they can discover the truth to their actions." She laid a hand on his chest. "But those that find it sooner are better men for it."

"I—" he stopped as she held a finger to her lips.

"I only ask you to consider the why of it." She disappeared inside the minaret.

He glanced at the water basin in the courtyard. Then back at the sky. "A woman who thinks too much is always a problem." He laughed to himself, "It's either kill or be killed. That's it."

The bottom floor of the tower was dark and dank even for this region. A candle sat on an overburdened table illuminating Hugh and Mohammed. Ulf leaned on the wall, axe in front of him. A single-person bed was wedged in the corner. Bookshelves filled with tomes lined one wall and barrels rested along another.

Arnulf and Marya stood near the stairs leading to the next floor where there were more books and more chairs for quiet study and contemplation.

"Mohammed, may we use your minaret to see out over the land?" Hugh asked.

Mohammed smiled, his eyes staring. "You can see far from the very top. I am told even to the sea."

"It is imperative to our quest."

Mohammed frowned. "Do the Franks come again?"

Hugh and Ulf exchanged a glance before Hugh spoke. "We search for an enemy of all people."

"I see," Mohammed said with a nod. "You mustn't bother the people below; their privacy must be maintained. Do you understand? My voice was not the only reason I was selected to be the *muezzin*." He tapped the corner of one of his eyes. "Blindness has brought me closer to God than I ever thought possible."

"They shall be respected," Ulf said. With a nod at Arnulf, he jogged the steps.

"Would he learn the *Adhan*, these old bones would not have to traverse the stairs at dusk," Mohammed said. He wheezed a dry laugh to himself. "May I offer you bread? I am afraid it is all I have."

"We are not hungry," Hugh said, resting a hand on the old man's arm.

Cutnose settled to a seat on the floor, enjoying the coolness of the stones.

"Your friend, do I know him?" Mohammed said. He slumped in his chair, turning an ear toward them intently.

"I am afraid not, friend, my name is Ulf." He rested his long axe on the stones, using the shaft to brace himself.

"Ahh, I can tell by your voice you are a great warrior, but there is something else there that lingers." The blind man turned to Hugh. "You are kin?"

Hugh and Ulf exchanged a grin.

"There is much fondness for one another, but your tone is similar."

"We are kin long apart," Ulf said.

Hugh answered him. "Although, I thought I would never see him again before recent events."

Mohammed grinned, baring crooked teeth. "I sensed as much. I can't see a thing, but I can hear everything."

Marya raised her eyebrows.

"I know there is a young woman in this group," Mohammed said, turning in her direction.

"I am hardly young," Marya called over.

"Your voice holds wisdom, yet the sound is youthful," Mohammed said. "You are a contradiction."

"Aren't we all?" she asked.

He nodded, his blind white eyes turning toward Cutnose. "And another. A stink emanates from him." Mohammed's mouth twisted. "The stink of an unwashed Frank, or washed, I am not sure there is a difference."

Cutnose sniffed near his armpit. He smelled perfectly normal if a bit more ripe than usual. "The name is Cutnose."

"Aptly named for what one must do to tolerate your presence," Mohammed said with a twist of his lips. "Who could name a child as such?"

"It's more of a nickname. My mother called me Robert from what I can remember."

Mohammed sneered in disgust. "I offer you a bath in the pool outside." He held a hand up to his nose, wiping away his odor.

"I agree," Marya mouthed.

"I think I need a breath of fresh air," Cutnose said as he stood.

"That makes all of us," Mohammed said. "They say when one sense goes, the others heighten to compensate. This is one day that I wish my sense of smell hadn't."

Cutnose lumbered the stairs story by story until he reached the very top. A stone-ringed balcony encircled the tower and the view threatened to steal his breath away. He'd never been so high in the air. The land below was a quilt of greens, browns and tans stretching until turning into a salty haze.

"Beautiful, isn't it?" Arnulf said. His eyes scoured the land but settled upon the long cut of road meandering through the green-and-brown landscape like a dry riverbed.

"Never before have my eyes beheld such a thing."

Arnulf gave him a short nod. "To think, that old man is deprived of such an experience every day."

"Makes you thankful to have your sight." He shook his head about the unfairness of it all.

"Come this way." Arnulf led him to the other side.

"Deus vult," Cutnose said.

If the view to the east was breathtaking, the view to the west was a glimpse of Heaven itself. The coast was a blue sparkling haze, like God had sprinkled diamonds over a field of grayish blue. "The sea." Were the only words Cutnose could utter in his awestruck.

"There is Jaffa," Arnulf said.

The walls were not tall, nor the harbor impressive in size, but he could make out the shapes of the town, man's timid footprint on the horizon.

"I don't have words to describe it."

Arnulf smirked, the scars on his cheek resisting. "God's very own garden. One might say Eden." Mountains, green hills, the sandy tan of the desert populated by shrub-like trees, farmland near the sea filled with fruit, it was as if God had crammed every type of land into a single area.

"If it weren't for all the sorry whoresons killing each other over it."

"It is in our nature. No amount of time changes that."

"Far easier to kill a man than learn about him."

Cutnose leaned on the wall. He studied the town below. Houses upon houses layered one another like the opposite of a mosaic, haphazard and without uniform. The various colored stall overhangs overlapped with one another throughout the market, reminding him of a beggar's patched blanket.

The two men manned the tower for hours. In the chaos that was a military campaign, standing above the land was like peering down from the heavens itself. It was to be detached from the stink and the violence that came with people. It was to be on the very top of the world itself, almost as if Arnulf and Cutnose were gods on Olympia watching the workings of the mortals below. The lands stretched endlessly. The breeze wiped away the heat.

It was the most peace Cutnose had felt in a long time, and he lost himself in it. He couldn't take in enough of the scenery, almost afraid to blink and everything would disappear. "Who was the man? The one who killed your father."

Arnulf's lip twitched after a moment, his mouth tightening. "You would not know him."

"Lots of men I don't know. Lots of men I haven't killed yet."

"Ulf and I sought him for years and could not track him down." He waited a moment. "He is known as Kveldulf. The Night Wolf. I do not know if he lives, yet I pray that he does so I can be the last thing he sees before I take his head."

"The Night Wolf. Sounds charming."

"Not in the least. I know not where he came from. I believe him once a part of Thorkell the Tall's army, but I do not know, I was but a boy. He came in the night, asking for hospitality at our home. We knew he was like *us* and gave him shelter. When he tried to take my mother and sisters by force, he gave me this." He outlined one of the scars on his face. "He took them and disappeared, and I haven't seen any of them since."

"You think they yet live?"

"He wanted them alive. I had my chance and failed, and now they are gone."

"But you were just a boy."

"I failed them." Arnulf's mouth twisted. "Never again."

The two men continued to watch over the lands in silence

before Cutnose broke it once more. "I understand a lust for vengeance."

"Your wound is fresh. Eventually it festers in your heart. Then when it has corrupted every part of you there will be little joy to be found anywhere. All except the desire for vengeance." Arnulf's jaw clenched in misery. "When I try to recall my sisters, I can hardly remember their faces. They are just a presence, lingering outside my view. I know they are there, but only a shadow of themselves." He shook his head in frustration. "I have wandered for far too long." He continued to peer out over the land. "We are no pack, but Marya and Ulf are as close to family as I have ever known. When I met Ulf, I was almost gone to the Wilds." He smirked as if he relived that memory. "I almost slew him, and he me, but since he has saved my life in more ways than I can count fingers."

"Makes two of us."

Arnulf regarded him for a moment. "You will survive this. You have a certain stubbornness for life."

"War makes men harder, or it breaks them." A grove of olives in the distance caught Cutnose's eye. Two men walked among the trees, the men no bigger than bugs from the tower. They picked the small round fruit and placed them in bags draped over their shoulders. The gathered fruit would need to be placed in salt water to become edible, too raw and bitter to eat off the tree as many a pilgrim discovered on their journey.

One of the men stopped picking and crouched behind the tree. He faced the direction of Jerusalem. Cutnose's eyes followed where the man's gaze had frozen. He squinted, even though his eyesight had improved drastically, it was still much too far to see clearly.

A swirling dust cloud obstructed the road with alarming speed. Cutnose stood straighter, a soldier's wariness ringing the alarm bell in his chest. He shaded his eyes with a hand. Faint shadows grew more prominent, a sizable contingent of mounted men riding hard in the fading heat of the day.

"Arnulf," Cutnose said, his voice urgent. The archer took his place, glaring at the rising dust storm of riders. Streamers whipped near the lead of the procession. Red and blue fluttered in the cloud of war.

"Somebody important is coming," Cutnose said. They both continued to observe in silence, only their hearts pounding.

"And fast." Even at the distance, the cloud made rapid movement over the road.

"I'll tell you one thing. It's not the bloody Pope come to attend his own show."

"How many men do you think?"

Cutnose judged the dust, the banners, the lead riders he could identify. "I'd say an entire company. Over a hundred mounted sergeants. Twenty to thirty knights at least."

"We did not expect them to ride in such force. You have drawn the ire of many men." Arnulf flashed him a gritty grin. "Ulf will not be pleased."

"Can't take on a hundred mounted men?" A jest was the only thing a man could do when he faced the approach of insurmountable odds."

"He will growl in anger, but deep down, he will relish the opportunity to bring down so many." Arnulf bound for the stairs.

"At least that makes one of us that enjoys fighting grossly outnumbered."

"Two," Arnulf said from the stairs.

Cutnose gave the mounted men another glance. "I'm surrounded by fools with a death wish."

CHAPTER 17

Lance tips reflected the sun, steel implements polished and prepared to perform their deadly duties. Light reflected from the helms brilliantly as if they were God's own host. Most wore conical helms with nose pieces, others conical with metal earpieces dangling from the sides. Most knights and sergeants wore ringed mail, the richer knights donning mail coifs over padded ones, or scale armor over the mail for extra protection.

A contingent of lighter armed turcopoles, mobile horseman recruited from local Christian populations or tribal mercenaries, joined the column from distanced positions along the flanks. They were trained to fight as the Turks and Saracens did with hit and ride tactics and rode smaller mounts, recurve horse bows and light lances in hands, and quivers, maces, and long knives secured on belts, bearing light or no armor at all. Their defense was found in lightning speed and mobility in the field. They were instrumental in screening, delaying, and scouting for their more heavily armored Frankish allies.

The front of the column was composed of knights and standard bearers. Cutnose's heart dropped when he saw Tancred's standard and then Galahad as he walked his horse through the gates of Ramla. Ludolf of Tournai was near Tancred, ready for his every beck and call. Lord Robert of Limosano rode on Tancred's other side, his facial blemishes visible from a distance, his leaf-shaped shield was painted red with three black circles stretching diagonally across the length of it. Sir Attropius passed beneath them with his javelins holstered in a saddle quiver. Sir Rainald of Salerno was a few riders behind, scowling as he eyed doors and windows. Sir Hermann and Sir Guarin rode side-by-side, lances unwavering in the air.

Many additional knights rode with Tancred that Cutnose could only recognized by shield. One could tell the wealthier knights from the mounted sergeants, their gear more expensive and higher quality. Their shields bore more extravagant themes than plain metal, wood, and hide. A white swan on a field of blue, a red hawk spreading its wings over black, a silver mailed fist on yellow, a gray keep on a field of dark blue, three yellow fish on red, and numerous other colors split into thirds or fourths, dividing the shield. Most shields were battered with gouges and chips, holes where arrows had lodged themselves and been removed.

The mounted sergeants were plain grizzled versions of the knights. In many ways, a knight's equal in battlefield tactics and prowess but lacking in the best equipment. Their shields were mostly plain single colors, some bearing less extravagant versions of the lords they served. More had painted red crosses on white backgrounds that openly signified their oath to fulfill their holy quest. These men would fight. And five warriors, no matter their strengths, would never be able to stand before the domineering force of a heavy cavalry charge. Combined with the harassment of the turcopoles, there would be no escape.

"There," Marya said. She pointed at a knight near Tancred.

"That is the man from Tancred's mansion," Cutnose said.

"Galahad," Ulf said, violence coiling in his voice. "That man has plagued me for millennia. If I told you the number of times I'd killed him…" He spit onto the balcony. "Does anyone see Bors? Can you sense Bors among them?"

"The back of my neck aches fiercely, nearly as bad as the other night, but I do not see him."

Ulf furrowed his brows. "I am surprised Bors would split his force like this, he was always the hammer of their band. Blunt. Riding hard for the coast with as many as possible would be his way. Daring us to challenge him. But perhaps he is comforted by the presence of the crusaders. I know not his mind."

"It may be a diversion," Cutnose said. "Tancred has sought advantage before by breaking away from the main force to scout with the turcopoles."

Hugh crossed his arms over his chest. "Galahad has always been cunning."

Ulf ground his teeth, sniffing the air. "He has, but he has not the wile he believes he possesses unless he has inherited something better from his mother. Yet he is before us, and we would be amiss to not act." He sniffed the air again. "The air does not smell right."

"None of this does." Hugh's words were laced with his personal pain. He shook his head. "I came here to avoid this struggle."

Ulf reached out and gripped his friend's shoulder. "This war always finds us. Your kin have always been my kin. Time does not change that. It was the gods who set us along this path. Together."

Hugh watched the riders walking their horses, shaking his head. "My heart is empty." He breathed hard. "The only warmth I feel is that of revenge. I will follow you into battle, Ulf, as long as I can wet my blade in their blood and embrace a good death."

The mounted warriors paraded through the town. They stopped to water their horses near the opposing gate leading to the sea.

"We must divide them so we can manage the fight," Marya said.

"Without Bors in their ranks an ambush is foolish, but we mustn't let them escape us in case he seeks to join them elsewhere," Ulf said. He smoothed his long gray braided beard. "Hugh and I will follow Galahad's band. I do not fear a Second Son and his men. We shall see where they take us." Hugh nodded his head vigorously. "You three will stay and wait for the arrival of Bors. I know not their plan, but he will come." He watched the three of them with knowing eyes. "He is dangerous. Do not attempt him alone."

Marya regarded him coldly. "I do not like splitting our force."

"We must be sure the agents of the Order do not deceive us."

"I will go. Hugh can stay here," she said.

Ulf close-lip grinned. "It has been far too long since Hugh and I have ridden to war."

"He is ancient, and he said himself that his fighting days are over."

"You are too young to remember, but Hugh was once a fierce warrior. That old flame still burns in his chest, but I am saddened that it was the loss of his family that kindled it." Ulf dismissed them fiercely. Hefting Crowfeeder, he left with Hugh.

Marya watched Tancred's company with a shake of her head, the sun curving toward the west, wind ruffling errant strands of her raven's hair. "Leaves me to watch you."

"I could think of worse things."

"Is that so? Name one."

"Could be like poor Hugh, family slaughtered."

Marya blinked and sadly grinned. "Could be."

Tancred's men spent almost three hours lounging lazily in the shade near the stables, letting the afternoon heat fade away into dusk. The horses were more important to them than any other possession, for there was no quicker way for a knight to perish than losing his mount, and there were few enough horses around.

The knights disappeared into a house while the sergeants traversed the market, spending their pilfered gold and silver freely. The market vendors cautiously sold their goods, fearful that the soldiers would abuse or rob them. But these men were not like the first crusaders to pass through. They were mostly happy and content, not in a violent frenzy but merely armed pilgrims.

As darkness stretched over the lands chasing the sun, the temperature began to drop, and the shout went for the riders to mount. The horsemen begrudgingly obeyed, stiffly swinging into the saddle. Horses whined and clopped their hooves in irritation. Shields were secured. Lances gripped. They filed out of the gate in a long column.

Mohammed joined Marya and Cutnose, leaning on the walls of the minaret to give the Muslim call to prayer. Although Cutnose did not understand a word, he was impressed that such an ancient man still had such fierce conviction and air inside his lungs. The people of Ramla rolled out their rugs and prayed toward Mecca to their god, thanking him for sparing them another time from cruel Christian blades.

Hugh and Ulf saddled their horses in the courtyard then made their hasty goodbyes, clasping arms with Arnulf and Marya and lastly with Cutnose.

"Remember what we said, water around the flames. You mustn't let it burn too bright." Ulf eyed the rising moon in the distance. "Your time will soon be upon you. Do not falter." He swung a leg over the back of his mount and adjusted his long axe, so it rested on his thigh.

Hugh wrapped himself in a loose cloak, a simple sword on his belt. No armor or helm. Only the robes, and in the dark, he would be thought of as a nomad or ancient bandit. He nodded his goodbyes, but his eyes still burned with disdain for Cutnose.

"Once it can be discerned what Galahad's purpose is, we will return." Ulf's horse shifted beneath his weight. "If Bors arrives, track him, and if I have not returned in time, take his head. I would look him in the eye one last time." With a nod, they turned their horses and departed after Tancred's company.

After Ulf and Hugh departed, the three warriors took turns manning the tower's balcony. Cutnose drew the middle shift, the darkest of the night, the wolf's hour. He still marveled at the sky above him. The moon was close to the earth, a lustrous white orb that was almost completely round, only a day off from being full. He had little time left. From the top of the tower, it seemed even closer, and it bore down, making him itch from the inside out. He took a deep breath, trying to settle himself. "Water around the fire," he whispered. "Water around the fire." Beads of sweat formed on his brow, his throat drying around the words. He tried to focus, gripping the side of the wall until his knuckles popped.

"How are you holding, Sir Cutnose?" came Marya's voice.

He steadied himself the same way he did before a fight, his breath reverberating in his chest. He breathed in through the mouth and out through his nose, attempting to stifle his struggle in front of the beautiful woman. "I am fine."

"The Wilds call to us all. Its call is as fierce as a bear protecting her cub and as beautiful as the rising sun." She wore her black, gold-trimmed kaftan and wrapped her arms around herself to keep out the cold.

The moon felt anything but beautiful, more of a wildfire attempting to burn him to a crisp, all precipitated by the damn celestial light in the sky. "Could be my last night. Moon's almost full."

Her teeth flashed at him. "This will not be your last night."

"You sound so sure. I been around long enough to know nothing's sure."

Her grin deepened. "And I've been around long enough to know that what needs to be done gets done, one way or another."

"How will it happen?" he said.

She turned toward him. "Your Turning?"

"If that is your name for it."

She leaned on the balcony. "Your first true time is called the

Turning. When the full moon reaches the apex of its rise, it will overcome you. No matter how much you try to control it, the wolf will win. There is no word for it, but I would say it is his 'right.' You will become the wolf in its ugliest form. How bad, all depends on the man. Some are uglier than others." She glanced at him. "If you do not eat Bors's heart, you will be plagued by this uncontrollable affliction, unable to return. It will be best to cut you down early before you have gained more experience and strength from killing."

"More dangerous than Bors when he was in his beast form?"

"You could be. More feral over time. You will be extremely dangerous to everyone, including yourself. If you fall into the Wilds, other wolfskins like us will hunt you. The Order will hunt you. Regular men will attempt to slay you while you sleep for you are an abomination of them."

"Why would you hunt wolfskins like yourself?"

"Because if the wolf rules you, you are a threat to our existence. You will be wild and untamed. An uncontrollable monster. Your only companion will be slaughter, and we cannot let that happen."

"But if I kill Bors, I won't be?"

Her eyes studied the recess of the night. "Killing Bors after being bitten tempers the hold. Stabilizes it. I've seen it done only twice." Her grin saddened. "Like Ulf, I was born this way, my abilities are innate. However, we can fall to the Wilds if we are not careful and become feral all the same."

"I've lived a long life compared to most men. I do not wish to exist as a monster." He regarded her. "You will give me a clean death?"

She faced him again. Her ebony hair flowing freely around her shoulders, the moonlight glinting off her hair like the sun off a fresh black snow. Her full lips spread flat; her greenish-hazel eyes held the answer like precious gems.

"Yes. But know I will take no pleasure in it."

"I can now die in peace," he said morbidly. Death was simple to a mercenary. It was a contractual obligation that came with selling one's sword to a lord. A contract that promised riches or an inglorious demise on a battlefield. Life and death were bosom buddies to one another, and a mercenary never knew which teat they were suckling on until there was a spear sticking a foot out his back. It was always waiting for him just over the next hill, the next march, or the next river. If you met an old mercenary at a tavern, it was best to not cross them for they did not become old by luck alone.

"Perhaps a small sliver of pleasure," she said, her lips curving.

He laughed deep. Laughing at death was all a man could do, for it came for him all the same. "What happens if I kill him? Then what do we do?"

Her eyes bounced away from him. "You will eat his heart, and you will be one of us, Sir Cutnose."

"You mock me with titles, but I was offered a knighthood once."

"Someone saw something noble in you?"

"I think he didn't want to pay what I was owed." That dream was as dead as his men. He joined her at the balcony. "When we are through, I will find a new company or join a household guard. There's always a war to be fought."

"You cannot go back to Tancred," she said. "He knows the old Cutnose and the new, and he will continue to try to kill what you've become. You should be dead to him. In some ways, it is the hardest part. The men you marched with are revolted by you. They've already labeled you devil, something to be feared and killed. You will not be able to stay here, at least for some time. With time, memories will fade, and you will become a legend to them, a story to be passed on to frighten their children."

"If I survive."

"If you survive."

What he didn't mention was that Bohemond was north in Antioch. The ambitious noble had the power to pardon him from whatever false accusations had transpired here, but it would take all his powers to clear his name. But what if the man was like Tancred and only saw a monster? He would show mercy on his steadfast ally. Cutnose could throw in a cheaper rate to help smooth over any rough ends. He only needed to slay the whoreson, Bors.

"When we kill Bors, you must find a new life somewhere." She gripped his arm and he faced her. "A new life. Away from here."

With her touch, the wolf inside him pounced on his rib cage, the fire flared in his chest and loins, an animalistic lust billowing in the winds of desire. He reached for her, and his fingers touched her face, running along her cheek to her neck. She didn't move away but blinked at his touch. His other hand reached for her, grasping for her waist. She let herself be pulled closer, and he deeply inhaled her scent.

"Could be my last night," he whispered.

"You are not the first man to use those words to make a woman loosen her inhibition." Her eyes locked with his, there was pain and loss, but a desire to feel life too, and then her eyes descended to his lips. Her resistance crumbled. He stretched his neck trying to kiss the smooth skin running down to her collar bone. Her flesh was sweet and felt like silk as he skimmed his lips over it.

Firm hands pushed him away. "Control, Sir Cutnose," she said, and released him.

He exhaled sharply. "You can't deny this attraction."

"You have mistaken my kindness for attraction. Douse your flames." She shouldered her way back into her kaftan. "If you wish to survive this, you'd best be on the lookout for Bors instead of indulging your most primal urges."

He put both hands on the side of the balcony, then ran a hand through his hair. "Water around the flames. Water around the flames," he breathed. "You're a confusing woman."

"Aren't we all?"

He gave her a side eye. "Some more than others."

"You are not the first man to say so, and I am sure you will not be the last."

His eyes scanned the city. Night's black cloak shrouded all of Ramla, but the moon illuminated everything as if it attempted to be the sun yet could never be. It cast a yellowish mantle upon the tan buildings. Candles flickered in a few windows, but the night was quiet. He sighed, heady fog escaping his lips. "And you will not be the last woman to turn me down." At least he hoped.

CHAPTER 18

Weathered hands gripped cracking reins driven by hardened hearts. Dust tried to choke them, smother them into stopping, yet they continued, only drinking from their water bladders sparingly. Wind whipped Ulf's gray-braided beard. His cool blue eyes read every dip and incline of the terrain.

Hills rolled to the east, dark trees standing over top of them like an army of green-armored soldiers waiting to do battle with the sea. The sea roared its defiance, crashing waves onto the rocky shore, challenging the wooded lands to come closer.

The faint odor of horse dung and the stink of man marked the way, as if they littered pieces of themselves along the road, the dust settling in their aftermath. Yet something else rode the winds with them, its foul essence held no scent, it was a relative of fear, and could only be named desperation.

Ulf took solace in the man riding next to him. It had been so long since they'd hunted together. Ages had passed since the rivers of wind last flowed through their hair. Centuries since they'd last savored the blood of victory.

Once they had traveled in the same pack as wolf-brothers across faraway oceans and foreign lands, until their ways parted. Hugh had known when his time as leader was nearing the end.

He gracefully had bowed to his challenger during the Sundering and trekked into the outlands to fade away, but he did not die. He only assumed a new life in a distant place.

It was only by chance they had been reunited. On a dusty road outside Jerusalem, their paths crossed. He'd smelled his distinct scent first and when he neared, it made his nose wrinkle. He knew a wolf-brother anywhere. His scent was familiar and pleasant, but different, less vibrant, leatherier, and filled with reserved calmness. The calmness of a man who was comfortable with the idea of death.

The thought forced a smile onto Ulf's stone-like face. Hugh had in fact not perished, but embraced a far more peaceful life in Jerusalem, providing for and protecting a local woman and her children. They were not of his own blood, no, his breeding days were behind him. He only cared and watched for them as a grandfather would. Now they were more broken branches on the bonfires of war.

When men lived as long as they had, there were plenty of wars and feuds to fight. Years of war brought on oaths of blood stretching generations between rival packs. When your enemy lived just as long, for every one that fell, more filled their ranks. But it seemed that Ulf's people were only memories, and his enemies grew in number as fecund rabbits.

Hooves beat the earth like dual thunderclouds, and his mind raced alongside his steed. Galahad had been a thorn in his side for centuries. Ripping out his heart in a pass had been as satisfying as decapitating his progeny years later. He knew that killing this Galahad may be the most important kill of his life, for the Chalice could shift the balance of power further into the Order's hands. The land would be burned and his kind eradicated, and the Order would name it a most reverent peace.

He'd kept this knowledge from his companions. The Black Chalice had the power to turn them to dust, and if the legends were true, raise an unstoppable army. An army bent on the eradication of Ulf and all of his kind, and while he yet breathed, he would fight them every step along the way.

Hugh called out and they brought their horses to a walk. "They've stopped ahead."

Ulf's grip tightened around the haft of his axe as he tilted his head to the side, listening. "We must tread carefully." The two men walked in silence the same as when they wore a younger man's armor, stalking through the timber in search of prey. The horses' hooves clopped off the hard dirt road. "I am sorry for Agatha and the children."

Hugh sighed, sitting tall, his limbs holding sinewy strength despite his age. "I was foolish to think I could protect them."

"No man can stand against an army."

"I've heard tales of men doing as such."

"I should have died that day."

"Perhaps it is more noble to die then."

"No. You fight when there's a chance. Back there, there was no chance. With the Chalice at stake, we must not throw our lives away."

The noble Hugh kept his eyes on the road. He sat in the saddle naturally, like an old king off to battle one last time. Both men rocked in their saddles as they walked their mounts. "I left war a long time ago, and I should have known better that it would follow me. How can one so old be so foolish? Escape war?" He lowered his head for a moment in disbelief, tortured by the cruelty of fate.

"All men dream of peace as they sharpen their swords. You deserve to be at peace, brother. We all do."

"I suppose I should have just died in the Sundering or drank of Moonlight Lily tea. Instead, I wandered. I searched for God, and never finding him, I ended up in Jerusalem. I saw a woman begging with her children wrapped around her legs near the Holy Sepulchre. Every manner of pilgrim, merchant, and noble pretended they did not exist." He sighed heavily. "I bought them food. Then a home. And while I didn't find God here, I found peace in caring for them, even if it was simple and small and only for a moment in time." He swallowed with difficulty. "Only to have it stripped away by those vile men who live only to tear things down."

"Finding peace, if only for a brief moment in the chaos, is something to be cherished."

"What happens when you can't find the will to carry on? When each loss has made you harder and harder to life until you are more brittle than an over-quenched blade? Until you only see their deaths instead of the blessed possibilities of life."

Every man Ulf had known that wasn't a wolfskin, had been dead and gone for centuries. Friends, lovers, enemies, wives, brothers in arms, all gone, turned to the dust of time, yet here he sat in the saddle, still waging an eternal war against the enemies of their kind. Over time, one's sense of hope was eroded until only the pain of loss remained. The hope of life simply gone, perhaps that is what Hugh's adoptive family was, a hope of life that lay smoldering ash and bone in Jerusalem.

Death was a kindred spirit to their kind, and they walked hand in hand for lifetimes, not forever, for they were still men. Eventually death turned on them too. Its arrow still seeking them, but the arc long before it found its mark. "If nothing still brings you joy or hope, then perhaps it is time to pass on," Ulf said. The two men rode in silence until Ulf spoke again. "Only the man who walks the journey knows when it must end."

Hugh's brow furrowed. "Then we are close, but not there yet."

They tracked for fifteen miles in the dark, the roar of ocean waves concealing their pursuit along the coast. The company of mounted crusaders chose to make their encampment at the center of a fishing village. Small fishing boats lined the shore out of reach of the greedy waves, masts laid into the hulls, nets were laid over top of them to dry before the next day's venture into the shallow waters.

The villagers were sent into a frenzy as the mounted men entered the village, thinking they'd come to exact a vengeance upon them. Men and women knelt on the ground, hands outstretched, begging for mercy in front of their packed mud homes with layers of dried palms for roofing. Women wailed at the crusaders, clutching children to their breasts.

Tancred spoke to the village in their native tongue, and they calmed as the crusaders occupied their homes instead of cutting them down and torching the buildings. The men went to work constructing crude shelters out of the fishing boats and sails as their families cowered away from the knights and sergeants. Tancred gave strict orders to leave the people unmolested.

Ulf and Hugh watched from a distance atop a rocky bluff above the village, hearing the shouts and cries in the night. "At least they aren't slaughtering them," Ulf said.

"I fear for them. These people will be caught in the middle of every conflict to come between the Franks and the Fatimids."

"The common folk are often swept away in the winds of war."

Crusaders moved about the cluster of small hovels. A fire bloomed light over the village and men crowded around. A group of the mounted sergeants started to pass around a bladder filled with wine and cook food while others bedded down around the fire. The knights were taking whatever comfort they could find inside the tiny single-room homes. Their mounts were tied in a line running between two of the hovels, squires attending to the horses. The soft waves of the sea lapped the shore on the other.

The two elder warriors watched in silence as the crusaders ate and drank then curled upon the ground. Nothing appeared amiss. Yet they had not seen Galahad since their arrival, although there were at least a dozen sergeants and brothers of the Order intermingling with the other crusaders. The camp below became quieter as more of the men slept. Ulf kept an eye on the dozen guards standing vigilant in a rough semi-circle surrounding the village. Tancred was no fool. He understood they were in hostile territory.

A man barely recognizable emerged from a small hovel. He wore a coat of mail and sword, shield on his back, and a sack underneath his arm. He straightened himself to his full height, glancing toward the sea. "There," Ulf said, pointing. The knight walked through the camp. It was the way he walked that gave him away. A confident swagger, the same as his father's grandfather. "That's Galahad."

Hugh squinted. "Looks like him. You ever grow tired of killing him?"

"No." He thought about the countless times briefly. "I believe you were there for one."

"Was I? How we've grown long in tooth and soul." Hugh scratched his chin as he thought. "Near Paris?"

"It was."

"Should I add to your tally?"

Ulf rested a hand on Hugh's shoulder. His old comrade was eager to find his way back into battle. A fight that could get them both killed if they weren't careful. They needed to know what he was doing, and if he was isolated, an opportunity to cut him down would greatly level their odds against the Order.

"Only if we find him alone. The last thing I want is for a hundred men to ride us down."

"We've had worse odds," Hugh said with a dry laugh.

"Not when we had the choice."

"I know of your feud with his kin, but will you let me wet my blade for Agatha?"

Ulf nodded. "Yes, brother. I hope it will quench the flames of revenge burning in your soul."

"You and I both know that the flames never disappear," Hugh spat as if the words were a maggoty meat thwarting his tongue. "Only numbs the pain for a while."

"Yet we still seek it."

"We do."

The Order brother became a shadow along the shore trekking along the beach. Leaving their mounts, the two warriors jogged after him, weaving through short pines, white thorn, Valonia oaks and tall shrubs covered in pink, white, yellow, and red flowers. A goat trail took them closer to the shore, where the ground was sandier, slowing them. They knelt between short palms near the water.

The waves washed gently in the night, covering the sound of their approach. The moon cast an eerie glow with shadows three times longer than a man. Galahad made haste ahead of them, not running, but moving with purpose directly along the shoreline. He eventually stopped, and the warriors did as well, observing.

Galahad bent low and sparks flared outward from his feet, until he raised a lit candle high over his head. He hovered it in the air, using his other hand to shield the flame from the wind.

"He signals someone," Ulf muttered.

A dark shape moved along the water like a sea beast cutting through the waves for the shore.

"A boat," Hugh said.

"They whisk the Chalice away by sea."

The boat was manned by a single rower churning hard on the oars. It scraped the sand and rocks as it was driven on shore, and Galahad tossed the candle and waded into the waters to assist. The rower jumped into the sea with a splash, and with a mighty effort, both men beached the vessel.

"He departs?" Hugh asked. "Why leave Jerusalem with such a large escort only to sneak away in the night?"

"Safety in numbers."

Galahad handed the man a bag and they gripped forearms.

"The Chalice cannot be there?" Hugh asked, his voice swept away by the sea breeze. He peered along the beach. "I smell men in the wind."

"The wind is a fickle maiden this night." Ulf briefly considered the breeze, and the faint scent of men faded. His heart sped up as he watched the two men. *It cannot be.* If Galahad was secretly shipping the Chalice away, there was no time, only now. Once it left the Holy Land, the trail would be almost impossible to track. He bet it would go to the Order's lands in England, surrounded by hundreds of the Order's brothers and sergeants, locked away in a vault. Even with his prowess, he could not entertain attempting to retrieve the Chalice there. He would need an army such as the world had never seen, a thousand packs united, and those days were ash in the wind. A faint memory of another time, another army arrayed against the Order disappeared from his mind.

"It mustn't leave these shores," Ulf said. He glanced at his comrade. "We stop them."

Quietly, Hugh drew his plain sword, a soft sound scraping the leather. Ulf hefted his long axe into both hands. No words were needed. They walked along the abyss of death together, stalking forward. They picked up their pace and the two old men ran as stealthily as they could out of the weeds and onto the shoreline. Galahad and the boatman spoke quietly to one another, not noticing the two warriors gaining momentum in the darkness.

Ulf raised his long axe to his shoulder as they closed. Galahad and the sailor turned toward them. Neither fear nor anger crossed their faces, making Ulf's heart pound even harder, his perception of danger rising. *Why do they not react?* He had no time to consider the thought. For good or ill they would fight.

"Galahad!" Hugh shouted. "Meet my blade."

Galahad drew his sword, and the sailor raced back to his craft, splashing in the shallows. The Order brother braced for impact, taking a step back, swinging his shield from his back and over his torso, sword lifted in the ready behind him.

An evil scent flooded the air. The odor of many men both fearful and determined. It was accompanied by the distinct scent of horse sweat and dung.

"Loose!" Galahad shouted over his shield.

The two old warriors slowed their steps for a fraction of a second. A cluster of crossbowmen stood in the anchored boat. More peeled to the sides of the craft, aiming as they moved. The sound of crossbows loosing cut harshly through the night.

A step closer to the water, Hugh gave a soft cry as he took the brunt of the volley. The bolts sounding off as they hit him the same as a man tossing a dressed deer carcass on a wooden table. Hugh had no armor. No shield to protect him. The bolts layered his right side and arm. He fed his sword into his left hand.

Violent air crossed Ulf's cheeks as a bolt barely missed him. Then there was an explosion of pain. It shocked his body, crunching into his scale armor and through his mail, penetrating his flesh.

A rank of men-at-arms filed onto the shore with a shout, their armor dull despite the moon glinting from them, led by a brother bearing a red sun on a field of white. Galahad sprinted to them, catching himself as he stumbled, and they closed ranks in front of him in a protective shield wall. Exposed in the shallows, the crossbowmen hurried to reload while keeping their weapons dry. The thunder of hooves erupted the sands behind the old warriors, and a guard of mounted sergeants barreled down the sandy beach toward them, lances angled toward the moon, almost in salute.

"Hold your fire," called Galahad's voice.

Hugh and Ulf slowed and stopped. Each man's chest worked with vigor. Hugh bent over, haggard breaths sounding like a man breathing water. Six bolts buried deep, only the feathers visible. Ulf peered down at his own chest. He grimaced. Two bolts sprouted from his chest.

Ulf glared over his shoulder. The mounted sergeants slowed at a distance, raising their spear tips, a glinting black in the moonlight. There must be at least a Guard's worth of men. The cluster of men-at-arms was no less than twenty, the crossbowmen numbering roughly the same.

"Wolf, is it?" Galahad shouted at him.

Ulf stood taller, watching him over the rank of soldiers. He flung blood, running down his arm and off his fingertips. "It is Ulf Bodvarsson. Hand over the Chalice, and I will let you live longer."

"Chalice?" Galahad said with a laugh. "There is no chalice here. That is Bors's and Uthur's game." He studied Ulf for a moment, a small smile on his lips. "You want the Chalice as well? You ancients all want it for yourselves. Bors is already in Jaffa, soon to board a ship for England."

He is a deceiver by nature, yet it smells true. "There's a blockade. No ships will leave there."

"The Fatimids are men just like any other, they accept coin to look the other way. Your naiveté surprises me, but when you exposed yourself, the hunt began."

I am a fool. "He never could have traveled so fast through the wilderness."

Galahad smirked, trying to get a better view of Ulf in the dim light. "I know your name; my father spoke of you."

"You must have been young. Did you know him long?"

This brought a heavy silence from Galahad. "I did not. He was taken from me at a young age."

"I thought so. Which one was your father? The pox-marked bastard or the earless dog?"

"He'd lost his ears as a young man."

Ulf dug into his memories of how he had cut down Galahad's father. It had been raining for days in the highlands. The rain had decimated any means of tracking, but Galahad, the impetuous bastard, continued to try and hunt down Ulf and his pack. They never would have found him either, if Galahad hadn't decided to torch a town filled with innocents for not giving up their whereabouts. A town Ulf had no connection to, but Galahad would not stop until one of them was dead.

Galahad had rested in the massacred village with his company of spear and horse. They hadn't even known they were surrounded until Ulf and his men had torn through them like a scythe through stalks of tall grass, laying men low, until the last man standing was the earless bastard with a black eagle on a field of crimson red painted on his shield.

"I see you still bear his crest," Ulf said.

Galahad sneered beneath a sharp nose. "I was thinking about turning it in for the red cross of Christ. It may be time to start a new chapter for the kin of Galahad."

"Eagle or cross, matters not. I'm still death to your line."

"Brave words for dying men."

"I took my time with your grandfather. Did your father tell you this story?"

Galahad was silent, and Ulf grinned at him as he flung more blood from his hand. "He was an ugly bastard. Looked a lot like you. Saved him for last." His eyes stabbed at the men before him, and he coughed and spat to the side. He wiped his hand, seeing blood on his lips. The wounds in his chest were warming, instead of cooling.

Hugh dropped to one knee, using his sword to keep him upright.

Silver-tipped bolts.

"The sons of goats were ready for us," Hugh said with a hack.

"That's silver, Ulf, tainting your blood as we speak," Galahad shouted. "Difficult to heal with silver stuck four inches in your chest, huh? You wouldn't believe how easy it was to create them with the riches this land holds."

Ulf grimaced, turning his eyes to Hugh. His companion pushed himself to his feet, straightening his back, strength escaping him with every breath.

"I don't have long, old friend," Hugh said.

"Do not let the enemy see you falter." Ulf took a step forward, lifting his voice past the silver pain, his chin rising in defiance. "I took his hands first." He removed one bolt from his chest with an open-mouthed snarl. "Then I took his feet." He removed the other bolt and spat on the sand. "We let him cry in the mud. Handless.

Footless. He cried in the mud for hours and I sat and ate, watching him flounder about with his stumps. Until I tired of his cries for mercy. Then I took his head." He glared at Galahad, waiting for a rebuttal. "Didn't bother to bury him or his men. Let their bones bleach in the cold sun and the crows thanked us."

"You hear the devil's words, men? He speaks of the murder of our fathers and grandfathers," Galahad called. "He expects no mercy and shall receive none. He is a blemish on this land. When this is done, we will take his head back to Uthur and decorate our hall so all the brothers may spit upon the Hunted known as Ulf the Coward." The Order brothers and sergeants gave a defiant cheer, raising their weapons ready to charge.

"If you had seen what he'd done with those hands, you would have done the same, kin or not." He hefted his long axe with both hands eying the line of men-at-arms. Despite their courage, there was always a weak ring in the armor. He searched for the first man he'd bring down, the weakest shield in their wall. Blood trickled down his chest and soaked the tops of his undergarments, leaving them warmly damp.

"Many of you men have waited for a day to wet your blade in a Hunted hide. Today is that day. God guides us to victory."

"And what about those people in Jerusalem?" Hugh shouted; his voice stronger than it should have been. "What about that woman and children you slaughtered?"

"They were shadowkin. Bedding down with the demons themselves. We did the city a service by watching them burn. The earth will be a better place without *them* and without you, whitebeard."

Ulf gave Hugh a nod. "The journey is long. The journey is hard. But it is yours. Even your death is uniquely yours. And we do not go into the endless darkness without baring our fangs."

"We take as many of them as we can with us, brother."

Ulf faced Galahad's men. His focus took him out of his own body. A detached existence prepared to exact brutal violence upon his enemies.

The sun cracked the horizon over the hills to the east. Light poured over the beach. A horse whinnied behind them. Each wave that gently rolled onto the shore. Every creak of leather. Every man shifting his shield against the others. The sweat running down their necks. A crossbowman's eye twitching as he stayed his aim. Ulf's senses caught everything.

His inner wolf bit at its cage. It paced, ready to unleash its violent fury upon the enemy. His grip tightened on his axe. "You already shot first. What do you propose?" Ulf called to Galahad. The words were meaningless, blood would be spilled. Then softer he said to Hugh, "Have to make it to the shieldwall or the horses will ride us into the ground." Being crushed a horse wouldn't kill them, but it was damn hard to fight with three feet of lance sticking through your chest. Painful experience told him that. And if one landed an impaling below to the skull, it would be over quicker.

Hugh gave a short nod. "It has been a life well lived."

"Our song will be sung for kings."

"It will be a race to the shield wall."

"Wind in our hair."

"Just as the old days."

Ulf closed his eyes for a moment, remembering a thousand memories flashing before him. Love, honor, victory, sadness, and defeat, life was all these moments and more.

Galahad's voice interrupted him. "Uthur would see you in chains."

Ulf looked down at his weather-beaten hands then back at Galahad. "I cannot be caged."

"I have offered you mercy which is far greater than your kind deserves."

"A mule could kick your face with honor-cloven hooves and you would still have less than a pile of shit." His eyes searched the heavenly darkness. "By the steel of my axe, I make an oath to Odin to take your head as I have your father and grandfather before you."

There was no more point in waiting. Wait long enough and a man might lose his nerve or the initiative in acting as the aggressor. Ulf charged, Hugh a step behind. The two ancient *Ulfhednar* sprinted over the sand like men gone mad. They were berserkers of the old days wielding the Old Ways, enchanted warrior skalds, unfelled and undeterred by any spear or blade. Weapons were held high, their war songs overcoming the crash of the sea.

Galahad snarled and lifted his sword high into the air and screamed, "Loose!"

Bolts whispered death from their flank. The crossbowmen bent over, hurrying to reload, praying the enemy did not turn upon them. The sands shook as the horsemen charged from behind. Ulf sprinted for the center and the towering soldier anchoring their line braced himself for impact. *Brave man.*

Spear points and swords bristled outward of the manmade hedgehog. Always safety in numbers. Ulf's axe hovered over his shoulder as he prepared himself for a glorious death. He would meet Odin awash in a deluge of his enemies' blood.

At the last moment, Ulf adjusted his course, leaping suddenly for their weakest man. A spear jabbed at him, darting over his shoulder. He swept another to the side, the sergeant unable to adjust his aim. Crowfeeder's blade arced through the air then over his shield. The sergeant screamed as his chin split like a pink apple cleaved in two. Using the beard of his axe, Ulf ripped his shield from his hands, tossing the man out of line. He sprawled out to die covered in blood and sand.

A hole had been made in their line. A weakness exposed. There was a crash to his right as Hugh threw himself into their shields, but sword darting at their faces. There was no time to cover his friend's attack. Ulf rammed the shaft of his long axe into another sergeant's face, then raked his axe-head through the footman in the rank behind, who fell grasping a growing gash in his neck.

Ulf was the lord of the dead. Their line crumbled before him. A sergeant tripped and fell trying to escape. Crowfeeder showed him no mercy. The long axe crashed into the sergeant's skull, denting everything grievously inward. Warm crimson rain washed over his face. A raven god among corpses. He turned his head skyward and howled.

"Odin owns you all!"

CHAPTER 19

The battle song raged around them, the dusky morning magnifying every clash and each scream. It was a cacophony of crashing metal into metal interspersed with the slap of metal into flesh punctuated by the cries of the fallen. Donning his helm, Galahad anchored the right side of his line, the tall and slender Second Son Alymere in the center. Sergeant-Brother Edwin, as the most senior footman, held his ground on the left.

Galahad was not here by chance. His ambush had been plotted far in advance. He'd had the Order's infantry and crossbowmen under First Brother Mador circumvent the village through the rough terrain. He knew they had struggled navigating the lands, and they must be exhausted, but they held their tongue. If they survived this encounter, he would see them rewarded.

He knew the pack would follow Tancred's host but would never reveal themselves with such a formidable company of mounted men. Their lupine nature made them vile and deceitful creatures that only emerged when they thought the odds were in their favor. So, he manufactured a situation that would draw them from the shadows, and they'd taken the bait, walking into the trap.

To be the esteemed brother who brought down the infamous

Ulf Bodvarsson, Hunted of legend, would grow Galahad's prestige and standing as high as any of the other Twelve. His reputation would supersede even Bors. Most of the men in the Order were mortal men. They lived in the here and now, not in the past, and would wish to honor him as their champion.

His chapter in the tome of brothers would be earmarked for others to study his strategy for victory. The night Galahad the 9th slew the vile beast Ulf. Many brothers and sergeants would have their names listed as deceased before this morning was through, but they would all be given their honor, a scribe scribbling their mark over its pages, a bland and nondescript note of the horror that awaited them.

Sergeant Oswald was dead, his head split in two, his body face down in the sand. Brother Hector lay bleeding in a heap, the rings of his mail coat twisted and bent, the axe cleaving between his neck and shoulder with such force the crunch made Galahad's stomach turn. Sergeant-Brother Thomas dug his elbows into the sand, crawling as his insides stretched behind him.

Galahad's Horse Guard led by Brother Richard of Somerset, the best horseman under his command, an expert with spear and lance, had drawn up short in their charge for fear of riding over his own men, and the crossbowmen had ceased shooting for the same reason. Leaving the infantry to bear the brunt of the Hunted assault.

Galahad shoved his shield into a sergeant's back that was losing ground before the other Hunted, the swipes of his sword quick and precise for such an ancient man.

"Mador!" Galahad shouted. His feet slid in the sand as they were driven backward, straining to keep the man in front of him upright. "Mador!" He had hesitated to call in the spearmen so early, but he had no choice. Two more sergeants were already near the center.

"For the Pendragon!" came a shout. Twenty spearmen emerged from the trees. They jogged down the sandy slopes, mail shirts whispering. They formed the last wall in the box around the

Hunted, points outward in close rank. First Brother Mador led them from the front, bushy mustache flared out, holding a spear over his head, his shoulders thick, a scowl of determination on his face. He was quick and as strong as an ox, and he showed no fear in the face of the beasts. He kept his men together, holding the line steady as they charged.

The appearance of more footmen drew the attention of Ulf. The warrior swung his long axe wildly over his head, knocking away spear thrusts. The two Hunted grew further apart. Breathing heavily, Alymere shoved his men back into order. "Form up!" he shouted at them. The ranks rapidly closed over the fallen.

The horsemen danced uneasily around the edges. Brother Richard, his shield adorned with the stag and cross, drove his mount into the fray with a shout. If Richard survived this day, he may earn himself entrance to the Hunter's Rite, those elite warriors in their ranks who had slain one of the Hunted. At the least, elevation to first brother. He charged, lance couched, and drove it into Hugh's shoulder blade, blood splashing as the red point burst through his chest.

The ancient Hunted bellowed. He lifted his head to the sky, the force of the blow driving him to his knees. The footmen had been trained to press the attack, but they were not careless. They hacked at him from all angles. It was the only way to bring down beasts such as these. Cut them steadily to pieces. The removal of limbs always proved advantageous, as the beasts could not heal from the blows, hindering their ability to fight.

A regular man could not hope to succeed against one on his own. The Hunted were much faster and stronger than any man, even when they hadn't taken their wolf-form. The process to take one down took impeccable discipline and courage in the face of certain death. The Order's training focused on small unit cohesion; without it they would be slain easily. There was no room for individual bravery when facing the beasts.

The spear-wielding sergeants helped with their long reach; the possibility to pin the Hunted so others could deal lethal blows. The silver crossbow bolts helped even more. To engage a Hunted without silver-tipped bolts or arrows was a risky and often deadly endeavor. Each tactic his men employed to perfection.

Hugh's body shook, and his bellow turned into a howl. He gained his feet and reached behind him, spinning in a wild circle, his robes twirling red. Screams erupted from Mador's rank of spearmen. Ulf danced through them, wielding his long axe as if it were as light as a rose petal. A man fell, holding his belly. Before he hit the sand, another screamed as the blade bit through muscle and bone. He dropped like a rock, clutching a spurting stump below his knee.

"Richard! To Mador!" Galahad pointed at the other rank. Ulf could escape if he cut his way through them. Richard barked at his men. They formed a tight unit, stirrup to stirrup, and wheeled toward them, gaining speed. Ulf broke free of the enclosure of men. Three more spearmen lay dead or dying. Ulf flowed among them like a shadow of death, untouchable by blade or spear, and if they did touch him, he remained unfazed.

A mace crunched into Hugh's skull. The Hunted sank to his knees, two spearheads sticking through his chest. His sword still jabbed dangerously. The six silver-tipped bolts still stuck out from Hugh's right side, the silver diminishing his ability to heal.

Galahad's men continued to hack and swing at him, and Hugh could barely fend them off. Blades cut through his skin revealing deep shades of red. Each blow stealing more life and emboldening his men. Two of his spearmen rammed their spears through Hugh's upper chest, lifting him from his knees and pinning him to the sand.

The old man coughed and snarled. Lifting his head, his body strained against the spearmen, but he could not extract himself. More footmen rushed forward to deal the killing blow.

"Halt!" Galahad commanded. His footmen stopped, forming a circle with their shields around the dying man, weapons ready to finish it. Galahad shoved his way through them. He carried his sword on his shoulder. He gazed at the elder beast with as much pity reserved for a demon about to be sent to Hell. "Your curse will be extinguished in this morning light."

Blood dribbled from Hugh's mouth, running down his chin. He breathed hard, precious air difficult to come by. Galahad observed the wretched man. "Looks like we got a lung."

Hugh tried to lift his sword with his immobilized arm.

Galahad gently placed his sword on the elder's neck. "Are you going to Embrace the Darkness?" A wolf-head trophy was much more dynamic than a man. He cocked his head to the side. "It will be futile."

Hugh gave a short snort and lifted his chin. "I would not give you the pleasure. I will take the form I came in this world when I leave it."

"You accounted yourself well, all things considered." Three of his men lay dead, another soon to join them. The spearmen and horsemen were still corralling Ulf, keeping him at bay with spears and swords, the man seemingly made of endless violence.

"I sent men to the afterlife that should have been sent earlier." Hugh gulped. "Ulf will avenge me and the children."

Galahad turned his head toward the rising sun, the warmth of the coming day washing over them, the same as victory. God's blessing bestowed upon them. He tapped his sword upon Hugh's chest. "Those were your kin?"

"Not of my loin but of my love."

Galahad closed his eyes, embracing the rays of sun for a moment before he spoke. "A few less shadowkin in the world makes it a better place." He shrugged his shoulders. "They weren't the ones we were after, but it drew you out of your den to die."

"Fight me so that I may die on my feet. The old way."

"As you wish." The spearmen ripped their shafts free, and Hugh lay in the sand, gasping. The old man gradually pushed himself upright. Blood leaked from dozens of wounds. His arm lay useless at his side. If he was truly a man, his advanced age and severe wounds would have killed him in a minute, at least from the violent shock, but this man wavered before him still able to stand. Galahad regripped the leather handle on his shield, feeling its reinforced weight, and held his sword over the top in a defensive stance.

Hugh pushed the lance back through his chest with an exhausted sigh, then removed the bolts one by one. The wood hit the sands with a soft thump, and he grimaced and took in an uneasy breath. His blood flowed freely now. He bent painfully to the ground, hefting his sword with effort, then lunged at Galahad, but he had already anticipated as much. Galahad deflected his sword thrust with his shield, and another as the old man came back around.

"Rahh!" Hugh cried. He staggered and gripped his slick sword handle harder. Galahad kept his sword hovering over his shield in proper form. He was a scorpion, tail poised to strike.

The old man renewed his attack, this time swiping low at his legs. Galahad danced away, and his opponent arched his sword over the top, in a swing meant to smash in his skull. He sidestepped again. The old warrior stumbled forward. In a few steps he regained his feet, turned, and charged Galahad again. The elder threw his body into Galahad, who used his shield to spin away. The old man fell into the sand. He rolled to his side with a groan and tried to get to his feet, collapsing again.

"Are you sure you don't want to embrace your corruption? You may extend this pitiful existence."

"Never give you the satisfaction."

Hugh stood, wavering unsteadily from side to side. The elder couldn't have much blood left running through his veins. His next strike was overly slow, a mere snowflake fluttering to the ground. Much too slow for Galahad not to act. He parried it with his shield and thrust his sword with methodical precision, a movement he'd done thousands of times. His blade bit into Hugh's unprotected belly, sinking in deep, the old man letting out a gasp. Galahad held the sword in place as Hugh collapsed, clutching at the blade with gnarled hands, but Galahad would not relinquish his weapon.

"Your time has come to an end." He leaned closer. "Know this. The sun rises on a new generation of Hunters, and it sets on the abomination of your kind. You will only be remembered as legend and myth, an evil that has been swept away and forgotten."

Hugh's lips shook with hate. "The wars against our brothers are always the fiercest."

"We are nothing like you. I am nothing like you."

Hugh coughed, blood flowing from his lips, turning into a smile. "I leave this life with the knowledge of a thousand." His voice dropped. "You will never win this war."

Ripping the sword from his body with a crimson flourish, Galahad snarled. Hugh groaned and bent his head to his chest, ragged breaths were all he had left, exposing the nape of his neck beneath strands of hair the color of snow. Galahad dropped his shield and gripped the sword with two hands. He swung. The razor-sharp edge seared its way through flesh, muscle, and bone until the blade stuck into the sand. The old man's head rolled end over end; granules tossed into the air. The body soon followed.

Galahad drank in the smell of fresh metallic blood. Euphoria tickled the base of his skull. His men lifted a bold shout. "For the Stag!" He breathed it in with a grim smile, the taste of victory galloping through his veins. His legend grew with a sword stroke.

"Galahad," came a voice.

He blinked as he came back from the ecstasy.

Edwin pointed. "It breaks free!"

"Ulf," Galahad snarled. He pointed his sword. "Rally the men! This ends today." He turned toward the crossbowmen standing in the shallows. "Stay close behind us." He waved them forward. His line of sergeants had shrunk to thirteen, some bleeding from their last encounter.

"Awaken Hunter!" Alymere shouted, pounding his shield as he led them over the sloping sands. "For the Pendragon!" his men shouted, following behind. Galahad offered an arm to Brother

Vincent and hauled him upright. He collected Hugh's head from the sand and followed his men.

They topped a sandy crest and closed on the other fight. Bodies of the fallen lay writhing in the sand and rocks. The spearmen had made a tight double-line with Mador at their center. They were layered, giving off the impression of a badly ravaged hedgehog.

Brother Richard had formed his Guard along the other flank in a slightly looser formation, and Alymere with Galahad's men formed the last piece of their steel triangle. In the center, ensnared, was their wounded prey, a roaring bear surrounded by a pack of dogs. Galahad the hunter with his spear poised to deal the fatal blow.

Ulf howled as he spun his axe overhead in circles. He would feint a rush toward the spearmen, then turn, making for the horsemen. Every time he did, the other group would tighten the noose of armored men around him. Galahad was surprised he hadn't embraced the darkness.

"Ulf!" Galahad called at him.

The man continued his wild attacks, keeping the men around him at bay.

"Your friend is gone," Galahad called. He took Hugh's head and tossed it in the center. Ulf stopped swinging and came to rest, his axe held in both hands. His eyes lingered upon his comrade's. His chest heaved with battle-wind, his eyes aflame with a primal rage, but the sight of his ally dampened his fury with the sobriety of an impending death.

"He died on his knees," Galahad shouted. "Surrender and you will be shown mercy."

Ulf's eyes flashed a sparkling golden star, a sun reaching its fingers to set on a field of grain. His eyes diverted to the morning sun, casting its light over the dead men on the seashore. Waves tossed a man, rolling his body onto shore and then dragging him out to sea, only to be swept back to shore again, the process repeating itself.

The Hunted squinted in his direction. "Your mercy means nothing. Your word means less. Let us settle this as warriors. Let the gods determine who lives."

Challenging a man's honor in front of his men presented Galahad with a precarious situation. He had already gained the respect of his men by killing a Hunted in single combat, the likes of which would be immortalized in the Brothers' Tome. To kill two in single combat in a day, would only ever be topped by Uthur and a few others throughout their history. None would openly doubt his courage if he rejected the offer.

There was little to gain by risking his life. He would already receive praise for his ambush, and pending Bors's successful departure, he may even earn himself elevation to First Spear, greatest warrior of the Order and right hand to Uthur, for Bors would not vacate his position as Field Marshal, general of the Order's forces in battle. However, Galahad cared not for that rainy island which the Order inhabited, nor did he care for standing his post as Uthur's First Spear. Following the old wretch around, would be a living nightmare for him.

Chances of victory in single combat were slim. The Hunted before him was a warrior of infamous legend, far greater than Galahad, with enough strength to lift boulders and speed matching a galloping horse, driven by the endurance of a team of oxen. His wolf blood pure and ancestral. Galahad's bloodline was diluted at best, passed through generations, each one weakening from the first of his name. He knew it would be a fatal mistake, but he couldn't turn down the chance to avenge his forefathers. *Is this how my father and grandfather fell before this monster? Our pride threatened until we took action.* The moon and stars only aligned for this kind of meeting once in a couple generations. Two tidal waves crashing at the same place and time. If he could win, he could bring the monster's reign of terror to an end. Where there was opportunity, risk lurked nearby. As a calculating man, his stomach rolled inside him, knowing his choice was an illogical one.

"I accept your challenge."

"No," came Alymere's voice. Ulf's eyes turned toward the new champion of the Order. "I will stand in your stead. Do me this honor," Alymere shouted firmly, he bowed his head in deference to Galahad.

Galahad blinked, judging the ever-noble Alymere. *What do you hope to gain here?* Brave words from a brave man, who probably wouldn't be around long. Alymere stood to gain even more than Galahad from defeating Ulf. To bring Uthur Ulf's head would garner great honor to his name. It is possible even the position of First Spear may be bestowed upon him instead. It would be a suitable vocation for the noble knight. *Perhaps you may wear this animal down before I face him, easing my path to victory.*

"Your bravery is unmatched, brother. May your blade strike true," Galahad nodded to his fellow Second Son. *Fool.*

Brother Alymere stepped into the ring of men and metal. He steadied himself, loosening his wrist by twirling his sword in a circle. While his blood was as diluted if not more so than Galahad's, he had survived several encounters, his long reach was his greatest asset in a fight, his every movement embodying confident nobility.

A chant sounded out from the circle of sergeants and brothers. "Hunt. Hunt. Hunt." They beat their weapons upon their shields in time to the chant, banging them over and over.

Ulf grinned wide, a ravenous wolf sniffing out a fat calf. "A sacrificial lamb to the slaughter."

"I fear not Satan's words for God guides my hand. His Son my shield." Alymere lifted his sword high in the air, it sparkled with the rising sun. "Awaken, Hunter!"

"Evoco venatores!" Galahad said, whispering the ancient battle cry of the Order.

Deep sand consumed his footsteps as he charged. His sword was a blur as it cut the air. But Ulf was there, parrying them and dancing away from the knight. He countered with two overhead swings and Alymere barely moved his head from the second, his helm ringing. They circled each other, and Ulf switched his hands back and forth, threatening to strike from either side. The sergeants continued their chant.

The Second Son stepped forward, feinting left and lunging right, his sword razoring past Ulf's ear. Blood spilled; Ulf snarled. The brothers and sergeants let out a cheer. Alymere composed himself, gaining confidence in his enemy's blood. He went on the offensive again. Galahad was impressed by the brother's relentlessness.

Alymere parried an axe strike meant to cleave his shield, then slashed at Ulf's exposed leg. He rapidly followed by trying to cut across his belly, but Ulf rolled and spun around Alymere with more speed than a man of his stature should allow, as if he knew Alymere's every thought. From behind, Ulf hooked Alymere's sword arm with his axe, and using his other hand to pin him upright, sheared the arm from his body with a mighty rip.

Blood fountained skyward, spraying the nearest spearmen. Sergeants turned away. The chant died upon their lips. One of them vomited behind his shield. Weapons and shields came to rest. Ulf kicked the stunned brother in the back, sending him crashing into the sand. His blood pumped into the golden grains, disappearing.

A finger twitched on his separated limb. Unable to free his arm from his shield, Alymere flopped over the sand in silent horror. Ulf bent down and shook the sword free of his lifeless hand. He tossed it at Galahad, the limb rolling to his feet.

"Mere sheep. I tire of brutalizing your lessers." He pointed his axe in Galahad's direction. "Let me introduce you to your kin. Galahad the Cockless, Galahad the Limp, Galahad the soon to be Headless. Fight me now and show you have a shred of honor."

Scared eyes watched Alymere continue his struggle across the sand. His men may break if Galahad fell. Sergeant-Brother Edwin and First Brother Mador would attempt to keep them together, but he doubted if any of his men would walk away from here.

Once you ran you were as good as dead. The Hunted loved the hunt.

His cheeks reddened as his pride surfaced. He lifted his chin, peering at his men, his brothers and sergeants. Many faces were missing, but these men were steadfast, hard eyes and iron spines in the morning light. This monster had desecrated his kin for generations. A curse that was seemingly impervious to overcome, a bane upon the name Galahad.

He could not best this freakish monster in single combat. It was simply beyond his ability. His eyes found Alymere still crawling through the ranks of spearmen. None dared to give him aid for fear of exposing themselves to the deadly warrior. The brother continued onward, as if he wished to die in the sea.

He had no choice. He took a step inside the ring of men. He must have victory this day. No matter the method. "Show no mercy! Slay the beast!" he shouted. He pointed his sword in Ulf's direction. There was a glimmer of surprise in the man's eyes. *Never do as your enemy expects.* "Loose!" Bolts flew, sprouting feather and wooden shafts into Ulf's body. Finding what tattered shreds of bravery they still had, the circle of warriors surged forward.

The Hunted howled in rage. He bounded toward Galahad, chopping and hacking at the men between them. A spear took him in the side. He snapped the shaft with his axe, crying out in pain. He threw himself into the shields of the footmen in front of Galahad, driving them all rapidly backward. More spears darted at him, and he created space with his axe.

There was a blur, and Galahad ducked. The long axe crashed into the sergeant next to him taking him off his feet. Ulf stood weaponless. Galahad's men hesitated, fearing him. He ran a hand down the side of his scale armor stripping it in a flash. Then he flung his mail coat to the sands holding his arms out from his sides.

"Attack!" Galahad screamed. But no man moved as Ulf embraced the darkness. He howled as he transformed into a wolf.

If there was ever a doubt in his men's mind that they fought the devil's spawn, it was gone now. The silver should have slowed this progression, but this creature transformed in rapid speed. "More bolts!" Galahad cried.

Gray fur threaded together with Ulf's beard, thickening in muscle, flesh, and skin like armor. His wounds were still apparent, but they too diminished in severity. Its snout grew and spearhead-like claws took the place of his hands. Fangs like curved knives curled under wide open lips. Spittle dripped from his open mouth as it welcomed the flesh of man.

A horse reared in terror. They'd been trained for this, but many had been lost over the course of the crusade, and now all the mounts were not prepared to stand before such terror. The crossbowman behind him sucked in a breath. The spearmen wavered.

"Hold the line!" Mador yelled at them. Their spears shook in hands. They obeyed begrudgingly facing the jaws of death itself.

"Get those crossbows loaded," Galahad hissed behind him. The crossbowmen rushed to obey, fingers fumbling under pressure. His eyes found Brother Richard, his nostrils flared; he grasped a lance tightly in his hand. Sensing his tension, his horse stomped its front two legs.

"Charge!"

The horsemen charged. The beast turned to face them. The horsemen kept rank, urging their mounts forward, lances slanted downward to impale the beast. The wolf-man crouched low, tensing before springing into the air, a blur of fur and muscle.

There was a moment when every man watched in terror unbelieving the abilities of the man turned monster. That moment turned into reality as the creature landed atop the two nearest riders, breaking both rider and horse bones alike. Horses collapsed screaming, throwing their riders. Lances wavered, hitting air or the ground. Another horseman was flung from his mount as the beast ran a claw over its neck and head, shredding flesh and rending bone. The giant man wolf did not hesitate. It bounded after the disorganized riders as they tried to turn. A claw speared through a man's neck and ripped another man's belly as he passed by. Mail armor was silk before its razor-sharp claws.

"Pin him!" Galahad shouted at Mador. The first brother blinked, but he urged his men forward, voice shaking. "Slay the beast!"

The spearmen ran toward the wolf. It turned on them and threw itself into their spears. Shafts snapped. Spears grazed harmlessly off fur as strong as ring mail. One had to be intentional when the Hunted reached their most dangerous state, and Ulf was the strongest he'd ever seen, even in human form.

Helmets deformed into unrecognizable pieces of metal, crushing skulls. Knife-like claws diced across a man's face, separating his jaw, mouth gaping like a fish. Mador's men broke like dry kindling before Ulf's inferno.

Don't run. There is no surer way of death. No more than a man could outrun a horse. Richard was reforming his remaining horsemen, waving his sword over his head, his lance lost.

Ulf bounded onto a man who'd already dropped his spear, bending near his neck and ripping his head backwards dragging head and white spine with it.

"Shoot him," Galahad hissed at the crossbowmen, now staring dumbfounded at the beast. "Give me that." He grabbed the crossbow from the nearest man, aimed in on the beast's back, and loosed. The bolt struck true into its shoulder, and it roared in pain.

"Rush it! We have him!" Galahad shouted, but his words rang hollow. Sometimes it was enough to just believe the falsehood. He raced over the sand. He was faster than the others, closing the distance even quicker than he should dare. The beast turned. Galahad's throat dropped into his stomach. Blood sprayed from the beast's foul mouth. Galahad raised his shield. A claw penetrated leather and thick wood, and with a rip, Galahad, his shield, and his body were thrown into the air.

He clattered and rolled over the ground, his body rotating too fast to orient himself. When he stopped, he shook his head, blinking away the sand. He lifted a hand to his ribs. A few were cracked. *Far too close.* The screams and shouts of men carried into the air. His men fought bravely, and without the intervention of the horsemen, they would be slaughtered.

Two of the horsemen managed to plant their lances into the creature. It staggered the beast, giving the infantry time to regain their footing. Richard's horse danced around it, chopping at the beast's skull, cutting its snout and putting out its eye. His horse emitted a shrill shriek as a wild claw caught its belly, spilling its insides.

Galahad crawled on all fours and stood, unable to locate his sword. He drew the dagger from his belt. He had only drawn it a few times, and only in the face of the Hunted. It had been his great-grandfather's blade, only uncovered a hundred years after the fact, an artifact held in reverence within a monastery in the hills of Navarre. Local legend held that it had slain a great dragon, the dragon's breath having melted the blade, slaying his great-grandfather in the process and earning him a sort of local sainthood. It was said to bear mystical properties bestowed upon the dagger blessed by angels. He simply called it the dagger with the red hilt.

Truly, it had been a weapon forged specifically to kill the Hunted. The blade was a blend of silver, steel, and a one-of-a-kind ore they called the Sunstone. The result was a metal the founding brothers named Lightsbane for the way light appeared to fade in its presence.

He gripped the pugio-styled knife and blindly rushed forward. The beast backhanded a brother, sending him to the ground. It arched its neck, biting into a sergeant's mail around his shoulder. The man stood paralyzed as the teeth cut through the armor as easily as if he was bare chested.

"Face me!" shouted Richard. He sprinted at the Hunted, only sword in hand. Galahad ran faster. One of his men tugged at him as he raced past. "Help me," he cried, blood covering his hands. Galahad brushed him away and jumped over the bodies of two crossbowmen.

The beast held Richard over his head, claws wrapped around his neck. He reached backward for the killing strike. Mador's helmetless form barreled in from the other flank, blood running down his face. He rammed his spear into Ulf's side. *An opening.* The beast howled, swinging a mighty arm into Mador. The man sailed into the sandy ground, and a moment later, Galahad collided with it.

The dagger pierced both fur and muscle. It bit harder than a regular blade, sliding into the beast with ease. Ulf roared and released Richard. The brother fell to the ground with a yell and jangle of mail. He scrambled away. Galahad fell backward as the beast spun, trying to grasp the hilt. Unable to, it howled again. The wolf bounded on all fours, then on two legs, snatching the long axe before it disappeared through the trees. Galahad blinked, watching the trees shake where the Hunted had once been as if it all was a waning nightmare.

Richard rubbed his neck, gaining his feet. Five remaining mounted sergeants turned their horses in circles, looking down at the two brothers not wanting the orders to pursue. Richard coughed violently then grasped his sword. "Get me a horse. We must hunt it down."

Galahad shook his head, catching his breath. "It will die. My dagger struck true." His command was made of corpses and to-be-corpses, only about half remained of almost sixty brothers and sergeants.

A storm of riders galloped down the beach, flags fluttered in the rough sea winds, horse manes flew wild. Lances glinted in the rising sun. Tancred emerged as their leader. Lance in hand, he galloped right to them before yanking his reins to stop his horse.

"By God, what has happened here? Point the direction of the fight and we will avenge thee."

Bodies and limbs were strewn about the beach. Two men rolled in the waves where they had crawled only to expire in the sea.

Galahad's arm screamed where its claws had cut evenly interspersed lacerations over his forearm. It would heal much quicker than the average man, but not quick enough. His own blood flowed down the tips of his fingers in crimson rivers of red.

"I am afraid this battle is complete."

"I beseech you, my good knight. Point the way they went, and we will exact our vengeance." Tancred turned his horse in a circle. A crossbowman held his belly while his comrade tried to push back in the tentacles of his insides. He cried piteously, his head rolling back and forth.

"It was one of them," Galahad said, catching his breath.

The color drained from Tancred's cheeks. "One that we've spoken of? The demons?"

"Two. One lays over there, dead, by my own hand. The other will die before the day's end."

"How do you know this?"

"I placed the blade into his heart."

Galahad sheathed his sword, using his other arm sparingly. He reached for his shield and found it broken and maimed beyond repair. He tossed the shredded wood back onto the beach, and finding another painted white with a red cross, he hefted it.

"I would see this monster."

Galahad spoke over him. "I have wounded that need care." The Order and their allies had been savaged by the two beasts, but while the cost was high, so was the reward. They had brought down two ancient Hunted, renown warriors in their own right. It should be a time of great celebration.

Two of the spearmen carried Brother Simon's headless body, draping him across the back of a horse. Richard assisted Alymere onto his own mount. *Alymere yet lived? Perhaps his bloodline is stronger than we know.*

Galahad stared down the beach. "There are greater threats than those animals. Threats to Jerusalem." The sun was rising on a new day and a new world. "The Saracens are coming from the south."

Tancred squinted and waved a couple of leather armored

turcopoles. He spoke to them and pointed. They galloped down the beach, bows in hand.

"They are coming in force," Galahad said, raising his chin. His true purpose would lie in these lands, and the Fatimids stood in the way of that future. Now, it was time to carve out his place in the new world. Bors could handle the rest. He approached an unmanned horse. He raised a hand, and the horse jerked its head back. "Shhh, there, there." He grabbed the reins and leapt atop him. The horse tossed its head.

"First Brother Mador, see that the wounded are cared for in the village."

He wiped blood from above his eyes. "I would go with you, lord." His mustache pushed out, both deliberate and dutiful.

"We will be back by nightfall. We need our men able to ride by then."

Mador nodded his head fiercely. He pounded his chest in salute. This day had earned Galahad the respect of many amongst his men.

"Brother Richard, gather those horsemen that are able."

"Yes, lord," he said, calling to the mounted sergeants. Galahad saluted, fist to his chest. He turned to Tancred. The young lord understood the bond between warriors. "You may have this honor, sir."

Galahad gave him a smile. "Deus vult!" he shouted and spurred his mount. The men responded in kind, and the sea breeze ushered them southward.

CHAPTER 20

The day passed in an uneasy stagger. The three warriors took turns manning the minaret, scouring the land around Ramla for signs of Bors. With each passing hour, the candle dripped, and precious time melted away for Cutnose. Marya's words became tenser with each passing shift. Arnulf was distant. Each embrangled in their own worry. Repeatedly, they asked if he felt Bors's presence, yet the dull ache in the back of his skull remained distant. His own end loomed before him like an executioner's axe lifting higher and higher until it fell upon his neck.

Dusk came for him, and he settled in at his humble table, sharing bread and water with Mohammed and Marya by candle-light, the stones refreshingly cool compared to the mid-day heat. Cutnose did not begin eating ravenously as all soldiers do, but slowly munched each morsel of bread, trying to contrive a way out of his plight. The blind man sensed their dread and ate quietly, ingesting the meager sustenance and internal thoughts.

"They should have been back by now," Cutnose said. He waited a moment, watching Marya eat. "Night is upon us."

"I am not blind."

Mohammed gulped down his bread. "Blind men see too."

"I meant no insult."

"I could hear it in your voice."

She stared at Cutnose with venom.

"What are we going to do? No Bors, no Ulf, and my time is running out."

"I am well aware of our current predicament. I have not decided on a course to take."

"There is no true path that your heart doesn't take," Mohammed said.

Cutnose ate more bread, but it was plain, and he wasn't hungry. He wondered if this is what men facing the gallows felt, an excited desperation with no way out and no relief.

"I'm going to relieve Arnulf," Marya said, standing.

"Courage and effort mean nothing if not put to purpose."

"Don't mean to dampen your philosophical rant, but none of it means nothing if you're dead neither," Cutnose said.

Mohammed smiled, eyes staring beyond Cutnose. "And we all die. Does anything a man does mean anything? Are we all lost to fate? Or do the actions of men ring through the passages of time, reverberating through the lives of our kin?" He grinned at Cutnose.

"I hate riddles." Cutnose waved him off. "You'd be more tolerable with wine."

The old man leaned back from the table. "And you would be with a bath."

Cutnose shook his head at the old, irritating man.

"You two try not to kill one another," Marya said.

"Are you sure I cannot teach you the Adhan? It is not difficult to learn. I keep forgetting you are a woman. Perhaps you could learn?" he said to Cutnose.

"I'd rather piss in my boot and drink it."

"You fear salvation. If you are lucky, someday you will find it."

Cutnose stood, calling to Marya, "You want to switch watches?"

"No," echoed back down the steps.

Cutnose sat down again, eyeing the blind man. "You sure you don't have any wine in here?"

"We do not indulge," Mohammed said. "But I can expand your mind."

"Tell me more."

"I have plenty of books."

"Can't read."

"What a lonely life you lead."

"Not as lonely as being dead."

The door swung open, startling Mohammed. Cutnose's axe leapt into his hand, half-standing.

The man leaning on the doorway was barely recognizable. Feathers of crossbow bolts stuck from his chest imbedded deep within his body. He had a long open gash along his skull and his tunic was tattered, what remained completely red. His face was white and his lips were cracked with open sores. His gray beard was darker with dried brown blood. Everything about him appeared older, his hair grayer, wrinkles deepening on his face. He clung to his long axe with a battered hand.

Cutnose raced to his side, wrapping an arm around the warrior. "What happened?" He called at the stairs. "Marya! Arnulf!" He eased the wounded man into the room, allowing him to settle abasing the wall. "Stay still," he said quietly.

Mohammed joined them, holding a shallow basin. "Here."

Cutnose took the cloth and began to wipe the blood and grime from his face. He eyed the man's open wounds. He'd been around enough wounded and dying to know when a man was going to perish. Ulf did not have long, and some semblance of comfort and care was all a man could do to ease another's passing.

Marya leapt from the stairs. She knelt beside him, taking stock of his wounds. "What happened?"

Even Ulf's voice had aged. "It was a trap." He let out a wet cough and grimaced, letting the pain pass over him like a funeral shroud.

"Galahad and Bors?"

"Just Galahad."

"Hugh?" Marya asked.

Glassy eyes glared in pain. "Has joined his ancestors."

Mohammed let out a soft cry and whispered a prayer in a foreign tongue. "He was a noble man, even for a Frank."

"Galahad doesn't have the Chalice. I believe Bors has it." He rested his head on the wall in exhaustion. "I fear we have failed."

"Get me bandages," she said to Mohammed. He brought them one of his robes and Cutnose tore ribbons from it, handing them to Marya. She wiped the blood from the exhausted warrior then wrapped cloth around his head, covering the gaping hole of his eye. Then she began stuffing the ribbons into the wounds riddling his body.

Arnulf emerged from the tower steps, taking a place near Ulf's side. "Ulf, no." Cutnose took a step back and Arnulf gripped the dying man's hand.

Ulf sighed, and his breath came with a struggle. "Marya, there's no point." She ignored him, trying to mend his dozens of wounds. "The bolts were tipped with silver and this." He pulled a blade from his belt and handed it to her. The dim light from the candles shied away from the blade.

She held the knife in her hands. She felt its weight and eyed it closely. She rubbed a finger carefully along the blade. "This is a Lightsbane forged blade."

"Aye," Ulf managed.

"That is one that you spoke of?"

"These are especially dangerous to our kind," Marya said, handing it to him.

The knife was that of an older style that Cutnose had never seen in use. It was wide in a leaf shape, a hand and a half long, the point sharp, meant to be used as a stabbing weapon like the Roman gladius. There was a short crossbar to protect the hand from other weapons in a fight. A quick way to lose your fingers. Then again, a man using his sidearm in a fight was in a dire place.

Whereas most soldiers had utilitarian, almost workman-like weapons. Plain, rugged metal chipped and worn, kept to the highest standard possible, for weapons were expensive, and without one you were a man open to any number of evils. This dagger was different.

The dark gray metal repelled the light away, yet a faint ripple of silver ran throughout it like oil over top of boggy water. The end of the blade was slightly curved, coming to an offset leaf-shape. The hilt had been worn down, at one point having been made from a rich wood like chestnut or cedar.

"Still holds its edge, if a little aged."

Arnulf viewed him in disgust. "Deadly. Most other wolves would already be dead."

"Listen, my time is short," Ulf spat, his breathing becoming more labored.

"No, you will recover," Marya said. It was strange to see her in such distress, she always held herself with regal authority.

Ulf shook his head painfully. "I'm done. My tale ends here, but we can still stop them."

"How?" Arnulf asked, his voice hardening.

"The full moon comes, and we haven't found Bors," Cutnose said, his head pounded in the presence of Ulf as if he'd drank half the casks of wine in Rome.

"Bors has bribed passage through the Fatimid blockade. He may already be gone."

"He has not passed through Ramla," Arnulf said.

"The foul troll is smarter than I thought he could be. Perhaps he's learned something after all these years." His eyes glazed a fraction, realizing that after all this time, he'd been bested by his enemies, and shaded by a hint of sadness that he'd failed in his quest.

"I must try then," Cutnose said. "Jaffa?" He knew in his heart it was futile, but a man must fight to live, or he was only waiting to die.

"It must be Jaffa."

Cutnose stood. "Then I must depart now."

No," Ulf said.

"If Bors is in Jaffa, then I must try to beat him there." Cutnose shook his head. This man would not stop him.

"No," Ulf said louder, his voice becoming that of a dying king. "You will not depart until I am gone."

Marya cocked her head, her sable hair shifting with the movement. "No, Ulf." She glimpsed at Cutnose, tears forming in her eyes, then back to the aged warrior, and shook her head vigorously. "No. Do not do this. There is still time." Arnulf ran a hand through his hair, eyes staring a thousand paces away.

"It is the only way," Ulf said, pushing to his feet. He wavered and steadied himself. His blue eyes settled upon Cutnose and flashed a dim gold. "You are about to become a famous man."

"I don't understand."

"Silence. You will do as I say."

Cutnose shut his mouth.

"You need to be blooded or you will fall to the Wilds. Marya and Arnulf will need every bit of your fighting skill to bring down Bors."

"We need you," Marya said to Ulf.

"You will do whatever it takes to deny them the Black Chalice. Swear it."

Marya nodded, her mouth twisting. "I will deny them the Black Chalice."

"And I will as well," Arnulf said.

"And I," said Cutnose, not knowing the full extent of his words.

"You must pray he has not escaped these lands," Ulf said. He reached over to Arnulf and gripped the back of his neck. He pulled the young man closer and pushed his forehead against his. They locked eyes. "You are a noble man and fierce warrior. You will find your family one day, and I regret not being with you when you are joined. You will lead your own pack, and your reign will be long." Ulf's mouth formed a grim smile. "I am glad we found one another despite the grief you caused me."

Arnulf gripped Ulf tight. "I am sorry for that. My anger controlled me."

Ulf grimaced. "I will miss traveling in your company."

"And I you. It has been an honor to be your companion."

Ulf pushed him away and slapped his cheek. "May your path be filled with women and worthy opponents."

Then he turned to Marya. He rested a hand on her shoulder, and she flinched.

"You can still overcome this. You are the strongest I've ever known," she said, her eyes not leaving him.

"I've never seen a man survive this. I've only seen them wither and die, mere husks of what they once were. That is not a warrior's fate."

Tears glittered in her eyes like sparkling hazel-green diamonds.

"The journey was long. I regret some things I've done. Acting in anger or haste. But never joining paths with you." He moved to hold her shoulders. "I've loved you like my own kin. One day you will have your kingdom. Rule justly with fairness and they will respect you and die for you, rule with fear and they will only do enough to not incur your wrath. It is better to fight and fall than to live without hope." He hugged her then, and her fingers grasped his tunic, clinging to him.

He leaned back and kissed her forehead like she was his very own daughter.

Ulf hefted his long axe into his hands as if it were his fondest memory of life. His hands ran along its haft, and he examined the engraved axe-head, running a hand over the rune markings. He took in a deep breath, glancing at Arnulf. "Take Crowfeeder. May she wet the ground with the blood of your enemies and keep the eaters of the dead well-fed."

Arnulf shook his head, denying him while holding the weapon like it was the most revered of holy relics. "I am not worthy to wield such a weapon, nor am I the right man. The longbow is my weapon." He bowed his head and returned the gift to Ulf's hands.

Ulf nodded. "Knowing one's path is a blessing, for many do not." He turned toward Marya. "And you?"

"Nor I."

He turned to Cutnose, his eyes settling. "The man who slew Ulf Bodvarsson. I must bestow this weapon upon you."

Cutnose took a step forward in confusion, and Ulf watched him with sure eyes. "You have no son to bestow such a beautiful weapon?"

Ulf raised his chin. "That is not possible. Care for her, and the mere sight will send your enemies fleeing. She often sings for blood. Do not let her go too long without having her fill or you will risk angering her before battle."

"I cannot take such a weapon." Cutnose shook his head.

"You will need it in the coming battles."

Cutnose marveled at the excellently crafted axe. He turned it over in his hands, fingers gliding over the carvings. It was heavy, but lighter than he thought it should be. He ran a hand over the bearded axe-head. The hook of the beard was long and pointed. The top edge of the axe-head also came to a slight point to be used as a spear-like thrusting weapon, using the long axe's reach to the wielder's advantage.

"Set it aside, Cutnose. She is full this night. Let us finish this."

Gently, Cutnose leaned the axe against the wall. "What would you have me do, my lord?"

Ulf smiled grimly at him. "No need for pleasantries. That was a past life. You're going to plunge that dagger into my heart, cut it out, and eat it."

Cutnose grimaced. He had killed plenty of men over the span of his life, but eat their heart? The barbarity spoiled his hard stomach. This man was mad from the loss of blood. "I thought I was to kill Bors?"

"You were. There were two wolves who marked you that night. Bors's bite took your life and my blood stopped you from dying. By killing either one of us and eating the heart, you would have completed your Turning and become blooded, joining us as Ulfhendar. Since he is not here, you will complete your Turning by taking my life."

Marya stared at him, greenish eyes still glittering with emotion. Arnulf's were the same, his held a saddened disdain as if he blamed himself for the fall of his beloved lord.

"You are strong. Young and raw, yet you have a noble heart."

Never had a man called him noble. He was a soldier and a warrior, but nobility was a societal status held by those in power, and he was no noble. He was a man they used to keep the lower class in check with violence and brute force, and they fed him coin to keep him happy. He took care of his company like they were his own, but one could hardly name that noble. He considered it maintaining business in a short, brutish world.

"I am but a simple soldier."

"There's always a need for soldiers. But you must be more than that, or our kind will be lost. You have strength in you to overcome the trials ahead." Ulf paused, weighing the soldier before him as blood still trickled from his many wounds. "Your name will be known. For there are still many packs that roam these lands. They will want to see the man who slew Ulf, for many have known me in life and in death. Many will fear you. Others may seek to challenge you. The Order hunts us all. For you will be known as the one who took the life of Ulf Bodvarsson, Gray King, slayer of Galahad and his kin, Ector, and Kay, Father of Ulfdane Ulfsson the Young, Dalla Ulfsdottir the Fair, Bjorn Grimshield, and Ivar, commander of the Wolf Guard, champion of Jutland, vanquisher of Genthel, Shadow Traveler and Wolfskin. Jarl of the Lochlainn and King of the Isles." His voice lowered in volume.

"You forget one," Marya said softly.

"I do not forget. I choose to omit him from my story."

"He always loved you."

"And my love was lost upon his blade," Ulf said then coughed violently with a glare at her. She stayed silent, pain clouding her eyes. His found Cutnose once again. "With my life, I give you one anew and a quest like no other. Do not let the Black Chalice leave these lands. It must not." He held out the Lightsbane knife. "Take the blade and remove your armor, it will ease the turn."

Cutnose stripped his coat of mail over his head and took the knife, glancing at the blade as Ulf removed his tunic with Marya's help. He was lean and muscled, having been much larger as a young man, now age had turned him lean and long, his chest and arms covered in coarse hair. His braided gray beard hung down to his chest. Streaks of red trickled through it, racing for the tips. Arnulf helped him unbind his hair. Ulf shook his head, letting the gray hair laced with dingy brown fall to his shoulders. Shirtless, dozens of severe wounds covered his body, blood leaking. "I am ready to begin my journey anew." He turned his head toward the ceiling. "I would see the sky and moon for one last time."

The group walked outside to the courtyard. Marya and Arnulf with their arms wrapped around Ulf. The old warrior spoke to the sky. "Odin, old friend. We will meet soon." His eyes took in the heavens with fond wonderment as if all his questions would soon be answered. He breathed in as much air as possible, let out a short wheeze, and then coughed. He gritted his teeth. "It is time."

Cutnose held the pugio loosely in his hand. "If there is another way, you must tell me now?" He'd mercy killed men after a battle to ease their crossing, but this warrior had been indestructible.

"Cutnose the Timid, now?" Ulf shook his head. Arnulf handed Ulf Crowfeeder. "One last battle," he said to the axe. "Strike clean, soldier."

Cutnose took a step closer, gripping the knife. He eyed Marya; her face was set in a storm of misery. She nodded fiercely to him. Ulf's blood streamed in slow moving rivers down his limbs, seeking to water the ground, and pattered softly on the stones.

"Do it, Cutnose. Embrace your destiny. Answer the Call."

Cutnose gripped the knife harder, the muscles in his forearm flexing.

"I hear the Valkyries circling. They beckon me join my people all the way to the beginning." He raised his chin, hand securely around Crowfeeder, the only comfort to a dying warrior. He spread his arms out to his sides, lifting his chin, eyes fixed on the moon. A soft smile traced his lips. "Thyra."

Cutnose adjusted his feet and rapidly twisted, ramming the knife into the center of Ulf's chest. The point melted into him, stopping near the hilt. Ulf let out a gasp, but no cry escaped his lips. He fell to his knees and uttered words in a foreign tongue, and Arnulf and Marya lowered him to the courtyard stones.

With tears in her eyes, Marya spoke. "Hurry now, before his heart stops."

Cutnose crouched nearby, and with a grimace, cut into the man's chest. Ulf's eyes shot open, the ringed blue flashing a golden sunrise. It made his stomach turn as he sawed in a circular motion, then reached into Ulf's steaming chest and tore out his heart.

"Do not falter now. Eat it," Marya ordered.

Arnulf nodded, a frown on his lips. "Give his death meaning."

The heart pulsed in his hands. It was a dark red hue. Breathing hard, the heart neared his lips. He bit down and ripped, the piece of organ reluctantly tearing free. The meat was spongy like muscle; it resisted his teeth. The blood tasted of metal and salt. The morsel struggled to travel downward into his belly, but he swallowed it down. It was fuel to his fire, a fire that grew with every bite he took. The pressure in his neck began to fade the more he ate.

Marya and Arnulf watched him with fierce conviction. His muscles began to seize. His senses went into overload, sparking like a sap-caked branch thrown into a fire. He heard every drop of water in the bubbling pool and could easily see the top of the minaret where he'd carved his name into the stone out of boredom.

His sense of smell embraced a life of its own. Every intricate weave of Marya's scent was known to him. It was peculiar, a woven tapestry of arousal, warrior, and deep sadness. Arnulf's woven scent was different. There was much anger and mourning, blended with steadfast determination. Cutnose went to take another bite of Ulf's heart.

"That is enough," Marya whispered, her lips quivering.

Cutnose's veins raged as if Greek Fire blazed green and bright through them, spreading faster and faster. His heartbeat strengthened. His muscles were flawless and pumped, and he wanted to hoist a boulder into the air and throw it a hundred yards. Crush metal between his fingers. Bound ten feet in the air. Run like the wind. All these things were within his ability, and satisfaction squeezed its hold on him.

"How could a man not desire this?" he said, flexing his fingers. He was being reborn faster, stronger, better than anything he ever was. Then he felt the wolf inside him. It had been lurking, and it too was stronger. It burst from Cutnose.

He could not stop the beast from wrenching control. The flame of his wolf was as brazen and bright as the desert sun, and he couldn't stop himself from turning. He grew in size. The forced turning caused him an agonizing ecstasy. The pain should have made him cry out, but the result was the most gratifying sensation he'd ever felt.

His legs elongated. He stood taller than the tallest man he'd ever known by at least a half head, but he felt natural resting on all fours, muscles tight and ready to lunge. The people around diminished. Claws replaced his fingers. His forearms were weaves of thick sailing ropes. His mouth and head grew into a powerful muzzle and jaw capable of tearing through armor. His ears pointed and dense mixture of blond and brown fur sprouted and enveloped his entire body, acting as armor against man-made weapons. His muscles rippled over his back and neck as water turning into stone, spreading out like a sail over the meat of his neck.

He felt her presence now. It was different than his connection to Ulf by a thousand-fold. She did not cause him pain, but he yearned to be near her. The Moon Goddess shone upon him. He howled long and hard for her. Her form was full and bright, and it was a siren calling him to the feast of life. He bellowed his demand for her acknowledgment. *I am one of your children now. See me for I am alive.*

The two-legs before him were like him but refused to embrace their wolf. The man knew their names, but the wolf did not. They were only a faint memory to the wolf. As wolves, their scent was opaque but distinctly them. They were *Night Wind* and *Lost Eagle.* He was bound to them, but they were not his pack. He had no pack.

Night Wind called to him in her two-legged voice, her words a frail parchment turning to dust, and he roared his indomitable spirit in her direction. The other one like them laid upon the ground, his blood-life had pooled around him, and he no longer took breath. His wolf spirit no longer resided in his body. The noble scent that lingered was of the Gray King.

The man inside Cutnose called to him faintly. He grasped at the reins of his wolf form, trying to reel him back inside. Water and fire danced desperately to subdue the rival. Both his pack mates called in their man forms, pitiful and weak. He stretched his neck, finally free. He roared at them. *Join me, fools. The night is our kingdom. The Moon Goddess calls us to join her pack in the Great Hunt.* He peered at the Moon Goddess, she glowed a savage shade of yellow and white, ever the seductress, always calling from above. She sang to him with the voice of an angel, and she led him away from the ones he once knew.

Bounding over the courtyard, he ran on two legs and on all fours. He leapt onto the wall, claws finding hold in the stones, and crawled over the top, throwing himself to the other side. He hurtled through the streets. Dens of the two-legs blurred by him. A two-leg fell to the ground with a cry, yellow-fear poured down his leg, but Cutnose never gave him a second glance. He charged into the surrounding hills, goaded on by the moon's wordless song. *I am Scar.*

CHAPTER 21

The wind ran along his fur like a cool mountain stream after spring melting. He ignored the limbs of the shade-givers that scraped and scratched at his thick fur coat. He leapt over a rock-pile fence and stopped at the sound. The bleating of food.

There was a two-leg term for it but that was lost in the recess of his mind. Goats? He knew them by other names now. *Little horns, fat bellies.* He raced for them. They must have caught his scent, but he was far too close before they spooked into a run with tiny cries and high-pitched bleating. They were pitifully slow, and he ate among them with impunity.

He snatched one with his jaws and crunched around its midsection, splitting the animal in half. He chewed unfulfilled, the two pieces falling to the ground. He leapt onto the next one. They scurried in every direction. They were even slower than the two-legs. He mauled another. Each one sating his blood lust only a droplet. He continued his rampage on the herd until he smelled the stink of the two-legs. He raised his snout and tested the air, seeking the wind's guidance to his location. The odor drifted closer. Sour, bitter, weak of flesh, fear laden.

He turned around and a young two-legs stood before him. *A naked-chin.* He wore a rough-spun tunic and a goatskin belt wrapped around his waist. Black hair ran down to his eyes and over his ears. He held a simple crooked staff in one hand. A mere stick. He wavered, terror gripping him by the throat.

Scar's lips quivered as he let out a low-pitched growl. This creature would run now, and he would chase, that was the way of the Wilds. The hunt would be quick and end in a shower of blood. The young two-legs dropped his stick and scrambled away. With a jolt, Scar followed.

The naked-chin scrambled around trees and rocks, emitting audible fear. Scar trailed behind, with every bound of four legs, he closed the distance. The urge to hamstring the naked-chin and sink his fangs into the stringy heel of his leg grew inside the wolf. Then he would finish the kill, after he was done feeding upon the fat-bellies.

The naked-chin let out a terrified wail as he fell to the ground. Scar stood over him, blood and saliva dripping from his jaws. The naked-chin tried to crawl away, grasping at dirt and plants, mouth shaking in terror.

Pain crashed through Scar's chest as he was taken off his feet. His shoulders joined the pain as a weight pressed him into the ground. The snarling fangs of another wolf bore down on him, and he twisted in its grasp, rolling to throw the creature away from him. He held in a crouch ready to attack the new threat.

The naked-chin escaped into the trees. He would find his scent and the hunt would be renewed, after he dealt with this rival. The shadowed form of a wolf shifted before him. Its fur was as black as the night. Its eyes a greenish-hazel ringed in gold. Its lips curled back, baring its fangs at him. There was a familiarity with its scent. Known but unknown. It tickled the spot in the back of his neck. The other wolf stopped growling and took a submissive step backward, lowering its head.

Female, ran through Scar's brain. The man knew her as Marya, but this wasn't Marya. She smelled like something else completely. *Night Wind.* He padded over to where she stood on all fours.

She let out a soft growl to let him know she was not to be pressured to submit. He circled her, taking in the thousands of strands of her scent that weaved a tapestry of emotion and complexity which composed her. Yet it was also as simple and refreshing as a warm spring rain. Then her scent was as deep as the deepest ocean, yet as clear as a cloudless day. She was all of these things, a twisting of a thousand individual scents into a single thread.

Wolves could not hide their scent. It was open to all, and if a wolf could grin, it did so lightly. For he detected something else in her scent, the soft prickly smell of desire.

Before his eyes, she transformed back into a two-legs. It was rapid, and it confused him. *Why would one want two-legs when four were fast? Why suffer the darkness of night when one saw as clear as day while wearing wolfskin? Why bear man-flesh when a wolfskin brought great strength and freedom of the land?* No obstacle was too great in this form. And he remembered he had once been like her. He had once been a two-legs. The fires inside him tempered beneath the distant memory of man.

She spoke softly, but for his ears he heard easily, the sounds meant nothing, yet there was command and tenderness in her voice. He stepped closer, taking in her female two-legs scent, trying to understand her meaning. His rage subsided. He knelt in front of her, and she rested a hand atop his head, fingers lacing through his fur.

The man in him yelled as he watered the flames of the wolf, and they sizzled inside him. The wolf howled at the Moon Goddess. *Wild. Free. Hunt.* The feelings and scents faded, the Moon Goddess's song decreased in his ears, and the night grew darker and darker. The fires inside him began to subside as he uneasily slid back into the world of men.

As he returned to the form of man, it felt as if a weight had been lifted from his entire body. His thickly muscled limbs receded, and his frame shrank as his claws retracted until they were calloused fingers again, not the sharp claws of a vicious wolf. He held his hands in front of his face, and they were the calloused palms that he remembered. *I am Cutnose.*

Marya stepped toward him. Her kaftan was gone, revealing more of her womanly form. Her hair pulled back and tied with a leather thong, but loose strands encircled her face, raven wings over the snow.

"It took me. I had no control." He breathed heavily. "It was amazing." He stood upright and regarded the moon once again, wiping the blood from his face. It was dimmer and only the faintest song called to him. "Can you hear her?"

"Loudly. She calls to all of us. It is said we are her lost children." Her eyes lifted toward the sky, wondering as to the purpose of her song. "The mother cannot reach us, so she sings so we may know her."

She paused after a few moments. "Deva's story is a sad one, one of longing." Her eyes wouldn't leave the moon. "She is married to Dazhbog, a mighty, beautiful and jealous god, and the sire of men. The Moon Goddess made all other life—the plants and animals—but is a protector and death giver. She culls her herds and packs, and protects the young, ensuring that while some lives fade others grow. One day, she goes hunting with her great bow, tracking a giant wolf, but as she prepares to shoot the wolf, she is overcome by its beauty. She cannot bring herself to slay the beast. Many think him Veles, the adversary of Dazhbog's father, Perun, god of the sky. She is so taken by the wolf that she lays with him. Many believe her tricked by Veles. Others believe that he is her true love, and it is not trickery at all, for she couples with him willingly."

"Every spring, after a winter of hunting, she bathes in the Lake of the Morning, renewing her maidenhood before she rejoins Dazhbog. Soon after, she gives birth to my kind. Our kind. Dazhbog sees the monstrosity, and with the aid of his father, and despite Deva's powerful bow, they banish us from the heavens. Perun then ties Deva to Dazhbog's chariot with a twisted rope of her hair. He drags her behind him every day in the darkness, so she is unable to see her children here on earth. She sings so that we may know her and her love, and we sing back so she may know her children still seek her. One day, the Sun God will stop his chariot and consume her, and both gods will perish. There will be great turmoil and war, bringing an end to all man and wolf."

He couldn't take his eyes away from the round, golden-white celestial body. He had so many questions as to why but couldn't put them to words. She reached up and cupped his cheek, her eyes peering at him. "You would do well to keep your wolf in check. You've been bestowed a magnificent gift. If you squander it playing in the Wilds, killing goats, and scaring shepherd boys, then we are lost."

"It was much stronger than before." He shook his head, catching his breath. "I want to turn again. It is the only thing I desire." Far greater than any lust he'd ever fallen into. Even the Contessa's embrace paled before it, the mere love a stone beside the beauty of the flower.

"Shhh." She lifted herself onto her tiptoes and kissed him long and deep. Her tongue darted into his mouth, and his shock at her bold stroke turned into enjoyment. He put his hand around her waist and started to pull her in tighter. He was familiar with this game, if a woman was this bold, he was closer than half-way there. And to his chagrin, she abruptly pulled away. "We ride for Jaffa, Cutnose. Pray to the Moon Goddess that Bors has been delayed."

"What was that?"

"A reminder."

"Reminder of what?"

"Come." They started to walk back to Ramla, side-stepping mauled goat carcasses. She spoke over her shoulder. "A reminder that you fight for more than the Chalice. Good comes in many forms, mercenary."

"I could use another reminder," he said with a smirk. "For a noblewoman, you kiss like a commoner, and you picked a mercenary in a foreign land with a scarred face to give your virtue away to."

"I will take your crudeness as a compliment. I've loved many men, Sir Cutnose, and many men have loved me. To share in love is a gift from the gods."

"Once you love a soldier of fortune, no man will ever be the same to you."

She sighed in front of him. "Love takes many shapes."

"And let that be a reminder to you to not fall in love with me. I know how you ladies love songs of undying love and knightly virtues."

"You do not know high-born ladies as well as you think."

"I seen enough of 'em."

He could smell her wolf faintly in his human form. The breadth of intensity was there, yet it was only a glimmer of itself, a mere shadow, yet it was there under the surface.

"You should feel lucky to have received such a gift. Many men across many lands would kill for such an opportunity."

"And I've received it by chance?"

"It was not by chance. We could have let you die or killed you at any time, but Ulf saw something that it took me longer to see."

He grunted his acknowledgement. The world had been a very simple place only a week prior. Men fighting for their lords against a foreign enemy. Men fighting for their God. Easy. Lords paid, soldiers fought and died, and the regular folk either celebrated their lord's victory or were held to the whims of new overlords.

The world he'd been thrust into was one subject to the madness of the gods. Wolves the size of a horse. Enemies as devious as they were terrifying. The Black Chalice. A price upon his head. And this mysterious woman, a lady, a wolfskin, who hated him as far as Cutnose could tell, and now fancied him enough to give him a fair maiden's kiss, although she was no more maiden than the goddess Deva she spoke of. He'd embraced terrifying powers beyond his imagination and now felt as invincible as a mortal man could get.

"You were the man that presented himself in our time of need. Ulf was a match for Bors in battle, with Arnulf and I to support him against the Order's brothers and sergeants." Her eyes betrayed her. "With you, I am not certain. This is not meant as an insult, this is the truth of the situation. We must be at our very finest to stand a chance."

"I am no foreigner to battle, and my blood burns for vengeance for my men. I will not falter before him."

"Then it will be enough," she said with a nod. She unsheathed the Lightsbane pugio knife on her belt and offered it to him.

"Crowfeeder will be enough."

She shook her head. "Your powers are raw like a fresh wound. You need every advantage you can get. If the opportunity presents itself, do not hesitate to end Bors."

He took the ancient knife from her. "Won't you want it?"

"I can hold my own."

"Or Arnulf?"

"He hates the whole idea of it. He will not carry it."

A warrior's weapon was his most prized of possessions, and to be carrying two elegant weapons that were once another revered warrior's made Cutnose slightly hesitant. He'd always valued plain quality over elegance, these were the tools of his trade, but to have such finery on his person sprouted a weed of doubt that he deserved them, that perhaps he'd risen too high from his position as mercenary captain. In the East, he'd known other mercenaries to decorate themselves in finery, reds and purples trimmed with gold and silver, but that was not his way.

"I will not hesitate to plant the blade in his heart."

After retracing his steps back to the town, they entered the courtyard to the White Mosque where Mohammed was helping Arnulf prepare Ulf's body for burial. His pierced and battered scale armor had been placed back over him, covering the gaping hole in his chest. His beard and skin had been wiped clean, ghostly white in the moonlight. His hands were clasped in the Christian style, fingers interlocked and scrubbed of dirt and grime, his long knife pointed downward beneath them.

Arnulf had brushed his hair, and it hung gray and long draped over his shoulders. His beard was kept beaded in Norse fashion and stained with the blood of the many.

"You will hold him until we return?" Marya asked.

"I will. A friend of Hugh's will be kept safe. It is my desire to reclaim Hugh and make sure his mortal remains are cared for," the blind man said and gulped. "But I am afraid, everything you've spoken is beyond my imagination. Nightmares. Frankish djinns. We all knew they were infidels, but knowing they are communed with the devil shakes my core. God watch over us all."

Marya gave him a grim smile that he would never see. "Not all have ill intent. There are few, and we are going to deal with them."

"Then may Allah guide your way."

Marya bowed her head. "You have our thanks."

"Rid this land of the evil."

"We must." After a somber glance at Ulf, she said to the men, "Prepare your weapons and armor. We ride through the night for Jaffa."

Arnulf rested a hand on Ulf for a moment longer and stood, gazing down at Ulf's body, and nodded as if a silent oath had been sworn. He retrieved his longbow. He pushed his weight overtop the bow, bending it. Then he pulled a string from a pouch on his belt. Each end was notched, and he looped them over small inlets in the bow staff while it was bent. "I would normally wait until I knew we were close to battle, but battle will find us quickly." When he was finished, he started to check his quiver of arrows tied to his saddle, running his fingers over the feathers, ensuring quality and uniformity.

Cutnose hefted the long axe, Crowfeeder. The long axe had a rugged elegance with runes carved through the shaft, the head holding a vicious beard. It had been a long time since he'd used a long axe, preferring a hand axe and shield for cover over being exposed with an unwieldy long, two-handed weapon. It would be an insult to not use the axe, and if wielded properly, it was terrifyingly effective against one or many foes.

The long axe was a weapon made famous in the hands of the Danes and Anglo-Saxons that fought all over England and the kingdoms presiding over the continent. Cutnose had seen them used by the Varangian Guard, a savage unit of westerners and Norse under the employ of the Eastern Roman Emperor. They were much like Cutnose and his men, mercenaries for hire, northerners and westerners, adventurers who traveled south and east to find employment, many stayed in the East creating legacies within the guard. He flipped the axe over and rested it carefully on the wall.

He secured his coat of mail and threw it high in the air before donning it. The lightness of armor surprised him; it was like wearing an additional tunic. It hung below his waist almost to his knees, where it split down the middle to allow for riding a horse and movement of long strides. He secured his belt around his hips. He would carry his shield, a strap wrapped around his body so it could be slung if need be in combat. He kept his hand axe on his belt as a sidearm. He could throw the axe if need be or wield it. On his other side, he slid the ancient Lightsbane knife through the belt. Secondary weapons provided a quick transition in battle if his main weapon broke or was lost. He placed his nose-piece helm, letting it rest over the mail that enclosed his skull.

"A proper Norman," Marya called to him. She walked her horse, leading the reins of a fresh mount. The horse didn't shy from him like he'd expected. Her hair was pulled tightly back atop her skull. She bore leather-scale armor and a buckler, her queenly curved saber on her hip. Her kaftan embroidered down the hem in gold, every part a warrior queen.

"He doesn't spook," Cutnose said, resting a hand on the horse's flank.

"It was accustomed to Ulf. Not all are capable. Beasts or men," she said.

Cutnose swung his leg over the saddle. The extra weight of the shield, axe, and mail coat felt like nothing at all. The horse felt his weight but didn't complain or stamp his feet. Cutnose expected he was about the same weight as Ulf. He was shorter than the old warrior, but he was at least as thick. He rested the long axe on his thigh. "I am ready."

Marya looked upon him fondly. "How does Crowfeeder feel in your hand? Does she resist?"

He eyed the axe. "I find her welcoming."

"She does not like to rest for long," Marya said. "Mohammed, we will return when our hunt is over. You have our thanks."

The elder nodded briskly with a grim grin. "I will see you then." He walked to the gate door and opened it for them. Arnulf nodded at their host, lowering his head. Mohammed wrinkled his nose as Cutnose passed. "No need to call when you arrive. I will know this one's stink."

Marya gave Cutnose a smirk. He leaned off his saddle. "I will roll in the mud before I return."

"It cannot make it worse."

Marya spurred her horse, and with vim in her voice shouted, "We ride for Jaffa! Ulf Bodvarsson demands vengeance!"

CHAPTER 22

Bors's journey took an extra two days in the hot scorching sun, traveling first north, then west, then south, adding fifteen more miles. As was his nature, he disliked the broad-ranging evasive maneuver. He had wanted to take all the Order's men and ride straight for Jaffa, but Galahad had convinced him otherwise. At least along the coast there was a pleasant breeze from the sea. By the time they reached the port of Jaffa, his men and their mounts were worn out and layered in dust from the road.

Jaffa was the closest port to Jerusalem, yet despite this fact, it had the feel of a neglected backwater town frequented by smugglers and a few ambitious merchants. It had changed rulers a handful of times during the crusaders' campaign. After a brief occupation by the crusading army, then a slightly longer hold by Fatimid marines during the siege and sack of Jerusalem, the town was back under crusader ownership, the Fatimids settling for a blockade of the harbor.

The fortifications were in dire need of repair, the walls crumbling, stones scattered on the ground. The central keep, situated on the seaside portion of a hill, leaned toward the water, sinking into the sandy ground in which it was built. Nestled in next to the keep was the richer part of the town, facing the coast. The further it sloped down to the docks below, the shoddier the homes became, much like the refuse that poured down the street during the mornings after the town began to awaken from slumber.

The harbor was protected by a rocky sea wall enhancing a natural inlet. The waters were calm and a light-green shade of blue. The harbor was almost empty. No traders had been allowed in or out for over a month. Fishing skiffs and other small boats lined the docks that normally held trading vessels, cogs, and galleys. Further out, he could make out the Fatimid fleet sitting at anchor not far from shore. Green flags hung from every mast of the fleet, some holding black crescents and a single black star.

The Fatimids had blockaded the port to deny the crusaders logistical support from the maritime Italian city-states. The blockade would have been detrimental to the siege of Jerusalem had the Genoese ships not sailed into port just days before the Fatimid fleet arrived, providing the crusaders with much needed supplies, and more importantly, wood to construct siege engines.

Bors's men passed Jaffa's markets, the stalls nearly devoid of goods. Local people gathered to watch his Banner, composed of his and Percival's Guards, march through the town. He saw the looks upon their faces. Fear and anger, but mostly fear ruled their humble existence. Enough that most turned away or even hid from his men.

As he passed the keep, he briefly met with one of Godfrey's knights, Sir Geldemar Carpinel, who rushed from the sinking keep, to walk with them to the docks. He'd offered them residence inside its walls, but Bors was short with the knight, telling him they would not stay long. The knight begged for them to stay, for his small garrison of footmen and archers was small compared to the Fatimid forces outside the harbor, and the Saracen brigands in the nearby deserts were bound to strike at any time. He didn't trust the Armenian mercenaries employed to assist in holding the town. But Bors was unsympathetic to the man's plight, instead making for the docks and leaving Geldemar shaking his head and cursing beneath his breath, before he retreated inside his eroding fort.

Near the docks, a swarthy man waited for them, dressed in just fine enough garb to make him liable to be robbed. His nose was hooked and his hair black curly ringlets. He wrung his hands together, then gestured at the harbor. "See, Lord Bors, not a seaworthy ship in the harbor. Even if we had one, the Fatimids lie in wait like sharks near a carcass."

"I see that, you fool. That is why I'm paying you. Find me a ship." He reached out and snatched the Genoese captain, Arduino di Narbona, by the scruff. The captain stood on his tiptoes, trying to balance himself. "The blockade, lord."

"You need only find one seaworthy enough for your crew and me," he hissed. "By nightfall, you will have a ship."

Arduino raised his brows, struggling in Bors's grasp. "I have no money. My ship was my money, and Godfrey had the beautiful girl dismembered piece by piece."

Bors breathed in through his long mustache and released the thieving bastard. He untied a coin pouch and handed it over. He knew Godfrey had compensated the man greatly for his contribution to the crusade, making the sea captain bolder in his requests. "I already paid you once. This should be enough to acquire a ship. You only need get us back to Genoa. Understood? I've now paid you enough for a ship and triple the cost of passage. We cannot delay."

Arduino took the bag, balancing it in his hand. The coins clinked as he felt the weight with a greedy palm. As quickly as the man weighed the coins, he pocketed the pouch with a sleight of hand in the blink of an eye. "My men are able, you see, but this may take time." He looked out at the harbor. "I must speak to the right people, pay off the right people. No blockade is perfect, but one must know the right places to delve. You understand, my lord?" His eyes equally regarded him as a foreigner with no sense of this world, and a healthy amount of fear of Bors's anger.

The captain had more fabrications and excuses than an

overfed horse had a steaming pile of dung. "You understand for every extra hour I wait, I will take a piece of you, starting with your tongue, so you can utter no more lies. Then your greedy fingers one by one until you are a fingerless thieving bastard. Finally, I'll take your cock to ensure you can't ever breed another of your skulking kind for as long as you live. Then when I get to Genoa, I will make sure to wipe out your entire stinking brood of kin, but keep you alive so you can watch, both mute and cockless." He paused, taking pleasure in the fear painted across the captain's face. "Tonight, I will have a ship and passage out, or you will begin to understand why you fear me."

Arduino bowed his head to his chest. "Yes, my lord."

"Sundown, at the docks. In the meantime, you will find me at the only tavern in this backwater port."

Bors took refuge at a deplorable excuse for a tavern near the docks. It was filled with soiled, out of work sailors, and other lowly personage. It was viewed as an inferior and sordid part of the town where foreigners and sailors frequented for their wanton pleasures. The coastal cities usually had taverns, despite the angst from the local Muslim populations to service the Christian traders from across the Mediterranean. Jaffa was no exception.

Men shuffled away from the Franks when they entered, yet stared with hard, unrelenting looks. They had been taught harsh lessons by the crusaders the first time they'd marched through. When Bors drew up to his full height, hand on his hammer, the men scattered like chickens before the fox, others gawked, while most turned away, avoiding his gaze.

Over thirty of his men filed in behind him, adding to the threat of violence, raising the tension of the patrons. Bors gave the nervous barkeep an unamused glance, and the tavern owner rushed to unseat a section of the establishment for Bors's men.

The patrons vacated for the Order soldiers, and the owner retreated behind his bar.

"Do not get too drunk," Bors ordered. "We must be ready for a fight any time." His men nodded and went about ordering food, whatever stringy piece of street meat this crook would feed them.

The barkeep approached with a jug and earthen cups, gently setting them on Bors's table. He gulped his nervousness before he spoke. "That'll be one dinar."

Bors slid over ten coins. "Make sure my men are fed." He wouldn't have them starving. The journey would be long, and he may need them in a fight before they reached England. Once back in England, there would be more relative safety, but he would never let his guard down until he placed the Chalice in Uthur's hands.

His command would be sufficient for traveling safely. Over thirty mounted sergeants, two first brothers, and five brothers, all well-armed, should be more than enough to deter the boldest of bandits or pirates, but in these times, desperation made men brazen. He would not hesitate to sacrifice every single one of his men to accomplish his quest, and if they didn't think so, they did not understand the blood oath they swore.

Yet, they were all still young, mostly unlanded sons, and soldiers that had shown promise with spear and horse. Intense training by experienced warriors made them better than most knights in the field. All understood they were the armored line that stood against evil.

Bors sipped his wine and wiped the clinging droplets from his mustache. He rested a hand atop the bag holding the Chalice. The bag masked its presence, but he felt it ebbing, pulsing from within, calling to him from inside the sack. It took a man of discipline to resist a lure so strong. He removed his hand from the bag, ignoring the humming allure. His mind drifted to Galahad.

Little verpa. A grand idea splitting ways, but he always knew the weak-blooded brother wouldn't have devised anything that didn't directly improve his station. Bors couldn't see any advantage in lingering in this land of deserts and palms, barbarians and heathens, and holy sites of the prudish Christ, the Jews, and now the Muslims. New religion after new religion took root in the fertile soils of men's minds before blooming into the flowers of conflict and war.

He couldn't see why Galahad had such interest in this uncompromising conflict, but if the bastard wanted to escape England on his own quest, then he'd let him. He poured himself another cup of wine. It was a hardly palatable swill, tasted more like forage for livestock than wine he had once known, and lacked any sort of punch. The era of worthy wines had long spoiled into vinegar, and for centuries he had been forced to raise inferior drinks to his lips as the art of winemaking had long since faded. In this part of the world, it was even worse, the wine having to be transported over the sea.

The first brother of his guard joined him, adjusting a chair to sit. "Brother Bors," he said gruffly, with a thick accent of the northern Scots.

"Osbern."

The high-born brother gestured at a chair. "May I?"

Bors didn't answer but nodded his head in the chair's direction. He offered the knight a cup and the Scotsman took it and poured it to the rim. "Excellent," he said, and took a long hard drink. He waited a moment, eyeing Bors before he spoke. "The men and I were wondering."

Bors raised his eyebrows then let them fall into a consternated scowl. They were not to question the orders of one of the Twelve at any cost. With a natural dread that accompanied Bors, he'd thought his reputation was enough to deter any thinking or dissent. But he would entertain the brother. He needed them in high spirits if he was to complete his quest. "What?"

Osbern was the bastard son of a claimant to the lordship of Moray, meaning if he was legitimized, he would have a claim to the title, unless a lot of dying happened in the family. Most high-born bastards, if they were lucky enough to be recognized, found their ways into the clergy or another county, perhaps even mayoral positions. If they weren't so lucky, they were visited by a paid thug in the night to make the claimant problem go away or exiled to a foreign land with nothing but a bag of coin and a host of inflated ideas of self-worth. Or in Osbern's case, shuffled off to a secretive knightly order to serve God. He leaned in and wiped reddish hair from his eyes before lowering his voice. "I don't trust Captain Arduino."

"You and me both, but we have no choice. We need a ship, and he will complete his task for the right price."

"The Genoese are an untrustworthy lot. No better than pirates."

One could name the Scots as much, he thought. "It's of no matter. We need them." The same way the Romans had used his tribe to fill their ranks. Except he paid these men much better. It was the hierarchy of power. Those with money and power used those with less to fulfill their ambitions.

"I don't like it." Osbern eyed the room over his shoulder. "This lot be as much to throw us overboard or knife us in the back while you're having a drink."

"That is why I need your men prepared."

"Will Galahad or Percival return to us?"

Bors had kept Percival's death from the men to ensure they did not lose morale. His death would be explained after they'd completed the quest. Galahad's disappearance with over half the men he could not avoid. "They will not return before we reach England. The enemy will try us again, we must be ready."

Osbern turned back to him and downed his cup. "I'll make sure the men are ready."

"Then I need you to do something."

"Aye."

"You must take this letter to Uthur."

"When we land in Genoa?"

"No. Over land."

Osbern snorted, a half-smile forming on his lips. "Over land. That must be a couple thousand miles. It will take months."

"It will."

"By myself? That's a dangerous venture. Between the Saracens and the Greeks and the Godforsaken Saxons. I'll find myself in a kettle over a fire to be cooked."

"I can find another if you are not up to the task."

Osbern's brow furrowed, his cheeks reddening, there would be no man that named him coward. "What of Percival's first brother? He lacks a command. The men will be distraught to see me leave." Osbern gave Godric a sideways glance.

"I do not trust him with a quest such as this, but I will order a sergeant-brother if you are not able."

"I am afraid of no man." His voice lowered. "Nor beast. You know this more than most, my lord." Bors had known Osbern for years, the man was brave beyond imagine, if not reckless and even more lucky, having the scars to show for it. "I can handle the journey."

Bors knew the man would bristle at the threat of being seen as afraid. "That is why I selected you, First Brother Osbern. Pick two sergeant-brothers you trust and depart immediately. Tell Brother Odo he is to fill in your absence." Bors produced the letter from hidden inside his clothes and handed it over. "You know why we are here. If I do not reach Uthur, it must find its way into his hands. He must know."

Osbern stood, taking the letter and shoving it inside his boot. "I will see your orders done."

"Depart at once. Keep your colors concealed. You are returning pilgrims. You know enough to avoid Constantinople."

"I do, my lord."

"You were not picked by chance, Osbern. I trust you to complete your journey."

"I will not rest until the letter is placed safely into Uthur's hands."

"Carry on."

Osbern turned his back on Bors, rejoining the men. He spoke to a table and two stout bearded men rose from their seats to follow him. Sergeant Gamelin and Sergeant-Brother Peter of Summershire. Both veterans had a broad range of skills. They were adept woodsmen and hunters that would serve them well traveling in the wilds. Exactly the two men he would have picked for such a task. They departed the tavern.

The day wore on, and Bors passed his time by downing a jar of wine, feeling little effect. Bors poured himself another cup and drank it with an ounce of pleasure. A handful of his men had departed to sleep near the horses when Arduino returned to the tavern, looking the part of a scoundrel. He crept inside as if he were a thief planning on robbing them. Bors gestured him over.

Sweat stuck Arduino's black curls to his forehead. He wiped his brow and glanced around the room before he sat down. He reached for a cup, and Bors snatched it from him before he could speak. Arduino rubbed his fingers together.

"News?"

The ship captain grinned mischievously. "You'll be happy to know. A ship has been found."

Bors didn't let himself grin, only a faint glimmer of content, curling on his face. He knew enough from swindlers like Arduino that there was always something more to tell, something more masking the truth.

"But—"

"You carry lies as a woman collects flowers. Speak plainly."

Arduino put on an apologetic smile and raised his hands. "You ask for the impossible. The blockade. My ship is gone. Come, Bors. Not even a king can create ships from nothing."

"I paid a king's price for passage." He stared expectantly, reached over and poured more wine from its jar, keeping it out of Arduino's reach. He took a long draw, watching the swarthy pirate.

"You see, we aren't very popular with the Fatimids at the moment." He spread his arms wide. "Yet not all men are above coin." The Genoese captain rubbed his hands together. "I have made contact with a man here in the port, who in turn has reached out to another trader, who knows a captain in the fleet in the harbor."

"I do not need every nuance."

Arduino licked his lips with a smile. "The trader has a vessel that will come in tonight. It must be after dark. You do not know how many palms needed coin for this. In fact," he paused. "We'll need more." He gulped after he said it. The man wasn't dumb, most criminals had some cunning.

"How much more?"

"One hundred dinars."

Bors snarled, his voice booming. "One hundred?"

Arduino shrugged his shoulders apologetically. "I had to bribe a lot of people. You want me to escape a blockade. That takes a lot of coin. It'll be a small window. No more than an hour when the ships will part, the trader will arrive, and then we must depart. You know what is at stake. Those ships in the harbor will row us down and sink us with ease. We will be sailing in the midst of a thousand enemies." His eyes averted. "Perhaps we should wait for a better time."

Bors slammed his fist onto the table with a crack. His men stared his way, the tavern owner glanced up and fled to his kitchen.

"We go this night. Your men are the best."

Arduino's grin deepened. "We are."

"Then you will get us through without a problem."

"We will need more money," Arduino said, holding out his palm.

Bors's hand leapt like a snake striking. Gripping Arduino's tunic, he pulled him over the top the table in an iron vice-like grip, one that could crush a man like Arduino in a heartbeat. "We leave this night," he growled into the man's face. He didn't bother to grin, only pushed the man away.

"Of course. Of course. It's only a matter of coin." The sea

captain gave him a friendly disarming smile then straightened his tunic.

Bors unsheathed his knife from his belt, and in a flash, swiped the captain's ear off. For a brief moment, Arduino gaped at Bors, holding his ear and a knife in his hands. Then Arduino blinked slowly as crimson liquid flowed down his cheek. He brought a hand to cover his ear, and he scrambled backward out of his chair trying to escape. He spoke rapidly in a slang Bors could barely understand, but it amounted to a horse and sheep and a man.

"Tonight, Arduino. I don't have time for your horse shit."

"The coin," Arduino said, his voice quivering in fear. His hand held the place where his ear had once been. "I can't do it without more coin."

Bors tossed him another bag of dinars, the man catching it with his chest. It was Bors's last to be sure, but nothing mattered aside from escaping this land in haste. He hoped that Galahad had been successful in his diversion of the pack, but if he wasn't, Bors and his men were in a hard place until they escaped. It also meant that the pack may be larger than they suspected. Five, six, seven wolves would present a deadly obstacle.

Arduino took the coin and tucked it away in a hurry.

"Do not make me wait," Bors said.

Blood leaked from between the captain's fingers, but he bowed, nonetheless. "Wouldn't. I swear an oath to God."

"Tonight."

"I will return when we are ready," he said, bowing again.

Arduino sped from the tavern, bowing as he went. Bors watched him leave with no remorse. Men were weak. Men like Arduino even weaker because only money motivated them. No higher purpose or standard or cause. Their lives short, brutal, and indulgent. Bors blinked and they were in their graves by the handful.

Therefore, they could be swayed, manipulated, or maneuvered by money or loss thereof. That weakness seeped into other things like rotting garbage left too long in a heap. Bors knew men like this could be brave and cruel beyond belief when fighting for their future coin, but it was a craven motivator. While it motivated men to take risks, and sometimes their lives, it could always be found elsewhere. They would sway with the political and financial winds with no regard for loyalty. In the end, they were only opportunistic dogs, brave when food was near, cowardly in the face of resistance.

Whereas the sergeants sat with no qualms, for they were cared for monetarily, but knew they fought for something much greater than how many whores they could afford at the local brothel. They fought for good over evil, and therefore weren't swayed so easily by pain or pressure because their cause was greater than all those motivators, and most men in the Order only knew the half of it, having only been at war for a fraction of their lives.

Bors turned his cup upright and poured himself more wine. They were on the precipice of wielding a relic that would change the war and the very fabric of the world itself. Armed with that knowledge, he rested easy, for the tides were turning, and the Order would be the victor in this war over the bestial darkness lurking in the shadows. Perhaps his days fighting would shorten and end in a *pax*. He doubted any true *pax* existed; *faux pax* were all there ever was. He wouldn't know how to handle himself without a war to fight. The Noctis Bellum was his singular quest in life. *Auribus teneo lupum* — I hold a wolf by the ears. And only one of us will walk away.

He glanced at the bag. Could he drink from the cup like Percival and end his near eternity? No. His fate was one of blood and lust, he had more honor than picking his own time and place. The gods held that distinctive fate, and they had deemed him worthy of fighting for hundreds of years in his very own version of the Northman's Valhalla.

He held Arduino's leathery ear between his fingers. Worthy of his saddle? He judged it for a moment. No, not this puling whoreson. He tossed the ear to the floor for the rats. Nearby patrons stood and made for the door. He took a sip of wine. How soft the world of men had become. They'd been coddled for far too long. Long gone were the days of the rider. Days of free men living under the sun. Days of the warrior.

Since the culmination of the Dark Years, Bors urged Uthur to spread his reach and build an empire. Yet for centuries, Uthur rejected his advice and bade his brothers to work in secret, staying reclusive and almost entirely separate from the world of men. Despite generations of leadership and centuries of knowledge and wisdom, he'd almost completely withdrawn from ruling over the mortals, which Bors knew was not only an obligation, but a right bestowed upon them by their longevity. Bors cared not what the mortal men thought of him, he wanted to rule kingdoms with an iron fist, establish order in this chaos left in the wake of the collapse of the western Roman Empire, ushering in a time of great encroaching darkness.

He found his hand hovering over the bag once more, a slight waver in his fingertips. They would be able to establish their Order over the entirety of the civilized world, driving the taint of the Hunted into the very fringes of existence. They were on the cusp of decisive victory, and Bors would see it done.

CHAPTER 23

A lone torch illuminated a scarred wooden gate, hewed by a number of axes. Yet the gate still held enough integrity to perform its function, impeding their entry to the town of Jaffa. The walls were made of sandy stone, appearing as if a mighty gust of wind may blow them over. They waited a long time before two Armenian turcopoles under the employ of Godfrey hefted a heavy wooden beam, granting them entrance, not bothering to ask them their cause or reason for late arrival. The trio of warriors walked their horses inside the gate.

"We make for the docks. If Bors wishes to depart by sea, he and his men will go there," Marya said.

The town gradually sloped downward to the waters of the Mediterranean Sea. The houses rose with the land, and then over the apex of the hill they were built onto the slope, clustered together as if they clung to the hill in order to not fall into the sea. A woman tossed a bucket of night waste from the window, and it splattered onto the street in front of them.

"Watch it," Cutnose snarled.

A curtain flapped, but there was no response. The citizens of Jaffa were not fond of paying tribute to the Franks, and especially were not fond of being blockaded by the Fatimids because of their new occupiers. The local populace caught in the middle, resisted in other ways.

Near the docks, the three reached the edge of the houses, sitting nearly atop the sea. A pathway ran along the shore, following a stone wall and wooden docks that led out to moored merchant vessels and smaller fishing boats.

"I don't see how Bors is going to find a ship to sail him away from here," Cutnose said. He gestured to the edge of the harbor. "Those dark shapes are the Egyptian fleet."

"He will find a way. He is neither Christian nor Muslim, he worships his own gods. This conflict here, these mortal men killing themselves in the desert, means nothing to him. He will swear fealty or pay his way through their lines. Never doubt a force such as Bors."

"Sounds like a pagan."

"That's exactly what he is. Those heads he carries on his horse are a custom of his tribe from long ago."

"He must be ancient."

"Older than even Ulf."

"How has he not perished?"

"Your gift offers you many benefits. Long life, although not eternal, is one of them." To Cutnose, long life was sixty, but hundreds of years was something unfathomable in his mind. He would be a demi-god. The possibilities were limitless and filled with danger. Men feared what they did not understand, and to them he would be something of another world.

He gestured with his head along the sea-side street. "There's a tavern this way. Sailors and the like frequent it. Caters to the Christians."

"An expert on Jaffa now?" Marya asked.

"We took Jaffa on the march to Jerusalem, and a mercenary knows where he can spend his coin."

"I should have anticipated you would hold such knowledge." She snorted a laugh. "Lead the way."

The tavern had two floors, all made of stone. Candlelight

shone from the upper windows. The sound of a woman's laughter carried out from above, followed by the laugh of a man. Marya exchanged a glance with Cutnose. "I can't say I am surprised."

"Can't be ashamed of what men and women do."

Dozens of horses were tied to heavy iron rings bolted directly into the stone tavern's walls. A stone trough stretched the length of the wall, and the horses bowed their heads as they drank their fill. The three managed to fit their mounts near the edge of the crowded trough.

"Not surprised this is a popular place," Marya said.

"No competition with the Franks. It's the only place that serves wine."

"These mounts are well-fed," Arnulf said with a glance at all the horses.

"Plenty of armed pilgrims in these parts now. Men trying to find passage back home," Cutnose said. He opened the door to the tavern for Marya, candlelight trickled through. "You have my thanks."

He nodded to her and followed her inside. In the doorway they stopped, standing completely still. Soldiers and knights were deep into their cups. Their shadowy forms illuminated by candles. A brown-and-gray haired man with stubbly cheeks regarded them with hard eyes, his mail rustling as he set down his cup. He leaned to the man next to him whispering something.

"This is wrong," Marya said, holding a hand out to stop her companions from going any further.

"What?" With a glance at the tavern, it became clear that sergeants and knights filled at least half the seats. The few that had surcoats had crosses sewn on them, all wore coats of mail. He assumed most were part of a garrison Godfrey left to keep the critical port under his control, and act as a warning bell if the Fatimids decided to attack from the sea again. They all gave off the impression of veteran soldiers. Cutnose could always tell men who'd been in their fair share of fights, they held themselves differently, a prepared coolness to them.

Eyes slowly found the newcomers. Cups were set down. Men eyed spears, propped on the wall. Tension began to invade the room, taking each of them hostage. Then he saw their shields lined along the wall, green stags upon iron crosses on fields of white. *The Order.*

A scent caught Cutnose's scarred nose. It ruffled him. He knew it yet he didn't, like a lost memory, but it struck him as foul, like spoiled meat. *There is another wolf here.* Hands reached for swords. The sergeant at the table nearest them, with a scar running from eye to jaw, slid a knife from beneath his plate. The metal of his blade gently scraped the table.

Cutnose's hands instinctively tightened around Crowfeeder. With the low ceiling, he would be constrained with the types of swings and cuts he could make with it, dangerously narrowing his options. He'd be forced to switch early to any of his shorter weapons strapped to his belt.

Marya's hand settled on her curved sword while Arnulf ran his fingers over the goose fletching of his arrows. A shadowed man rose from his seat in the back. Broad-shouldered, he pushed through the tables, more bull than man. His mustache was long and golden, hanging far from his chin like twin ropes. His jawline was broad and set. A grim smile settled on his lips. "I knew you were close."

"I could smell your stink from the city gates," Marya said.

"I can see we have the same taste in fine establishments," Bors said.

"I led us here," Cutnose said. He took a finger and ran it over the length of the scar on his nose.

Bors stared at him as a man who guts a fish and feels nothing for the animal's life, for its intelligence and significance is far below his level of caring. "This man speaks as if we are equals."

"Come a little closer, I have a friend to introduce you to." Cutnose brandished his long axe.

"The young pup growls," Bors said with an amused grin.

"Give us the Chalice," Marya said. "And we will let you live. Hear me when I say, it will pain me to allow you such a mercy."

"You are in no position to make demands." Sergeants and brothers from the tables all stood, weapons loosening in sheaths and belts.

"None of your men will survive this encounter," Marya said with the confidence of a queen.

Bors squinted at her. "You'll be the second prettiest head I've ever taken for my saddle." He turned to Cutnose. "Yours the ugliest."

Dozens of armed men crowded the way between the three and Bors. They all wielded swords, axes, daggers, and maces. Cutnose ran his eyes over them, deciding which would be the most advantageous to eliminate early.

Bors growled and the wolf inside Cutnose began to rattle in his ribcage. He felt Marya tensing beside him, as she prepared to spring herself forward. Arnulf was as tight as his bowstring would be in a fraction of a second.

"Make way," said a man trying to get past them through the door.

"Arduino," Bors growled.

"I am hurrying, my lord. The time is upon us. My men and the ship are waiting."

Cutnose eyed the Italian, by the looks of him a Genoese captain, bandages wrapped around his skull, a patch of red where fresh blood seeped through. The sea captain stopped and took a step away as he realized the conflict brewing in front of him. Then another, hands in the air. "Haste, my lord," he called to Bors. "Our time nears."

Bors bared his teeth, fangs pointing long, then charged. Arduino threw himself on the ground. An arrow softly thrummed from Arnulf's bow and Bors moved his arm in a flash to take the arrow in the forearm punching through the other side. Using his chest, he snapped the arrow point, shoving his men to get to his enemies.

Chaos erupted. Cutnose lunged for the three men at the table nearest him, the furthest sergeant grasping for a spear on the wall, before Cutnose kicked the table into his back. He fell beneath the table. A knife swept past Cutnose's face, then slashed at his chest. He brought the haft of his axe across the man's mouth, knocking teeth and man, tittering across the stones. The sergeant fell into the table behind him, clutching at his face.

The third man had darted behind Cutnose. He sensed the sergeant preparing to cleave his skull in two, but the narrow room forced the sergeant to take a limited swing. The slight hesitation gave Cutnose a critical half-second to bring his long axe back around. He dragged it over the man's face. The sergeant screamed, holding his nose and mouth.

The steel song sang loud within the stone walls. Marya's sword was a foggy blade turning the air into red mist around her. She cut a man from groin to neck and danced through two more, her blade a deadly serpent among them. Bors snarled, throwing a table, shoving his men out of the way. Arnulf shot an arrow into a man's eye and then whipped his bow like a staff, sweeping another off his feet.

In a blur, Bors's hammer sought Marya. She rolled to the side, dodging as he slammed it into the stone floor, sending stone shards airborne.

Cutnose left his long axe in a portly sergeant's skull, drawing his long dagger in a reverse grip, his hand axe in the other. In the close proximity, he awkwardly fended off a sword strike. On the soldier's second angled strike, Cutnose hooked his sword with the beard of his hand axe and sliced through the man's forearm, opening a gash that would need the care of a physician, but he had no time to worry as he fended off jabs from a spearman reaching over his adversary's left shoulder. The brother in front held his arm close to his chest, switching sword hands. The two men were effective in their dual maneuver to drive him backward.

Bors and Marya ducked and dodged, swung and stabbed. Sparks fell as weapons struck with the strength of a dozen men.

The Order soldiers were forced to the flanks of the battle. Cutnose rushed the man in front of him, keeping himself centered as he barreled into the brother and rolled him over his back and onto the floor.

The spearmen reacted, attempting to drive Cutnose into his fallen comrade with the shaft, but Cutnose hooked the spear with his hand axe while simultaneously forcing his long knife through his belly. The sergeant's eyes widened.

Her scream pierced the air. It drew every man in. It was both fierce and vulnerable at the same time. Cutnose kicked the sergeant backward into a brother, sending them crashing into chairs. "Marya," he breathed.

She lay in a heap upon the stones. An arrow sprouted from Bors's chest. The giant brother roared, lowering his hammer forcefully over the butt of the arrow until it snapped. A sergeant stepped in front of him and took an arrow through the skull meant for Bors's neck. Bors wielded the dead man like a meat shield, using his body to absorb arrows. Then he lowered his head and charged for the door.

Cutnose lunged for him with his knife. The two men collided. The knife buried itself in the dead sergeant, and Bors threw them both to the side. Cutnose crashed into the tavern floor, and he untangled himself from the body. A sword blurred his way, and he parried it with his knife, scrambling to stand. He dodged a backswing and stabbed the man in the belly.

He rushed to Marya. A sergeant made for her with his axe and Cutnose shoved his dagger in the way, deflecting the strike. Cutnose changed his level and swung his hand axe into the sergeant's thigh. An arrow sprouted from the man's throat, and he fell to his back to die. Cutnose dragged Marya by her kaftan toward Arnulf.

Every man in the room huffed trying to catch his breath. A dozen sergeants and two brothers remained upright, including a tall, formidable-looking brother standing in the rear of the tavern. The tall brother with a haughty glance commanded his men to formation. "Form the Stag!" he shouted, bearing a shield with the green stag upon it.

The Order soldiers breathed heavily, arming themselves with shields, spears in the rear rank, swordsmen in the front. Arnulf aimed his bow from one man to another, shifting his sight frequently so no one man would be brave enough to try them.

Cutnose bent near Marya, her face was rapidly purpling where the hammer had struck her. "Marya, wake up."

Arnulf loosed an arrow at any weak point in the formation. One of the sergeants went down, grasping his boot. "Bors escapes. Grab her and move."

Cutnose hoisted her in his arms. "Forward," shouted the tall brother. The Order soldiers marched forward aggressively, recovering lost ground and their wounded. Cutnose rushed out the door while Arnulf kept them in check.

He made for their horses and hoisted Marya into the saddle. Arnulf exited the tavern and tossed Cutnose Crowfeeder. "It would be a grave insult to leave such a weapon behind."

"Won't happen again." He pointed toward the docks. "Bors is escaping."

Arnulf climbed onto his horse and grabbed Marya's reins. Cutnose hurriedly unraveled the other mounts, slapping at their rears to get them running. The horses bolted into the town, thundering in the darkness. A sergeant shielded himself as he exited the tavern, and arrows drove him back inside. Cutnose scrambled back to his mount and saddled.

"Ride!" Arnulf called. They spurred their mounts for the docks. Order soldiers cautiously filed into the street, shouting insults and anger for their missing mounts.

A merchant galley docked in the harbor. The galley was the most prevalent vessel throughout any land that touched the Mediterranean. It had been in use since ancient times, an oar-propelled vessel with various modifications for war or trading. This one was a round galley, designed for hauling more cargo and less for maneuvering, which aided in naval warfare. It was a stubby broad-beamed ship with a high freeboard and multiple decks. A single mast stood near the center of the ship. Bors skillfully led his mount over a gangplank to board.

The ship teemed with thirty or so sailors. Sailors clustered on the bulwark and crossbow bolts flew in Cutnose's direction. Cutnose reared his horse, shielding Marya with his mount and body. Ropes were removed from the mooring. Oars stretched outward, the sailors bending them to reverse the ship from the dock. Bolts whispered through the air past them, others skidded along the stones falling short, keeping the riders at bay. The Order men gave a shout from the rear. They marched in formation, steady and poised to strike them down from the rear.

"They escape," Cutnose said with a glance back at them.

"Shield me," Arnulf shouted.

Cutnose steered his horse between him and the ship and raised his shield to cover his body and that of Marya as best as he could. Arnulf quickly wrapped three arrows in rags. Then he took a flint and struck them alight, keeping them between his fingers. Bolts thudded into Cutnose's shield. His horse repeatedly tossed its head, threatening to run with each arriving projectile. The final sailor on the dock clutched a rope and jumped aboard.

"Hurry, Arnulf, or we will never see him again."

Arnulf raised his bow, stretching the string taut, and aimed it skyward. The arrow's tip flamed, illuminating all three riders, sparks spilling from the head. Arnulf frowned as embers seared his hand. His concentration unaffected by the flames. The arrow became a comet across the nighttime sky. It arched downward into the furled sail. Flames spread from the arrow and the sail burst alight, raining fire upon the sailors below.

Shouts carried over the water. Oars were lifted into the air. The galley floundered near the docks. A sailor scrambled up the mast. A blanket unfurled, and he beat at the flames wildly. In desperation, he cut the lines holding the sail in place. It went crashing onto the deck. Men stomped at the flames, but they continued to grow.

Arnulf loosed the other fire arrows. The inferno spread with a fury. Oars were released and the crew dove into the harbor. Men splashed as they hit the water. A horseman leapt from the galley deck and onto the docks. The mount's hooves slid, but it stopped itself. The rider heeled its sides and the horse galloped for the city gates.

"Awaken Hunter," came a shout from the rear, the Order sergeants and brothers closed, spear points outward, but all eyes were upon the retreating Bors, speeding toward the town gates.

Cutnose snarled with a glance at Arnulf. "He's mine."

"Not if I can take him now." Arnulf grasped an arrow with a gray fletching, guiding it upon his bowstring. He tracked Bors, the arrow blurred, and the bowstring was left vibrating near his fingertips. Bors let out a roar, but Cutnose was already several horse strides ahead before Arnulf could protest.

CHAPTER 24

The chase went on for some time. Jaffa was long behind them. The moon illuminated the road and country, a stalwart guide in the night. The horses heaved with exertion. Dust caked Cutnose's face, drying his nostrils and splitting his lips. He crouched low in the saddle as they ventured miles north. With the armored men, the mounts would never be able to sustain the pace for long, yet each man was willing to ride the animals until they breathed their last.

As Bors's mount floundered, Cutnose began to salivate over his coming victory. Soon he would sate his vengeance with blood in the sand. Crowfeeder would feast. His enemy cut down to mere pieces of flesh and bone.

Bors spurred his horse's flanks, drawing blood, but the animal continued to falter. The beast buckled beneath the added pressure, sending Bors flying. He crashed into the ground in a cloud of dust and sand. He rolled before bouncing upright as Cutnose bore down on him. If he could take Bors's head without letting him gain solid footing, he may be able to end the fight before it began. There were no rules in this war, only living and dying. He let the long axe extend to an unwieldy grip. It was meant for two hands, but he would use one or risk tangling his reins.

Bors braced himself, orienting his shoulders for a strike, war hammer held in both hands. Cutnose swung his axe, but Bors ducked beneath it, bringing the hammer with him into his mount's front leg. His horse piteously cried out in terror before slamming headfirst into the ground.

The ground came for Cutnose next without mercy. His shoulder struck first, his face following close behind. He didn't roll, merely slid forward before his legs followed overtop. His helmet disappeared. Skin from his cheek scraped off and filled with dirt. The horse rolled onto its back, horrible shrieks crying out. The animal flailed its hooves. Cutnose threw himself to the side as the beast rolled in his direction.

His hands grasped dirt. *Axe?* He blinked away dust, knowing his opponent was as fast if not faster than him. The horse screamed. He felt the wind from the hammer. He threw his body sideways as the hammer whooshed into the ground next to him, spraying sand. Fighting from his back was not an option. Scrambling backward, he tried to stand. Bors followed, a killer's rage flaming in his eyes.

Cutnose gained his feet. He staggered away from Bors, gripped his axe with both hands, and spit dirt from his mouth. Bors moved between him and his mount, picking up his shield.

"You are quicker than I last remember," Bors taunted.

"And you're slower."

Bors sneered. "So, you took one of them? Who marked you?"

"Ulf Bodvarsson."

"The King of the Isles?" Bors said, his eyes lighting in surprise. "He was here. I was in more danger than I knew."

"He sends his regrets," Cutnose said, brandishing his axe.

Bors grinned beneath his golden rope of a mustache. "You killed a legend. I envy you in this moment. Many of our brothers have hunted him. Many would have killed for that honor." He slowly circled Cutnose, war hammer switching between attacking angles, his shield light on his arm.

Cutnose kept his long axe bladed backward, his left hand forward, right hand handling the middle of the shaft, each reach to block, deflect, or swing into action like a bladed catapult ready to explode with pent-up force. The key was not overextending himself and exposing himself to a vicious counter.

His heart pounded with the rhythm of Hugh's hand drum. The wolf fire blazed with a fierce rage, desiring freedom from inside, and he watered its flame, keeping the beast in check. The man, Cutnose, wanted the kill more than the wolf.

"You killed my men at the Temple."

"All this for a few sword-brothers?" Bors lowered his war hammer. "More honor than I've seen in some time. What is your price? You are a soldier of coin? A man who values payment? I will make you rich."

Cutnose licked his dusty lips, feeling the sand grind in his teeth. "Vengeance is my only price."

"A man with no price?" Bors shook his head in disbelief. "Then you've chosen to join your sword-brothers in whichever afterlife you believe in."

Bors ran for him, raising his hammer over his shoulder, red boar on green decorated shield held in front of his body. He sprinted over the rocky sand and dirt, boots kicking it into the air. Cutnose waited until he was near before launching his own attack. Surging forward, he swung his axe into Bors's shield, the weight of the attack throwing him off course. Cutnose shifted, then swung the axe wide to separate Bors from him, keeping a long axe length distance from his enemy.

Bors circled, shifting for a closer advantage. His eyes were steel spear points searching for a weakness in Cutnose's stance. The brother's hammer was ready to strike like a blacksmith waiting for his metal to glow orange before he struck. Cutnose thrust with the edge of the long axe, keeping it between them. He jabbed at Bors's face and then his feet, careful to not overextend and expose himself to attack.

Have to keep him off tempo. Must control the flow. He swung and Bors parried shifting his shield's point at Cutnose's face. Everything was angles. Angles of attack and angles of defense. *Must keep him guessing*. Cutnose swung with the butt of his axe at his face and the brother caught the blow with his shield driving Cutnose away.

Sweat beaded over Cutnose's brow, running down his back. His thigh still bled where the sergeant had caught him with his sword, slowing his movement. Bors used his shield with expert precision, jabbing with the tip to trip Cutnose more than once. Until with a sudden rush, Bors charged him, deflecting a feint with his shield. His hammer chopped through the air like an arrow on a downward journey. Cutnose threw himself to the ground, using the long axe to catapult himself forward and past Bors.

The hammer slammed into the ground, but Bors did not wait. He charged Cutnose another time. Cutnose swung with all his might and the axe-head cleaved through Bors's shield, splitting as one cuts a loaf of warm bread with a knife. The blade bit down and only the bones of Bors's forearm stopped the axe. Bors roared in pain and only the strength of his shield and his mail prevented the hand from completely severing.

Cutnose struggled to free the blade from the confines of the wood and iron, and Bors tore his shield from his arm and tossed it to the side, taking the axe and Cutnose with it.

"Lightsbane," Bors spat.

"Ulf's own." He kicked at the shield, but it was still wedged deep in the wood. *Must end this now.*

Bors's cheek quivered as if he read Cutnose's thoughts. He growled with an overhead swing of his hammer intended to crush his skull. With the additional weight of Bors's shield, he was slow to raise the shaft, hefting the shield and axe to deflect the blow. The hammer grazed the crown of his skull with an explosion of light in his eyes. He found himself on the ground, church bells ringing inside his head, breathing in the gritty sand and dust, blinking away the shock.

Bors stood over him. Blood dripped along his fingers, involuntarily bending in a claw-like form. Air puffed through his mustache. "You give good contest, but you are not the man to take Bors's life. I will honor you by taking your head for my saddle." He lifted his hammer over his head and Cutnose rammed the pugio into the brother's belly. It crunched as it penetrated the mail rings, biting through flesh.

"Lightsbane, whoreson," Cutnose growled. He drove the man backward with the knife until both fell onto the ground. Bors wrapped massive hands around his neck. The brother's mouth shook as he squeezed. Both men gaped at one another, eyes brimming with battle rage. Each man exerted the strength of a dozen men, each man finding only pain and struggle with no victory.

Flexing his neck, Cutnose drove his weight down on the blade, shoving it deeper into the brother's belly. Blood pounded in his head. He released the hilt and punched Bors in the face repeatedly until his grip loosened and Cutnose was able to roll away. He scrambled for his axe on all fours. His hands settled upon the engraved shaft, and he stood, shaking the axe-head free of the shield.

Bors got to his knees, knife still stuck in his belly, face bloodied and battered. He rested both hands on the hilt and ripped it free, tossing it into the sand. He spat bloody phlegm. "Where did you find that?"

Cutnose warily approached, long axe in both hands. "A parting gift from your friend Galahad."

Bors roared in rage, halting Cutnose. "You will dine with Hades headless, mocked by the shades."

"On your knees or on your feet, warrior. You choose."

Bors stared him at him with glowing golden eyes. "I'll die a thousand deaths before you take the Chalice from my possession." In a matter of heartbeats, Bors had tossed off his coat of mail and transformed into the wolf that had murdered Cutnose's men with impunity. With open jaws that dripped, it howled its rage toward the sky.

Cutnose could never win man versus beast, but the wolf inside him was ready to embrace battle. Cutnose, the man, slid away along with his mail as he relinquished control. His blood simmered inside his veins until it transformed to a roaring inferno and the wolf exploded forth. His transformation was easy this time, almost a seamless metamorphosis, a dozen breaths and he was Scar.

The long axe fell to the ground. The wolf neither wanted the weapon of a man nor wanted to touch the poison metal. This animal before him was wounded, ripe for the slaying, yet the most dangerous beast he had ever encountered. No fat-belly or two-leg, but an ancient one of his kind.

Smoky tendrils traveled through his golden fur. Thickly built, neck muscles almost connecting directly to his shoulders. Powerful, meaty legs and razor-sharp, knife-like claws. Saliva dripped from the wolf's mouth, but he knew this enemy not by a given name, but through his weave of scents. It came to Scar like a whip landing across his shoulder blades. *Long Tusk.*

Strong, fast, resilient and deadly beyond his imagination. Long Tusk's nose wrinkled, lips revealing canines like daggers. He let out a guttural growl, moving from two legs to all four.

Both wolfskins were unrelenting in the face of the other's gaze, seeking weakness and submission that was only found in death. The first to break eye contact would be the first to admit defeat.

They stalked one another in a circle, bristling man-wolves of claw and muscle. Long Tusk trailed blood behind him, the smell of decaying autumn leaves, favoring his front leg. He was dying. The weakness of his enemy was too much to ignore, and Scar leapt into the air. Long Tusk met him mid-flight, and the two collided with a thunderclap. The two wolves rolled. Claws darted in and out, fangs pierced thick coats of fur, and the wolves battled with a primal ferocity only known in nature.

With a rip, Long Tusk removed a gouge out of Scar's shoulder. In the next instant, Scar's claw left a jagged trail of skin and fur in its wake. The wolves cared not for time nor their wounds, it would only stop with death.

Claws swept through air and flesh alike. Jagged teeth ripped through muscle as the beasts fought to the song of the night. Scar bowed low, muscles tensing, then lunged for Long Tusk's jugular, but the ancient wolf swept him from his feet, landing atop him. Long Tusk's jaws clamped around Scar's neck. It was a domineering move, one that would gain submission or death. *Not again,* screamed the man inside Scar. *Not again.*

But this time it was different. He was not beholden to the laws of men. He was wild and free, of the forests, and of the moon. Scar dug his claw into Long Tusk's metal wound. The man inside Scar knew *poison metal* had caused the wound, and now it stunk of encroaching death.

Long Tusk's jaws loosened until he reared his head and howled in pain. Scar flipped him to the side and sunk his teeth deep around Long Tusk's neck. Muffled cries leapt from Long Tusk, surprising Scar, but the taste of his rival's blood unlocked an even greater bestial strength. Long Tusk clawed his shoulders and sides attempting anything to break Scar's hold. They rolled and Scar gained a position of dominance, never relenting his bite. Long Tusk tried to squirm beneath him and escape, but Scar's jaws only clenched tighter.

The strength disappeared from his opponent, yet he held him down all the same, never letting up from his attack. Until Long Tusk's scent changed to that of the two-legs. Scar stared down at his opponent with smoldering golden eyes. He released the two-legs and took a step back, breathing heavily, panting, the exhilaration of the kill taking hold of him. The two-legs would be one with the earth soon.

Scar turned his muzzle toward the Moon Goddess and called to her to see his prowess in overcoming the enemy. He sang long and proud and her voice hummed from above. *You have my tribute.* Cutnose, the man, shouted in the background, calling for Scar to return to his home, but home was a cage, and here he was a king. The man wanted subservience; the wolf only wanted to be free. To hunt, to kill, to breed, that was the only way. The wolf resisted the calls of his two-legs.

Scar stood upright, claws hanging at his sides, and howled with the blood of his enemy drenching his fur. The man wanted his vengeance, and the wolf fought him internally for control. Water flowed over the wolf's flames. Scar's powers waned, the collar and leash around his neck. He reluctantly let himself join the man, for he was never free of him, they were joined, two spirits as one. Scar lowered his head and let his fury be doused with man's water, the man wresting control over him. Scar took one last glance at the Moon Goddess and rested his head. *It was a worthy victory.*

Cutnose took charge of the wolf and transitioned back into the form of a man. He breathed heavily. The beast had been close to seizing control from him permanently. The Wilds still rung in his ears. The wolf still baring its teeth inside him. He pushed himself from his knees, stepping closer to the dying brother.

Bors lay on his back, breathing his last, his throat destroyed by the wolf's teeth and jaws. Even now, his eyes still darted around, and his fingers grasped for his war hammer but he weakened with every heartbeat, barely holding enough life-blood to stay among the living.

Cutnose searched the sands and reclaimed Crowfeeder. He ignored the pain surging through his shoulder and the puncture wounds around his neck. Blood escaped, but he would live. It would heal and his pain was temporary. He limped back to the fallen brother.

Bors gasped breathlessly, his mouth working, his throat a mangled mess of meat. His fingers reached for his war hammer. Cutnose found the hammer, lifting the weapon. He debated whether he should allow the ancient warrior the respect to die with a weapon in hand. While a hated enemy, he was a soldier and warrior, and had earned the right to die as such. He placed it in Bors's hand.

"For my brothers. For Ulf and Hugh." He watched for some sort of recognition from the fallen warrior. "Know that your Chalice will never fall into the Order's hands as long as I live."

Blood spurt from Bors's lips as he tried to utter something, Cutnose assumed some sort of curse upon him. In his experience, a dead man's curse meant little when you were the one left standing.

"We shall battle again in the afterlife." He held no pity for the dying wolfskin. "But you will fight headless as you made Ralph." Bors's eyes narrowed. The long axe sang a short song as it threaded the air and ended with a thump, biting into the sandy ground. Cutnose breathed in the scent of the fresh blood. He leaned on his axe, staring at the dead man. The pain of his wounds crept upon him slowly, some more grievous than others.

He did not know how long he stared vacantly at the severed head and its body. The sound of hooves drew his attention south. Two riders emerged in the distance, galloping hard, kicking up a dust cloud behind them. He gripped Bors's long hair and picked up his head. It was heavy in his hand, like holding a sling with a boulder in it. The shadowed riders became Marya and Arnulf.

He went to Bors's mount. In death, its tongue hung from the corner of its mouth. He knew the bag that held the Chalice immediately for its song was intoxicating. He cared little for his trophy, and he dropped Bors's head. His fingers hurried to untie the knot like a boy about to become a man for the first time.

The riders slowed and brought their mounts to a halt, both peering at him intently.

"Do you have it?" Marya rushed.

Cutnose held the sack into the air. It called to him with a wordless note, entrancing as it was terrifying, a man on the edge of a great unknown precipice. He wanted to toss the bag and run, yet at the same time, deep inside his soul, he desired to protect it until his last breath.

Marya's head was wrapped with a jaggedly cut piece of cloak, her cheek and eye swollen. She dismounted and approached slowly. "Give me the Chalice. We do not have time to waste. The Order will regroup before long. Galahad is still out there."

Unrelenting, he stared her in the eyes. Blood trickled along his brow dripping from his face, the rest finding a way into his eye. "Why?" The coarse bag felt silky in his fingertips even as his hand prickled into numbness.

"Because we have to protect it." She gestured for him to hand it over.

He retracted it away from her as if struck. It was more precious than any sack of gold. "Can you hear it? It sings to me." He studied the plain brown sack. He found his fingers untying the strings shutting away such beauty to behold.

"Do not. It holds more power than we could know."

He ignored her and thrust his hand into the bag. His fingertips grazed the Chalice. A cold numbness akin to death, crawled from the stone into his hand, sending shockwaves through his person. The chill of an endless night settled into his bones, a rapid frost crystalizing over his soul.

"Don't!" she called out.

Arnulf's bowstring tightened audibly under the pressure, arrow nocked, but none of their protests or threats of violence meant anything to him, only the Black Chalice mattered and its place in his hands. It was a singular compulsion, driving him onward with no regard to his friends. The bag fell away empty.

He lifted the rough-hewn bowl toward the sky. His bones began to turn brittle as a frozen tree branch. The light of the moon bent and absorbed into its reaches. Arnulf lowered his bow in awe, and Marya's jaw dropped, eyes shying away from it.

He held the bowl, and all sensation was lost from his hands. He forgot to breathe. He didn't need air when he had the Chalice. He needed nothing except the bowl, as it promised to send him to the cold oblivion of death or life everlasting. "My eyes have never beheld anything so pure. It is perfect," he whispered.

"Put it away," Marya called. "It is not meant to be handled lightly."

"How do you know?" His eyes would not be pried from it.

"Look at your hands," she shouted.

His eyes revolted. It was a struggle to pull them from the abyss of the bowl to see his fingers. They were as white as bone growing paler by the moment, his hands appearing as ashen dust of a forgotten fire.

"Yet I feel nothing," he uttered. His eyes were unable to part from its ghostly entrancement. It was as if the bowl drank in his life-force drip by drip, and he would allow it, for it gave him an indescribably pure, almost numbing pleasure, one he struggled to release himself from, for one moment away from it would be an eternity too long.

Marya dismounted, stepping closer, raising her hand. "Cut-nose, put it away. It is too powerful. It will kill you."

He didn't bother to look at her until her hand touched his. He slowly looked in her hazel-green eyes. "I hear it too. Its song is beautiful. Now, let's cover it again." Her eyes held something in them. Life. Love. Pain. Fear. Strength. Command. They all flashed through her. She held the sack. "Put it in here." He blinked away the temptation of the bowl and placed it back into its sack with a shudder when it left his fingertips.

He lowered his head for a moment, catching his breath. The feeling of warm blood poured back into his arms and body, the sensation of numb ecstasy lingering. In the back of his mind, he knew that only the bowl could fulfill his desire. It called to him to take it back.

Marya held the sack gingerly and nodded to him. "You did well."

He stared at his white hands for a moment. "What was happening?"

She shook her head. "I know not for its knowledge is arcane, but it holds immense power, and must be kept hidden from men that would use it for ill."

He flexed his fingers in his hands, pins and needles riddling them. "I don't even remember why I was holding it, but I knew I only wanted to hold it. It was the only thing I could think about. Nothing else mattered."

She nodded gravely, securing the sack upon her saddle.

"Come, we must leave here. It is only a matter of time before Galahad finds our trail." She tightened the knot and remounted. "We go north."

Cutnose grasped Bors's head and Crowfeeder. His body hurt; his leg would need some sort of binding. He was tired and blooded. His horse dead.

She offered him a hand. "We must depart."

He stared at her for a moment. She was an oasis in a desert sea. The truest noblewoman he'd ever met. Yet he was beholden to his own path. "I'm not going with you."

Her face twisted in scorn. "What do you mean? It is not safe here. We must stick together."

His eyes sought an answer in the sand-swept road leading back to Jaffa, and in the far distance, the water from the sea. Wolfskins were his people now, how else could one be accepted, yet he couldn't break away from the man he once was. A man of war and coin. "Whatever I am now," he said, regarding the blood on his hands. "I'm still a soldier."

She cocked her head to the side, her eyes reflecting betrayal. "You can be a soldier anywhere. You can be a soldier with us."

He disconnected from her and looked in the direction of Jaffa. Tancred was back that way. The army he'd served in for years. An army that was on the lookout to slaughter him on sight. "A man's reputation is all he has. I'm going to clear my name. I won't have them hunting me the rest of my life."

She shook her head. "Then you still do not understand what you are. Naivety is no excuse. You have joined something ancient that must be respected. The ideas of men are of no matter to you now. You must be above them if you wish to survive."

"I've never been a fast learner."

"There is no doubt in my mind of that," Marya said with disdain.

Arnulf gave him an understanding nod. "Let the man go, Marya. You do not force a wolf to travel in your pack."

"His path is with us," she snapped.

"All those that wander are not lost. You know this, Marya. It is how we found each other."

She looked back at Cutnose, her eyes sparkling in the moonlight.

"Where will you go?" Cutnose asked.

"We gather at the only place left for our kind. The only place we can protect the Chalice."

"Where's that?"

"Constantinople." She shared an uneasy glance with Arnulf. "It has been a long time since we've been there. I am not even sure we are still welcome, but there is one there even older than Hugh that will know what to do with the Chalice."

"Throwing in with the backstabbing Greeks? They welcome everyone with a smile on their lips and a knife behind their backs."

She peered down her nose at him. "Those people have given us a chance. They have made a pact and upheld their oath." She eyed the land. "When you are done playing war with these zealous men, you can find us there."

"Who says I'll come looking?"

"You will. No matter how long you wander, you will end up seeking ones such as yourself. You will yearn to find your pack." Her eyes confirmed the truth. She knew he would eventually seek them once more. Was it a reluctance to let go of the past? Was it wanting to leave with a clear name? He had avenged his slain men. None yet remained to make amends with. Yet there was something here that kept his feet on the ground, drawing him back toward Jerusalem.

"Maybe I will," he said with a smile.

Her grim stare softened. "The Order has brothers all over the known world. You would do well to take care of yourself, Sir Cutnose."

"You do the same." He glanced at Arnulf. "Good shooting back there. Perhaps if I start a new company one day, I'll need a man to lead the archers."

Arnulf turned his head to the side. "Perhaps I will start my own band and you can join me." He gave a half-smile. "We will meet again."

"That's what they keep telling me."

"We will, Sir Cutnose," Marya said. Her horse danced beneath her, anxious to depart. "Be careful here. Godfrey is an ally of the Order, and it appears that your friend Tancred is as well." She paused. "This land will change with the Franks. The Order will seek advantage in the chaos. Their roots run wide and deep. However, this day is ours, and you have my thanks. Know that the Chalice will be protected with our lives."

"I can't think of a better keeper."

"Then we must begone, for time is against us and Constantinople is far away."

"Deus vult, Marya." The hilt of a knife poked out from the sands. "Wait," he said, bending to pick it up. "If what you say is true, you'll need this Lightsbane weapon."

He flipped it point first in his hand and gave it to her. She nodded to him fiercely, slipping the knife into her belt before shouting, "Vetar!" Spurring her horse, she galloped along the road followed closely by Arnulf. He watched them until they faded from sight.

He took everything of value from Bors's saddle and body. He pilfered a worn stag and cross ring from his left hand and placed it on his own. "Must be worth something." He felt along the man's tunic and undid his belt, finding a hidden pocket concealing a bag of gold coins. By the weight alone, it was enough to buy six horses. *Always need coin.*

Taking his axe, he dug a shallow hole and buried the three heads hanging from Bors's saddle in the sandy soil. There was nothing to mark the grave, so he piled rocks atop to deter the wildlife that hadn't already picked at their flesh. He said a quick prayer to Christ for their souls, especially Ralph's, hoping he could finally find rest.

He marched back to Bors's body. "You're one big bastard, aren't you?"

He prayed to God there was not any truth to Bors's pagan customs, but on the off chance there was any truth to it, he would keep his head. He bent down, took Bors's long blond graying hair, crossed his hair in sweeping swathes making Xes. The man's head was heavy and unmanageable in death, but Cutnose ignored it and tied his weaved hair just below the bearded axe-head.

Bors's mouth hung open, his blue-and-gold ringed eyes staring vacant at the nighttime sky, reflecting the moon.

"Shall we go, you thick-skulled whoreson?" Cutnose said. He waited a moment for a response. Not hearing anything, he said. "We shall."

He propped his long axe over his left shoulder and walked south toward Jaffa, the head of his enemy swinging with the motion of his gait.

CHAPTER 25

Through the night he limped southward along the crashing waves of the coast. As long as the shore was on his righthand side, he would eventually reach Jaffa. The sun made its appearance and began to bake him inside his coat of mail. Sweat ran down his skin and every wound stung with its salty touch.

He stopped beneath an olive tree, tore a piece of his tunic and wrapped the wounds still open, the worst being his thigh. "That should hold until someone can care for it." Some wine, meat and bread would do him right, prop his leg on a pillow and get a good night's sleep, and hopefully it would be healed by the next day.

He felt the wounds around his neck that could have been his end a second time. The puncture holes were already sealing closed. He felt the pain of every wound and the terror associated with being stabbed, feathered, and sliced, but it faded fast. Even the scars. He felt his nose and the scar that still ran down the center, ridging his nose to the tip. Not all scars.

A caravan of traders in flowing robes and head scarves riding camels passed him. They took one look at his wound and his long axe and gave him a wide berth, departing off the road to avoid close contact with him. He called to them and offered coin for a ride, but they ignored him and continued onward, leaving only a cloud of dust in their wake.

It took him hours to reach the walls of Jaffa, the gash on his thigh already lessening in pain and irritation. He fingered the tear in his leggings, getting underneath the bandage. The skin was already sealing shut around the edges. "By tomorrow, you'll be new as a babe." He shook his head in wonderment. "I'm basically invincible, huh Bors?" He removed his axe from his shoulder, holding it out in front of him so he could get a good look at his ghastly accomplice.

The agape brother was silent aside from his entourage of black flies that buzzed around him. His canine teeth were not fully retracted, extended too long in his human form, making his appearance even more frightening.

He considered the large brother's head again. "Well, not quite invincible, huh?"

He walked along the crumbling walls until he came to the main gate, which was open. Two guards stood outside the gates in as much shade as the walls could offer. Both leaned against the stone, one with his head down, the other staring vacantly at the wind-swept lands. They wore formerly white plain surcoats, now dingy shades of brown with red crosses sown on their breasts and open-faced helms atop their heads, spears in their hands, shields resting on the ground.

Posting guards after the melee at the docks?

They both were short men, Frankish commoners, in the service of one of the Crusade's main lords, he'd bet Godfrey or Robert of Flanders.

The closer of the two's eyes widened when he recognized the man walking toward them had a head hanging from his axe. His face was grizzled, and his skin tanned into a brownish leather.

"Gregory," he hissed, kicking at the other guard dozing with his head down.

Cutnose pulled a scarf over his face, concealing his distinguishing scar on his nose.

The other guard lifted his head and joined his comrade with a rub and a squint of his eyes. "What's it, Henry?"

Henry gripped his spear a bit tighter and tilted it in Cutnose's direction. "You. Stop there."

Cutnose complied and slowed to a halt. He set his feet casually spread in case he needed to run or fight.

Gregory joined his companion, and his voice croaked. "What you doin' here?"

"Traveling south. Looking for a place to rest."

"Jerusalem is east. You on pilgrimage?"

"Aye."

Henry frowned at him, his eyes darting nervously toward Cutnose's decapitated comrade. He licked his lips. "Who's head you got there? He looks like a Frank."

"Came across this traitor at a watering hole and did him in. Trying to find Lord Tancred so I can deliver it. Good enough reward for it."

Gregory planted his spear in the ground and scratched his cheek. "Which traitor?"

"The one with the scarred nose. Killed all them heathens at the Temple."

Henry pushed up his helm to get a better look at the head. "By the blood of Christ, his nose is ruined. You be in luck, traveler." He pointed along the road further south. "Godfrey's whole army is traveling in that direction. Every last one. 'Cept this small garrison under Sir Geldemar to hold off any Fatimids raiding from the ships." He snorted. "And some of those Armenians. But they're never around when it's time to stand watch. That's why Geldemar has his best out here now."

"Next time we shouldn't be around neither," Gregory said. His eyes darted over the landscape as if he looked for the Armenians or Saracens, viewing any local resident as one in the same.

"What are fifty spearmen and half as many crossbowmen against an army?" Henry asked.

"We don't do nothin'. We get word to Godfrey and hold up in

that keep over there until we can be relieved. Pray we don't get betrayed."

"You don't think the Fatimids come this way?" Henry asked.

"They sit in the harbor. Could be waiting for a fleet to transport a whole army straight into Jaffa's backside."

"They wouldn't."

"Why do you think Geldemar is so skittish, won't leave the keep?"

"I thought his stomach was bad."

"His stomach is bad cause he fears the Fatimids slitting his throat. They aren't going to just let us take all this unopposed."

Henry gulped at Gregory's words.

"But the army went that way?" Cutnose asked. He scratched a fleck of dried blood from his cheek.

"Aye," Gregory said.

"If you hurry, you could catch them by dark, but I'm not sure I'd be in such a hurry," Henry said. He rubbed his upper lip nervously.

"Why's that?" Cutnose asked.

Gregory gave him a look like he was a bad dog. "Where you been?" He waved southward. "One hundred thousand-man army of Saracen whoresons are marching this way led by al-Afdal Shahan-shah, shah, shah, I can't say it. He's the one who took these lands from the Turks in the first place, and he doesn't want to give it away. Godfrey has called all God-fearing men to join him in the defense of Christendom."

"Thought we were through with the defense of Christendom. We took the Holy City."

The guard barked a laugh. "Not sure we'll ever get home. Just too many bloody Saracens roaming the hills."

Cutnose gave him a nod then squinted as he judged the way southward. "One hundred thousand?"

Henry nodded. "Aye. Makes one glad to be on guard duty here."

"What you think those Saracens going to do after they get done riddling those men with arrows?" Gregory said.

Henry rubbed his upper lip again. "I don't know."

"They're going to come up here and shoot us full of arrows." He turned back to Cutnose. "Traveler, if you're looking for a fight, you'll find one that way. Heard there was a nasty brawl in the tavern earlier. Over a dozen killed and a ship sank. You ever known a sailor that couldn't swim?" He shook his head and leaned closer. "Rumors have it the Saracens were trying to burn the only tavern in the town to the ground. Don't like us drinking all the wine. Trying to get us up here." He patted his helm, and it softly rang. "Make it so we want to leave."

"Sounds like them," Cutnose said.

Henry raised his chin and puffed out his chest. "But we made sure to check everything out. Not one enemy left in the city."

"I best be on my way. I mean to get my reward for this ugly arseling. Deus vult," Cutnose said.

"Deus vult," both guards repeated.

"Friend, fill your water bladder in the pool." Henry gestured toward a watering hole for horses and animals. "If we learned anything, can't never have too much of the stuff on the march."

In clusters and as individuals, he passed the stragglers from the column of marching footmen of Godfrey's army. Those that were too injured or sick were allowed to fall back, dragging spears and polearms, shields barely grasped in worn hands. Some shed their armor and tossed it on the side of the road. They could be craven, looking for a way out of the impending battle, but at this point, the craven were gone or dead, trickling back to the land of Franks, most likely killed by raiders in Anatolia on their return journey. There was no room for the craven in these lands. For even the land itself could easily take a man, whether from lack of water or the bites of snakes, spiders, or wild beasts.

The stragglers hurried as quickly as their ailments allowed because they were in immediate danger of being slaughtered or captured by enemy scouts. Cutnose eyed some of the discarded armor but found most of it battered and dented in need of repair by a master armorer or blacksmith, only of interest to an unarmored man. A few footmen lay beneath trees unmoving.

Before the light had dissipated into full darkness, he stumbled upon the outskirts of the Christian camp. The encampment was smaller than he expected. Not nearly enough men to face an enemy with over five times their number. Toward the outer edges, the common men camped in spartan tents that encircled larger and more colorful tents of the lords and knights. Most of the lords' tents were faded from the sun and the countless days on campaign. A few of the knights resided in the vibrant colors and floral decorated tents of Saracen lords that had been looted.

Sentries didn't bother to stop him from entering the camp, figuring him to be one of the stragglers. They needed every man they could muster for the upcoming fight against an enemy who required no deception.

He settled near a fire along the perimeter of the encampment. A cluster of four crossbowmen warmed themselves around its flames.

"Can I join?"

Their leader, a bearded sergeant with an eye patch, eyed him up and down, deeming him a threat, as a thief or otherwise. "Where'd you come in from, stranger?"

"The road. Fell behind," he tapped his thigh and bandage.

The sergeant eyed the bloody rags. "Recent?" he said, frowning. "They get behind us?"

"No, the rear is clear. Took it in the capture of Jerusalem. The wound broke open on the march and is enough to hinder."

"There's space over there." The sergeant gestured with his chin and Cutnose found a spot to sleep under a cluster of palms.

He sprawled out and lay listening to their conversation. His heart jumped when he discovered that Godfrey's army didn't include Raymond's contingent.

"Raymond's men aren't here?" he called over from his tree.

The sergeant squinted. "Where've you been? He's been in Bethlehem. Refused Godfrey's call."

"That has to be a third of the army."

"Aye, we're only six thousand men. Mostly foot and crossbow. 'Bout eight hundred knights."

"The Saracens number over a hundred thousand."

The sergeant licked his lips. "Don't think we don't know that, but I ain't in charge. Them dressed up fools are, so we go where they tell us. Kill whom they tell us."

"Or get killed," said one of his men.

The sergeant eyed him before saying somberly. "Or get killed."

"I understand," Cutnose said. That was a soldier's life, not to question why, but to go and fight and die.

"With Christ's True Cross, we will prevail!" said one of the younger men. He made the sign of the cross, blessing himself.

"Bugger that piece of wood," the sergeant said. "Better off using it to make arrows, spears, or wood for this here fire." The sergeant watched the flames. "Godfrey knows we can't survive a siege, which is why we march. Hope that the horses last long enough to make a charge." He shook his head. "Or we'll be showered with arrows until we're dead."

The other men nodded grimly, the flames providing comfort to their worries.

"He can't hope to succeed with so few men," said Cutnose.

The sergeant snorted. "But we have the True Cross."

Cutnose gave him a short grin. "Ahh, but the Cross."

"Perhaps we can goad them into a close fight, where our men can do the dirty work. With their numbers they may take us up on it."

Cutnose never questioned whether he'd joined the right army, for the right price, but this may be the wrong army without a price. Despite his newfound abilities, a Saracen sword could decapitate him like anyone else.

"Looks like you've already seen some dirty work," the sergeant said with a gesture at Bors's head.

"We had a disagreement."

"What kind of disagreement?"

"Over a woman."

The sergeant eyed Cutnose with wariness, then nodded as if he understood. Whether or not Cutnose told the truth, war made men do things that others may find odd, including carrying the head of an enemy around on an axe. The men around the fire nodded quietly, peering back into the flames of comfort.

"You seen Tancred's banner?"

"Don't believe we've caught him yet. He's the one who discovered the Saracens. He's got a company of horsemen scouting with him."

"He's my lord."

The sergeant nodded. "Strong lad. Heard he was first over the walls. Him and brave Ludolf of Tournai."

Cutnose barked a short, hard laugh. "Tancred was. I was with him. Ludolf was there too. Pissed himself."

The sergeant laughed gruffly. "Should have known they'd have you men do the work and then take the credit."

"Isn't that always the case?"

"Suppose it is." The crossbow sergeant cracked a twig and fed it into the flames. "The priests will write poems and songs about them while we do all the bleeding and dying."

"No one remembers the soldier, only the general."

"Say, I like your company," said the sergeant. "You're a wise man, like me, but with two eyes." He eyed Cutnose's face, noticing his facial scar. He lowered his head, staring at the fire. "Can never believe any of the poems and songs anyway. Written by a bunch of eunuchs who'd rather line their pockets with gold and silver than tell the truth of it."

"Men die for the gains of others."

"But we free the land from the Saracens," said a young crossbowman.

The sergeant gave the man a frown. "Look around you. Godfrey started this campaign a lord, now he is a king."

"Protector of the Holy Sepulchre," the young man said.

The sergeant cuffed him upside the head. "That is a lord's speak for king." He gathered himself. "I'm not saying this land shouldn't be free but look who stands to gain from it. It's not you and me. By the time we get back to Normandy, any coins you've gained will have been spent on passage and whores."

"But we've made our pilgrimage and have been elevated in the eyes of the Lord. No greater accomplishment."

"Aye, we have, but I'd like to cuddle a few more bosoms before meeting him, in case we was wrong."

"We've been absolved. We cannot be wrong in God's eyes."

"Aye, we have." He shared a glance with Cutnose. A fellow veteran knew the truth of the ways of the world. "We could use a man like you in our ranks. Help me get these arselings back to their mothers."

"I am afraid I will need to seek out my lord as soon as he rejoins the army."

"Until then, stick wit' us. We'll watch each other's backs." His eyes settled upon the trees in the field next to them. "Can't have too many eyes when your enemies lurk behind every tree and rock."

"Fair request, sergeant." Cutnose bowed his head and dozed off.

By the end of the next day's march, Godfrey's army was within two miles of Ascalon, the coastal fortress under Fatimid control. They made their encampment with bitter resolve, knowing that no path led to easy victory. Shouts sounded as allied horsemen approached. Cutnose watched the riders from afar.

Tancred's company of horsemen drove a vast herd of goats, sheep, camels, and oxen before them. Ragged cheers lifted from the soldiers; it had been a desperate march with little hope but faith that God would send aid. He had listened to their prayers and sent them a herd to fill their bellies and strengthen their bodies before the coming battle.

The towering, golden-haired lord lifted a fist to the cheers of the men, Ludolf bearing his standard of red and blue. Cutnose moved through the crowds, scarf wrapped loosely over his head like a hood. Godfrey emerged from his lofty red and white tent to welcome him as he would a son.

"I come bearing gifts," Tancred said.

Godfrey nodded to him in deference. "A very welcome gift indeed."

"The enemy is camped between Ascalon and where we stand, even now unaware of our presence."

Godfrey turned to the congregating soldiers. "Eat well tonight lads, for tomorrow you will need all your energy for a fight." The men cheered. Tancred dismounted, and Godfrey hugged him, peering at him with fondness. "Join me in my council of war. Vizier al-Afdal Shahanshah will not walk away from this field." The two disappeared into Godfrey's personal tent.

The crusader army went about the slaughter of the herd as they would the enemy, energized by the prospect of a feast. With glee, they cooked the animals over raging fires, eating their fill, until all bellies were round and grease-splattered smiles took shape beneath sleepy eyes. Cutnose enjoyed a huge piece of mutton, tearing into the meat with the happiness of a good meal before an impending battle. Despite his hunt of Bors, he was beginning to feel comfortable and at home among the crusaders. Morale surged in the camp despite the proximity of the massive Fatimid host.

In the night, shouts of alarm sounded forth, but were dismissed as Raymond of Toulouse and his contingent joined Godfrey's army. Their ranks bolstered with every available Frank in the Holy Land; the men were unable to find rest. The fervor of the pending battle pumped their blood faster and their spirits soared. Backs were slapped and hands shook, for now they had the best chance for victory. After an hour of reunited cheer, the camp died down into a fitful slumber, the men struggling to sleep with the battle waiting with the rising sun.

Cutnose did not tarry. He left his coat of mail and helm behind, taking Crowfeeder as his only companion. In the darkness, he split between the sentries in the direction of Ascalon. With less weight upon his healing leg, he traveled the two miles.

Fires blazed like a horizon of stars in the night's shadow. The enemy camp sprawled before Ascalon's formidable walls. The city's walls were as tall as seven men standing on one another. They formed a half circle, cutting the town off from the land and only exposing her to the sea. An assault made even more difficult by the sloping hill the city had been built upon, that would deny most siege equipment from reaching the walls.

Two massive towers covered the main gate. The gate was wide enough to fit six horsemen riding abreast at once. The gatehouses were studded, the closest gatehouse smaller than the others but no less formidable, embattlements rising and falling in intervals to conceal archers. More men would fall here without reinforcements and better siege equipment. Ascalon was structurally the older brother to Jerusalem, bigger, stronger, and holding better ground.

He edged closer to the Fatimid camp, using shrubs and rocks as cover in the darkness. He tested the scent of the air for either horse or man of which there were many, but none were close. Surely there were not a hundred-thousand men, but he estimated roughly thirty thousand. Even with Raymond's contingent, they were outnumbered at least three to one, even more if he included the Fatimid garrison from Ascalon. Far too many for victory.

The crusaders didn't have enough knights or turocpoles to effectively combat the Saracen light horse. They would tire and be stretched thin until their mounts faltered and the knights cut down in their weakened state. Then the Saracens would shower the footmen with arrows until they were wounded and exhausted, sending their infantry to finish them off. The battle was win or suffer utter annihilation for Godfrey, his kingdom never growing from infancy.

The crusaders were not without some advantage. The Saracens camped here were either confident that they could master any army the crusaders could muster or were unaware that the rival army was so close. An enemy's recklessness was another man's advantage. Vicious surprise could level the scales, and if Godfrey meant to fight, then he would have to use it.

Cutnose stalked closer, keeping his back bent and his long axe in both hands. Sentries lined the Fatimid camp yet far too few to adequately guard a camp of its size. Perhaps there was truth to the rumor that they did not know Godfrey's army was on the march. He snuck even closer, moving before lying prone in the dirt.

A soldier in robes with mail dangling from his sleeves leaned on his spear. His head touched the shaft in sleepy repetition. An idea struck Cutnose. He counted the sentries down the perimeter. *It could work. It would work.* Without more thought, he raced forward like a wraith in the night and brought his axe into the man's skull with a damp thud, Bors's head dangling the whole way. The smell of his blood incited the primal beast residing inside him and the wolf burned bright with the scent.

He dropped his axe. *I will return for it.* Then he relinquished control to the wolf, and he cut down the sentries one after the other, no man able to call out before his throat was crushed or his head ripped clean from his shoulders. He fed upon the flesh of his enemies. Only muffled cries escaping them before they perished in terror. Dousing the wolf flames in the land stretching between the armies, he collected his long axe, and he slunk back into the crusader camp, making his way for the center of Tancred's contingent.

CHAPTER 26

Tancred's campaign tent was sewn from dual colors, blue and red of his house, along with a new standard hanging from a pole near the entrance. There were no guards posted outside, but Cutnose expected that his squire slept near the entrance.

He carefully pushed the tent flaps to the side and crept in. The young lord was still awake, standing with his hands splayed out on a table, a single candle casting light over a map. His squire slept on a host of blankets near the foot of Tancred's campaign cot in the corner. A jug of wine and silver chalice stood at attention near his hand. He reached for the cup and took a sip and set it back down.

"Tancred," Cutnose said with as little excitement as possible.

Tancred lunged for his sword in the corner, ripping it from its sheath. Cutnose held his axe to the side, blade downward and his other hand up in the air.

"It is me," Cutnose said.

Tancred squinted; his sword held across his body. "Cutnose?" His eyes narrowed as he noticed Cutnose's blood-splattered clothes.

"Don't call your guards."

"What devilry has driven you back here? I shoved a knife through your heart."

"Yet I have not died. I have something I must show you." Cutnose drew his long knife and Tancred braced himself for attack. He held the knife disarmingly and sawed through Bors's hair tied to his axe. "I bring you the murderer's head from the Temple." He took the head and tossed it at Tancred's feet. It hit the ground like a stiff piece of meat. Tancred took the point of his sword and rolled the decapitated head to gaze upon its face.

"Brother Bors?" he asked. "He is a sworn brother of a military order."

"And the murderer of my men and those innocents."

"How can I believe such a devil? You should be dead. Even now, you deceive me, wearing my captain's flesh."

"I am still the man you once trusted with your life."

Tancred shook his head. "It is not possible. Twice I have seen you mortally wounded."

"And each time I have returned, asking you to believe my word."

The tall lord's lips pressed shut. "Thrice Lucifer tempted Christ in these very deserts. My eyes do not lie. You stand here before me. Living. Breathing. But I know not what evil pact you've made to cheat death, but I fear that it is a curse that plagues me." He made the sign of the cross.

"Then know you will never see me again, but my parting gift to you lies in the Fatimid camp."

Tancred lifted his chin and lowered his sword. "What do you mean?"

"The guards near the center of their camp are all slain. You can catch them unawares if you move quickly in the dark. It will change the course of the morrow's battle."

Tancred judged his words. "Why? Why are you doing this?"

Cutnose eyed his benefactor turned hunter. "I want to clear my name, if not before all men, at least in your eyes, but I guess some things will never be the same." His nose caught a faint vestige of another wolf, but it was so distant he thought it must be himself.

"We cannot go back." Tancred shook his head. "Robert Cutnose the mercenary is dead to me. You would do well to crawl back to whatever grave you came from and lay in peace."

Cutnose grimaced with a shake of his head. "I suppose he is. Suppose he's dead to me too. Was never comfortable in peace." He smirked at his lord. "And without payment for my service. Your uncle and you owe me a debt."

"The devil comes asking for money after what he's done. I should call my guard and hang you as a traitor." He lifted his wine cup to his lips again with a short, angry shake of his head. "You would do well to be gone of this place. Ride as far as you can. Leave me and my kin be. For if I come across you again, Cutnose, I will do everything in my power to burn you at the stake."

Humbert, Tancred's squire, stirred. His eyes widened as he recognized Cutnose, and he shot from his makeshift bed. "The. The devil is here, lord." The young man shook, pressing himself against the cot.

"I am no devil, Humbert. I only came to clear my name."

Humbert breathed hard. "I cannot hear your devil's tongue."

"Remain calm, boy," Tancred said. "I need you to find Galahad and have him bring his men."

Hugging the wall of the tent, Humbert crawled along it, his eyes never leaving Cutnose. If Cutnose remained, blood would be spilled of his fellow soldiers. As a Christian man, he wasn't sure he wasn't a devil himself, but he was something new, a being with powers he hardly understood. The boy scurried from the tent. Cutnose's time was short before he resumed his place as the hunted. "Be careful, Tancred. Not all your allies are friends. Galahad is one of them. Make sure he sees that head. He will know."

"Be gone."

"As you wish." Cutnose slipped through the entrance and

raced for the rear of the camp. He put distance between him and Tancred's tent as to not tempt the young man to hunt him down. He heard the shouts echoing from Tancred's contingent, but he was already almost a thousand steps north along a lonely road to a place only his feet would find.

Tancred sat in a folding chair in his tent still in his mail coat, sword in one hand, wine cup in the other. Dark circles puffed beneath the young lord's eyes as if he were plagued by spirits. Galahad had responded quickly to his summons and even now crouched near the dead man's rotting head. "I am afraid that this is indeed my fellow brother of our Order, Bors." He stood and eyed the young lord, slumped in his chair, cup pressed to his temple. "Who is the man who brought you his ghastly remains?"

"Robert Cutnose. The one responsible for the deaths at the Temple. Whom you stabbed in Jerusalem. The one who had his throat ripped out and still lives." He gestured at the head with his wine cup. "He claims Bors was the one who murdered all those inside against my wishes." He eyed Galahad. "I believe him a curse on my name."

Far less a curse than Ulf was upon my name.

Tancred stood and poured himself another cup of wine. "Perhaps I should have offered him more coin, and we could have avoided this mess."

"My Lord Tancred, these things cannot be negotiated with. They are the spawn of Satan. The only way to deal with them is with axe and bow. Decapitation and fire. You did right to come to me. I will send my men out now to track him. You've seen what they can do on the beach. I lost many men in a pyrrhic victory." *But the curse of Ulf Bodvarsson no longer plagues my name.* Galahad bowed his head to Tancred and went to leave.

"Wait," Tancred said.

Galahad stopped near the entrance to the tent.

"He said he'd killed all the sentries on the northern perimeter of their camp. He said it is open for an assault. A man does not make that claim frivolously."

"He is no man. It could be a trap to lure us into ambush and defeat. We know not which lies his forked tongue speaks."

"I want to know if he speaks the truth." Tancred rested tired eyes upon him. "Our position in this land teeters on the edge of a knife. If we can take their army unawares in the night, we will have won this long campaign. With no help, Ascalon cannot hope to hold out against us. They will surrender and we shall have a great fortress to protect the kingdom's southern flank."

"My men and I must begin our search for the beast. Time is against us."

Tancred raised his chin. "First, you send men forward and scout their camp. I would know if all he speaks are lies."

"It is dangerous to leave such a foe unaddressed."

"It matters not if we do not prevail here."

"I will have my men scout the enemy camp." Galahad went to leave.

Tancred gestured back at Bors. "You may want to take your friend?"

Galahad bowed his head again. "Of course, Tancred. He deserves a proper Christian burial; he was ever a faithful servant of the Lord. I will report back as soon as my scouts return."

Galahad sniffed the air, however weak his blood was, he could tell if one of the Hunted lingered nearby like a wet dog who'd shaken himself. He caught the domineering scents of campfire smoke, unwashed men, but nothing to indicate this Cutnose still hid somewhere within the encampment. The Hunted always lurked like rats fearing fire, never showing themselves until an advantage had been found. Yet Galahad had a way of luring them into the field for extermination. This creature Cutnose would be no different.

There was an unsteadiness to his thoughts, a lingering fear. If Cutnose could defeat Bors, what else could he be capable of? He must have taken Bors's head close to turning back into his man form, for his canines to be extended in such a fashion. While Bors was unafraid of utilizing his skin-changing skillset, it would be an ugly day for his Order if they were labeled to be the very evil they hunted. They must be associated with order and justice, administering God's will, as Uthur had always preached to them, forbidding such wanton transformations for those who held the ability.

Their secret was to be kept at all costs. Each man within the order swore upon the Bible to uphold God's work and the secrets held within their community of warriors. Those that were initiated into the higher ranks of the Order swore to uphold the Order's will under penalty of torture and death to their entire line. He supposed that swearing upon a Bible meant nothing to Bors, another oath to another god, he always held true to his old tribal ways, or he simply was unafraid of Uthur.

Galahad tossed Bors's head into a campfire, letting the flames lick away his flesh and turn him to ash. Any evidence of his secret should be burnt to nothing. He did not need over pious lords asking questions now, not when he was so close to carving out a foothold in these lands. He would not have all the political maneuvering be stolen by Bors's death.

But Bors's demise meant that the Black Chalice was gone, and most likely in the Hunted's hands. He doubted the animals had any idea how to deploy such a relic to their advantage. He wasn't sure any of them did. Having it lost gave Galahad the perfect reason to remain in the Holy Land seeking its retrieval. It was a cause which Uthur would support. He may not even know it was recovered and lost, but eventually Galahad would have to send word of Percival's and Bors's deaths, which the old warrior would not take lightly as few of his original brothers remained.

He stood on the edge of the camp, awaiting the return of his scouts. His command waited in loose array behind him. Two dozen footmen led by the venerable First Brother Mador, his bushy mustache twitching as he leaned on his spear, and the horsemen led by Brother Richard, a scarf wrapped around his neck that was almost discolored beyond recognition with hues of purple and yellow from Ulf's vicious grip. He wondered how many, if any, of Bors's Banner remained. Someone must have survived to tell this grisly tale. They wouldn't disappear into the wilds; they would seek passage back to the Order or travel to Jerusalem in search of Galahad's Guard. He would need them all to establish his presence here, but with only a depleted horse guard and spear banner under his command, he would need to recruit more men. He needed wealth to rebuild, which meant it was imperative to acquire lands to tax.

From a distance, out of the eyesight of most his men, he could see the forms of three men running, crouched as to avoid detection. Edwin, his most senior sergeant-brother, and two archers with the short horse bows the Turks so loved. The compact bow was much easier to conceal and wield in close quarters.

The heavily-bearded Edwin sucked wind from the run. Galahad had known him since he'd joined as a young eighteen-year-old man. Now, he was in his upper thirties, and Galahad had seen him slowly lose the vigorousness he'd once had, to the drippings of time. A piece of mortality that did not concern Galahad like a regular man. Despite being of similar age, he felt as youthful as a young man in his prime, a benefit of his lineage.

"They're dead." Edwin gestured over his shoulder. "Every sentry on the northern edge of the camp has been slain. Throats torn out."

Galahad digested the information. Cutnose was sympathetic to the crusader cause despite them wanting to burn him at the stake for crimes Bors had committed. *A noble mercenary? What a thought.* "Our mercenary doesn't just fight for coin, but the love of his brothers in arms," he said to himself.

"Mercenary, sir?"

"You did well to slay the sentries on your mission."

Edwin furrowed his brow. "But I didn't, they were already dead, lord."

Galahad addressed the sergeant archers over his shoulder. "You men did well to slay all the sentries."

Edwin slowly nodded his head, eyeing the two archers behind him. "You heard Brother Galahad, we done well this night."

Galahad removed coin from a pouch on the inside of his belt. "You men are rewarded this day for your brave deeds." He pressed coins into Edwin's hand, and he turned, giving one to each of the archers.

"Ensure the men are ready. We will have a fight before long," he said to Mador as he passed by. He went directly to Tancred's tent. He found the man still sitting in his chair talking to himself.

"Lord, I have urgent news."

Tancred looked up with half-lidded eyes. "Yes, Brother Galahad."

This man may be too drunk to ride. "My men scouted the Fatimid camp."

"And?"

"The sentries were alive, standing their posts."

Tancred turned away in disgust. "The devil's tongue. I should have taken his."

"Do not dismay, lord. I sent my best men. They killed the sentries on your behalf."

Tancred sobered under the other warrior's gaze. "Your men killed them? With such ease?"

"Sergeant-Brother Edwin and his comrades are excellent scouts. With great risk to themselves, they struck true. We must move now while the enemy is still unaware."

Tancred stood, tossing his cup to the floor. "Humbert!" he shouted. His squire bolted upright from his blankets where he'd fallen asleep again. "Saddle my horse. We ride to battle."

Humbert scrambled from the tent, fumbling with a belt around his waist.

Tancred approached Galahad. He gripped arms with him with a fierce smile. "Tonight, we crush the infidels."

With light creeping on the fields outside Ascalon, nine crusader divisions, each led by one of the nobles, charged over the open ground toward the massive Fatimid encampment in front of the coastal town of Ascalon. Each noble's household knights rode in the forefront. Twelve-hundred horsemen followed by seven-thousand footmen. Galahad rode with his personal Guard in the vanguard with Tancred. In the early morning light, banners fluttered with the horse's gallop.

Tancred's cavalry closed on the enemy camp, the chilling shouts of 'Deus vult' traveled down the line. Horses leapt over the bodies of the sentries, and they crossed the threshold of the camp with no alarm rising. Fatimid soldiers stumbled from tents unarmored. Few held weapons, only shocked expressions. They were swept into the ground. Pummeled to death by iron-shod hooves. Others ran for the city walls and were speared in the back.

Galahad brought his sword down upon a routing man. He swung into another's neck as he exited a tent, cleanly cutting through his throat, blood waiting a moment before spilling tendrils of red. Behind him, Edwin skewered a shirtless soldier standing his ground, lance removing him from his feet.

The crusaders were a flood of cavalry among the Fatimids, riding with unchecked impunity. Resistance was almost nothing. They were wolves, the enemy a thirty-thousand-man herd of sheep. He couldn't remember when he'd slaughtered with such impunity. Over the dust, Godfrey's contingent swept into the flank of the camp, butchering more men as they sought to escape.

A triple-layered line of spearmen had formed with cohesion, spears outward, round shields in hand. Every man was the color of night beneath their black robes draped in blue cloaks. The retreating men ran around them to relative safety. A deep-voiced

Tancred and Galahad's men reared their horses to a halt. The two groups glaring at each other over shields and spears.

Tancred snarled. "We charge."

"Wait," Galahad said.

"They're escaping. Everyone left is another we face later."

Galahad pointed. Godfrey's men were running off a light cavalry squadron's attack. His infantry making quick work of the wounded as they ran past. "Give Godfrey time to flank them." Tancred sighted Godfrey's men. "It will give our infantry time to arrive."

"You're right." Tancred shouted while twirling his sword over his head, "Hold the line, good Christian men." Disorganized volleys of arrows landed about the knights, most grazing harmless off mail and helms. It was the mounts that were most precious, and several knights were unhorsed, and they begrudgingly joined companies of infantry arriving breathlessly on foot.

In the end, waiting for a few minutes men's lives in Tancred's contingent, as well as many mounts. With the thunder of hooves, Godfrey's knights slammed into the left flank of the black soldiers, and they shattered into pieces.

"To victory!" Tancred shouted, and his knights and infantry charged in, trampling the bravest men they'd see all day.

In less than an hour, the rout of the Fatimid relief army was almost complete. Those that reached Ascalon were admitted to the city, strengthening the garrison with the fastest runners. The crusaders had lost but a few men killed and wounded, most due to friendly forces clashing in the low light. Galahad's small company had maintained discipline in the face of the rout and all his men were accounted for, while the crusaders pillaged the camp.

A waist-high wooden chest, banded in iron, from the vizier al-Afdal Shahanshah tent was brought to Tancred and he smiled at the gold, silver, and jewels inside. "Spoils indeed," he said, and tossed a sapphire studded necklace to Galahad. "For your woman."

"She will be honored by such a gift." He had yet to marry, but where there were jewels, a suitable match could be found, preferably along a noble line to further establish himself, despite the Order's strict rules of celibacy that applied to both brothers and sergeants. The upper echelons of the Order bred with impunity.

Banners waved in the air as Godfrey and his household guard moved through the ransacked camp. They came to a halt as Godfrey held a hand in the air. Battle grime splattered his white surcoat. "We have won a glorious victory this early morning. Thanks to Christ and you, brave Tancred." He eyed the chest that Tancred sat upon, sharing wine with his men.

Tancred stood. "I do not deserve all your praise, Godfrey." He gestured to Galahad. "It was Brother Galahad's men who slew the sentries opening the way for us to attack."

"Sir, you have solidified our hold on this land. I and Christendom owe you thanks."

"I only do what is for the good of all men."

"Guy," Godfrey ushered a squire from his horse. The squire took his reins after he dismounted. "Let me see this brother." He approached Galahad. Godfrey was a tall man for his age, graying hair hanging around his shoulders. He held fierce, calculating eyes, and as far as Galahad could tell, a gray beard with a black mustache, a rocky boulder sticking from a pile of snow on his face. He appeared pleased with what he saw.

"Walk with me," Godfrey ordered. Galahad joined him. They walked through the tents, ignoring the cries of the dying. A wounded Fatimid spearman crawled in their path and a Frank stabbed him in the back, then hurried away. Godfrey stepped over a man impaled with a spear, guts running along the shaft, before asking, "You came here with Tancred? I've seen you before?"

"I did not, Lord Godfrey. I am from a humble order of knights hailing from far away lands of north England."

"Ahh, I see. Yet you have allied yourself with young Tancred?"

"He has been a most accommodating lord to myself and my men."

Godfrey walked in silence, hands behind his back. "There are men who can be more accommodating. Men with lands and titles to give." He studied Galahad for a moment as if he were a game of chess to outmaneuver and win. He was just deciding which piece to play upon Galahad to earn his trust. Yet it was Galahad who needed this man to further his goals, their movements seeking the same outcome. "If we are to hold this far outpost of Christianity then we need knights such as yourself to remain here and your men to defend it."

Galahad bowed his head. "You do me and my men honor. We only did as we thought would carry the day, or the night. Alas, my men must return for our crusade is complete now."

Godfrey reached out, resting a hand upon Galahad's arm. "Is there any way I can entice you to stay? Gold. Silver. I owe you a debt."

"I would not ask for such things."

"You may ask freely. I only ask for your loyalty."

Galahad grinned. "Then I humbly request a small parcel of land and funds to build a keep to defend the pilgrims and these Christian lands."

Godfrey eyed him curiously. "Many men ask for such things. This land is ripe, its people seek our protection."

"We seek to make this a safe place for all men, but we must establish a permanent presence that can be defended."

"What is the name of this order?"

"The Order of the Stag and Cross." He showed Godfrey his ring displaying the same symbol. "An ancient order. One that seeks to vanquish the darkness in this land."

"Yours is a noble calling. I know one of your brothers, Bors. He is a noble warrior of Christ. I treated with him. He assisted me in rooting out traitors within Jerusalem. Certain actions must be taken to ensure our future here is bright."

"Alas, brave Brother Bors is gone now."

Godfrey frowned. "I did not know. He fell this day?"

"Near Jaffa, skirmishing with brigands."

"He deserved a far more noble death."

"The agents of the devil are many. His death was noble enough."

"Then he sits with the saints at an endless feast."

Galahad wanted to tell him that the old pagan brother would rather burn in Hell than feast with the martyrs and all the saints. He'd have beaten them bloody by the end of the first course. If there was anything he despised more than weakness, it was choosing to be weak on a god's behalf.

"He was a pious man. We serve a higher cause."

"As do all brave Christians who have taken up the cross."

A mounted knight waved at them madly, reins in his hands. "Godfrey. Raymond is meeting the Fatimids in Ascalon now. It is rumored they seek to surrender to him."

Godfrey's mouth flattened. "That insufferable weakling is constantly placing himself in the way of our holy mission. He seeks to claim our victory for his own." He turned back to Galahad. "I must stop him before he ruins any chance we have at success. Not all are as welcome here as you Galahad. Come to the palace in Jerusalem, and we shall continue this conversation of your Order and lands."

CHAPTER 27

Lord Godfrey of Bouillon rode with a hundred knights followed by as many mounted sergeants at his back. Banners rippled with the pace of their horses. Turcopoles screened their movement while scouting for ambushes and enemy reinforcements. Dense dust kicked high into the air, and he was certain the Fatimid garrison had seen his force marching from miles away. A little over three hundred spearmen followed with two companies of archers and crossbowmen each. Most were experienced soldiers, leftovers from the crusade, a very few were locally recruited militia from the city. Jerusalem was virtually undefended save for a hundred men left to garrison the citadel.

Only a year after the successful crusade to take Jerusalem, Christendom's furthest outpost maintained a garrison of less than eleven hundred men, and that was generous. Only three hundred knights defended swaths of land stretching from mountains to the sea, numerous cities and towns falling within their purview. The knights were critical, and he could ill afford to lose any of them or their mounts if he hoped to remain in power long. They neared the fortified coastal city of Acre, the city's submission essential to keeping trade and supply routes open to the west for Christian reinforcements from the Frankish kingdoms.

It had been a year since his coronation as protector of

Jerusalem, and it had been fruitful. *Advocatus Sancti Sepulchri.* Despite his meager army, he held a certain divine confidence, he believed that God had guided him to this place and chosen him to be his shield on the earth for all Christians, a role he happily embraced. Jaffa, Haifa, and Tiberias had all been encompassed into his protectorate, other smaller towns reduced to tributary status.

He had moved rapidly in his first year to make his position tenable, for there were many wolves at the gates, his kingdom practically surrounded by enemies who wished to see him collapse. But Acre was the crown jewel to holding the region, as it connected the other crusader counties and principalities with the Holy Kingdom itself.

Acre would become the trading hub at the center between the East and the West, Godfrey was sure of it. With a protected harbor and massive walls, it could withstand an assault from land or sea with relative ease. The land jutted into the sea, creating a harbor that faced south, shielding it from the winds and waves. The narrow inlet was further defended by a giant chain that would be lowered into the waters to admit ships. Many men would become rich within her walls, especially the man who controlled the coastal city.

The merchants of Venice, Genoa, Pisa, Rome, and others all eagerly waited for a place to establish their trading enclaves. They only needed the commander to take the city and the transformation would begin. The walls materialized, and soon he was near enough to make out soldiers defending them. They were prepared to make a show of defiance.

Out of bow's reach, he drew his men to a halt. His infantry would arrive soon as they trailed behind on the road. There would be no delay in starting negotiations. Their position was weak, bending the knee was the only option for them. No army was coming to their aid. The last sizable force to enter his lands lay in piles of bones in the sand, whitening in the sun.

Most of the Saracens inhabiting his lands were quick to capitulate if enough force was arrayed, yet they resisted like mad if they thought there was a chance at relief. They exploited divisions within the crusaders' ranks like after Ascalon, where they sought to surrender to Raymond instead of himself. He could not let the wretched man hold such a critical outpost in his kingdom, so he'd stopped the negotiations. He'd rather have the enemy Fatimids sitting on his border poised to strike than allow such subversion within his kingdom. He would deal with the Fatimids in Ascalon later, for they were cowed in defeat. Now, he must ensure he was logistically sound, and Acre was this assurance.

He did not take his eyes away from the city as he spoke, "William of Esch." He waved the mustached minor lord forward. He was the third son. Where Henry and Godfrey had returned to their familial lands after the crusade was complete, William had stayed in hopes of winning a claim to lands here in the kingdom. He had proved the most diplomatic of the brothers and had learned the Fatimid language in short time, making him indispensable in negotiations.

"You will bring these terms to Zahr ad-Daulah el-Dschuyuschi or his emissary. If his men lay down their arms and open the gates, they will be free to leave with the true God's peace. The same holds for any Muslim who wishes to depart. I do not wish bloodshed this day but am unafraid to shed it."

William bowed his head. "Yes, lord. It will be done as you ask." He spurred his horse at a trot to the gates.

"Gunter," Godfrey signaled another one of his household knights. "Go hurry the infantry. I want a display of force." There was a back and forth of shouts between the gate captain and William.

Godfrey sat impatiently waiting for the governor's response with the rest of his men. Eventually, the footmen and archers began to file in, led by Sir Gunter. "Have them stand in formation. Bring those ladders forward so the enemy can see them."

The column of footmen hurried and began forming a long line. The archers shifted ahead of them in a loose formation to mitigate losses in return fire. They would be largely ineffective from a distance, but it was about a display of force. All the Saracens understood was force. As soon as the odds dipped out of their favor, they backed down and asked for clemency. His problem was the odds were almost never in his favor. But he had spies all over his territories, and the garrison here was less than two-hundred and fifty men. Two-hundred and fifty men could stand atop a wall fifteen times the height of a man for days raining stones and arrows with impunity.

William returned, his horse whinnying as he pulled him to a halt. "They have rejected your terms, my lord."

It was a common tactic among the infidels to stall and send for help, always seeking better terms than provided. These were the ways of this strange land, but he was familiar enough to play their games. He'd expected as much and that negotiations would continue back and forth for days. "What exactly did he say?"

"He said that you can come and take Acre if you..." William stopped speaking and grimaced.

"If I what?"

"If you have a pair of…" He stopped speaking again.

"Pair of?"

William averted his eyes trying to think of the words.

"Out with it."

"He said that if you had a pair of balls, you would attack and take the city by force."

Godfrey's lip curled. "The insolence of that man. I will see every one of them put to the sword." He would not be denied this city. He calmed himself, squeezing his reins in a white-knuckled fist. While he hadn't expected such outright hostility in negotiations, it wasn't beyond the infidel to banter with defiantly harsh language. "We will wait for the rest of the infantry and see if the infidels wise to their situation. Bring me Fabian when he arrives."

"Yes, lord."

The jangle of mail surrounded Robert Cutnose as he hurried among the footmen. He and a half-dozen men carried a siege ladder between them, most men having slung their shields behind them, gripping spears in their free hand, ladder in the other, the sounds of their shields softly tapping their backs as they ran. Most were seasoned soldiers from years of constant conflict on crusade and defending the kingdom after its culmination at Ascalon.

"Keep moving, you pox-marked maggots," shouted a sergeant.

Cutnose eyed the contingent of horsemen and Godfrey at their head. The lord's face was flush with the sun or anger, he knew not which, most likely both.

"You, leper!" shouted a sergeant, pointing toward Cutnose. "Bring that ladder to the front."

"Aye," Cutnose said. He and his men hefted the ladder and set it in front of the ranks of footmen, joining the line of hard-breathing infantry, each man hoping they'd have time to rest before testing the walls. Tugging on his shawl, Cutnose ensured it wrapped tightly, concealing his face. He stepped back in line.

"You don't think he means to rush the walls today?" said Osbert, a blond Saxon next to him, his front teeth bashed out in a shield wall giving him a slight lisp.

"It would be ill-advised after our long march," Cutnose said.

"Aye, it's supposed to be a siege, not an assault. Like the other towns," said Guillard from the other side. "We set up camp. Wait for them to negotiate terms. Then we march back home."

A knight came and went, parlaying with the men on the walls. He couldn't make out what they said from this distance, even he had limitations, but it did not appear favorable. Neither did an assault on the city. The walls were built even higher than Jerusalem, to name them formidable was an understatement. They formed a semi-circle on land and a high bluff protected them from attack from the sea. A long ramp led down to the harbor the same as a water basin crumbling seaward, providing an easy platform for archers to shoot downward into attackers who penetrated the well-defended harbor.

The walls were made from thick stone wider than a man was tall, yet these stones were not simply set upon each other, but were held together with cement. The ramparts had cutouts for archers to fire upon enemy soldiers below. Critical weak points in the walls were protected by two larger towers. Shadowed heads of those waiting men peered over the walls at their enemy arraying before them.

Cutnose hadn't planned on assaulting the city or waiting around in a camp for the defenders to give in while the men around him died from pestilence. He'd wandered for nine months before finding himself back in Jerusalem, the thought of making right Godfrey's past wrong gnawing at his conscious until he took action. The kingdom was desperate for soldiers, or really any man willing to fight, and Cutnose found it was easy to join the garrison.

The guise of a leper kept most men at a distance. He slept in a stable near the barracks, alone save for the horses. Came and went as he pleased as long as he wasn't on guard duty, face covered as if he were a Bedouin. Nobody asked questions from a leper, as they feared the wasting disease.

Over the last few weeks, he'd gotten closer and closer to Godfrey, yet the watchful eye of the silent Sir Clarembald of Vendeuil kept Cutnose from striking him in his palace. He was always left wondering if somehow the man knew it was him. Even more threatening was the presence of Galahad and his men, but their visits to the city were infrequent, and he assumed they had taken residence in another town or castle. Yet their presence, even in passing, was a threat to his existence. Therefore, he would complete his task this night. He would sneak into the man's tent and end him for the role he played in the death of Hugh's family and depart before he took an arrow attacking Acre's walls.

His eyes caught a man moving swiftly along the ramparts. The defenders cheered as he walked past, lifting bows in salute. Cutnose strained to make out what Godfrey said to his knights.

Godfrey's voice boomed louder than the rest. "Look at this." The knights around him laughed. A few raised lances in a challenge to the archer.

"Take your shot!" shouted Gunter, captain of Godfrey's guard. Horses danced with the din. Cutnose watched curiously.

The men of Acre's garrison had named him Pale Bow, for the whiteness of his skin and his preference for the long yew bow. The length of which they had only seen in the hands of the Franks, and even then, only in the men from the far away island of the Britons. It was even longer than the Franks' normal bow and it added an aura of wonder to the Frankish traitor.

They avoided the quiet archer and he kept to himself, but he stood his watch when asked. Captain Abid al-Ashri had him watched day and night for fear he was a spy, waiting to open the gates for the infidel. However, he had sworn off Christianity and made an oath to never betray them. The man easily stood out among them, and the captain doubted he could do anything in secret.

The garrison's archers were more boys than men, only a few actual Fatimid warriors, the rest conscripts from the city's poor. It was an unfortunate posting for the captain, and while the walls were tall, the garrison was small. It was only a matter of time before the Franks came to seek submission, but Vizier Al-Afdal Shahanshah did not wish to spend the money nor the troops securing the city in anything but name, only leading to the conscription of the city folk despite Acre being the place of his birth. The vizier's idea that the crusaders were Roman mercenaries had been shattered at Ascalon, and he hid in Cairo for another opportunity to assert Fatimid authority over the lands of the Christian Kingdom. This left the towns and cities he had fought so hard to wrest from the Turks to the mercy of the Christians.

The archer militia was dressed in simple robes and tunics, rough-spun, lacking any finery. There was no armor among the archers, no helms, a few had simple knives on their belts, quivers on their hips and backs, short bows in hands. Captain Abid al-Ashri had been harsh with them, lashing out with a long stick every chance he found, slouching, missed shots, broken arrows and bowstrings, or if the men hadn't hurried when he called. Yet with Pale Bow, he did not dare swing his stick in his direction. It was the glint in the Pale Bow's eyes that stayed his hand, the look of a wolf fierce enough to rip his throat out with a mere bite. So al-Ashri took it out even more on his company of archers, and the Frank's mystique grew among them.

As Pale Bow walked through the defenders, the young men cheered. They had seen him shoot in the practice yard, and his aim was the deadliest they'd ever seen. He stopped near the captain. The black man regarded him with wary confidence but didn't say a word. Pale Bow tested the tightness of his bowstring. The sea air had a tendency to ruin them, which was why he always had many extra in a pouch at his waist. It had the right stiffness and flexibility to it. At his hip, he ran a hand over the fletching, searching for the proper arrow.

He scanned the paltry force arrayed against the port city. He recognized a collection of the banners and a few of the symbols painted on the shields. The upstart house of Esch, his shield depicting a green tree on a field of red. A few men bore Godfrey of Bouillon's house colors of red, white, red in thirds. And others he knew not the name of, a red horn on a field of yellow, a white lion on a field of blue, a simple black and white half and half, a checkered blue and yellow, and numerous red crosses painted on shields. At the center of the mounted contingent, surrounded by banners beholding crosses and spears, sat the man he waited for. Godfrey of Bouillon, Protector of Jerusalem.

Godfrey wore a white surcoat with a five-fold golden cross, a large cross potent surrounded by four smaller Greek crosses of the same color in the center over his mail coat, embroiled with gold along the sleeves almost as if he were a warrior bishop. He donned no helm; it dangled off the side of his saddle. A shield hung on the other side of his saddle, a scrawling golden cross potent on a field of white. A neatly trimmed gray beard with a dark mustache. His cheeks rounder than the last time he'd seen the Protector of Jerusalem. Godfrey must have a spy within Acre to know just how weak the Fatimid governor's position was.

Captain Abid al-Ashri turned a white-turbaned head toward him. "Pale Bow, they are far out of reach. Save your arrows for if they foolishly attack." Even his command lacked in confidence, coming across as almost a question. He turned on his archers. "You boys will become men fast or be dead boys quicker."

Pale Bow spoke quietly, his eyes gazing over the array of crusaders. "I will issue a warning to them."

The captain shook his head. His discipline stick stayed at his side although the man yearned to use it. "You would be wasting an arrow. The distance is too far."

"I humbly request one shot."

The eyes of the young archers all stared at their captain in anticipation. They all feared him, but Pale Bow was a mysterious legend capable of anything their minds contrived.

The captain sneered. "If you can hit a man or beast from here, I will give you my month's pay."

"Loosen your purse strings," Pale Bow said. He drew the string taut, his right shoulder thicker than the left from thousands upon thousands of draws over the many years, each one taking immense strength. His eyelid closed to a sliver, eye focusing on the precise angle to strike his target. His hand held the arrow at its zenith and bow pointed high in the air. He licked his lips steadying himself and calmed his breathing.

The archers of the garrison gazed on in wonderment. To see Pale Bow in action was enough joy for them, but the potential to best the domineering captain out of a month's pay was worth even a retributive beating. All their eyes willed Pale Bow success.

The arrow hissed from the bow. The string hummed after it sang, ushering on its projectile. The archers leaned on the walls, shielding their eyes to the sun, trying to see how far the tall archer could sling his arrow. No man, no matter his strength, was capable of such a feat. Eager eyes prayed to see it strike. The arrow soared as an eagle in the sky before diving down to seek its prey.

Pale Bow watched the arrow, his mind feeling how the shot released. His eyes followed, ensuring it took the path he'd desired it to find. He took a step forward. His vision was clear. The knights in Godfrey's entourage curiously watched the sky. Bewildered amusement etched on their faces with no fear for they were far out of range for the other archers. But not Pale Bow.

Cutnose watched the arrow as it sped downward with incredible force. It took Godfrey in the eye, punching into his skull and out the back with a spray of red mist, ivory bone, and a blood-soaked arrowhead. The force was so great he was thrown from his horse. He fell rearward, doing an entire flip before landing with a metallic crunch on his stomach, the lodged arrow forcing his head onto its side.

The knights' horses danced away from the dead noble. Squires and knights clumsily clambered from their mounts to give aid. Men raised their shields in anticipation of more deadly projectiles. Anyone who'd seen a man take an arrow to the eye, knew the nobleman was already on his way to the gates of Hell.

"Jesus Christ our Savior," Guillard said from next to him. He made the sign of the cross. "I thought we were out of range."

"I've only ever seen one man make a longer shot," Cutnose said, running his eyes along the wall. *It must be Arnulf.* Two squires and two knights had stretched Godfrey's white cloak beneath the lord and hoisted him, carrying him farther away from the wall to avoid further desecration.

Cheers erupted from the defenders. Fatimid soldiers banged on their shields and archers waved their bows in victory. A couple more arrows were loosed, but they fell far short of the crusaders' position, certainly not shot by the same bowman.

"You think he's dead?" Guillard said with a curious look at Cutnose.

"He's as dead as you can get and then some." But he was distracted by the lack of purpose. He was to kill Godfrey, and now he didn't know what he was going to do.

"Who's in charge now?" Osbert said, scratching at a ragged blondish beard. "He got no heirs." The knights called to one another. Two riders galloped southward toward Jerusalem. The knights in the front argued what to do, horses tugging on their reins with the smell of blood in the air.

"The Pope?" Guillard said.

Osbert peered at him. "You think that tight arse is going travel all the way here to rule? Maybe that brigand Patriarch Dagobert, we'd be out raiding again for sure." The footmen licked their lips. Dagobert was no more than a brigand in priest's clothing, traveling with a Pisan fleet and raiding Romans, Turks, and Fatimids alike for plenty of loot.

"The Pope could rule from here. Jerusalem is the Holy City. More holy than Rome. I been there. Wouldn't call that place holy," Guillard said.

"The Pope isn't coming," Cutnose said. The knights still argued amongst themselves. The tall archer stood on the ramparts and raised a longbow skyward. Cutnose shook his head. "St. Peter's favorite whore." He took his long axe and lifted it high in salute. It was Arnulf. He gave Cutnose a fierce nod. Vengeance had been achieved.

Osbert shaded his eyes with his shield. "Saracens don't wield long bows. That man a Frank?"

"He is."

"Traitor's what he is then."

"Could be a slave?" Guillard said. "Muslims love slaves."

"Anyone with enough money loves a slave," Cutnose added.

The sergeant in charge of the spearmen marched to the knights, and a trio of men started to yell at each other.

"Come on," Cutnose said to the spearmen. "No use standing here all day until we're leather. Those knights are going to fit and spit at one another all afternoon before anyone decides what to do. Let's set up camp." They fell back roughly four-hundred yards to a grove of olive trees, and the men went about setting up tents before basking in the shade. Cutnose helped Osbert with his tent then excused himself to take a piss.

Instead of returning, he filled his water bladder, shouldered his shield, hefted his axe, and ventured down the road away from the small crusader army. He had no place. He had no people. While still a man, there was something else inside his blood, primal and bestial, something that needed to be let out. He was better, faster, stronger, every sense enhanced, the heat and cold were dim reminders of manhood, and while he felt hunger, it was faint, and he could go days without thinking about eating.

He eyed his boots, the sole was wearing thin, he'd need new ones before long at this rate. He marched on regardless. He did not know where this road would take him, but he was sure of one thing. There was always a place for a soldier in the Holy Land.

CHAPTER 28

The rhythmic striking of a thousand hooves startled Tancred awake in the night. The ground rumbled beneath him. He lifted himself from his camp bed inside his spacious tent. A table and chair were in the corner, in the other, hung his armor, a mail halbrek and coif along with his helm wiped clean of all dust and grime.

His surcoat was an off-yellow and white, while his cloak bore his household colors of blue with red crosses sewn on his sleeves. Hanging off the side of his camp bed was his sheathed sword, polished along with a knife strapped to his belt. He grabbed his sword as the wave of thunder grew louder. *Must be thousands*, his mind raced.

He pushed through the tent flaps, sword drawn, still in his night clothes. Torches had died low in the early morning. Light dimly scouted for the vanguard of dawn. On the horizon, a mass of misty riders raced for his camp obscured by a cloud of dust.

"Christ," he said. He ripped open the tent door next to his. "To arms! To arms!" His squire Humbert scrambled from his tent, eyes focused in frightened determination, the young squire was ready to take his oath as a knight now at eight and ten, and had grown over a foot since they'd left Jerusalem so long ago. "My armor," Tancred hissed in a rage. He continued to rouse the camp. His men stumbled from their tents, hastily donning armor and holding weapons. Shouts of alarm rippled through the tents.

Humbert brought him his mail coat, and he hurriedly helped it over his lord's shoulders. The weight was reassuring as it was heavy, yet for a man of his broad stature, it was an accustomed pressure that brought a comforting security with it. "Get my horse, hurry," Tancred said, securing his belt around his waist. His eyes would not leave the horde of infidels galloping to destroy his camp. The squire went for his shield. "No, horse." Tancred ducked inside his tent and grabbed the shield and settled his helm upon his head. He stepped back into the dawn.

Arrows whistled as the riders let loose a disorganized volley. He raised his shield. A man fell screaming as an arrow pierced his leg. Then another gasped as one embedded into his chest. The enemy riders retreated, and another wave of feathered death was unleashed. More arrows struck home, raining indiscriminately amongst the camp.

Ludolf of Tournai rushed to him, shield held high, followed by his brother, Engelbert. "I shall shield you, prince," Ludolf cried, but his shield mostly covered himself. Arrows continued to hail from above, flying serpents hissing death as they went for the kill.

"Get whoever you can mounted. Engelbert, form a line of spearmen. We need time to form."

His squire led him his horse and helped him into the saddle. The Turkish horse archers were riding forward firing their arrows, then rotating toward the flanks allowing additional archers space to fire. The arrow cover was smothering, with almost no respite to breathe unmolested. The harsh reality of movement meant exposing oneself to mortal danger. He circled his horse. Ludolf returned with a few mounted men. A meager line of footmen formed near the edge of the camp; spears pointed outward. The arrow shower clouded around them, and the spearmen hid beneath their shields.

"Christ have mercy on us." He could see the rest of the enemy army now. His adversary was as wily as he was smart. General

Sabawa, marshal to Fakhr al-Mulk Ridwan of Aleppo, had taken him by surprise. The horse archers kept them pinned down while thousands of Turkish spearmen and archers raced for the camp. A cloud of dust marked their fresh approach.

Engelbert swung his sword in circles over his head, urging the footmen to hurry into position, barking orders at them, his blue and white checkered shield riddled with arrows, his mount had one sticking from its hindquarters. Crossbowmen were joining them now in twos and threes. A few were still in their night clothes, less wore helms and armor. One man was naked, yet he clung to his crossbow with the rest. They would be overrun in minutes. Hacked to pieces while they slept or while they ran for safety.

Tancred's army needed a way out. His eyes swept over the hilly terrain around Artah. The city which he sieged now blocked his path of retreat. He picked this location for the camp to ensure the enemy was cut off from retreat, and his Armenian turcopoles were to let him know of any approach of the enemy. He assumed they lie in the sands, riddled with arrows and throats slit. He could ill afford such a defeat.

The defeat of the Christian forces at the Battle of Harran had all but stripped the principality of Antioch of any reliable troops, the loss of towns and tributes following the slaughter. It had forced his uncle, Bohemond, to travel back to Italy to gather reinforcements, leaving Tancred as regent over their dwindling lands. The Prince of Galilee was barely more than a title.

Another setback, and everything Tancred and his uncle had worked to achieve here in these lands would be thrown away, ground to dust by the Turks, Romans, and the Fatimids. He knew the end drew near, perhaps it was better to die and let the desert take his bones. "Treacherous infidels."

There must be a way out. If they made for the sieged city, they would be slaughtered at the gates. He searched the desolate lands for respite. The Turks were attacking through the only approach that was left, the relatively cleared fields to the southeast of Artah, avoiding the rough terrain of rocky hills and scrubby trees to the north and east.

Ludolf screamed next to him as an arrow lodged in his arm. "Jesus Christ of Nazareth, save me!" he cried out. Tancred raised his shield, more arrows burying themselves within. Shieldless Humbert held his standard, flinching with each passing arrow.

Sir Guarin snarled at him trying to control his horse. "My lord, it is a massacre!"

The only move was to retreat over the rocky terrain north and hope that the Turks cared enough for their horses to not follow, preferring to harass them from a distance. He knew he would be risking his knights' precious mounts, but if they stayed upon this ground, they would be cut down. He gritted his teeth. Many men would breathe their last among those rocks.

"North to the hills!" he shouted. "Retreat! Retreat!" He turned his horse, leading his knights and mounted sergeants northward. The terrain soon turned into jagged rocks and boulders, littering their path and forcing them to ride painfully slow with no close cohesion for attack. This gave a portion of his infantry time to catch them. The Turkish riders shadowed them out of range. Arrows crashed around them but far fewer than in the camp.

Behind him, the Turkish foot soldiers had reached the outskirts of his camp and were beginning to loot. He urged his horse carefully around a rock. A horse screamed behind him, throwing a rider, and a fellow knight hefted the rider behind him in his saddle. The ride was painfully slow, but eventually he crossed the summit of the hill. Men straggled behind him like a pack of whipped dogs. The sunlight grew among them, casting long shadows upon the destruction of his camp below.

They lined a crescent-shaped bluff facing south and east with good visibility of the surrounding terrain. To their rear, a valley rolled behind them and led to another hill. "Form ranks along the crest!" he shouted. He pointed with his sword, asking his men for more. The eastern edge of the bluff descended softly into a road that was much less rocky and covered with long grass. If the

Turks were going to try them, they would try to flank them there, where their light horse could be best utilized.

He felt more secure as more of his men joined him, closing ranks with exhausted gasps. *There is still some semblance of an army here.* His losses weren't as bad as he'd initially speculated. At least half his force of infantry and cavalry had reached the summit. Enough to fight a battle in their favor.

The trickle of footmen limped along the rocky hill to where he rallied. Many were stuck with arrows, but most could still fight, their armor absorbing much of the blows. A suitable rank of spearmen took shape, followed by enough crossbowmen to make the Turks think twice about trying them.

The Franks that had stayed in the Holy Land fought with a certain determined desperation. In most other engagements, the men were not far from home, escape to family and friends was close if one wanted to make a run instead of perishing on the field. Here, in this inhospitable land, men had homes, but it wasn't the same, they were adopted abodes. In time this may change, but these men were transplants. In this land, there was nowhere to run. It was stand with the Christian men at your sides or be slaughtered like lambs in a pen of wolves.

"Look, Tancred, our men still fight in the camp," Engelbert said. He pointed near the center, where Tancred's tent had been. "The enemy has stopped?"

The sun crept a sliver over the horizon, and Tancred shaded his eyes. A single man walked through the tents, a long axe in his hands. A Turk tried him and lost his head with such force that Tancred flinched. Then another found himself cleaved from shoulder to groin. Another Turk was butchered and the axeman spun in a circle, bringing down another in a whirlwind of death. This happened repeatedly until the Turks formed a rank of footmen against him, curling around the edges to envelop him.

The soldier worked like lightning striking; moving quick, slashing here, overhead strike using the haft of his weapon, shifting backward to avoid biting spearheads. A block of men attempted to rush him, and he swept his axe low along the ground, knocking four men from their feet and crippling several, slowing the others behind.

"Magnificent," Tancred whispered. "Who is this man?" he asked the men around him.

"I do not know, lord, one of the footmen, a man of no status," Ludolf said, nursing his arm across his body.

"But he fights as Michael the Archangel does," Tancred breathed. He eyed the camp. Turks bled around the man ransacking the place, none pursuing the last of Tancred's escaping footmen, preoccupied with looting or this mysterious warrior. The Turkish horsemen shadowing the retreating soldiers had given up with his men forming on the hill. They backtracked to loot the camp with victory whoops.

He turned back to the center of the camp, expecting the man to be dead and gone, yet he'd only shifted a few tents over and was fighting there, a running battle against his foes. He wielded a torch in hand lighting tents as he went. Black smoke whisped rapidly into the air.

Tancred estimated he had almost two hundred knights around him and three hundred mounted sergeants. Spears and swords in hand, some helmetless, but most wearing armor with shields decorated with red or black crosses. More than enough. "Ludolf, you take charge of the footmen. You lead them back down this hill and through the rocks."

"The men are tired, my lord." Ludolf grimaced, afraid of the orders.

"They can rest when they're dead."

"And my arm?"

"Can you fight, Sir Ludolf?" Tancred hissed.

The blond, naked-chinned man, blinked his eyes in painful worry.

Engelbert sneered at his brother. The rumors said that Ludolf had been the first crusader to take the walls of Jerusalem, and the man was a sniveling coward, something his brother had probably known since they were young. Then again, Engelbert had missed the entire assault due to illness, so perhaps it was a familial trait.

Ludolf felt the judgment from Tancred and his brother, gulping down his pain. "I can manage."

"Very well, Sir Ludolf. Lead the men back down the rocks. Engelbert and I will lead the horse around the eastern flank, scatter any riders, and rejoin you in the center of the camp."

"Yes, lord."

Tancred led his mount to the center of his knights. He hefted his sword high; his lance had been lost in the camp. He leveled it down at the camp below. "Our men are still in the camp. One holds the heathens at bay. First knight to reach him, gets a gold bezant."

His men cheered and he spurred his horse down the grassy sloping road to the east. His men formed around him in a mass of horse and steel. Many held their spear tips high. They bounded down the desolate grassy slope and into a shrub filled plain, trampling the grass down beneath eager hooves.

The Turkish horse archers saw his men in fits and starts. Clusters of horsemen scattered into the fields to escape, loosing arrows only in passing. He had no doubt they would return as a fly to dung to harass his men, but not before his mounted men could punish the looters.

He held his sword leveled with his campaign tent. "Deus vult!" he screamed. The Turkish infantry on the fringe of the encampment only regarded them with a slight indifference, easy riches stealing any concern for safety. Tancred's cavalry rode the rays of the rising sun. His men closed on the camp, mouths roaring a battle cry of revenge.

Turkish archers hurried to form a line along the camp's perimeter. They spread out, trying to give the knights space to pass by, in a loose formation. Terrified footmen dropped spears and broke into a run, leaping tents and wagons to escape. It would not save them this day.

Tancred brought his sword into an archer's unprotected skull, cleaving him down the back. The Turkish infantry crashed into tents and campfires as they tried to escape the horsemen, throwing themselves to the ground in terror.

In their panic, they did not notice the Christian footmen forming what was soon to become a wall of death closing upon them like an anvil of spear points, Tancred's mounted men the blacksmith's hammer. Unknowing which way to go, the enemy ran into the waiting spearpoints of his infantry like the sea throwing itself upon a port's breakwall. Blood splashed into the air, and the slaughter began anew.

Tancred took the tip of his boot and lifted a chain-mailed shoulder to peer at the fallen soldier beneath. It was a Frank, lifeless stare in his unclosing eyes, although one would hardly know any different with his deeply tanned skin and mustache. The red cross sewn on the breast of his surcoat labeled him as one of Tancred's men, but not the soldier he sought, as this man clutched a knife and no long axe. He'd set his men to search for the brave soldier who had held the Turks back long enough for Tancred to reform his men.

The sun loomed over them, baking everything with unforgiving heat. Any loot stolen from his camp had been secured and his men had started to collect piles of weapons and any armor that was serviceable. The lack of adequate armor on his enemies, was to their detriment, but revealed the desperation of Ridwan, as at least a sizable contingent of his soldiers were mere peasants driven to arms by the whip of conscription or the flagellating scourge of religious fervor.

The wailing of the dying Turks was less common now, a shout or cry for help as his men ran through the wounded with sword and dagger. His men looted the bodies before dragging them into oversized piles outside the camp. Over the years, the Christians had found it more efficient to create smaller piles to burn, as the higher the pile of dead, the longer it took to incinerate all the bodies.

Tancred wiped his brow, moving to the next corpse. A Frankish soldier reached for him with blood-covered hands. "Lord, help me."

He knelt next to the footman, placing a hand on his shoulder to ease him to his back. "Where have you been injured, man? I will find you aid."

The bearded sergeant lifted a hand from his belly revealing a gash, stretching as if his abdomen had split open into a red mouth. Tancred clenched his jaw at its sight. This man would not leave the field, but his bones would be left in the rocky sands of this land.

He gripped the man's hand, tightly placing his other hand over top of it. "I will pray for your soul. You have done Christ's work this day and will be rewarded in Heaven."

"I seen him." The sergeant swallowed hard. "The man you seek."

"Where can he be found?"

"They had me pinned down." He licked dry lips. "One of them was goin' crush me head with a mace. Then the angel came for me. He moved like lightning, lord." The sergeant coughed and grimaced as wide as the wound on his belly. "He killed all three and dragged me out of a burning tent. The axe of Christ I say. Slayer of the infidel. A warrior angel."

"That is the man I seek. Which way did he go? I would reward him for his bravery." *I would see if my suspicions are true.* The thought chilled him even as his veins pumped with the warmth of victory. The demon stalked his very existence, like a curse hovering over him, never far, gnawing at his courage, yet he saved us this day from slaughter. The two ideas were the very antitheses of each other. *Was he here to collect his final revenge?*

The sergeant continued to squeeze Tancred's hands. "I saw him run for the hills." He leaned back and rested his head, his breathing labored.

"My lord," said Ludolf, hurrying his way. His arm was bandaged and slung over his body. He could carry no sword or spear in battle. He would need to spend time at one of the hospitals when they returned to Antioch. Perhaps bathe in the healing waters of the Pools of Bethesda.

He turned, eyeing his knight. "Have you found him? I would pay my respects."

"No, lord," Ludolf said. He gave the sergeant a tepid glance.

Tancred pointed at two men. "Get this man out of the sun, call for the physician." He gestured at the wounded man. "Perhaps they have poppies to ease the pain."

"A most generous lord you are."

"Tancred," Ludolf said. "He is just a soldier. We have lords' work to do." An emissary has come from Artah. They wish to surrender."

With the relief army slaughtered save for the fleeing horsemen, they had no hope to withstand a siege, long or short. Tancred smiled to himself, another city reclaimed in his territory. He would be able to recover more towns and lands east of the Orotones River.

He was the regent of an almost overrun principality. Lands crippled by his uncle's defeat at Harran. It had been an ugly affair that sent political repercussions rippling and incurring the gaze of both the greedy Romans and Turks. Yet Tancred had managed to turn the tide while his uncle was away securing support.

It was rumored Bohemond had been welcomed by the French royal court with open arms, his uncle telling exotic stories of the east with the promises of more riches. His uncle's return was delayed if not indefinitely, so Tancred would continue to be the Prince of Galilee for the foreseeable future. This meant engagement in eastern politics which were as clear as the bottom of a mud pit.

"Tell him to wait in my tent. You may treat with him until I am ready."

"It would be my pleasure." Ludolf looked pleased to be asked to perform a task out of the saddle.

The pile of dead had collected their own army of black flies in the heat. The stack of bodies growing taller with each addition. He pointed to a cluster of his men looting corpses. They would be burned soon to prevent the pestilence brought by the dead. "I want his long axe. Any man who brings it to me, I will pay thrice the price of it. I want the man who fought here found."

His footmen grunted "yes, me lord" and went about their task of pillaging the dead. Tancred circled his camp. Round and round he went, staring into the lifeless faces of the dead, determined to find the warrior. Almost seven thousand Turks were thrown into a dozen heaps. He'd lost almost a thousand footman and archers combined, over fifty knights and a hundred mounted retainers. Every loss significant when surrounded by enemies that were as numerous as grains of sand. Despite the losses, it was a resounding victory and he still wondered if he could follow up the capture of Artah with a march on Aleppo itself.

With no hope of relief, cities and towns would fall back under Antioch's control again. *Fakhr al-Mulk Ridwan* had paid Antioch tribute only a year past. He waited for an opportunity to force his authority over any town or fort the crusaders occupied. The defeat at Harran was that opening. *I will go meet Ridwan and make him grovel at my feet and kiss my boots, pay an even greater tribute.* It was a far-fetched fantasy, but he nonetheless dreamed of it, if only for the breathing space it would give their domain. Constantly being on the defensive was a suffocating existence.

Humbert hurried to him, seemingly unfazed by the dead surrounding the camp. He'd seen more fighting than most men saw in a lifetime. A sword on his hip, a glint in his eyes, his hair longer, he had grown strong in body and acquired a war-like mind that came easy to their line of people. "Lord Tancred, Sir Ludolf requests your attendance again. Our infidel guests grow anxious."

"Tell Ludolf I will return when I am ready. Go."

Humbert dipped his chin in deference. "I will relay the message, lord."

The emissaries would wait. They had no choice in the matter and if they wished to return, they would be facing him again in any regard. The day melted by in the heat and the bodies began to stink. As the sun dipped behind the hills, he ordered the dead burned. The moon was a faint white circle in the sky waiting to make its appearance.

His men sparked flint and lit torches, walking around the piles with covered faces. The evening roared with the flames and gut-wrenching smoke. He stopped and rested both hands upon his sword, sticking it in the ground. He watched them burn in a tired daze, mesmerized by the flames. The faint sound of a howl caught his attention.

He squinted past the fire to a hilltop in the distance. The howl reported anew in the dusky light, long and sorrowful. Tancred ripped his sword from the ground and raced to the other side of the fire, shielding his mouth and eyes as he passed. His eyes ran along the hill. A man-shaped shadow faced his direction. It raised a long axe in the air. *Is that him? Is that the warrior?*

"Hail, friend!" Tancred shouted, raising a hand.

"Wolves be in the hills, my lord," said a nearby spearman, supported by his spear, face covered with a scarf. "They smell the dead."

"That is a man out there."

The spearman turned and gazed at the hills with a narrowed eye. "I see no man, my lord. My grandmother always told me not to stare too long in the dark, you won't like what you find."

Tancred disregarded the superstitious man. "I saw a man."

The spearman eyed the darkness. "All I see are scavengers, my lord." He pointed. "See there. Them be eyes."

Yellow eyes glowed in the dimming light from the hilltop.

"Wolves," Tancred said. His mind raced to a man who masqueraded as a skin-changer. Those that must be hunted. *Is it Cutnose returned to me like the plague?* "Cannot be."

The wolf howled a fierce ballad toward the growing moon.

"Told you, my lord. Smell the meat. Fire'll keep 'em at bay."

Tancred stared at the hilltop, searching for the man again, but he was gone. "I'm not sure you know them as well as you think."

"What's there to know? They are scavengers."

"Perhaps they know us better than we know them."

He wrapped his cloak around himself tighter against the chill, or to warm himself from the nerves, his suspicions confirmed that Cutnose did remain close. He turned away, making for the interior of his ransacked camp. Men raised tired arms and heavy weapons toward him as he passed.

The camp both lived and died in the night. Flames roared as they consumed the flesh of the dead. Shadows lurked around the fires. *Was Tancred the flame and Cutnose his shadow? Would he ever be free of the man he once called friend? Could he name this man fiend when he'd saved him and his army this day?*

He reminded himself the devil aided man when he sought advantage over his soul. He spoke in lies to draw a man away from Christ's path. Paths of glory. Paths of power. Paths of riches. Paths of lust. All enriching to the mortal man and detrimental to the man's soul. Yet all men sought these things anyway.

He reached his tent. Humbert had instructed two of the camp women to sew the wall shut where the Turks had cut their way inside. The stitching was crude and jarring to the eye. Two spearmen stood outside, armored in mail and crosses over their breasts. They held a fist to their chest in salute. He ignored them and searched the distant hills for a glimpse of the shadowy man.

Was his shadow a plague upon his soul or a guide along a righteous path?

Blessing or curse, there was no shadow without the light.

The story will continue with the second novel of the saga, ***Sands of Bone***.

THANK YOU FOR READING OATHS OF BLOOD

We hope you enjoyed it as much as we enjoyed bringing it to you. We just wanted to take a moment to encourage you to review the book. Follow this link: Oaths of Blood to be directed to the book's Amazon product page to leave your review.

Every review helps further the author's reach and, ultimately, helps them continue writing fantastic books for us all to enjoy.

Also in series:
Oaths of Blood
Sands of Bone
City of Wolves

Check out the entire series here! (Tap or scan)

Want to discuss our books with other readers and even the authors? Join our Discord server today and be a part of the Aethon community.

Facebook | Instagram | Twitter | Website

You can also join our non-spam mailing list by visiting www.subscribepage.com/AethonReadersGroup and never miss out on future releases. You'll also receive three full books completely Free as our thanks to you.

For all our books, visit our website.

AUTHOR'S HISTORICAL NOTE

As someone who considers themselves a historian, I felt like I would be doing my novel a disservice if I did not do my due diligence in my research. And in the same breath, this novel is fantasy, and I would like to think I am not entirely beholden to historical fact as one would be writing historical fiction. At least I hope you see it that way, but I do attempt to retain as much of the historical events, flavor of the times, and pertinent details as possible without sacrificing the story. My quest was to give you a satisfying introduction to the secret history surrounding the Noctis Bellum or the Night War, in the context of the greater conflict of the First Crusade.

I began this dive into the Noctis Bellum waged between the Order and the Hunted over three years ago in 2020. While I considered various time periods, I felt that the First Crusade was the perfect place to begin this journey, as it is already filled with dramatic conflict—East vs West, Muslim vs Christian—an introduction between two groups who not only misunderstood each other, but would fight each other viciously for centuries after, mirroring the fantastical factions of my novel.

As I researched and wrote, I found that the historical personalities crowded one another with their various competing wants and desires, many providing fascinating backgrounds with little embellishment. Tancred, Godfrey, Bohemond, Raymond, amongst others could all have their own novels in themselves. The period was also filled with persons only mentioned by name in the historical text giving me a wide breadth of historical characters to breathe life into or take away, if even just in passing like Ludolf and Engelbert of Tournai, Arduino di Narbona, and Pagan (Cut-nose's band).

Below is a breakdown of some of the facts and liberties that I believe a historical reader may find interesting. This is a work is fantasy; however, it is grounded in enough history to do a deeper dive for those that may be interested. Let us begin.

Most of the main battles depicted in the novel: sack of Jerusalem, Battle of Ascalon, and the Battle of Artah involving the Franks, Turks and the Fatimids are grounded in fact. The first two battles were critical to completing what is known today as the First Crusade. Taking Jerusalem was one of the primary goals of the crusade and defeating the Fatimid relief army at Ascalon solidified western Christian control over the region which allowed for the founding of the Kingdom of Jerusalem.

The First Crusade was one of the only crusades where the crusaders accomplished their primary objective, which in this case was the liberation of Jerusalem. It wasn't truly the first crusade as one came before referred to as the "People's Crusade." It was named so because it was more of an armed pilgrimage of commoners that had heeded the Pope's call to capture Jerusalem, departing before most of the lords has mobilized their armies. However pious they may have been, they did not make it far before they were annihilated by the Turks in Anatolia.

The participants in the First Crusade came from all over the various kingdoms and principalities from what is known today as Europe. The main factions broke down between northern France, southern France, Italo-Normans, and Germans who were all supported by the Italian city-states like Venice, Pisa, and Genoa. There was very little cohesion within the army, as most men fought under their own lords within their regional contingents.

Coming from different regions, with different languages, and their own rivals, the crusaders were only kept from killing one another by their single common goal of taking Jerusalem. Different contingents came and went over the course of the campaign as ambitious lords sought to sack towns or take lands for their own benefit as seen with Bohemond and others. This diverse group of foreign invaders started with roughly 30,000 men and after two years (starting from the Battle of Nicaea in 1097) of battling the Turks and Fatimids, they were cutdown to roughly 9,000 men when they reached their "primary" target of Fatimid-controlled Jerusalem.

Robert Cutnose and his mercenary band are fictional, however, there is historical record of a crusader named Pagan. The term mercenary in regard to Cutnose's band may be slightly misleading. Adventurers may be more accurate. Essentially, he led a band of soldiers who were looking for military campaigns and sought to sell their services to various lords. During this time period, the Normans were well known for their prowess in arms and adventuring.

Considering Bohemond's connections and campaigns in the Roman East, as well as his Norman roots, it would be assumed adventurers and soldiers looking for lucrative looting opportunities would find their way into the ranks of his forces. Mercenaries or soldiers for hire were not unheard of for the time. The crusading lords employed Turkish or local light cavalry known as turcopoles as "mercenaries" to supplement and counter the lighter horsemen of the Fatimids and Turks.

Romans, Eastern Romans, and the general crusader term "Greeks" are used several times throughout the novel to refer to what many historians would name today the Byzantine Empire. The Roman Empire was officially split between East and West in 395 CE with the eastern part of the empire surviving more or less until 1453. The Eastern Roman Empire was in a decline during the First Crusade due to several factors both internal and external. This includes the impact of Norman expansion throughout southern Italy and Sicily at the empire's expense as well as various Arab rulers. Probably even more critical was their defeat at the hands of the Seljuk Turks at the Battle of Manzikert in 1071. It was catastrophic to the empire leading to civil wars and the loss of the Anatolian heartland which supplied the backbone of their armies.

The Siege of Jerusalem (1099) was the climax of a chaotic two-year military campaign (starting with the Battle of Nicaea 1097) and was most certainly a bloody affair. With the Fatimid fleet cutting off supplies from the Italian city-states, there was little hope that a long-term siege would be successful. Combined with the threat of a Fatimid relief army, this left the crusaders, by now falling into two factions, Godfrey of Bouillon's and Raymond of Toulouse's, with only one option, to storm the walls and take the city by force. Both leaders sought to be the first to breach its walls. They split their army in two, seeking to divide the Fatimid garrison.

The Fatimid garrison was not defenseless, in fact, they had done an adequate job of destroying food supplies, poisoning wells, and burning any timber that may be used to create siege engines. They had received an elite cavalry unit weeks prior to the crusaders arrival and pushed out most Christians for fear of a traitor within the city collaborating with the Latins. One of the largest hurdles the crusaders faced was the lack of timber because they did not bring their own siege engines. In 1187, Saladin and his army would arrive with dozens of dismantled siege engines as to avert a similar situation.

Only by dismantling Genoese ships, who barely arrived before the Fatimid fleet, were the crusaders able to construct two siege towers and a ram. Although other sources say that Tancred found the wood while searching for a place to relieve himself. The truth is lost somewhere. Regardless of the source of the wood, the night before the assault, Godfrey had his siege engine shifted to another point along the northern wall with less defenses. In the south, Raymond did not. The next day when the assault began,

Raymond's tower was burnt, and Godfrey's was the one to take the walls. Raymond's men gained entrance to the city as the defenders fled to defend the breach to the north or escaped to the citadel.

There are conflicting accounts of which crusader was the first over the walls. Often Ludolf of Tournai is given the distinction of having been the first. Some texts also include his brother Engelbert or Tancred. What we do know is that a bloody religious fury descended upon the city, however, it was not likely a complete massacre as we have been led to believe.

It is a commonly repeated myth that the crusaders killed everyone (Eastern Christians, Muslims, and Jews) roughly 40,000 people during the sack of the city. The actual numbers are far lower probably between three and five thousand people. There are several reasons why this myth has taken hold over time. Many Christian sources used biblical imagery that would be simply understood by other Christians, in an attempt to glorify the crusaders triumph over what they considered as evil. Other sources sought to exaggerate the misdeeds of the crusaders to vilify the western occupiers of the city. Yet many eyewitness accounts and interviews with those that were there, stated that all were not slain. There are records of ransoms of both Muslims and Jews back to relatives. We also know many people were enslaved, a common practice for the time employed by most cultures.

There are several stories that surround Tancred, Prince of Galilee. One of the most widely known is during the sack when he offered protection to people hiding within the Al-Asqa Mosque (Temple of Solomon). It was this vague massacre that led me to write the fictional battle between Robert Cutnose's mercenaries and Brother Bors. It should be noted that the crusaders may not have known or referred to the buildings by those names when first seeing them. Later both the Dome of the Rock (Temple of God) and the Al-Asqa Mosque (Temple of Solomon) were repurposed for Christian use.

When the crusaders took the city in 1099, it was similarly,

although not exactly split into quarters like the Old City is today. The current walls and fortifications were created during Ottoman rule while the quarters are generally attributed to a British map from the 1840s. In 1099, the city was split amongst religious/ethnic sections: Christians in the northwestern part of the city, Armenians in the southwestern part around the citadel, Jews in the northeast section, and Muslims in the southeast. Most of the Christians were removed from the city prior to the crusaders arrival to prevent them from aiding the attacking army. I found the book *Jerusalem in the Time of the Crusades* by Adrian J. Boas incredibly helpful with its detailed information on every aspect of the city.

Students of religious history may have noticed I left out the place that Jesus was crucified in my description of the Church of the Holy Sepulchre. There are various beliefs regarding the location of Calvary or Golgotha "place of the skulls." Many believe that it resides within the Church of the Holy Sepulchre along with the nearby tomb that Jesus was said to have been placed after his death. This location was first decided upon almost 300 years after Jesus had been alive. There are alternative ideas as to where Calvary was in a city that has been built and rebuilt many times. There is a small hill outside the Old City, while a slightly more modern theory by Edward Robinson and reinforced by a British general Charles Gordon for which the hill is named after today, fits what some believe is the biblical description of Golgotha. The reason will become more apparent in the next novel, but during the historical time most people would have believed the place Jesus was crucified resided within the Church of the Holy Sepulchre.

The First Crusade culminated with the Battle of Ascalon (1099). The capture of Jerusalem had ended any kind of cohesion seen amongst the crusading factions. Within the city itself the Fatimid commander surrendered the citadel to Lord Raymond of Toulouse leading to a standoff with Godfrey of Bouillon's faction. The standoff continued until Raymond turned down the role of lord of Jerusalem, stating that only Christ could rule the city. Godfrey accepted the position as the city's protector adding even more fuel to the feud. A feud that almost snuffed out the Latin Kingdom before it began.

His crusading obligations complete, Raymond's contingent refused to join Godfrey as he marched for Ascalon to intercept the massive Fatimid relief army of 30,000. The crusaders knew the enemy army was mobilizing early in the siege which hastened their assault on the city.

Marching his small army into the field was a risky move on Godfrey's part. He only had about 6,000 infantry and 800 knights without Raymond's contingent. But he couldn't defend Jerusalem in a siege because he had no open supply chains with the blockade of Jaffa. What he did have was highly motivated soldiers who believed God was on their side. Combined with the desire to hold Jerusalem and return to their homes, they marched to war.

When Godfrey's men reached the outskirts of Ascalon, they must have lamented. The Fatimid relief army was encamped before the impressive fortifications of Fatimid Ascalon. As Tancred scouted the enemy positions, he was able to capture a gigantic herd of livestock. The ample supply of fresh meat lifted the fledging morale of the army. It is thought by some that the capture of the herd was a tactic used by the Fatimid's to slow, disorganize, or spread out the Franks to make them more easily to destroy. Yet the Fatimids never pursued any advantage against the feasting crusaders, who were soon to be reinforced by Raymond's faction.

In the dead of night, a change of heart by Raymond added another three thousand soldiers to the army. With the reinforcements, Godfrey ordered a surprise attack at dawn, leading to a rout of the far more numerous Fatimid forces. For most historians, this was the final battle of the First Crusade.

Godfrey of Bouillon, as Protector of Jerusalem, designed the **symbol of the Kingdom of Jerusalem** that was adopted in the 1100s, the golden cross potent surrounded by four smaller Greek crosses. I had him bear the symbol on his surcoat near the end of the novel and be the only one as it was a new crest. Godfrey died a single year after the capture of Jerusalem before he had been able to do much with his new kingdom. There are conflicting sources as to how Godfrey exited this world. Few say he was killed by an arrow at Acre, but most say it was due to illness. Acre wasn't taken by crusader forces until 1104 by Godfrey's successor, his younger brother, Baldwin I.

Lords and knights began using **heraldry** in the mid-12th century. As the great helm and its precursors became prominent and the face was covered in battle, heraldry displayed on shields and surcoats began as a method of identifying one another on the battlefield or tournament grounds. This wasn't an overnight development, and one could surmise that the practice would have started well before it was adopted by the many. Fact or fiction, it was a fun way for me to bring the knights to life with additional imagery. The use of a surcoat (a long garment/dress that went over a knight's coat of mail) did not come into use until during and after the First Crusade as it was adopted by the western Christians to block the sun from baking their armor as well as keeping mud and grime from corroding the mail beneath.

The Future King of Jerusalem Baldwin was not present for the capture of Jerusalem, as he was securing lands near his newly acquired domain of Edessa during the same time, but I wanted to add him because his kin are the future players in the Kingdom's politics. He was the youngest of the brothers Eustace III and Godfrey, two major players in the crusade but not second to them in ambition. As a third son, he was destined to join the clergy, but married instead, then joined his brothers on crusade. He quickly departed from the main army in Anatolia with another ambitious man, Tancred, where they eagerly attempted to take towns. This led to infighting between them. Baldwin seemed to have a better sense of local politics, allying himself early and often with Christian Armenians who aided his advancement, eventually creating the county of Edessa, the first crusader state. With the untimely death of Godfrey, he became the first Latin King of Jerusalem. Baldwin's previous campaigning and conflict with Tancred would lead to other disputes and infighting during Baldwin's reign as they squabbled for influence.

The Battle of Artah in 1105 was almost a knockout blow for the principality of Antioch. Tancred, ruling as regent for Bohemond, had been struggling to take back the lands lost after Bohemond's disastrous defeat at Harran, not to be confused with Hattin about eighty years later. Tancred was laying siege to the city of Artah where the Turks caught him by surprise, yet he managed to defeat them using a feint and effective counter-attack. This led to the recapture of several towns that Bohemond had lost.

The White Mosque was completely destroyed by an earthquake in 1030 along with a sizable part of Ramla. The mosque was rebuilt during the time before the First Crusade but may have only been partially complete. Today, the Mamluk-built minaret is all that still stands and serves as an inspiration for the minaret used to house Cutnose and his companions during the novel. There was most likely a minaret standing during the same time frame of the novel; however the architecture may have been different than described or that can be seen today. There was a courtyard and fountains associated with the mosque as were three cisterns that provided water for the building.

Arnulf and his long bow could be seen as a bit of a stretch. The first recorded use of the English longbow was in 1188, however, there is ample evidence that the war bow and great bow were in use from prehistoric times. There are many questions that remain as to when or how they became prevalent or if the innovation of various arrow tips precipitated its rise. While a longbow like Arnulf's would not have been common on the crusade, it is not outside the realm of possibility, and would certainly make an archer stand out.

The Esch brothers were a fictionalized family. The actual Henry of Esch died in 1098 of typhoid near Antioch, but I liked his familial backstory so I kept him alive. The second oldest Esch brother, Godfrey, survived the crusades and returned home. The youngest brother, William, was a fictional addition as was the depiction of their family crest.

I sincerely hope that you have enjoyed the first novel of **The Oaths of Blood Saga**. Having you along for the ride has been an all-around grand affair. What are you waiting for? The next novel awaits…

LIST OF CHARACTERS

(Those marked by * are in the historical record)
(Those marked by ** are in the historical record but may be legend)

Noblemen of the First Crusade

*__Godfrey of Bouillon__, main leader of the Northern Franks.

*__Raymond of Toulouse__, main leader of the Southern Franks.

*__Bohemond of Taranto__, leader of the Southern Normans.

*__Tancred of Taranto__, nephew of Bohemond, lieutenant of the Southern Norman contingent.

*__Gaston of Bearn IV__, siege engine expert.

*__Robert of Flanders__, leader of the Northern Franks.

*__Eustace Grenier__, a Flemish crusader.

*__Baldwin of Boulogne__, younger brother to Godfrey and Count of Edessa and future King of Jerusalem.

Minor lords, knights, soldiers, and less scrupulous characters of the Crusade

*__Bishop Arnulf__, a "bishop" serving the crusaders.

*__Ludolf of Tournai__, knight of Tancred.

*__Engelbert of Tournai__, knight of Tancred.

*__Henry of Esch__, knight of Godfrey.

*__Godfrey of Esch__, knight of Godfrey.

William of Esch, knight of Godfrey.

*__Rainald of Salerno__, knight of Tancred, bastard son of Lord Richard of Salerno.

*__Guarin of Apulia__, a landless knight of Tancred.

*__Attropius__, a Greek knight of Tancred.

*__Lord Robert (of Molise) Limosano__, a lord traveling with Tancred, but originally one of Bohemond's supporters.

Humbert of Hauteville, a distant cousin to Bohemond, serves as Tancred's squire.

Fabian Le Fleur, a thief and brigand in Godfrey's employ.

*__Sir Clarembald of Vendeuil__, a survivor of the People's Crusade and bodyguard to Godfrey.

Sir Gunter, a member of Godfrey's household in Jerusalem.

*__Sir Geldemar Carpinel__, knight, garrison commander at Jaffa.

**__Arduino di Narbona__, Genoese sea captain.

<u>**Order of the Stag and Cross**</u>

An ancient military order based in the borderlands of Scotland and England. Their vocation is combating the darkness of men. Their symbol is an antlered stag upon a cross, usually upon a field of white.

Hierarchy of the Order

Pendragon – title bestowed upon the leader of the Order.

All-Father, highest ranking Order member, one of the founding members or may refer to the commander.

Field Master, serves as commander of the Order's armies when in the field.

First Spear, serves as the Pendragon's highest champion and bodyguard.

The Twelve, twelve hand-selected brothers, serve as peers who hold council power with the Pendragon of the Order.

The Second Sons, progeny of the founding brothers.

Oath Brothers, a high and mysterious rank within the Order.

First Brothers, veteran brothers who have proven themselves in combat. Serve one of The Twelve, a Second Son, or as a commander in the field.

Brothers, a knight or lord who serves in the Order. They are known for their training in arms.

Sergeant-Brothers, a senior sergeant who has survived many campaigns, low-born.

Sergeants, the most prevalent rank given to low-born men who serve as the Order's rank and file soldiers. They often serve in both infantry and cavalry capacities.

Brothers of the Order

Uthur, Pendragon and All-Father

Bors, All-Father, one of The Twelve, symbol a red boar on a field of green.

Galahad, Ninth of this name, one of The Twelve and a Second Son, symbol a black hawk on a field of red.

Percival, All-Father, one of The Twelve.

Alymere, a Second Son, serves in Galahad's Guard.

Godric, a first brother, serves in Percival's Guard.

Mador, a first brother, serves in Galahad's Guard.

Osbern Moray, a first brother, a bastard son of the Lord of Moray, serves in Bors's Guard.

Richard, brother, master horseman, serves in Galahad's Guard.

Vincent, brother, serves in Galahad's Guard.

Colban, Percival's servant and squire.

Hector, brother, serves in Galahad's Guard.

Thomas, sergeant-brother, serves in Galahad's Guard.

Edwin, sergeant-brother, serves in Galahad's Guard.

Peter of Summershire, sergeant-brother, serves in Bors's Guard.

Gamelin, sergeant, serves in Bors's Guard.

Oswald, sergeant, serves in Galahad's Guard.

Robert Cutnose's Company

A mostly southern Norman mercenary band serving the Lords Bohemond and Tancred over the course of the First Crusade.

Robert "Cutnose" of Apulia, captain of the mercenary company known by a distinctive scar running down the center of his nose.

Ralph, known as the Gray, second in command of the band.

*__Pagan__, a pale Northman suspected of being his namesake.

Henry, soldier.

Roger Maule, soldier.

Geoffrey of Segre, soldier, claims to be a bastard son of a minor lord near Bari.

William, soldier, carries an axe.

William, soldier, carries a bow.

Hermann, soldier.

Peter, soldier.

Jan, soldier.

John of Lecce, soldier.

Jordan, soldier.

Unaffiliated Persons

Ulf Bodvarsson, an ancient Norse warrior.

Arnulf, an Anglo-Saxon warrior.

Marya, a female warrior.

Hugh, a Frank living in Jerusalem.

Agatha, Hugh's woman in Jerusalem.

William, Agatha's son.

Mary, Agatha's daughter.

Brother Beniface, a young monk.

AUTHOR BIO

Logan is the author of the acclaimed grimdark Arthurian fantasy series The Oaths of Blood Saga.

A lifelong traveler, he has visited over 50 countries for both for work and for pleasure. Lifted in Arnold's childhood gym in Austria, asked his wife to marry him in an abandoned castle in Ireland, bartered for jewelry in a Kuwaiti souk, drank beers and sang quite poorly German songs at Oktoberfest in Munich, and burned a Viking ship during Hogmanay in Edinburgh.

Fantasy, historical fiction, and history novels dominate his library. In particular, the works of George R.R. Martin, Steven Pressfield, Bernard Cornwell, and Robert Jordan inspire his work. He currently resides in Virginia, a place with enough history to keep him busy until the end of time, with his wife, son, and a dog named Ronin the Barbarian.

If he has free time, which is rare, he throws axes (usually at targets), is physically active, and loves taking his family on adventures.

And he's convinced his nieces he's a werewolf...

logandirons.com

Want to stay in touch? Do you want **The Oaths of Blood Saga** novella ***Bridge of Kings*** for free? Sign up for Logan's spam-free newsletter, **The Iron Brigade,** to stay up to date about future releases, deals, and more exclusive content.

Feel free to join forces with Logan on Instagram or Facebook.

Printed in Great Britain
by Amazon